The Hidden

Part 1

Keith Joseph Nickerson

E-Book

The Hidden

The Octology

Part I

by

KEITH JOSEPH NICKERSON I

WHAT WAS LOST.....

WILL BE FOUND.....

EXPLORE.....

Disclaimer Document

Printed in the United States of America

ISBN - 9781521806326

Contact Information:

Keith J. Nickerson
421 St. Charles St.
Lafayette, La. 70501
cldlucille@aol.com

ALSO

BY KEITH JOSEPH NICKERSON

My Malady – Cancer & Addiction

Confessions of the Incarcerated

A Classic Western – The Winning of Freedom

Silent Scream Trilogy – Part I – Complete Fear

The Coolest of the Cool Guys

The Revelation – A New Era

The Kee – Toe Saga / Volume I

The Kee – Toe Saga / Volume II

The Bachelor/Playa Diary – A How to Book aka The Rule Book

The Way We Were – A Book of Images

Coming Soon to E–book and paperback:

The Collection:
A Personal Tribute to
Lucille Bessie Mae Nickerson

PREFACE

A **SECRET** from long ago has resurfaced in the most unexpected way, and in the most unexpected place. It is a discovery that will forever change the course of a town, an unearthing that will alter the future. The inhabitants of the township will never be the same; nothing will ever be the same. A **BATTLE** for survival begins; it starts out simple, but will eventually determine the fate of all humanity. **EVIL** manifests itself, the source is unknown, a revelation made, and a fight ensues.

WHO WILL SURVIVE?

The answers are uncovered within this intertwining tale of intrigue; no one knows what the **FUTURE** holds, or what will come to fruition, only **TIME** will tell. An **INNOCENT** discovery alters the lives of two boys, two families, and all affiliated; witness **LIFE'S** consequences involving **TRUTH** and **DECEPTION**. Within the **SILENCE**, there are **SCREAMS**, unheard **CRIES**, silent for **THOUSANDS** of years; included are **YOURS**.

Acronym for FEAR.

F = False
E = Evidence
A = Appears
R = Real

KEITH JOSEPH NICKERSON I

ABOUT THE AUTHOR

Keith Joseph Nickerson I is the author of countless books, plays, sonnet compilations, short stories, etc. Among his most recent are: The Way We Were – A Book of Images, A Classic Western – The Winning of Freedom, The Coolest of the Cool Guys, The Kee-Toe Saga: Part I & II, The Bachelor/Playa Diary-A How to Book aka The Rule Book, The Silent Scream Trilogy, Confessions of the Incarcerated, My Malady, and The Revelation.

He is a self-described recluse and prefers it that way, totally removed from the public **EYE**, a single man and happy to stay that way. Encouraged by his publishing team, he carves out a unique niche in the writing community. A native of Broussard, Louisiana, his writing style reflects his early country rearing, a place where his imagination and love of reading took him on countless imaginary journeys.

Raised by a **SINGLE** mother and taught many of life's lessons by his four sisters and one brother, his stories relive his rural upbringing. The writer wants the reader to venture back to a period when respect, education, and knowing one's place were virtues. It's a long lost era, a time when the three **R'S** were vital:

READING,

RITING, and

RITHMETIC.

An **ERA** this author constantly reflects on and relishes!

Dedicated to: **Glen Raymond Simms** and **John Nick Simms**

BROTHERS for **LIFE**

GOD BLESS.

THE HIDDEN

PRINCIPAL CHARACTERS

MAIN CHARACTERS

Keith Joseph Nickerson - Dirt
Glen Raymond Simms - Bud
John Nick Simms – Silhouette Maker
Steven James Nickerson - "Hub Cap" - Colossal
Paulette Marie Nickerson - "Pooh" – The Negotiator
Claudette Ann Nickerson - "Dean" – The Rebel
Lucille Bessie Mae Nickerson - "Lu" – The Smeller
Susan Cecile Nickerson - "Sue" – The Genius
Carolyn Ann Leblanc - "Chew-Bus" – Through **BOX**
L.B.M.N. – Momma – The Prophetess
Shirley Simms – The Good Witch
Father Dauphne - Nobility
Gus Girouard – The SUG

SUPPORTING CHARACTERS

Scrunges
Ratwolves
Loup Garou
Night Stalkers
Coosh – Maa
The Dark Witch
EVIL
"IT"

Table of Contents

Marco Polo

INTRODUCTION

Beginning of ¼.

Who knows how long those skeletal remains have been there, I also found something else, not gruesome, but interesting. In the shrubs, partially buried in the mud, further up the coulee bank; under a Moj-Yah tree. The ground is stained purple by the fallen berries, an object caught my eye, releasing a colorful reflection. I pushed back the leaves, stained my shirt sleeves purple, and thought of momma, she's going to kill me. I know she'll get the stain out, a little Clorox will do it, the berry juice also got on my hands. I reached for the glistening thing, the reflection drew me, I'm intrigued, and have to know what it is.

It isn't completely visible so I dig it out, and realize what I've found; a **BOX.** A dingy, mud covered, wooden **BOX**, buried near the foot tub, covered in muck. I have no idea why, but I feel the two are somehow connected. I've passed this route numerous times and have never seen the foot tub or the **BOX**. I held the tiny BOX, looked it over; wiped it off, and then dunked it in the waters of the coulee. Once cleaned, magnificent, covered with jewels, and they shimmer as the sun hits them. I have found hidden treasure, and the **BOX** is mine, I'm staking my claim.

I've found it, no one else knows it's there, my, my, what a prize. I completely wipe it off, and it's stunning, the prism it creates is amazing. A sea of color, purple, blue, pink, red, and yellow, I'm mesmerized, and have seen nothing like it before. My mind races with questions, I look around, no one is near; and decide to find a stash spot. No one can know about the **BOX**, and I have to find the perfect hiding spot. I take a seat on dry ground at the bank of the coulee, wanting to inspect the find. Again, I look around, see no one, listen intently, hear no splashing or crackling of leaves, and can breathe easy?

OBSESSION - 1

I watched as the water streamed below my feet, the level is lower than I have ever seen, normally the coulee is at least half-full, but it has been a dry summer, and there is a drought. The low level exposed things I have never seen, I make finds never before discovered; it has a memorable day, more memorable than I know. The closer I examine the discovery, I conclude it isn't a **BOX** at all, but a small case, possibly a casket; I am totally captivated, and intrigued beyond imagine.

Juan Ponce DeLeon

The skeletal remains, a mini-casket, I begin to put two and two together and realize they are somehow connected. Was the dead creature, now only bones, once housed in the **BOX**, part of me is curious about the possibility, and another part scared. As I sit on the bank, I hear something; a rustle of the sugar cane, a splash of feet, it's something. I freeze, stuck, unable to hide, and caught red handed with the goods. Emerging out of the tall corn grass, Bud appears; I didn't even bother to try and hide the **BOX**.

"What you trying to hide?"

I said, "I don't know what it is, I just found it?"

"It's pretty, what you think it is?"

Nosey as usual, I said "I don't know Bud, I told you I just found it, and something else, some bones; a dead thing."

I oddly began to hear a voice, calling me to the **BOX**, growing stronger, beckoning me, I have to know who or what it is before Bud, he might try to claim my find. I could wait no longer, **CURIOSITY** ruled my brain; what is inside? I then realized, I have found something dead, maybe a baby; it is more important than some secretive **BOX**? I explained to Bud about the bones, he took a look, puked, and agreed. We both know the area, one of many ports of call on various coulee expeditions, and know the exact place to stash pirate treasure. A spot off to the side, a place no one ever goes, and no one needs to. A perfect hiding spot, if it rained would remain high, dry, and safe. We climbed up the bank of the coulee, and found the massive Chinee Ball Tree, the biggest producer. If having a war and you need powerful Chinee Balls, this is the tree, Bud and I both know it. We dug out a hole, as we unearthed the spot, something told me to remind Bud.

"Bud, you know this is my **BOX**, that's clear huh?"

"That's ashamed for you to ask me that. I walk up here and whose hands was it in, sure not mine. I know it's your **BOX**, let's hide the thing and get out of here, it's getting late. Nobody gonna be coming up here."

"We have to bury it very deep, no light can hit it, that thing glistens, it would definitely reflect. Now that it's clear who the **BOX** is for, we can hide my **BOX.** I pulled a few branches from a nearby Moj-Yah tree and covered the ground with the berries, if anyone came near, they would leave tracks; and drug a few branches over the ground to conceal our footprints. No one ever comes to the coulee, but it is better to be safe than sorry."

"You lead us out Bud, I'll dust away our tracks with the berry juice; I put some on the branches."

Bud took the lead, he is a great tracker, and has a hawk eye.

"Bud, keep your ears open, I feel funny."

"I wasn't gonna saying nothing Dirt, but I feel something too. Let's put it in high gear, and get out of here."

Bud sped up his pace, and I threw down the branches, we've gotten far enough away. We started running; needing to make it home A.S.A.P., and before long arrived at the Choplin's house. Out of danger; the expedition for the day is over, but in actuality, it has only just begun. We've found something special, after all these years, we've finally made a discovery. The **BOX** is beautiful; and I wonder what's in it?

The PAWN.

Glen led the way, as he walked, a voice, clear as day spoke, pulsating, and consuming his thoughts. The tone, possessing the pretty little **BOX**; it's Keith's because he found it, but I'm second in line. I wonder what's in it? It must have something good inside, and if anything happens to Keith, it's mine. We passed Byron's place, and could now see our homes, we both turned back to take one last look at the spot which held the treasure. The grass swayed, dancing in the breeze, beckoning, trying to persuade, calling us. We looked at each, seeing the influence, ran the rest of the way.

At my house, Glen turned left, headed home, and waved goodbye in the afternoon sun, his hair blew in the wind as he continued to run; he's fast. I ran into the back yard, sat on the step a while to catch my breath, and thought about what's under the foot tub; then thought of the **BOX**. I know no one will find it, a trick to concealing stuff, I learned on T.V., and I personally think the branch dragging is pretty slick; inside, my ingenuity prompted me to smile. In my mind, I could still see the bones of the dead thing; could it have been a baby? It's so little, I wonder what happened to it; and how long it's been there? My breathing regulated, it's scary to think of what the bones could be, I'm partly curious, but also scared. I know the discovery of the bones outweigh my **BOX**, but I can't help thinking about it. I hope it's safe, want to see it again, and it needs me. I want to know what's inside, and I'm not going to mention the **BOX** when telling of the discovery. All I found is the foot tub with the bones beneath, and that's all I'm going to say.

The afternoon sun set fast, night arrived, and along with it; a nice cool breeze settled my mind. Broussard is a small town, a one cop town, and all knows the Chief of Police; his first name is **GUS**, and his last name I don't know. Maybe you find it out if you get in trouble, I don't want to know it. There is a running joke in our town centered on the Police **Chief**. He doubles as a **Bus Driver**, and **Watcher**, wears numerous hats; and who knows, he might even be the **Mayor**.

"Don't fuss, call GUS.

He'll fuss for us."

I know when Gus questions me, I will have to be convincing, he is a good cop, but T.V. cops are much smarter. Now if it was **KOJAK**, I'm in trouble, and would crack under his intense interrogation techniques; the sucker would do it.

"Who **LOVES** you baby?"

STEVE McGARRETT, of Hawaii Five-O, his coolness would do me in, I'd spill my guts and he would simply use the silent treatment.

"Book him, Dan – O."

There will be many questions, and I have no answers for them. Who was the baby for, if it's even a baby? How did it end up in the coulee? What did I see, if anything? Did I find anything else? Did I move anything? The list could go on and on. I will be the center of attention, how do I prepare for something like that. I will be pressured, but have to remain cool, I'll try, but

"I'M SCARED."

Being scared is new to me. I'm an outgoing boy, enjoying the beginning of summer, there is no school, and I can be foot loose and fancy-free. I worry about nothing, and play my days away. Sitting on the step I pondered my situation, thinking as a kid, how does one act cool, and in front of **GUS**? I'm an explorer from Broussard, the first voyager braving the new world. There are days I'm **Christopher Columbus**, the leader of excursions, others I'm **Ferdinand Magellan**, circling the Earth, and even **Vasco De Gama**, first arriving in India. Just happens today, I'm **Juan Ponce De Leon**, on a personal search for the Fountain of Youth, but discover something else. By accident, I stumble upon buried treasure, a priceless plunder, the **BOX**. Momma opened the little kitchen screen door and it hit me in the back, my breathing had just settling down.

"Get in here boy, where you been, what you up to, sweating and breathing all hard?"

I stood, followed her into the little kitchen, she's cooking, it's almost suppertime. It's hot in the big kitchen, momma's soaked, her T-Shirt is wringing wet, and the stove is blazing. She has pots on every burner, no air's circulating inside; it's **HOT**. Momma checked the pots, stepped back from the stove, wiped her face with an apron, looked at me, and smiled. Tired is written on her face, I waited before speaking, not wanting to rush. I have to be on point or momma will know it's a fabrication.

TRUTH or CONSEQUENCES

Momma – 1

Before I could get out a word, Tote arrived, hearing the back door open or seeing me run past the side of the house. My chest rising and falling, she knows I have been running. With a puzzled look on her face, she asked.

"Maaay Keith, what's wrong, who chasing ya?"

I turned, Tina is a temporary distraction, allowing me time to plan, and perfectly timed, I can always count on Sue. Momma wiped her face again, waiting, wanting to hear what I have to say. Her ears are keen, her memory **ETERNAL**, I have to be careful. I paused, the **TRUTH** involves the **BOX**, I have to make a decision, tell the **TRUTH,** or **LIE,** both have consequences. The **BOX** is mine, I found it and shouldn't have to share it. I want it for myself, deserve it, and will **NEVER** tell.

I began, "I thought one of ya'll called me, it's not **SUPPERTIME**? I'm hungry enough to eat a cow."

That did it, momma smelled something fishy, we just ate bologna sandwiches for **DINNER;** my own words did me in. Momma began playing **PERRY MASON**, hearing, seeing enough, and without looking at me, asked,

"What you done, done boy?"

I'm put on the spot, she knows the signs, and sees what no one else does; my quirks, eye contact, tone, and if I get tongue tied, that's a wrap.

"I'M LYING."

I'm a **KID**, have to act a certain way, and began trying to be cool. I went into **LIE** mode, put on my "**A LIE**" game, Tina might fall for a "**B-LIE,**" but not momma. A simple lie you throw out, off the cuff, the person I have to fool is no Huckleberry Hound, she's a veteran. She can smell, see, recognize, hear, probably touch, and taste a **LIE**. Uncovering her face, sweat dripping, forehead covered in perspiration, we made eye contact and I'm busted. I don't know what to do when Dean appear and asks,

"What you done, done Keith?"

COLUMBO is already investigating, and on my butt, now **DETECTIVE JOHN SHAFT** arrives on the scene. Another **LIE** sniffer, I now know what is required.

"TELL the TRUTH."

Momma spoke, in pause position, I had to wait, and she has the final say. I was an inch away from getting the dish towel popped on my butt or leg, momma was winding it as she calmly said.

"Claudette, mind your place, I'm Keith's mother. Both of ya'll, to the front room and I better not hear a pin drop, I better not see ya'll either."

They turned and disappeared toward the front room, I watched as they walked off. Momma was serious, for her to put them out, it was one on one, I had to spill my guts. Claudette turned back once she got out of momma's sight. Her lips said,

"You in TROUBLE."

You couldn't hear the words, she lip sync'd them, and I suddenly realized,

I could "LIP READ."

Tote and Dean disappeared down the hall. Quiet consumed the two kitchens, and I was now alone with momma, it was a showdown; I had to fess up.

TRUTH vs. LIE.

HONESTY or DECEPTION.

"Boy, what I'm gonna do with you, always playing explorer. You don't have Roger no more, you better be careful. I know you gonna miss him that old mutt."

My mood instantly became somber, just that quick, I had forgotten. That fast, I had overlooked my boy, the **DODGER**. He was my **DOG**, a German Shepherd, he was fearless, my protector, I missed him. A tear came to my eye and I realized this is good, I can use this, momma was giving me an opening; all I had to do was step in. I didn't hesitate, it rarely happens, I had to seize the moment. I let the tear come to my eye; I faked a grimace, made a tearful face, and put the act into full display mode. I ran to momma and smothered my face in her apron. The smell was musty, but I was willing to pay the price.

"I miss him Momma. I didn't know how much I would, it happened so fast. I still wish he were here, he was **MY** dog."

Momma hugged me tight. I fake sniffles and snorts, even a shortness of breath, I thought it pretty good; no tears, only sounds. I was now, "In Like Flynn," the tightness of the hug confirmed it. She then began to rub my head, and that did it; spared.

She said, "He was **OUR** pet, I told you about being selfish. It's not all about **YOU**, we all loved **ROGER**. You did good with dog, I'm proud of you."

Momma is forever teaching, in her own way giving lessons, I got quiet again. I was feeling out momma, it was only us, she and I, one-on-one. This is rare, I have four sisters, and she rarely has time for me alone, I was gonna go with the flow..

"The next few days are going to be tough on you, you my little man, huh. You and that dog were close; Roger was a good dog, a family dog."

Her words were comforting; the direction of the conversation was perfect. The mood was ideal, I seized the moment, the perfect time.

"Momma, I was walking the coulee, thinking of Roger; just exploring, I'm used to him always being there, it was weird."

I paused, sniffled, and then momma squeezed me even tighter. I had almost pulled it off, the door was still open, all I had to do; fill in the blanks and be **COOL**. She continued to rub my head; buried deep in the center of her breasts. Momma has some big tay-taws, my lil head fit perfectly in the center. She squeezed my head into her chest, smothering me, I needed to escape; get air. I tried to smother my chuckle, it sounded like a sniffle. I could now finish my tale of deception, I now had options, and the **BOX** was totally out of the picture; with the **BOX** gone, the **TRUTH** exited also. Momma continued to rub my head and held me tightly. I had to play this to the max, if I didn't, I would be found out; the death of Roger was sad, but perfectly timed.

"This is going to be a trying time for you boy, I know momma's been busy lately, I have to work. By the time I get home, Kee-Toe, Momma tired, now tell me, **'What's Wrong.'**"?

The truth would burden momma, I could see the weight already, I didn't need to add to it with the **BOX**. Something had her tired and drained, I would tell of the dried bones; that's all.

"I was exploring, the coulee is really low, like never before, it's almost dry."

I began to shake, still in momma's arms, she could feel my body, shivers overwhelmed me, thinking of the bones did it. She could feel the onset of fear, she let me go a little, looked down at me; and we made eye contact.

"What has you frightened boy? I can feel you shaking, tell momma."

I began to cry, was afraid, and needed to tell all, but I couldn't; I lied to my momma. She deserved to know the truth, but I couldn't tell her about the **BOX**, at least not just yet. With a puzzled look on her face, she asked me.

"Don't be afraid, has anybody done something to you; tell me the truth."

Holding my shoulders, she demanded.

"What is it boy?"

"I found a foot tub in the coulee momma, under it, there was something dead."

Momma pushed me further back, the puzzled look returned, she was now curious.

Christopher Columbus

THE FINDING.

"What do you mean something dead, some kind of animal, a fish; what was dead?"

"It was a baby momma, the bones of a baby, Bud saw it too."

Immediately, momma sprang into action. Without hesitation, her mind began to click. She had no more questions; she released me, grabbed the potholder, and began removing the pots from the stove. She removed the stove lids and used them as potholders too. She sat the hot pots on the lids, and then began removing her apron; simultaneously she was talking to me. Part of her mind was still on the meal, another part of her mind was curious about what I just told; confirmation was necessary. If her son is correct, the police will be involved; her son needs no police problems in Broussard. La.

"Go get Paulette. Tell your other three sisters I said to stay put. They better listen to their big sister."

I went to the front room, as I did, I could hear momma's footsteps in the kitchen. I could hear pots clanging, and spoons stirring, momma was getting busy. There was a lot of banging coming from the kitchen, that's unusual for momma, she likes quiet and peace. I arrived in the front room.

"Pooh, momma called you. Dean, Lu, and Sue; she said,

"STAY PUT."

I didn't release the words, I didn't voice them, I lip synced them; it was payback to Dean. I had to get even, I looked directly at Claudette, silently forming the two words, but saying nothing.

"STAY PUT."

Dean gave me the evil eye. Pooh and I walked to the back of the house, as we walked, she lightly spoke to me. She is the negotiator, when in charge, Pooh never whips, it isn't her form of discipline. She challenges you mentally, uses logic, listens, and always reaches a compromise.

"What have you done, boy?"

Always the same question, always my fault, we returned to momma. There would be no more talking by the children, the only speaker was going to be momma, she was now running the show. Pooh and I stood in front of her as she spoke.

"Paulette, watch your sisters, I have to go somewhere with your brother. We won't be long."

Momma took me by the hand and led me out the kitchen. We went out the back door to avoid curious eyes. She literally pulled me as we walked. She was now leading. How she knew where to go, I had no idea. She was incredibly going in the right direction. As we walked, she talked.

"If this is what you say boy, this is serious, there's going to be a lot of questions. What do you have to tell me? You and that Simms boy, Shirley sure got her hands full."

"I found the bones momma, I didn't do anything wrong. They were under a foot tub, you can ask Bud, he looked. I had never seen anything like that, it scared us, and we ran home."

She could tell I was shaken, she observed me, as we walked, looked me over. It was the detective coming out and she saw me looking at her.

"Don't look at me, which way do we go?"

I had to stop watching her eyes, I could feel them inspecting me. She leaned forward as we walked to get a full frontal. She slowed down to inspect me from behind. Anything out of place, momma would notice.

"How you got that berry juice on your shirt?"

She caught me off guard, I wasn't ready for questions, my mind wasn't sharp; we were talking. I can't do two things at the same time, much less three, I paused to think.

"Don't LIE, I know you boy."

She knows her son, his secretive, and curious sides, she also hurts because of his loneliness, prays for his success, and supports his dreams; she **LOVES** her boy. She stopped, and we both stopped, and she knelt down in front me, sweat was on her face again, but a different kind of sweat; it was perspiration from fear. It was knowledge of what this finding might bring; attention to her family. It would put her son under the spotlight, she had to be certain, and looking into my eyes said.

"Tell me everything before we get there. I want to know how you got berry juice on your shirt and dirt under your finger nails?"

LIES have a snowball effect, once you start, you have to continue; I knew I was in trouble, one **LIE** leads to another. I couldn't spill the beans, not about the **BOX**.

"I'm not lying momma, you have to believe me. I didn't want to find that, it's bones; that's all I found."

"Show me where, I want to see for myself."

We continued to walk. It was a hurried walk, almost a run. I took the lead, Momma followed closely behind. Her head was on a swivel, she was checking out everything, and looking at everything. As we arrived, she began to ask more questions.

"Is this the normal spot where you explore; Christopher Columbus?"

I chuckled, momma was trying to be funny, she's always serious, it's nice to see that side to her, it was different, laughter made her come across different; I like that.

"Yes, ma'am, we have to turn right here. It's a little further up, I can see the foot tub. I covered the bones back."

"If this is a body, there is going to be trouble. Gus is going to have to get involved. It's gonna be a big commotion."

"I just want to show you what I found. I wasn't looking for that, now I'm sorry I found it."

"Is the bones all you found?"

"There is the foot tub, just like I found it."

As we walked, momma was now in the lead. She walked toward the foot tub, I slowly dropped behind her, she was going to turn over the foot tub and see. I know it will have the same effect on her. Momma bent down and slowly turned over the tub, I stood back; I knew what was under it. I didn't want to see it again, one time was plenty. Momma gasped when she saw what was under the tub, it took her breath, the inhale was intense, a sign of fear, I had the same reaction; she instantly put the tub back down.

"Lord Jesus."

She made her sign of the cross, turned and looked at me. Her look was strange, her eyes were suddenly filled with tears, it was compassion. She wiped her eyes, and quickly a new look appeared; **ANGER**.

"Let's go, we have to get Gus out here. That's a baby's bones, no child deserves that kind of burial. Someone just dismissed this baby, which is not right. A baby is dead boy."

We began to walk home, momma was running the show, and her pace was near running, momma in shape. As we walked, she spoke.

"You didn't answer me son, how did your shirt get full of berries? The Moj-Yah tree was off the bank of the coulee, how did you get from the foot tub to the bank?"

We walked and talked, she was waiting for an answer. She expected an answer; I had to come up with something.

"I stumbled back when I saw the bones, it scared me, and I must have fallen onto the bank. I might have bumped into the branches of the Moj-Yah, I fell and messed up my shirt and dirtied my hands; I was afraid momma."

I think momma believed me, I hoped she did, her look did not reveal anything, but her facial expression was intense. She had one thing on her mind; we walked at the fastest pace I have ever seen momma move. **TIME** had passed so quickly the last few days, Rogers' death was tragic, and it left me in a funk. I felt so alone, Roger was my boy, and he was my friend. He gave me courage, he was fearless, I wished he were here right now; he would be leading us home.

"Did you find anything else son, if you did; now is the time to tell me."

It was a crossroad moment; it was now or never, the final straw; I had to tell the **TRUTH**. It was all or nothing, I could smell trouble, **LIES** are normally followed by trouble; I knew trouble was near.

"You're going to be questioned; it's not going to be easy. It's the police were dealing with, just tell the **TRUTH**. Say the same thing every time."

"O.K. momma, will you be there? Will you stay with me?"

"Of course boy, I won't let you out of my sight. You're my **SON**; I'm going to support you through all of this."

"Momma, why would they leave that baby like that?"

Momma was fuming; I could see the anger written on her face. We were home now, the curious **FOUR** were waiting, by our walking pace; they knew something serious was going on. Their eyes showed curiosity, I know they wanted to say something, but they didn't utter a word.

"Pooh, take Keith and ya'll go to the police station, get Gus. Bring him back here."

Pooh and I began our walk toward the police station. In the distance, I could hear momma talking to Dean, Lu, and Sue, her tone was on point; she was serious and going make preparations.

"Let's go inside, we need to get the house ready, we're gonna have company."

Pooh and I walked fast, she was curious, she had to know what was going on; it was tearing her up inside. The pace was fast, but not too fast to talk. She was looking at me as we walked, expecting me to bring it up, when I didn't, she began.

"What you did boy, why we need Gus; this is a first."

"I found something in the coulee. Momma said we need the cops. That's what we're gonna do."

"Well, let's hurry, you know momma expects us back pronto."

The City Hall wasn't far and we arrived in no time, there was one police car parked in the front. Pooh took hold of my hand, we walked in together.

"Don't be afraid, I'll tell him momma wants to see him, you don't have to say nothing. Don't talk until we get back home."

I figured it was a good time to listen, I always want to put in my two cents, but not today, Pooh took the lead. I had seen Gus in passing, but had never met him face to face; I was anxious. We entered the front door and a bell rang, attached to the top of the door, some kind of alarm. We looked around, a little woman was sitting behind a desk to the right, she asked,

"How can we help ya'll children?"

Pooh said, "I'm Bessie Nickerson's daughter, my momma asked Mr. Gus to come over to our house."

Gus must have been listening, the bell might have drawn his attention, but from out of the back, a tall, slim, black haired man appeared. He smiled as he looked at Pooh and I.

"What does your momma need me for?"

I said nothing, I just looked at Gus, and then I looked at the lady. I listened to Pooh, she has a way with words, always playing mediator, the negotiator for the children.

"I don't know sir, she just told us to come fetch ya. We'll be heading back home now, we delivered the message."

As we turned to leave, Gus spoke.

"Hold your horses, if I need to go talk to your mother, I can bring the two of you home. I'm going that way, let me get my hat."

He turned and disappeared into the back. Pooh looked at me and smiled. The lady behind the desk watched suspiciously. I looked at the inside of the station, it was my first time inside, I had to check it out. Gus reappeared from the back, his hat was now on his head. He was strapping his gun belt on as he approached, it was a big, black handled gun. I wondered,

"Why would he need that?"

We sat in the back of the squad car, looking around; it was our first time in a police car. Gus looked at us through the backward mirror; his eyes shifted from Pooh to me, then back. Pooh eyed me, she whispered,

"What's going on, what you did?"

Before I answered, I looked forward at Gus, he acted as if he was focusing on driving; he wasn't. His ears stretched to the back, they looked strange, and they were long, like dog-ears. I used my chin to get Pooh's attention and with my head pointed toward Gus. She looked toward him and saw; I could tell by her facial expression, she was shocked; it was a strange surprise. She silently turned her face to me, made sure Gus wasn't looking, and slightly puckered her lips. Almost unheard, she said.

SSSHHH!!!

Broussard is a small town, we passed our cousin Carolyn on the way home, and she recognized us in the back of the police car. She began to run behind the car toward our house that was the fastest we ever saw Chew-Bus run. We got to our house in no time, as we pulled up; momma came out of the house. She was waiting, and prepared, I could see the confidence in her face. Gus stopped the car and he got out, Pooh and I got out of the back, he approached momma, we were close behind. She waited for us on the side of the house.

Gus began, "Hello, Bessie, your children summoned me; what is it you need?"

Momma said, "Girls, ya'll go in the house, its supper time, I've made biscuits, use the clear Karo Syrup, don't make a mess, and leave some for ya'll brother."

Momma made the first power move; she cleared unnecessary ears, now it was three. She and I were of one accord, I could see her intention. The four gathered and began to walk off, I could see their dejection, and they wanted to be a part of whatever was going on. **Tote** looked back at me, her look was innocent love, she cared for her brother's well-being, and was filled with wonder; most of all, she loves Keith.

Lu looked back at me puzzled, she had no clue, she couldn't break herself out of a wet paper bag, and the girl is Foo-Foo. She has something though, she is always in the right place, at the right time; she smells trouble, it's that pump nose. **Dean** didn't look back at me; she had her eyes on Gus. She was watching him, I sensed she didn't trust him; she is keen as a bloodhound when judging people; an uncanny ability she possesses. Once on your trail, there's no shaking her, and she is relentless. **Pooh** is the arrival of diplomacy, she was behind looking at her little brother, eyeing me. She was trying to read me, and she knows what we saw in the car.

Something's up?

Carolyn arrived as the four left, she was huffing and puffing, trying to catch her breath. As she squatted, hands on knees, she looked up at momma, it was a look of concern, her eyes then shifted to me, and then she looked at Gus.

"What's wrong Aunt Bee?"

"Lynn, go in the house, your cousins are inside, it won't be long. What Edna Mae doing, letting you wonder the streets this late. Girl, get inside, they eating supper."

She looked at Keith; she had now caught her breath, she began to waddle toward the house. Keith know his cousin, he instantly thought of his biscuits, he tugged on his mom's blouse.

"Tell Chew-Bus about the biscuits."

Momma yelled, "Lynn, leave Keith some supper."

She never looked back, just waved her hand acknowledging she had heard; Dirt knew the biscuits were history; their attention returned to Gus. He now had our full attention; his stance was relaxed, just waiting. His ears were back to normal, I had a growing feeling inside about Gus; I couldn't **TRUST** him.

Momma began, "Mr. Jeerwaa, I asked you here because my son found something in the coulee. He took me to the location and I looked at what he discovered, it was disturbing."

Gus listened quietly, he glanced over at me as momma spoke, he was sizing me up. I couldn't conclude anything from his facial expressions, he kept an unassuming smile on his face.

"The boy just lost his dog, they explored in that coulee all day. The coulee is the lowest it's ever been, I think you need to see what he found."

Momma said his name funny, I just knew him as Mr. Gus. As she spoke, I could see all my sisters in the windows, they had their bionic ears working. They wanted to hear what was going on, it's the not knowing that's killing them. They hated being left in the dark, especially Pooh and Dean.

"Where is this strange discovery, Keith?"

My name rang in my ears; it rang in my mother's ears too. It was unexpected confirmation, a clue; instantly I wondered, as did my momma.

"How did he know MY name?"

Momma played it off; she reassumed control of the conversation. She was making sure everything done on her terms; she was not going to let Gus manipulate her.

"The boy took me to the spot, it's past his supper time, and I'll take you to the spot. Let me talk to my chillin."

Momma grabbed my hand and we walked together toward the front door. Gus followed, but stopped on the walkway into the house. We opened the door and the Curious Five greeted us.

"I'll be right back, it's gonna be O.K. We won't be long, ya'll listen to Paulette."

I walked into the house, momma closed he door, from the front picture window we watched, all jammed in it together. Momma and Gus disappeared into the bushes and down my trail; turns out momma knew it too. Momma incredible, she never ceases to amaze. My attention now turned to the biscuits and syrup, I made it to the table, but couldn't eat in peace; it was the most intense Q & A session ever, everyone had questions. Pooh was in charge, it made sense she should ask the first question. I didn't care where the questions came from; I was worried about biscuits and syrup, that's all I had on my mind.

Pooh began, "What's going on Keith, what you found in the coulee?"

I swallowed the mouth full, and washed the sweet glob down with some Borden's milk, it is milk from heaven. It tasted refreshing and cooled my entire body as it flowed into my stomach. With my mouth now clear, I could now speak.

"I found a foot tub and it had something under it. Let me eat, I'll tell ya'll when I finish."

I uncovered the second biscuit pan and found one and a half biscuits, I was hot; I looked around with a mean grimace, and Claudette began to chuckle. Lu smiled, Sue shrugged her shoulders, and Pooh raised her eyebrows.

Carolyn said, "I thought about you."

Pooh said, "We caught her on the last 1 and a ½ or you would have none, and she has the nerve to say she thought about you."

Carolyn erupted into laughter, I gave her the eye, but she is my Supergirl. She is tough as nails, strong as an ox, and fearless. She loves us and enjoys hanging out at our house, she is one of us, and especially loves Aunt Bee; she calls her Sexy Bessie.

The Queen

As momma walked with Gus, they spoke, she directed the conversation, and led them to the spot. It was now late afternoon, the sun was setting fast, and she needed to take care of this A.S.A.P.

"My child is a good boy Gus; he spends a lot of his time alone. He has sisters, but he needs a boy playmate. He just lost his best friend, his dog; he found this strictly by accident."

Gus listened as they walked and said nothing, just looked and listened. They arrived at the foot tub, momma stopped, and she pointed.

"It's under there; I'm going back to my children."

Gus walked toward the foot tub and momma turned and began walking back home. Gus approached cautiously and momma exited hurriedly. Gus was in for a surprise and momma knew she needed to talk to her son. As she returned, her mind raced, she wondered about the origin of the bones; whose child was this? She never did trust Gus, or cops; she walked, silently wondered, how did Gus know her son's name.

<u>End of ¼.</u>

1492 COLUMBUS SAILED THE OCEAN WITH A BLACK NAVIGATOR FROM SPAIN NAMED PEDRO ALONSO NIÑO. HE WAS CALLED "EL NEGRO" (THE BLACK) FOR HIS NOTABLE TRADE IN AFRICA.

SCHOOLS WILL TEACH OUR CHILDREN WHO CHRISTOPHER COLUMBUS WAS BUT WON'T TELL THEM WHO THIS MAN WAS PEDRO ALONSO NIÑO

Explorer Pedro Alonso Nino

Beginning of ½.

THE DISCOVERY IN THE COULEE.

I finished the last biscuit and a ½ in no time, and before I could get the last gulp down, the questions resumed. My sisters had me surrounded, they were ready to fire away, the questions will be coming at me from the left and the right; my food hadn't even digested yet, it was Dean's turn.

"What did you find?"

The suspense was killing them, Gus was involved, and it had to be serious. It was all so secretive, they had to know, I wiped my mouth slowly, and I intentionally left them hanging as long as I could. They were about to bust with anticipation, I ate it up, I had the power; I jokingly said,

"The biscuits were great, fine ladies, I would love a cup of warm milk to wash them down; don't overheat the milk."

Dean said, "Boy, if you don't tell us what you found, you're gonna wind up missing."

Lu said, "Tell us Keith."

Tote asked smiling, "What was it?"

Carolyn sat observing things, she listened, and I laughed; it was their inquisitive minds needing to be satisfied.

"I found a foot tub, a plain old foot tub; that's all."

Dean said, "Stop lying."

Just then momma walked in, it was dusk, she was quiet, like a cat, she snuck in; we didn't even hear her approach, just suddenly she was there.

"Quit questioning the boy, ya'll start getting ready for bed. Ya'll have school tomorrow."

Momma then turned to Carolyn, it was a weeknight, and she knew the child needed to be home, just like her children. Carolyn and momma are close, she's close to all of us, she really is our sister, and she especially likes her Aunt Bee's cooking.

"Lynn, you need to start heading home, I'm gonna watch you until you make it to the other end. Cut behind Broussard Elementary and you're home, hurry, it's getting dark."

Carolyn rose form the table, she was going to go out the little kitchen back door, and it was getting dark rather quickly this afternoon.

"The biscuits were good Aunt Bee, I heard momma talking to a man about you, and he called you Sexy Bessie."

Momma chuckled and then smiled; she caught a flashback of her fresh days. She pulled on the collars of her blouse, and then straightened out her skirt, almost instinctually, to momma appearances are everything; all the children stayed in the kitchen, momma was going to walk Carolyn and we were going to wait. Momma got to the door with Carolyn, paused and turned back, and calmly told us.

"Come on ya'll, we gonna walk Lynn a piece."

We sprang to our feet and ran to the back door. As we exited the house, the sun was slowly setting. The bare trees allowed rays of the sun to stream through, light pierced the darkening shadows, and we walked quickly.

Momma said, "To satisfy all your curiosity at one time, I have this to say. Keith found the bones of a dead body today, an old, possibly a little baby. It had been there a long time, and that is what this is all about."

We were now at L.D. Bernard gas station; it is ¾ of the way to the other end, we stopped, Carolyn continued to walk; momma did say we were going to walk her apiece. We watched Carolyn for a while and she began to shrink on the horizon, she became smaller the further away she got. At the very last moment, she turned and waved to us, we all waved back, the night was falling fast; I had to get the last word in, I yelled at the top of my voice to Carolyn.

"See ya tomorrow Cheww-bb."

Momma gathered us and we began our walk back home. Carolyn was damned near home by now, we turned again, but she was gone. As we walked back, momma explained her plan to us.

"No playing around, ya'll get to bed when we get home, it's not a school night, but that sill don't matter."

Momma is a stickler about getting to bed early, especially on a school night, but it was summer, she was just getting us in the practice, always teaching. We began to mentally prepare, we knew the routine, and it was

Shut Eye Time.

We arrived home and knew what we had to do, the girls began going their way, and I began to go mine. Momma first stopped in on the girls, and told them goodnight. They whispered some stuff I couldn't understand, they knew it was time to clean up and go to bed; no questions asked. Next, she stopped in one me and walked up to my bed. I was sitting on the edge o my bed, undoing my Chuck Taylor's, beginning to undress and prepare for a bath.

"Come in my room Keith, it won't be long; we need to talk."

W slowly and quietly walked to her room, she had me to herself now. She knew tomorrow would be intense and didn't want any surprises. We arrived in her room; she sat me down, and looked me straight in the eyes.

"In the morning, it's going to be difficult, you have to be ready; there will be questions. Gus is going to grill you; he will be able to tell if you are lying. Do you have anything else to tell me, now is your last chance."

I looked momma in the eyes and stuck to my story, I could not mention the **BOX**; it is my secret, my **BOX**, and I will never give it up.

NEVER.

I said nothing else, momma told me to go to bed, but I had to wash up first. As I walked to my room, there was a knock on the front door, no one ever comes over at this time of night, I was curious. Momma went to the door; the sun had already set, she put her ear o the door. It was pitch dark outside; there are no streetlights on West Railroad, which made momma even more cautious; through the door, she inquired.

"Who is it?"

"It's Gus, Bessie."

A few hours ago, the voice would have been unrecognizable, no longer. The voice was now familiar, it was Gus, and he was back to the house. Momma cracked the door, she never puts herself in a vulnerable position by fully opening the door at night; it's a precaution and she never puts herself in a compromising position. We could hear her talking through the wall and through the door to the room we were in, I know if my ears were keen, and so were my sisters.

"How can I help you Mr. Jeerwaa, it's getting late."

"Bessie, I don't mean to impose, can I talk to Keith a minute?"

"It's too late, the boy is already in the bed, and you'll have to come back tomorrow."

I was glad momma answered the way she did, if Gus was just leaving the coulee, he had been there a while. I hoped he hadn't found my secret, I didn't feel like being bothered either. It had been a long day; I wanted to be left alone; at least for the rest of the night. Gus left and we could hear momma walking toward the room we were all huddled in, we scattered, I ran to my room and jumped in the bed, thinking about the day.

I thought about how momma dismissed Gus, I was proud of her, he didn't sound too happy, but wasn't persistent; that's a good thing. The bones had been there a while, and whatever it was had been dead a long time, it could be a long, drawn out investigation. One more day wasn't going to be that big a deal; all of us heard Gus' last words.

"I'll come back in the afternoon, I'll wait until he is for sure home, and I can get a better look around the area by day; maybe I'll find something."

His words came through "Loud" and "Clear." I think that was his intent, he wanted me to hear or maybe I was just being paranoid, he spoke loud enough. I think he wanted all of us to hear them, he stressed them, momma shut the door, and that was the end of that. She cut off the living room light and as she walked to the girl's room, she spoke.

"I hope ya'll all done took ya'll baths, don't make me come in there and check on ya'll; Nosey Rosie's, I know ya'll were ear hustling."

All the girls looked at each other, momma had some hip slang with her, they erupted into laughter, and I chuckled quietly in my room. After my sisters bathed, I did a quick wash off, if I didn't, momma would be on me; and she doesn't like me to take a wash off. I hate the big foot tub, and I hate sharing the water. Tonight, a wash off was going to do, I quietly lay in my bed. Momma entered my room; she had some last words for me, and said them loud enough for my sisters to hear.

"We'll talk first thing in the morning."

My mind now raced, Gus was a strange man, and he was scary. He came across calm and collected, but there was something about him, I couldn't put my finger on it, he was odd. I wondered why momma called him Mr. Jeerwaa; I had never heard her address him that way. I had never heard her talk to Gus period, everything about today was a first, also, how did he know my name and, what was up with his ears?

Astronaut John Glenn

My eyes began to get heavy, running around at the coulee, the death of Roger, and the pace of the day; I was burnt, I was "foo-tee," that is one of momma's French words. We speak Creole here, the language of secrets. I tried to slow my mind, my thoughts were jumbled up; slowly, I floated away and sleep invaded my mind. I began falling, I was tumbling, out of the sky I plummeted, the speed of my descent was incredible. My legs and arms flailed wildly, as I fought to get my balance, trying to stop the free fall.

I was out of control, dropping to Earth like a doomed plane. I was going to crash and there would be no survivor, I was scared. I could see the surface of the Earth rapidly approaching, from high up; I could begin to see the surface. On the ground, there was a huge snake and it was directly below me. I was going to fall or land on it, the impact was going to big. The snake captured my attention as I continued to fall, fighting, but it was to no avail. Falling fast, I fixated on the snake, the closer I got to the surface, the bigger the snake got, and it was weird. The snake was in the process of shedding its skin; it slowly, yet meticulously, oozed out of its old skin. The discarded skin collapsed, nothing kept it open any longer, it left a white trail of dead skin. It was a huge snake, its length was unbelievable, it seemed to stretch for miles, and as it emerged out of its old skin, it glistened and shined; it reflected the sun and bathed in it.

The body of the snake creature had no bones as it slid out of its old skin, and then it began to coil. The old skin began to coil too and there were two coils, one of the live, huge snake, and a second coil of discarded skin, they both rose to the heavens, side by side. Suddenly, the snake began to look up, as if it sensed me falling, and I was still rapidly descending; I was right over it. I tried to do what I could to slow my fall, but nothing worked, closer and closer I descended. The size of the snake increased as I neared the surface, it's mass and bulk was incredible, it was like nothing I had ever seen; it was breathtaking.

As my descent brought me closer, the snake readied itself and opened it's mouth, it was filled with jagged, razor sharp teeth, I saw the teeth and fear enveloped me. Falling, yet frozen, I tried to comprehend what I was seeing, and prepare for the inevitable. I was heading directly into its mouth, the snake seeing me falling, slivered its body preparing for the meal falling from the sky. It was now ready to strike at its falling prey and I couldn't stop the free fall. He snake was a monstrosity and began to reach to the heavens, springing skyward to capture its prey.

It opened its mouth wider and I saw the billowy cotton inside, it looked soft and inviting, the perfect place to land without injury, and cushion my fall. I was now close; I was about to be devoured. I could even see the belly of the snake as it arched its body skyward, a majestic yellow, so intensely bright and almost blinding. The suns reflection bounced right off of it and into my eyes, I tried to shade my eyes with my hand, but it was to no avail. My fall seemed to be increasing by the pull of gravity and I was completely out of control, headed straight into the mouth of the beast, and I could do nothing. I was doomed, either the fall or the snake were going to do me in.

Suddenly, my descent decreased, I began to slow down. I had no idea how, but the intensity of the fall lessened and I put out my arms like wings. I tried to slow my fall even more knowing what lay in wait; the teeth. Blinded by the yellow reflection, I couldn't see my direction any longer. The snake was intentionally blinding me with it's belly reflection, a tool it uses on its victims and it was working; I was blinded and did not know what direction I was headed.

I couldn't redirect myself and realized, blind or not, I was going directly into the snake's mouth, there was no missing it, it was my destination; I was doomed. I lost it, and began to scream, a loud scream, at the top o my lungs I screamed for help and looked around, but there was no one and I plummeted into the mouth of the giant snake.

TEETH,

NO,

HELP,

MMOOOMMMMAAA!

"AAAAAA!"

From nowhere, I felt my body shaken and my mind began to regain consciousness, my awareness increased, and I became cognizant of my surroundings. I woke from my dream state, momma was shaking me free, from darkness, to haze, and then clarity, I woke; my heroes face I stared into,

MOMMA.

"Wake up boy, wake up."

She shook and shook, and I finally woke, the screams ceased and I realized it was a dream; the giant snake was only a dream. I struggled to catch my breath, but fear consumed me, the snake seemed so real, and believable; thank **GOD** it was a dream, I reached up and hugged momma. I began to cry; she shushed me, and hugged me tight. She was my hero and I had lied to her; maybe the dream had something to do with that, come to think of it, it wasn't a dream at all, it was a nightmare.

"What were you dreaming boy?"

I trembled in momma's arms; fear enveloped me, and hugged her tightly. I now had a chance to tell the **TRUTH**, still had a chance, the question was, would I? I began to explain the nightmare to momma.

"I was falling from the sky, from way up there, and I was falling fast. I was out of control, the closer I got to the surface I realized a snake was below me, a giant snake, and I was headed directly into its mouth; I couldn't break my fall."

I paused a moment, still catching my breath, and fear still had a hold on me. Momma's hug was reassuring and gave me the courage to continue.

"I screamed as loud as I could as I fell into the mouth of the snake, it ate me. What does that mean momma?"

"Stop crying boy, it's gonna be O.K."

My mind was now clear, the house was quiet, my room was quiet, and I could hear the rain falling onto our tin roof. Momma laid me back down onto the bed and held me a while. She felt my trembling body and lay with me. She began rubbing my La Tete that was all it took; I was off to sleep again in no time. When I woke the next morning, we all gathered around the table for breakfast. Momma had been up early and had one of our favorite dishes waiting, coffee milk, and saltine crackers, I had a whole sleeve of crackers, momma was making up for the prior nights biscuit shortage.

We couldn't afford chocolate milk, the closest thing to Nestle Quick was coffee milk, it served the purpose, and we never missed nor thought of Nestle. We quickly finished breakfast and went to play in the backyard, there was summer school, and momma encouraged us to go for the day. We walked and talked as we took our excursion to the other side of town. My sisters grilled me about the **FIND** and wanted to know everything. I avoided as many of their questions as possible, but they were persistent. It had rained last night, there were puddles of water everywhere, I splashed my sisters, and they chased me, we arrived at Katherine Drexel.

The day seemed to fly by and for lunch we all sat under a pecan tree and ate Potted Meat and crackers, Aunt Edna had sent lunch, we all knew what to expect; either Potted Meat or Vienna Sausages Carolyn passed out the cans and crackers and we relaxed and ate. I sat there, feeding my face, wondering what Gus was doing at the coulee. I knew it had rained, the water level in the coulee would be back to normal, and the foot tub may be under water again. The **BOX** may have washed off, I hoped it didn't, I couldn't stand to lose it,; I still didn't know what was in it yet? If Gus finds it, he would keep it. It's my **BOX**, he has no right to touch it, I found it.

FINDERS – KEEPERS,

LOSERS – WEEPERS.

Anyway, you **KEEP** what you **FIND**, the day went fast, lunch came and went, and by the afternoon, it was a wrap; the day was over. We began the walk back to the other end, Pooh watched over us as we walked to the house. We passed behind the City Hall, but Gus's car was gone, it was a relief.

Dean said, "Gus is gonna get ya."

Pooh said, "Stop it Dean, leave him alone. He didn't do nothing wrong, you always pickin,"

Lu reminded me, "You know he's gonna come by the house this afternoon."

Sue suggested, "Just tell the **TRUTH**, and that's it."

Pooh added, "Keith, momma won't let Gus do nothing to you, she got ya' back,"

Before long, we were home, but momma hadn't arrived from the Billeaud's yet. We began to do our homework, we had a regular routine, and we even had little desks from the throw away pile at St. Cecilia. A little hammering here, nails there, and they were as good as new. We all heard a knock on the front door, but it caught us by surprise; we never have visitors while momma's away. Pooh was the designated adult in momma's absence, she stood from the desks and began to make her way to the front the rest of us stayed in the back, but listened; we all knew it was **GUS**.

You could cut the tension in the house, instantly it got completely quiet, and you could hear a pen drop as Pooh walked to the front. The diplomat, she is made for situations just like this, how was she going to wiggle herself out of this was a mystery to us all; if only **MOMMA** were here. Pooh let the stranger knock again, she was using the stall technique, we all knew what she was trying to accomplish, and she knew it was Gus. We all went to the girl's room window; we would be able to see Gus through a crack in the curtains. He knocked louder the second time and listened, putting his ear to the door, listening for whispers, footsteps, or anything.

Pooh asked, "Who is it?"

"It's Chief Girouard, is your mother home?"

Vasco Da Gama

Pooh paused, allowing some time to elapse, she didn't immediately reply. She was a cool cookie, Pooh was smart, and so Gus then asked another question.

"Is Bessie in?"

"My momma not home from work yet, we can't open the door, and you can't come in."

We could hear him chuckle from the other side of the door, he was probably thinking, Bessie has raised her children well. We quietly, on tip-toes walked to the front room, we could now go see for ourselves; all of us together against Gus, a united front. Through the door Gus spoke.

"You're taught well, which one are you; Paulette, Claudette, Lucille, or Susan."

Pooh turned and looked at us, we all looked back, surprised; Broussard is a small town, ask the right person a question and you can find out anything. Gus had done his homework, he knew the inner workings of the Nickerson family, and he knew all the pieces to the puzzle; we were impressed, he's not as dumb as he comes across. I stood in the shadows with my sisters, Gus was on the prowl, and he wasn't going to take "**NO**" for an answer. Pooh again got quiet, we could see her thinking, and composing herself. It was incredible, she was **COURAGEOUS**, I saw, for the first time, what Pooh possessed.

Dean whispered to me, "Ah, hah; you in trouble."

Lu stood still, almost frozen, she was motionless, and petrified. She was scared stiff, and looked funny. Sue watched, always the quiet one, always watching. She made mental notes, almost a daily log, was the historian, and a **BRAIN**.

"I'm not going to go against what my momma said, Mr. Gus. She should be home soon, come back later."

"Can I at least talk to Keith?"

She stepped on the floor as if walking away from the door, trying to deceive Gus. She tip-toed back to the door and could hear him, he was smelling at the door jam, sniffing, recording her scent, like an animal. Pooh pointed for us to go to the window, we tip-toed to it, out of the window we could see Gus on his hands and knees, sniffing at the foot of the door jam. He was inhaling Pooh's scent, recording her aura, he looked around suspiciously, but stayed on all fours, smelling.

Sue said, "Let me see."

Gus heard, even though it was a whisper, the canine in Gus heard. His hearing was acute; he immediately stood upright, and straight, and looked around, seeking any on looking eyes. He backed away from the door and looked at the windows on the house. We silently and slowly retreated into the shadows, he stood in front of the house, looking; it was bizarre. We then heard the voice of our hero coming from down the street, momma had arrived. From a distance, we heard her greet Gus, her approach was quiet, and she surprised him.

"I know my children told you I'm not there, why you still here?"

"Bessie, don't bite off more than you can chew, know your place woman. I need to talk to that boy of yours."

Momma stopped and looked toward the house, she knew we were watching, this was a showdown moment, would momma have the guts to stand up to Gus? It was a huge moment.

"Would MOMMA back down?"

"Mr. Jeerwaa, you're here, my children are inside, let me change, get my house ready to welcome a guest, and I'm only now knocking off; give me a few minutes."

Gus didn't reply, he simply stared while momma walked past him. They made eye contact, as she passed turned her glance downward; it was almost a sign of respect or submission. Pooh opened the door as Momma approached, she had a serious strut; just before entering, she looked back at Gus. Again, they made eye contact; she then turned and entered the house.

"Pooh, close that door and lock it. Where's your brother?"

I came from the back, the others were behind me, momma looked worried and shook; she had a lot on her plate. She spoke to all of us.

GUS.

"Gus is acting strange, the people I work for were acting strange today, intentionally trying to keep me longer, I could see it. Something is going on, I don't know what you found boy, but this entire little town knows about it."

Momma went right past us to her room, she talked, walked, and commanded; she was perpetual motion.

"Pooh, straighten out that front room."

"Claudette, Lu, Sue; ya'll sit on the sofa, I want all ya'll to witness this. It is a part of lie for people like us, get use to the cops being in your business."

She slammed the door shut to her room; you could hear her moving around inside, her footsteps going everywhere. We went back to the windows to observe Gus, while Pooh got the front room ready; we all now had a part in this. Momma appeared from her room lickity split, no longer wearing an apron, and no housekeeper attire. Unbeknown to us, momma had planned this; she had on a pair of black jeans, black Keds tennis shoes, and a black blouse. We were shocked, Momma was dressed to impress, she was on Fire.

"Keith, come here boy, we gonna sit Gus on the recliner and you gonna talk on your home turf. Let's invite Mr. Jeerwaa in."

She walked to the front door, unlocked, and opened it, opened the screen door, and addressed Gus. Momma was making a statement; I was "**WOW'D**," all the children were "**WOW'D**."

"Come in Mr. Jeerwaa. The roof ain't gonna fall on top of you, and if it do, I don't have no insurance."

She laughed to ease the mood and waved him in. We waited, this was a big moment, and I could see, I wasn't the only nervous one. The tension was incredible, the moment was anticipated, and now it's here. Momma was going to kill him with kindness, a skill she has molded, tweaked, and finally mastered; Gus was in for a big surprise.

"Come on in here, Gus."

CORTÉS

We gathered in the front room as Gus entered. He took off his hat showing manners, we all stood back, watching him, and looking at his eyes, wherever they went, so would ours. He suddenly seemed bigger, for some odd reason he looked more intimidating. Momma welcomed him in and directed him to the recliner. Company always sits in the Recliner/Lounger, it is momma's pride and joy, and for "Company" only, the only time it's sat in, strange, but that's momma.

Gus sat in the lounger and I sat next to momma on the love seat, the girls all gathered on the sofa, everyone was there: Gus, Momma, Me, Pooh, Dean, Lu, and Sue; there were eight of us present, unseen, **CURIOSITY** was also in attendance. As I sat next to momma, I thought about the rain of last night, it was hard, I could tell by the ruts the runoff created; it takes strong water current to wash away soil. A lot of rain had fallen, it probably contributed to me sleeping so hard, and dreaming.

OBSESSION – 2

I thought about the rain all day and wondered about the **BOX**. I pondered if it was still there, had the current washed it away, or had Gus found it. I wanted confirmation, I wanted to know it was still there, I had to know it was still there, I wanted to sneak back so badly; but I chilled. I didn't need to draw any unnecessary attention to myself, I know I'm being watched, I hope Glen chilled too. The **BOX** has been there who knows how long, and the entire focus is on the bones under the foot tub, the gruesome discovery. I must keep it that way, and stick to my original story, momma told me, "Say the same thing every time." That's what I'm gonna do, I've been practicing, I'm ready, I'm set, and all there is left to, **GO**; I'm prepared for the mysterious creature named **GUS**.

Once everyone settled in, it began, the room was hushed, quiet; momma spoke first, this is her house, and she's in charge. She directed her first words toward Gus, then finished with me.

"Mr. Jeerwaa, remember, my son is a child, and your average teenage boy. Thirteen is barely teenager, he's my son."

She paused, her eyes were glued on Gus, once her point was made; she turned her attention to me.

"Be honest son, just tell the **TRUTH**."

I said, "O.K."

I took a deep breath feeling pressure, it was about to begin. Momma was now taking off the kid gloves. All eyes were on **ME**. Gus smiled with me, trying to ease the situation.

He asked, "Are you nervous Keith?"

I smiled back, but didn't reply. I took another deep breath and without a word said, nodded my head as confirmation, I was very nervous.

He said, "I'm nervous too."

We both chuckled when he said it, an unexpected surprise; Gus had a sense of humor. He looked around the room, gauging our lifestyle, witnessing our taste, and judging us. He gradually returned his focus to me.

"Keith, have you ever seen anyone back there before?"

I thought about it and quickly realized I needed to say "**NO,**" without further hesitation, I did exactly that.

"No, no one goes back there but me; me and Roger."

"Yes, I'm sorry to hear about your dog, he was one protective dog."

Everything Gus said was being analyzed, every reaction, every reaction, facial expressions, head gesture, he was the one being inspected, and he was auditioning for the Nickerson family. You had: Dean - Inspector Gadget. Pooh - Inspector Clouseau, Lu and Sue - Sherlock Holmes and his sidekick, Dr. Watson, and the one sitting on the Bench – Bessie Nickerson is Judge Judy Sheindlin. This was a tough bunch.

Gus continued, "Do you go back there often?"

The front room was silent, everyone awaited my response, it was a Q and A session, Gus asked the questions, and I answered them. I shrugged my shoulders up and down.

"Not really. The coulee runs under the tracks. I play along the tracks more than I explore the coulee, I'm not that into exploring."

My sister's faces said it all, I was cold busted; a bald-faced lie. I'm never on the tracks, I'm always at the coulee, momma knows it and my sisters know it. Gus probably knows it too.

"Are you being truthful to me son?"

I used a trump card, and I told you, I've been practicing, I had a Ace in the Hole. I could use an excuse that would fit the situation. I was ready.

"I'm just nervous, I don't know what you want me to say. I don't want to get in trouble, I don't know what to do."

Calmly, Gus replied, "Tell the **TRUTH** Keith. You know I can sniff out a **LIE**."

He touched his nose and smiled at me. I knew exactly what he was saying, he knows that I know, he is a **DOG;** Gus is a **DOG** disguised as a human. My imagination was in overdrive, I reminded myself not to talk about the **BOX**. I had to re-think this.

"Momma, Mr. Gus, I'm sorry for lying. I love to play along the coulee; I thought if I answered yes, it would be a problem. Momma knows if she's looking for me, I'm usually not hard to find. It rained last night; the coulee had been low, lower than I had never seen it."

"Why were you there yesterday?"

"It was just a normal day, I was thinking about Roger. He always used to lead the way, his nose was great; he could sniff things out too, Mr. Gus."

"Yesterday was just a normal day?"

"Yes, sir, like most."

"Your mom said it was a difficult day for you. Was it normal or was it difficult?"

Momma said, "Mr. Jeerwaa, the boy is not on the witness stand; don't try to use my words against him. He stays at that damned coulee, Mr. Explorer."

"I'm sorry son, I apologize if I got harsh. I'm just trying to get a handle on this."

"I know the rain last night didn't help, that's why I found the foot tub. The coulee was really low."

"Did you find anything else?"

"I object your honor. He is leading the Witness."

The room went completely silent, Gus had thrown out a nugget, his trump card, if I gave the right answer, it was a closed case, the wrong answer, and there was drama. I had to play this right, it was the ultimate Lead Question. Again, I respond quickly to reflect confidence and honesty, any delay insinuated doubt, and we can't have that. Doubt infers a **LIE**, and inferences are deadly; the demise of many a good liar. Hesitation on my part generated suspicion; I had to leave no doubt. If the **BOX** is still there, it is mine, in the midst of this, I was thinking about the **BOX**. I don't even know what's in it, yet it draws me, attracts me, and beckons me. If Gus had it, he wouldn't be here, he is fueled by curiosity, I realized he ain't got **SQUAT**.

"No, sir, all I found was the foot tub with the bones under it, and I'm sorry I found that. How long do you think the baby has been dead?"

I tried to throw Gus off, use a distraction technique; Barnaby Jones always does it. I flipped the script, now I was the **Q**, and Gus was the **A**, you are one wise kid, **DIRT**. Today has been a growth experience; I'm learning things about our Police Chief. Things that aren't always seen by the naked eye, if he had the **BOX**, he wouldn't be playing this Q & A game, and he's fishing. I now realized the questioning was a piece of cake, my confidence grew, and then Gus threw a monkey wrench in the mix, making an inquiry very unexpected.

"Did you find a chest or box of some sort?"

He came straight out and asked; I was surprised, and wondered; did he know? Why ask about a chest or box, did he find it, or see us, again I quickly responded.

"No, sir, I keep telling you, all I found was the bones; that's all. You can ask Glen Simms, he was with me."

"Don't get short with me boy, I'm only being thorough, you never mentioned the Simms boy before, why wait until now?"

Momma, sitting next to me, felt compelled to speak, she came to my defense, at this very moment, I could use another objection.

"That's an odd question Gus, how does a box or chest fit into this? No one mentioned a chest or box, like you said, 'Why wait until now?'"

"I'm asking the questions Bessie Mae, please shut up."

"This is my house Mr. Jeerwaa, you're not going to come into my house and disrespect me, and especially not in front of my children. I expect an apology or this interview is over."

Gus sat quiet, fixed his eyes on momma; we could see it was a stalemate. He was pissed and momma was perturbed, someone had to give or the Q & A session was over.

"My apologies Bessie, we have never had bad words exchanged, let's keep it that way. I'm simply frustrated over this case, I can't determine the rate of decomposition, the baby's sex or race, and the rain last night didn't help. I'm no further along than when I started."

His voice, filled with frustration revealed he was clearly unhinged, he hoped I could give him something, and I had nothing; I stuck to my first story.

"Just a few more questions and it's over. I want to say, you've done well Keith."

"Thank you sir."

Momma hugged me tight after my response, she saw herself in me, she always taught us to respect our elders; today would be no different.

"Under a Moj-Yah tree a few feet away from the foot tub I found a few footprints, they're gone today, but they were there yesterday. Also I found a branch used by someone to camouflage the ground; do you know anything about that?"

Gus was now hot, if I would have hid the branch there would be nothing, now he was burning hot, and we were playing a new form of Hide and Seek. I am doing the hiding of something, and he is seeking my knowledge to locate it, sorry Charlie, "I'm selfish."

"No, sir, I saw no box or chest. My footprints should be around the area, and Glen's. As for a branch, I don't have any idea what you're talking about."

"I just noticed an imprint in the ground, on the bank, I was square like a small container of some sort, and footprints were near the area. The square, the footprints, and the branch washed away with the rain. So much of the crime scene the rain destroyed, and the place where the foot tub sat is underwater."

Gus paused and gave me a long look.

"Are you telling me everything Jacques Cousteau?"

I felt good about what he revealed, the crime scene, no more, I sat quietly listening, I now had the upper hand. I had to dismiss the box/chest insinuation, and my current positioning had me feeling like anyone of the three mystic monkeys.

I see nothing.

I hear nothing.

I say nothing.

"Whatever was taken from the crime scene is valuable, it may be the vital piece of evidence needed to solve this case, think again; are you sure you saw nothing else or took anything? If you did, you're not in any kind of trouble, listen to what I'm saying."

I denied it for the third time like Peter denying Jesus, Gus could hint all he wanted to that I have something, but he couldn't prove it. You're innocent until proven guilty, I have or saw no **BOX**.

"No, sir, I saw no Box or Chest, sorry, and I k now Glen didn't see or take anything either. We were startled when we found the bones, I slipped in the mud and fell backwards, that's why my footsteps are there, and why my shirt was full of the berries; I saw nothing on the bank, I was just scared."

We had been at it a while and my sisters were getting restless. The sun was beginning to fall and I knew momma was about to step in, we would have to continue this tomorrow. As I sat thinking, a rooster crowed, I thought it was very ironic. I don't think anyone else put the two together, but I did, it was the third time I denied the **TRUTH**.

Gus said, "Bessie, I know you were just getting in from work, and the afternoon has quickly turned to evening; it gets dark early, I hate this new time. Maybe I could talk to boy again tomorrow, I'll try to set something up with Shirley Simms also; I need Glen's side to this."

Momma smiled, but said nothing, it was Gus' turn to have the floor, we were all quiet, there wasn't much more I could tell him anyway. His suggestion was perfect, he was in our house long enough, and it was time for the police to go. Everything about Gus felt wrong; I wondered if I was the only one feeling this way.

Gus continued, "Maybe tomorrow afternoon you and Glen can show me how you happened upon the foot tub, I would like to know the direction you were coming from, and a couple of other things to give me a better picture."

Momma replied, "Whatever time I get off of work, we'll show you. I'm going to accompany my son as long as it's Police Business."

I didn't have to answer, momma was on top of her game, she had been down that road before. She and the Broussard Police Department weren't exactly on speaking terms, her eldest son had a previous run in with B.P.D., was railroaded, and given a bad reputation; we knew the accusations were lies, but it still was out there. Momma stood and began to escort Gus to the front door.

"I'll make sure to be here when you arrive, if I'm not here, please, don't be snooping, or sniffing around my house. Thanks for stopping by Mr. Jeerwaa; children."

Together we addressed the chief, almost in harmony, that's how tight we are as a family. We tease, fuss, and fight, but we also stick **TOGETHER**. We think alike, and respond a certain way because we know it is expected; momma has high expectations, we responded.

"Thanks you Mr. Jeerwaa."

I said it the right way, pronounced his last name as it's spelled.

"Thanks for stopping in Mr. Girouard."

New Day

The day flew by, the entire school was a buzz, and I was the talk of the town. In a small town, news travels, people speculate about the investigation, and they talk to their spouses. All of it fuels wonder, contributes to conjecture, and when a police car is parked in front of your house the last two afternoons, people are naturally curious. Eyes watched me everywhere I went, it was weird, I was getting the kind of attention you don't need; the spotlight isn't always a good thing. When the day finally ended, it wasn't soon enough, and the walk home was interesting, we talked about the odd mannerisms of our Chief of Police. Pooh and I shared with the rest about Gus' ears in the squad car, and Pooh saw it, I wasn't making it up. We described to Pooh how Gus was on all fours outside the door, sniffing, trying to pick up her scent, smelling her.

Claudette said, "Yea, he smelled you through the door."

"I didn't see," Sue complained.

Lu made a funny face, she didn't like Claudette's tone, and what it insinuated; it was a bad thing. She spoke up.

"Claudette, you make it sound **NASTY**."

We laughed at Lu, her innocence is refreshing, expressions are strange, and is just different; sometimes I think she can read minds. She knows what you're thinking before you even say it, she is **MENTAL**.

"I didn't see," Sue complained.

We continued the walk home, all commenting about Momma's performance. We were proud of Momma, and saw her **STRENGTH**; she waited to reveal it at the most opportune time, momma never ceases to amaze.

I said, "I also must confess, Momma was stunning all in black."

They all erupted into laughter.

"Gus must be a dog," Pooh surmised.

I said, "I was Roger's master, I know dogs, the chief is a blood hound; twice, I've witnessed it, the **DOG** in him. I don't trust him, and what's his claim to fame around Broussard?"

"Once He gets on the Case, that's a WRAP."

He brags about always getting his man or woman. Broussard isn't a newsworthy town, it's a small, rural, country place, it's as rural as you can get; not much happens here, and when something does, everyone is in the know. There isn't much crime to speak of, and the residents are the who's who of Cajun Creole lore, names like Girouard, Ducrest, Janin, Hodges, Malagarie, Landry, Choplin, and Billeaud. The origin of the names, French/Creole, and they are all of one ethnicity. The town has the feel of an old fashioned, small, rustic town of the past. The people think small, crime is virtually non-existent and based purely on rumor, and I think Gus is batting 1.000. He has **NEVER** lost a case, and always gets his person.

UNCANNY

UNCANINE

We arrived home, it was Friday afternoon, and we could smell something delicious in the air; momma was home, she was cooking. She was home early, and catfish etouffee was on the menu, one of our favorites. We were excited, any time we spend with momma is a plus, she works a lot, and never gets off early. For her to be in at this time of the day, she was looking forward to this afternoon, her son is involved, and it's obviously important to her. She wants to make sure he gets justice, and treated fairly.

We rushed the back door, we knew where she was, in the kitchen, and the quickest access to the kitchen was the back door. Catfish etouffee, our mouths watered at the thought, every Friday there is a tradition at the Nickerson household; we eat seafood. It could be crawfish, catfish, garfish, fried fish, shrimp, crabs, etc., the choices are numerous, and that's why we love Friday;

T.G.I.F.

Momma is a devout catholic, tradition recognizes Friday as a day of fast, meaning no meat, and if she fasts, then so do we. All of us stood in the kitchen watching her cook and sweat; we began to put away the dishes, the dried clothes, and I was going to take out the trash. Before we began our afternoon chores, she asked,

"Children, how was the day?"

Pooh said, "It went by fast, on the way home we were talking about Mr. Gus. We didn't tell you, but Keith and I saw some strange stuff in the car when he brought us home; at times he acts like an animal, a **DOG**."

Momma chuckled, she couldn't imagine what Pooh was talking about, and probably concluded it was childish foolishness, and a product of her overactive imagination.

I added, "He is a **DOG** momma, he crawls on all fours, sniffs, and smells like a dog does; he's more Dog than Man."

Momma laughed harder, and began to remove the pots from the wood burning stove, she has no way of lowering a burner; with our stove, it's all or nothing.

"I need to start getting ready; ya'll know Gus is going to be here any minute."

Before momma exited to her room, she stopped and addressed me.

"Keith, quit exaggerating, Gus crawling on all fours; boy your imagination is in overdrive."

We all looked at each other as she made it to her room, from behind her door, as she changed, she directed us; we could hear her and she could hear us. She didn't believe what Pooh or I said about Gus, we continued to tell her.

"Momma, we all saw it, Keith and Pooh not lying. Something is wrong with Mr. Gus," Claudette added.

From behind the door, momma barked out a few commands, even though she was changing, she could multi-task; that's Momma.

"Pooh, check the pots, he'll be here soon, let's get ready. Keith and I are going to go with him to the coulee, while I'm gone, listen to Paulette; Keith, get ready."

Momma emerged from her room; we were all waiting to see what she had on today. Out of nowhere, Sue rushed into the kitchen, she was nervous, jittery, and her eyes were huge; she was scared, something shook her.

Stuttering, she said, "Momma, Mr. Gus is in the back yard, I saw him. He crawled to the back on his hands and knees."

Momma looked at Susan questionably, doubting what Tote had said, we could see it in her expression; she probably thought Sue was in on this, and we were all pulling her leg. Just then, there was a knock at the door, our attention turned to the front, all expecting the same person, and there was only one person it could be

GUS – The PAWN.

Momma and I began our walk to the front, the rest stayed in the back; momma gave some last minute instructions.

"Pooh, watch the food and the rest of ya'll, listen to Paulette; do whatever she tells you, we won't be long."

<u>End of CHAPTER ½</u>

John Cabot

Beginning of CHAPTER ¾.

We walked out of the house heading in the normal, no different than the one Momma led Gus on the prior day. Momma and I noticed Gus dusting off the knees of his pants and wiping off his hands, confirmation of what Sue saw, we both logged what we witnessed. The walk wasn't long, it wasn't far from the house, I led, momma was second, Gus was last, there was no talking, and I had nothing to say. Momma simply watched, looking at the area and Gus' mannerisms; Gus requested the audience. He opened with the first question.

Using LIES as ALIBI'S.

"Is this the route you normally take?"

"Yes sir, you can see the trail I take leading to the coulee, the grass along the trail is long, I try to stick to one route. I don't' know what's in the grass and I don't want to find out."

We continued to walk and he asked no more questions, then he added a strange comment, almost an observation.

"Roger was your protector, he handled anything you encountered, and fought off any animals."

"Yes sir, he was fearless."

Momma listened taking it all in, she asked nothing, and let me handle matters myself, I felt capable as long as Momma was near. We winded our way through the path, deeper into the tall grass, and it got denser.

Gus asked, "How often do they cut this stuff?"

Momma said, "Gus, my son doesn't work for the town, you would know the answer to that question before he would, please don't intentionally try to confuse him."

"Bessie, your son knows much more than he's putting on, I know he does, and he's not being truthful."

"This is the way I came Mr. Gus, I always come the same way, and I'm telling the **TRUTH**, I don't know anything."

"Let's keep going." Gus replied.

We made it through the brush, the coulee looked different, and the water was higher, higher than I had seen it in a long time. The drought had revealed a new coulee, but the recent rain returned the coulee of old, all the discoveries the drought exposed were now gone.

"This is the route I took Mr. Gus, that afternoon I started walking this way, no particular reason, I just started walking."

"Did you notice anything out of the ordinary, anything caught your eye?"

"What do you mean different, yea, I didn't have Roger; that was different. Also, the coulee was low, not like it is now, all the rest looks the same."

"You're a very observant boy aren't you Keith, you do notice your surroundings, don't you?"

"Yes sir, I try to, I have to be even more cautious now; there is no more Roger."

Momma said, "You and that damned Roger, that boy even made us have a funeral, he loved that dog."

Gus smiled finding what momma said humorous and then gave us his reasoning.

"A dog is man's best friend, I had a dog when I was a child, and he was a good dog. We had to put it to sleep, he got bit by a rabid raccoon, and my dad shot it after it bit me."

We listened to Mr. Gus as we walked along the bank of the coulee. It was very slippery, the rain had created plenty of mud, and our feet sank into the mud as we walked. Momma felt very uncomfortable, it was dangerous, and at one point, she almost fell in.

"What more can my son explain Gus, he showed you the path he took. You have the foot tub with the bones, that's all he knows, and I'm taking him home."

"One more thing before we leave, the Moj-Yah tree over there, that's where I found the imprint of the box. I noticed you had berry stains on your shirt the first day, did you find something under that tree?"

"No sir, I slipped and fell by the tree, that's how I got the berry stains on my shirt. I was startled when I saw the bones, I didn't know what it was, I was afraid. It was the bones of a baby, I ran home afterwards to tell Momma."

"I guess the chest shaped indentation in the ground was a figment of my imagination, and the branches used to hide footprints, all imagined on my part; and how fortunate the water washed it all away. I just want it known that I know, the rain was convenient; son you're protected by angels."

"O.K. Gus, that's enough, he is only a child. Your suspicions are simply conjecture, that's all it is. It's time for us to return home, my son has chores and he gets to bed early."

She then paused, her eyes fixed on Mr. Jeerwaa, and I suddenly saw it again, **STRENGTH** reared its head and rose out of Lucille Bessie Mae Nickerson. She was the picture of **STRENGTH** and Gus recognized it. She then turned to me. There was a silent pause amongst us all; Gus then made a startling revelation. He disclosed a finding that put a different variable into the mix it was disturbing.

"The crime lab determined it was not bones of a baby, the bones weren't human at all. It was the casing of a creature, the remains of a transformation, the discarded bones of the immature creature turning into the mature. It was an evolutionary step in a growth process, growth of what is yet to be determined. It was not human, not animal, and almost an insect."

Momma and I were surprised; we both thought the bones were of a little baby, to our surprise it was not. What a strange revelation, if not a baby, what was it? Momma pointed for me to go forward.

"Give me a minute son, let me talk to Gus."

I walked off, but watched, I almost walked backward keeping an eye on Momma and Gus, and she saw me stop.

"Keep going boy, just stay in sight."

THE KING

I was now out of listening range, didn't know what they were discussing, but I just kept an eye on Momma, and made sure Gus wasn't out of line. If he was, as if I could do anything about it, I knew Momma could handle herself.

"Gus, I don't know what you think my son has found, he told you what he knows, that's the last of it. Please, respect my wishes, I'll talk to him, and if he tells me anything, I promise to share it."

Gus was motionless, momma's was turned slightly to me, all I saw was the silhouette of her lips moving, and before I knew it, she was walking toward me. I thought I saw Gus' lips move, I tried to read his lips, he did utter something. I understood Dean's unspoken words, why couldn't I understand Gus? I was puzzled, then it dawned on me; Gus hadn't said a word, his mouth didn't form a word. I shockingly realized,

He Growled.

Momma walked hurriedly toward me, I greeted her as she approached. The mud no longer hindered her, she was high stepping, really moving.

"What's wrong Momma, what did he say?"

She didn't talk, only grabbed my hand as we hurriedly left the coulee heading home. She didn't look back, got to the turn in the trail and it was my final chance to look back, I had to. I had to see where Gus was, and what he was doing.

The Prodigal Son

Steven knocked on the door then stepped back and waited, he could hear footsteps approaching the front door, he then heard a high pitched scream, and heard running within the house. The running was of more than one person, rushing to the front door, the sound of running grew as it arrived at the front door. To be safe, Steven backed up a little more, he figured it was better to be safe than sorry. He heard the door unlock and as it opened, the screen door obstructed his view; he could barely see through it, dust had collected on it, and it hadn't been swept in a while. The person in the house was shadowed, he couldn't make them out, but Claudette recognized her brother, she tried to disguise her voice.

"What you want here boy?"

The running within the house was now silent, Steven didn't say a word, Claudette saw the confused look on her big brothers face, and could hold it in no longer. She erupted into laughter, Pooh then came out, then Lu, and Sue followed, they all opened the screen door and welcomed their big brother home. It had been four years since he went to live with Aunt Tuut; they all loved their big brother, and missed his **LEADERSHIP**. He is steady as a rock, the anchor, and he steadies the ship, after they all exchanged hugs he asked.

"Where is Momma and Dirt Man, I heard about Roger, I know he's hurt."

The sun was setting, Friday was coming to a rapid end, Pooh remembered about the pots on the stove, and before she answered Steven's question, she began to walk toward the kitchen; she needed to check on the pots. Dean locked the front door behind Steven and they all followed Pooh to the kitchen.

Pooh said, "Hub Cap, come to the kitchen, I have to check on the etouffee. Momma has on some Irish potatoes, she's gonna make a potato salad, she knew you were coming?"

Steven laughed, as if momma wouldn't know, she knows all, orchestrates it all, and is the author and the finisher.

"Of course she knows, she told Aunt Tuut to send me. She said I needed to talk to Keith, I figured it was about Roger; ya'll know if momma needs me, I coming."

As they walked, Dean said, "With momma, there's no telling what's up, I should have known. She and Keith should be back soon, they're with Gus."

Steven's facial expression changed, he remembered Gus, and their last interaction was not pleasant. Fear invaded his mind, he began to worry, and he needed some questions answered.

"What they doin with Gus; what Dirt did?"

Hub Cap knows Gus, their last confrontation left Steven with battle scars. He was used to being the scapegoat, and at times he allowed it and intentionally took the fall; the sacrifice of one to save all. All the girls stood silent, no one dared to answer his question.

Momma heard Steven's voice as they turned the corner entering the backyard, she paused, put her hand on my shoulder, and we both stopped. I knew the voice too, it was Hub Cap, I missed him, my heart jumped for joy, he is the **LEADER** of the family, and momma defers to him.

"Ssshhh, quiet, let' sneak up on them. Slow your breathing, your mind, quietly think, and slow down your thinking too."

I watched Momma as she crept, and like Bruce Lee she walked silently. She had skills; I couldn't hear her and I was right next to her, I know they couldn't. She whispered,

"Do like you Momma."

She put her pointing finger to her lips and rose to her tiptoes, then stayed on the balls of her feet, noiselessly creeping, and quietly approaching.

"Come over here."

Soundlessly we snuck away from the back door and stopped behind the outhouse, once there, momma's normal tone returned. We stood behind it, no one in the house could see us, it was our private moment.

"I know you found some kind of **BOX**, you're not being honest to me, I'm hurt that you can't **TRUST** me; maybe you'll **TRUST** your big brother. You have to **TRUST** somebody; this might be your last opportunity to tell the **TRUTH**."

Her words resounded, she knew, without a doubt, I was lying, Gus' suspicions confirmed it, and the mood of the townsfolk added fuel to the fire; they were all suddenly acting strange. I listened to momma, and had nothing to say; I was a **LIAR**. She now walked normal as we left the outhouse; we approached the back door wanting to surprise her eldest. Momma has a different nickname for Steven; he is Gumbo because of his insatiable appetite for the dish. His siblings, his brother and sisters, we call him Hub Cap,

Steven James Nickerson

"Look what the CAT drug in."

Entering into the back door, and then into the little kitchen; all eyes turned to momma as her voice rang out. Steven, by his lonesome, walked up to Momma. Hub Cap's eyes filled with tears, his heart became heavy; he was back home, and about to enter the arms of his mother. Momma's eyes filled with tears too, I think we all got emotional, and it was a bonding moment. Steven, our **LEADER**, was back in the fold; we were now complete. Momma and Gumbo embraced; a powerful hug, a hard squeeze, and a welcomed reunion. We could see the intensity of it, and feel the emotion involved, they hugged forever; all right, already, the catfish etouffee. You could hear both of them sniffling, we stood quietly watching, it was a special moment, very touching, and we were all awestruck. In a muffled, mumbled, weakened voice, Steven spoke.

"I missed you so much Momma, I missed all of ya'll."

He reached out his right arm and gathered me in, I was pulled into the embrace, it was now he, Momma, and I, and suddenly the last four joined us, once again, we were eight present, **CURIOSITY** was ever-present; never a dull moment at the Nickerson's. The family hug was the longest ever, tonight was special, and now were all back, we all missed Steven tremendously; his departure left a void in us all. Momma was now in the middle of us, the hug centered around her, as we embraced, she spoke.

"This family is finally all back together, I have dreamt of this for a long time, and prayed for it also. To see my dreams come true is unbelievable, and having my prayers answered; only of **GOD**."

She paused a while, the hug felt so good, and was long overdue. Momma was our queen, Steven was back, old Hub Cap, and though I lost Roger, I regained my Big Brother. I can't call it a trade-off, **GOD** knows what you need before you ask, he is watching over us; as we broke the embrace, Momma spoke.

"Steven, you asked what Keith and I was doing with Gus, we had to talk about something your little brother found in the coulee. I hope that all of this is over, what Keith and Glen found in that coulee, who knows? Gus says one thing, Keith says another, and I believe my son."

Again, she paused to allow her words sink in, we stepped back and continued to listen, momma had something on her mind; it was important. It was time for a lesson, we could feel it, no on interrupted, we let her do her thing.

"Once before, I believed Gus and not my son, not believing my son built a wall between us. I allowed that wall to grow and take full responsibility for my actions. I was wrong, I gave in too easily, should have fought than I didn't; I regret that."

Again, she paused, gathered her thoughts, and continued.

"I now have a chance to do it over; this time I will back my son to the end. As a family, we will support him to the end; I want you all to remember what momma always says,

'A FAMILY that prays together stays together.'"

After momma spoke, a hush invaded the room, the silence needed to be broken, but no one dared talk; Steven then took the lead.

"Momma, when you told me you were cooking catfish etouffee, I've been thinking of catfish etouffee all day, my mouth is salivating, and my stomach is making that springy sound. Pooh has the potatoes cooling to make the potato salad, we'll set the table, it's time to Maw-Jay."

In French that means eat, momma laughed, **GUMBO** hadn't changed a bit, he still had appetite. That's the brother I know, Hub Cap can eat 24/7-365, and Chew-Bus ain't got nothing on him. We all began to disperse, before long it would be suppertime.

SUSPICION

Gus walked along the banks of the coulee pacing back and forth, his mind raced, and he was pissed. His extra sensory ability was hindered, scents were washed away, and tracks were gone. There was nothing left, no trail, or leads to follow; his few advantages Mother Nature destroyed. The one scent he did recognize, Keith's, it was all along both banks of the coulee, he could also now smell his accomplice. Their scents, there before the rain, were still there, around the foot tub, on the trail, under the Moj-Yah tree, and by the little indention in the ground, it held a **BOX**. He exited the trail and began to walk to his car, as he passed Bessie Mae's house he caught a whiff of an old scent, a scent not too pleasing, Steven was back, and Gus smelled him. He stopped in front of the house and smelled the stink, he thought, "That boy is **TROUBLE,**" a terrible time for **TROUBLE** to return.

We all gathered around the table, it had been a long time since Steven's placement was set, it was years, his absence left an incomplete circle, an opening, an empty spot, and no one there. He's back and we're all excited, he protects the entire family, it was now intact. Momma called us to the stove, one by one, as she dished out plates; she and the girls served first.

"Keith, put my plate in my spot."

I took her plate in hand and put it on the table, there is no head of the table, our table is round, we are universally connected, all one body, and no one part is more important than the other; at a young age momma taught us that. I returned to the stove, she had dished me out a plate, it was heaping high, she had outdone herself, she knows I love her cooking, I gladly took the plate, and she then told Steven,

"You can finish it Hub Cap."

I almost lost my mind as I sat there; I had a full plate sitting in front of me, but felt a twinge of jealousy. The last four years, he was gone, that was my role, quick like that, Hub Cap returns and gets first position on the leftovers, momma could have at least shared it 50/50; **COLD BLOODED**, I felt slighted.

"Thank You Momma,"

He stood at the stove and looked back at me, the smile on his face irked me, he began serving himself; we waited knowing what had to be done, there was one prerequisite before eating. We had already washed up, momma was silent, watching, she wanted to see if her teaching was absorbed, and taken root? She also wanted to see if the temptation of hunger outweighed prayer, no one dared slip up, and once Steven sat, she suggested.

"Hub Cap, say grace."

He smiled, knowing it was coming, he expected nothing less, that's how momma operates, he had to take back his rightful place, and he is the oldest. We all knew Hub Cap was going to bless the food, it was his "Welcome Back" prayer; silence consumed the table.

"**GOD** is **GREAT**, **GOD** is **GOOD**, let us thank **HIM** for our food, Amen."

Hub Cap's prayer was straight to the point, he was obviously hungry, we all were, time to get our **GRUB** on. No one talked, only ate; catfish etouffee, Bessie Mae Nickerson's recipe; it's the **BOMB**. After the meal we talked at the table for a while, momma designated the girls as the dishwashers. Steven made his way over to me, put his arm around my shoulders, pulled me tight to him, and then put me in a headlock.

"Let's go talk lil' brother."

He led me out the back door, as we got to the screen, I looked back, momma was filling the dishpan with water, she watched. She and I made eye contact as we exited; her smile confirmed she liked what she saw. Steven and I began to walk down West Railroad, night had fallen, it was dark, and our road was even darker. At the end of the street was a dead end, there park was there, it gave access to the coulee, and St. Cecilia School. The school is whispered about, holds secrets, myths told by the elders, tales of mysticism, and stories of **Coosh-Maa**.

On the same dead end street was the church, and West Railroad gave access to the graveyard, a little street like that had many things on it. Legends spoke of origins linked to St. Cecilia, tales told by townsfolk of ghosts. The park, coulee, graveyard, or playing at St. Cecilia, those were the places Steven and I established our bond, an the places we first learned to explore. He was my teacher, the original Captain Ahab, at times, he was Captain Nemo, and when he felt the most adventurous, he was Captain Kirk; I was taught by a true Captain. There was never a thought of mutiny by the shipmate, the captain knew the one man crew was loyal, and he was in possession of precious cargo; he took excellent care of his little brother. I walked next to Hub Cap, darkness consumed the night, stars flickered overhead, and as I looked up to the stars, I could see Steven. He was a big boy, a giant dude, a huge brother, and even now, as we walked and talked, he seemed so much larger than **LIFE**.

He ain't heavy, he's my brother.

The strangest thing, just as sudden as he left, he's back, I'm glad he's home, I need him right now, we all need him right now. We reached the dead end and looked out at the darkened, lifeless park, looked toward the basketball court, and darkness covered it.

He said, "In the morning, I'm gonna put it on you like old times."

"Hub Cap, your memory must be fading you bro, your mind is playing tricks on you; before you left, you passed the torch. Actually, I took it, I'm the Kaa-Bopper."

He chuckled, but liked what he heard, the confidence, his little brother was talking trash, and he would have to put an end to that; it was intolerable.

"You talkin shit huh, wait till in the morning, and don't make me wake you up either."

"Don't worry about that Big Brother, I'll be up and ready. **REVENGE** is a dish best served cold."

"Old St. Cecilia, I've schooled many a homeboy on that court."

I laughed as Hub Cap reminisced, both of thinking of the times the two of us played together, two-on-two, unbeatable brothers, knowing each other's tendencies, and St. Cecilia is our home court; our advantage, a field of dreams.

"We have schooled many a homeboy, you schooling me, never, only in your dreams. Those days are over my brother, this is my home court, and there is a new **SHERIFF** in town, his name is Keith J. Nickerson."

"Wow, claiming St. Cecilia, how can you claim something you haven't earned?"

"Hub Cap, we'll settle the matter in the morning; won't we."

"I guess we will," Dirt man.

We just witnessed male testosterone in full effect, macho men, also little brother is trying to take claim of what he now feels is his, there can only be one bull in the pasture. Keith wants to be **KING**, wants to take down the reigning champion, and wants the crown; only one problem, Steven isn't going to hand it over, Dirt is going to have to wrench it away from Hub Cap. To the victor, goes the spoils, the local St. Cecilia champion and main man in the Nickerson household when it came to hooping, a **PRICELESS** title. We finished talking, and began to walk home; we have an appointment in the morning.

Steven said, "Now let's talk about Gus."

THE SCRUNGE.

Girouardville

The KING.

It ran along the exterior boundary of hallowed ground, low, just the right height, designed that way upon conception, mortar and stone in place; it is a hedge, a source of protection, the intention of the founding fathers of **Broussardville**. Originally, a Catholic haven, a little outpost along the Vermilion River grew into a village, became a town, and expanded into a city. Population explosion and migration necessitated a new categorization, a classification leading to its demise.

It sprinted in the dark of night, ran past the St. Cecilia administrative buildings, thoughts flashed through it's mind, recalling history witnessed, the hub of this once Catholic community; a landmark, located strategically, and significantly defines the town. The blackness of night camouflaged it perfectly, it smelled along the ground as it galloped, on a reconnaissance mission, and blending perfectly into the night. As it passed the cafeteria, it slowed, the grounds are familiar territory, a predator knows it's area. It has had many kills in the area, and stopped to mark it's turf; pissing. It once hunted here, the Alpha dog, and none dared challenge.

His hearing was keen, smell acute, silently it advanced, silently; it is the perfect killing machine, devours it's prey completely, nothing lingers, nothing is left over, and it's appetite is insatiable. It crept closer, past the gymnasium, and smelled something; another animal was near, on that side of town, his number one nemesis was Roger, no longer, it took care of the inferior human **DOG**. The Shepherd was a temporary nemesis, only a thorn in it's side.

Goodbye and good riddance.

It recalled their last encounter, the dog was older, smart, a fighter, and the canine knew when to pick its battles. The final battle with Roger was intense; the Shepherd was a formidable adversary, well trained well, and well fed. It had strength, quickness, and smarts; the one thing it lacks is the ability to rejuvenate. After numerous slashes, bites, and cuts; compiled with the loss of blood; the **DOG** fell, but not without a battle. Once past the gym, it got to the basketball court, using the huge trees as protection, it blended into the night. It hopped over the stone fence and crawled on its stomach ever so close; silently, unseen, and unheard.

It now could the humans, they were near, and as they drew closer, it stopped, and quietly sniffed. It savored the scent, inhaled the humanness, the aromatic odor was a familiar one, it then saw them, the two. Big trouble accompanied by Little trouble, the order was to eliminate both, but it had to be the right time, and the right situation. It listened as the two humans spoke, male humans are particularly aggressive; they hunt his kind, and seek to eliminate them from the face of the Earth. Not if it has anything say, it's race will reign again, they have for centuries and will continue.

It is one of the founders of the coven, selectively bred with others, creating a magnificent specimen, a creature feared, and a being meant to rule, and will rule. Hidden for centuries, they have assimilated with the humans, bide their time, and patiently wait. They blend in, become valued members of the community, and have previously witnessed the fall of humanity. They now see man's futile attempt to control its fate, all their efforts will fail, it's being aided by a convert partner. It closed it's eyes, no reflective glare, only complete darkness, the two boys continued to walk, unaware o the predator. It's breathing slowed, it recoiled, frozen, still, but present; invisible to the human eye. Human sight is limited at night, the dark is nocturnal supremacy to the creature; it stalked it's next prey. It silently crawled along side as the two humans casually walked right past it, and didn't even notice it.

The two boys spoke softly in the night air, but it could hear them clearly, smell them, and imagine the taste of their flesh, tendons, bones, skin, cartilage, and it's favorite; organs. Hearing is one of it's best qualities, a hunter, the instinct is natural. As they passed, it slowed, and from behind, entered their path. It stayed close, tracking, recording their scents, marking a new territory, undetectable, in it's innately nocturnal element.

"What's going on between you and Gus?"

Keith stopped abruptly, he didn't answer the question, something caught his ear, he turned. A strange look invaded his face, he needed confirmation, he asked Hub Cap.

"Did you hear something?"

"Like what, It's just me and you out here, Lu is starting to rub off on you; she's the one with the nose, not you."

CHECK

"I heard footsteps, I know what I heard, I come out at night all the time. Roger and I stayed out here; I wish he was here, he would flush out whatever it is stalking us."

"You think something is out here, O.K., let's start heading home. I don't want to have to kick no animal's ass."

I laughed, Steven is courage personified, will never back down, is a warrior, but can't fight, what he can't see.

"You are one bad mamma jamma, huh Hub?"

Now it was Steven's turn to laugh.

"Let's race; I want to see if you can beat me."

I didn't hesitate, took no stance, or gave no forewarning, I immediately broke out in a sprint; Steven began chasing close behind, the creature was left in their dust, they sprinted off. I beat my big brother by the hair of his chinny, chin, chin. Once home, they laughed as they struggled to catch their breaths, Steven said..

"You cheated Dirt, now I know what to expect."

"I learned from the best."

Steven knows his little brother was talking about him, they are a close duo, and it was nice for him to be home. He cherished the moments spent with his brother; there are four girls, and only two boys. They had to stick together, he had so much to share with Keith, they hugged as they entered the back door, Steven said.

"This Gus thing isn't over, first thing in the morning, before we ball, we're going to talk; I want to know what's going on."

We quietly entered the back door. Time had passed, it was now after 10:00p.m., and everyone was asleep. I quietly headed to the bathroom, Steven walked toward Momma's room; it was **SHUT EYE TIME**.

Outside, a creature stalked, invisible, circling the house, prowling, can't be heard, or seen, the ultimate predator. It rules the night, is present, hunting, it has located the prey, and now all it has to do is wait. Momma heard someone running water in the tub, her curiosity was peaked, and it was late. The water also let her know the boys were home, that gave her peace of mind, and she could rest comfortably. When she heard footsteps approaching her door, she began to ready herself; it was Steven, an opportune time for them to talk.

She also knows her youngest boy's habits, Keith's habits, notoriously known for his quick baths, in and out of the tub in the blink of an eye is his calling card, tonight was no exception. When she heard a knock on her door, she sat up in the bed, perfect timing, now she could talk to her son.

"Come on in here Gumbo."

Steven opened the door quietly and walking lightly, entered the room, for a big boy, he was agile; and light on his feet. Momma sat on the front edge of the bed, Steven took a seat at the foot. He was the oldest, the first, he had a special bond with his mother, always did, and always will.

"Ya'll just getting back?"

"Yes ma'am, Dirt and I talked, he's growing up momma; four years, he smelling his piss. It's been a while, we did a little catching up, and trash talking. He has a lot going on momma, we didn't discuss the coulee, we eventually will; we have time."

"Hub, don't wait too long, Gus is up to something, I feel it."

"I know momma, Gus has a hidden agenda. He doesn't like us, never did and never will, and the sentiment is mutual."

Momma laughed, "Like us or not, he's not going to get the best of us again, not if we can help it; welcome home my son."

He crawled up the bed and hugged his mother, talks with momma, the stuff he missed the most. As they hugged, it was emotional, a touching moment shared between mother and son.

"Thanks Momma, I know the importance of home and family; I missed ya'll."

"We missed you boy, what happened in the past is the past; let's put that all behind us, we can't relive the past. What is important, your little brother needs you right now."

"I can tell, he's bottled up, and losing Roger didn't help either. He's growing, turning into a man, and my role is to help him."

Momma released a huge yawn, it had been a long day, work was hectic, the coulee stuff was taxing, cooking, cleaning, and caring for the children, it is difficult, she's tired.

"It's late Hub Cap, I'm tired, we'll talk in the morning; you still like coffee, huh?"

He smiled, knowing the big breakfast was in store. In the morning, he would have grits, eggs, biscuits, bacon, and coffee milk; breakfast is his favorite.

"Yes ma'am, I'll get up early and help with breakfast; I love you Momma."

"I love you son."

Steven made his way to the boy's room; I had just gotten out of the tub. We sat in the room sizing up each other, talking trash, and hanging. I respect Hub Cap, and I know he loves me. I adjusted myself and once completely in the bed, shut my eyes, weakened, and sleep took over.

"Good night Hub Cap."

"All right Dirt, we'll talk in the morning."

Sleep quickly overcame the two brothers, just before the invasion of darkness; there was scratching at the back door, they both heard it, then it stopped, and there was silence. Both boys looked at each other, having heard the same thing, knew it wasn't a rat scratching, something was out there. They calmed themselves, lay in their beds listening, just as they began to doze, a loud howl was heard; evil sounding, long lasting, and it sounded very close; it scared both boys, simultaneously they wondered,

"What kind of animal was that?"

They both sat up in their beds, I thought it was a dog, Steven thought it was a wolf, the strength in the howl was felt, it echoed into the night, and through the night. It was a call, a type of communication; both Hub Cap and I knew it, we also realized the creature was near. We fell asleep wondering what was it, and it was definitely close. The howl was very distinct, an old cry, and the animal releasing it was

BIG.

St. Cecilia

Saturday morning came quick; I had just fallen asleep, someone was shaking me; my eyes opened, began to clear; and it was Hub Cap. I also instantly recognized the sweet-smelling scent of breakfast, I began to stir, if I waited too long; it would be a massacre.

"What time is it, Hub Cap?"

He smiled, that personality filled, infectious smile of his, I smiled back, we both knew the itinerary, St. Cecilia, a showdown was waiting for them, but first they had to make a pit stop, get refueled, and after that, **BALLING**. We slammed our breakfast, momma insisted we slow down, but neither of us could, we had basketball on the brain, one-on-one, and defending our home court. As we walked down West Railroad, I talked trash, giving Hub Cap the lowdown since he's been gone. Things have changed, young boys he left four years ago are now running things, and some are going to give him a run for his money.

As they approached, the court was packed, there were so many guys, both Steven and I were amazed, our home boys had turned out in droves to welcome him back, the word was out. Many of the faces, Hub Cap helped raise; now those same kids are young men. The change was drastic and eye opening, Steven had to acknowledge, and even his little brother changed, once boys, now young men.

"Dirt, you look anxious, you ready to peel some heads?"

"When you're home, I feel different, it's like I have something to prove, I have to measure up. I feel confident though. You make me feel like I can take on the world."

Steven chuckled, "Hold your horses little brother, I just got back yesterday, it hasn't even been 24 hours yet."

"Broussard hasn't changed, it's still the same old country town; nothing changes here."

"You've changed; I see that, you're no longer Dirt Man, that youngster has been gone for four years."

"You think so Hub Cap."

"I know so, I see it, and you do too."

We were at the court now, the boys saw us walking up West Railroad, it was the only way in, you are automatically recognized, and right when we arrived, curiosity reared its evil head. Questions began; all eyes were on Steven and I, even the shooters stopped, and they began to walk our way. The questions were for me, the rumors needed addressing, and what did he find in the coulee; it was the talk of the neighborhood, and the town. There was rumor, innuendo, and speculation; they wanted to hear it from the horse's mouth. Forget the he-say, she-say stuff, that is drama, they want facts, and want to know what is going on. Not 2nd hand information, from me; the home boys gathered around, we prepared to choose teams, and talk.

Calvin greeted us, "Well, well, look who's back, it's Gumbo, Mr. Sky Hook, and his rusty sidekick, the little **DOG**."

Steven laughed, as did I, then I obliged Hub Cap the opportunity to respond, he always has the correct responses. He didn't hurry his reply, being a veteran, wise **SHIT** talker, baller, and shot caller, he chilled.

Steven replied, "There can be only one, also, only one bull in the pasture, this is my pasture, **RECOGNIZE**."

I laughed, his answer drew a few laughs and chuckles from the others, Calvin didn't like it, he didn't like being clowned. Steven's response was his Highlander reference, Connor McCloud, from the clan McCloud, the immortal.

I said, "C.J., leave Steven alone bro, we came to hoop, fellas it's not about the coulee, it's about b-ball; that's all."

"What, you're speaking for your big brother now, cat's got his tongue, he no longer walks it, like he talks it?"

I replied, "Don't trip C.J., Steven is back, he's my brother, and I always got his back."

"The question is does he have yours?"

"You trippin man, Hub Cap just got in yesterday; take a chill pill."

Old Lion vs. Young Lion

A rivalry between Steven and C.J. has always existed, in Hub Cap's absence, I assumed the nemesis role, and was quite successful, but I'll gladly relinquish the crown to Gumbo. Calvin is a hand full, and some, his number one aspiration, to be the H.N.I.C. of St. Cecilia, before his departure, the distinguished title belonged to Hub Cap. Calvin always has to get the last word in, he whispered to me.

"I owe your big brother; he knows why."

"C.J., it seems personal between the two of you, I really don't get it, and I know Steven can handle his own."

"Keith, you may never get it, like you said, this is between Gumbo and I."

It was now time to choose teams. We had played some horse, and put out, it was now time to get our shine on; it was time to **BALL**. I was one of the youngsters, if picked; I had to be wise, smart, and couldn't afford to screw up. If Hub Cap picked me, I had to carry my weight, and represent.

Aaron asked, "Who's gonna pick teams?"

Click suggested, "Hold up, let's wait a few minutes, you know there's always stragglers, and I'm expecting somebody."

The fellas were growing impatient, it was nearly 9:00a.m., and normally we've played a few games by this time. It was a nice Saturday morning, perfect for basketball, but we were running behind schedule. At this pace, we were going to be playing all morning, while we waited for the late arrivals, questions were asked.

Choo Choo asked, "Sheik, what you find in the coulee bro?"

I said, "What makes you think I found something, I'm not some kind of explorer, and I haven't discovered the New World."

"Oh, you got jokes," Choo Choo replied.

Johnnie said, "Don't be a smart ass, Sheik"

"All of ya'll get this, I didn't find anything, or see anything, it's just talk, that's Broussard, and my momma said it's nothing but

CAWNT."

They all looked at me puzzled, what does that mean, they knew it was Creole, but had no idea the translation; Steven saw the confusion on their faces.

"It means **GOSSIP** fellas."

Down West Railroad came Snoop, Hick Say, and Junior Walker, it was now time to get our roll on. The three late arrives were the old **BIG** dogs. Word had gotten out about Steven's return, his homecoming brought out all the real balers, they made rare appearances; it was going to be a hot time at St. Cecilia this morning. Teams were picked and we played into the morning, some of the guys felt the **THRILL** of victory, and others, the **AGONY** of defeat. I was excited to be on the court with so many legends from Broussard, many of them I really look up to, they are talented, and have impacted my life. They were real athletes, I wanted to be just like them, and was awed playing beside them; it was the thrill of a lifetime.

By 12:00p.m., the sun was blistering, we played beau coup games, the competition was intense, we were spent, and had accomplished what we had come for. After play, we all gathered under a huge oak tree in the graveyard, it was the gathering spot. We unwound, rested, and got ready to split, before we did, I was questioned by Perry Mason, Jack McCoy, Matlock, and Johnny Cochran; I quietly sat as they disclosed the **CAWNT**. Some o the B/S, I found intriguing, they may want to consider the sources, some of it was hilarious, disturbing, and total rumor. That's how it is in Broussard, what starts out as a little thing gets blown out of proportion, and I was now the center of attention; even the old school ballers stayed to listen.

C.J. said, "I heard you found a dead baby."

"I found no such thing; I found a bunch of bones under a foot tub. I don't know who's supplying your info, but they're wrong."

Click asked, "So you didn't find a monster, a girl told me you found some kind of coulee serpent; you always at the coulee."

I laughed, "Man stop it, there is no coulee serpent, that's all legend. Next thing they'll tell you, I found Big Foot."

Steven, Snoop, Junior, and all the others laughed, they liked what they were hearing. It was good cool down talk, and it helped to clear the air.

Tony Curtis asked, "What happened to Roger, I heard the coulee serpent ate him."

Again, I laughed, the things people say, and hear, the gossip people start; the origins of all this foolishness is a mystery to me. It was ridiculous, and actually comical.

I said, "All the stuff ya'll hearing is lies, if people don't know the facts, they make things up. If you're gullible, you fall for them, don't fall for the banana in the tail pipe."

Aaron asked, "What did the bones look like, were they human, or animal?"

"Gus told me and momma it wasn't human bones, and it wasn't a dog, he couldn't tell us what it was."

Snoop asked, "What did it look like?"

I figured I had better chill with the coulee talk, I saw Steven's face. One of the questions, when I looked at him, he shook his head; it was a silent "NO." At the same time, he was telling me to stop, I did what my big brother suggested, and fabricated a little white lie.

"Gus told me not to talk about this with anyone, I've already said too much, ya'll know everything gets back to him, he's everywhere, or has spies."

Hick Say said, "Man forget Gus, don't be no scardy cat, tell us what you know."

Steven said, "Fellas, that's enough, that's all he's told me, ya'll know as much as I do and I'm his brother. It's dinner time, I'm hungry, and we are heading home; Dirt, let's go."

They laughed and teased me, calling me a coward, they called Steven and I momma's boys; we could care less. We picked ourselves up off the ground, and began to leave, as we walked off, Steven put his arm around my shoulders, he had kicked some butt this morning, it was a good morning.

From behind C.J. yelled, "Sheik, we gonna play again after church tomorrow, all of us want rematches."

Steven said, "The same thing is gonna happen; open up a can of whip ass."

Junior said, "Tomorrow Gumbo, same Bat time, same Bat channel."

It was funny, that's Jr., we all laughed at the designated time, Hub Cap then gave me a bit of advice.

"Dirt, remember, loose lips sink ships."

When dispensing advice, Hub Cap wasn't one to use many words, trash talking is a different story, that involves athletes and egos, guidance was something totally different. He knew I hung on his every word, and made sure what he advised was sound.

<u>End of CHAPTER ¾.</u>

Ferdinand Magellan

CHAPTER 1

THE FINDING.

THE DISCOVERY IN THE COULEE.

It was a great summer morning, we arrived home and Momma was alone, in the backyard on the swing, she called Hub Cap and I over, she wanted to talk. Pooh, Dean, Lu, and Sue had gone to Billeaud's, momma needed a few things from the store, she sent the girls, they would be gone a while. She intentionally made a long list hoping to spend some time with her two sons. I always told my mother the **TRUTH,** and I felt it was time I came clean, especially after all the talk at the courts. There was a lot of rumor swirling around, and I need to put an end to it, the only way is to tell the **TRUTH**. The pressure of a **LIE** was beginning to weigh heavily upon me, with momma and Steven present, I figured it was the perfect time. We approached Momma and she began by addressing me.

"Kee-Toe, I want you to know **I LOVE YOU**, I will always be there for you, and there is nothing you can tell me that will change that; there is nothing you can tell me that will change how I feel about you, it's time to tell Momma the truth. What you tell us stays between the three of us, you understand that Steven?"

Hub Cap nodded his head in the affirmative, it is **NOW** or **NEVER**, the girls are gone, and only three pairs of ears is listening. I knew whatever I said would go no further, it was time I spilled the beans, I knew I could **TRUST** Steven and Momma, inside I wondered if I could **TRUST** myself.

"I'm sorry for not telling you the entire story Momma, it has been eating at me, lying to you, I couldn't take it anymore; I'm sorry. I should have told the **TRUTH** from the beginning, you always tell me to be honest, and it's how you raised us. I never meant to lie to you, and I never will again."

I began to get teary eyed, they saw my sincerity, Steven walked up to me and put his arm around me, and it was reassuring. Momma walked up and began to rub my head; it felt good to get this off my chest.

She said, "Tell us everything, it will be alright."

Steven added, "Just be honest Dirt."

"Besides the bones under the foot tub, buried in the bank, I found a pretty little case. It was in the mud and I saw it reflecting at me, under Moj-Yah tree, it released beautiful light. It caught my attention, I had to see what it was, and I was curious."

Momma asked, "What did you do with it?"

"I buried it along the bank of the coulee, Glen and I. We were afraid, but I admit, I wanted it all to myself."

Steven asked, "Did you open it?"

"No, I didn't open it, it was beautiful though, I washed it off with water from the coulee and it sparkled, covered in all kinds of jewels. It even had gold nuggets on it, I think it's worth a lot of money."

"Where did you bury it," Momma asked?

"I put it in one of my private spots, it's safe, Glen and I buried it deep. It's near the Moj-Yah tree, but in the roots of the Big Chinee Ball tree."

Steven asked, "The one that produces the monster balls?"

"Yes, you showed it to me, I hope Gus hasn't found it. The questions he asked me made me wonder, I wanted to go back to see, but I didn't want to get in any trouble."

Hub Cap said, 'You did the right thing, let things cool off for a while. When the time is right, we will go get the **BOX**."

"It's mine Steven."

"Keith Joseph Nickerson, there you go being selfish again, you don't even know what's inside of that **BOX**, we all know it's yours. First, we have to determine if it's safe to keep it, and in the future, it is important to be totally honest; honesty is the best policy."

"Yes ma'am."

Momma's words calmed me, I cherish the **BOX**, it's mine, and it's always on my mind. I struggle to resist the pull of **SELF**, the lure of the **BOX**. I am sure of one thing, no one is going to get the **BOX**, but me. I felt better after my disclosure, it is simple to tell the **TRUTH**, and **TRUTH** or not, I am still of the belief,

You Keep What You Find.

All the girls returned and the afternoon quickly turned into night. All afternoon, Steven and I talked, away from the girls, a catch up session. It wasn't about sports, girls, or money, he shared the specifics of his previous experiences with Gus; it was meant to warn and enlighten me. He explained to me a little history of **Girouardville**, an original religious haven for persecuted Catholics. It was information I never knew, history, and very eye opening. Our home is next to the graveyard, a cemetery housing many of the founding fathers, the originators of the village. Carved out of sugarcane fields and bayous, it is rural, once expanded to a thriving city, but has reverted to its original formation; the desire is to keep it a plain and simple place.

He told me of the migration of our family to the area, originally slaves, our family arrived as some of the first freed blacks. The attitudes and beliefs our ancestors possessed were not popular upon their arrival, they caused uproars, led rebellions, and then Hub Cap began to mentally read off names I had only heard of as lore; inner family legends. Men like **James Noah Nickerson**, one of the first free black men to read and write, teaching a Negro to read or write was punishable by death, he was self-taught. He was an innovator, long existing animosity lingers between the Nickerson's and the Girouard's, it goes back to our grandfathers, and fathers.

Momma has a picture of him sitting in front of Ducrest Drug Store, eyes covered by a pair of sunshades, a little Kangol cap, and he's smoking a King Edward; dressed to impress. He sits in front of a huge display window, and in the reflection of the window, there is a man and a boy; the man looks exactly like Gus. I know it is impossible, but it is a striking resemblance; it can't possibly be Gus, James Noah Nickerson died over 100 years ago.

Women like: **Madora Charles Nickerson**, the wife of James Noah Nickerson, together they traveled the Bayou Teche and eventually landed in St. Martinville, Louisiana. Sugarcane was king, they gradually migrated to Girouardville, which is now re-named as Broussard. She was the local medicine woman, a term that can be interchanged, aka a traitor; a healer. She had cures that were only hers, whatever ailed you, Mom Dora could cure it. She wasn't a licensed practitioner, she was a local woman that all turned to when doctors couldn't find the solution.

Her potions, rubs, and herbal blends were revered, she was held in high esteem, but also hated by the locals of Girouardville.

She and James were ostracized, labeled as witch doctors, and their reputations destroyed. It was an attempt by the powers in place to destroy them, and run them out of town; instead, it made them two of the most respected people in the backwoods community. Momma has a picture of Mom Dora, she is naturally beautiful, has bi jolly cheeks, is a plump woman, and she dawns a white dress; it seems to be an immaculate, sunny day. The smile on her face is one of total contentment, there is a glow about her, a halo of light surrounds her; it's her crown. It isn't really visible to the naked eye, but if you look closely, you can barely see it.

The things Steven told me are fascinating, he has so much knowledge, I wondered how he knew so much. I wasn't told any of this family history, I was intrigued, and wanted to know more. I was impressed by Steven's knowledge; he's a bad dude, and never ceases to amaze. The history lesson captivated me, my brother's grasp of family history, mind boggled. How could he know so much, and where did he learn it from; who shared their knowledge with him, then the most impossible thought entered my mind.

"Was he actually there?"

We entered the house and the girls were preparing the table, momma had cooked a quick meal; grits and liver. She can whip up something quickly, she's a master chef, no one does it like her. I have never tasted anything cooked by momma that isn't delicious, and she has passed on her gift to Pooh. There are times I can't see how momma has the time to do all the things she does, in the blink of an eye she can create a meal, in a flash clean the house, and in a wiggle of her nose she appeared. There is a twinkle, a glimmer of light emitting from her constantly, maybe her smile or even a touch, but to her children, it is always obvious. We gathered around the table and as usual, before we began to eat, grace must be said, who would she choose, the wonder was quickly removed; momma took the lead.

"Lets' bow our heads and thank **GOD** for this meal."

We all stopped whatever we were doing, the girls got quiet, and we all bowed our heads. When I looked over at Steven, he was looking at me, and he kicked me under the table. It was right on my shinbone, it hurt, the pain made me frown, and I was going to get him back. I was about to kick him back when Momma spoke, how she knew I had no idea.

"Keith and Steven, I said let's pray, the kicking under the table; stop."

I looked at Hub Cap bewildered, how she knew; she knows all, sees all, and even knows about the **BOX**, before I told her. Momma is strange and has powers. She began with her usual prayer, taught to her long ago, and she has since taught to us.

"Grace before meals,
Bless us, Oh Lord, and these thy gifts,
Which we about to receive,
From thy bounty, to Christ our Lord;
Amen."

It's our traditional family prayer before eating, we all know it by heart, it has been with us all of our lives, all of the family recites the prayer. If you go to Aunt Seve, Aunt Edna, Aunt Toot, Aunt Beanie, or Aunt Lal, the prayer's recited. It is a family prayer handed down by Mom Dora, powerful, and effective. After supper, we all took baths, and were sent to bed. Steven and I had our own room; the back porch, located on the back end of the house. A house built many, many years ago by James Noah Nickerson, our room was once his. When the house is very quiet, we can hear him walking or smell a King Edward cigar.

Tonight, when the coast is clear, Steven and I are going to sneak out. We are going to our neighbors, John and Glen Simms, childhood friends. They would be glad to see us, and especially excited to see Steven. Glen and I have grown close since Steven left; he's my only friend on this side of town. We explore the coulee together; Glen is my Ace Boon Coon. In Steven's absence, Glen and John became Dirt's surrogate brothers. The three of them are close, and they share everything. They needed to talk about the happenings at the coulee; Gus will soon come a knocking.

The Four Musketeers

Silently we eased out of our back door, normally the screen creaks, but it didn't tonight, it was quiet, and going along with the plan. I led and Steven followed, pulled the door closed ever so slightly, Hub Cap is a vet. Usually Roger would be with us, but not tonight, it is only Hub Cap and I, going to visit the Simms brothers.

Out the back door and through the hedges, the night was musty, and dark, there are no street lights, it is pitch black, you could barely see in front of you; I suddenly wished Roger was still around, he was perfect for moments like these. The Simms brothers have been both our friends since boyhood. We walked through their back yard, and snuck up to their window. I knocked, but no one answered, I turned to Hub Cap.

"They're asleep."

"Knock harder, we're out here; we might as well wake them up."

I knocked again and a light came on in the room, Glen moved the curtain to the side and looked out of the window, he couldn't see me, it was dark. He knows who regularly comes to the window; he peered into the darkness and saw me. He opened the window and recognized Steven too, at the same time John Nick woke up.

Glen told him, "It's Keith and Steven."

John Nick said, "Tell them come around, I'll go open the door."

We went to the side door, and sure enough, John was already there waiting, he walked right past me to Steven, they are the older brothers and have a storied history together. They've done so many things as a duo, things Glen and I only hear tale of, things that make them legends. John Nick and Hub Cap embraced.

Glen walked up to me and softly said, "Gus been poking around here."

We know Ms. Simms is up and can hear us, we have to be respectful, she is like a mom to us, like momma is a mom to John and Bud. She can hear when no one else can, is wise beyond her years, and never intervenes in the boy's friendship. She encourages the friendship; she is a lot like momma. We followed John and Bud to their room, we know the way also, the four of us are like brothers. Of all the fiends we have in Broussard, the Simms boys are our closest. Once in their room, we began to catch up. John and Steven had the most to say, they've always been especially close. Since Steven moved to Lafayette, he and John had been out of touch, now is the time to reacquaint themselves. We listened, but at the same time talked, Glen and I had some things to talk about too.

I told Glen, "I need your help."

"Whatever you need, tell me, we are the talk of the town."

"I told my mom, my family, and Gus about the foot tub. Our secret, I kept our secret."

John Nick looked over at Bud in amazement, his face was puzzled, I now had his undivided attention. The two older boys listened to me, Glen sat quiet, I talked. The information I shared intrigued them.

"Besides finding the foot tub and the bones, I found something else, some type of chest, I think. It might be an old piece of treasure; t is beautiful, and is covered in jewels and gold."

Glen said, "I snuck up on him and he had found it already, it wasn't my place to rat him out, he asked me to keep it a secret; I did."

The two older boys had a look on their faces, it was curiosity, and wanted to see the **BOX**.

Steven asked, "Where is the **BOX**, Dirt?"

"We stashed it under the Big Chinee Ball tree; I think it's still there. I haven't been back since the day we found it; I think Gus is watching the spot."

John Nick asked, "Do you think he found it?"

I replied, "I don't think so, he came to the house and questioned me, he knows something. How, I have no idea, Gus is slick."

Steven said, "Don't think Gus is a fool, he's sneaky, and never underestimate him. He knows things no one else in this town does, he's dangerous, and if you get on his bad side, he's relentless."

John said, "Listen to Hub Cap Keith, I never did trust Gus. He will do anything to get what he wants"

Jokingly, Glen said, "Get on the bus Gus, make a new plan Stan, don't need to be coy Roy; just listen to me. Hop on the bus Gus, don't need to discuss much, just drop off the key Lee, and set yourself free."

John said, "Bud, be serious, this isn't the time to be joking, and we ned to have a serious talk, you held back on me."

Glen said, "I'm sorry John Nick, I you would ask me to keep a secret, I would, I'm not a blabber mouth."

Steven asked, "John Nick, ya'll have a flashlight or two?"

"We have two."

Glen asked, "Are we going to the coulee tonight?"

Steven replied, "Now is a perfect time, all four of us are going. We're going to find the treasure chest, and look at what's in it."

Bartolomeu Dias

The Coulee Re-Visited.

Steven and John were the oldest, they aimed the flashlights, I let them, but know I will have to be given one; who knows where the **BOX** is hidden. I was the one that found it, and without my lead, they won't know where to dig. We snuck out the back and began our creep, but first we had to get a few essentials.

Glen said, "Let's take a cane knife, and the machete in case we run into anything out there."

It was a good idea, there is no Roger, Steven and I recalled the scratching and the howl last night, and I felt something in our presence, in the darkness; Steven might not have noticed it, but I did. He hoped they wouldn't encounter whatever it was again, but if they did, they would be ready; Glen grabbed the cane knife, and Dirt picked up the machete.

Hub Cap & Dirt

The four of us snuck out of the Simms's house, and through our backyard, we tried to remain as quiet as possible, and knew the terrain. We all grew up in the area, and knew it like the back of our hands, it's our stomping grounds. I turned and looked at our darkened house in the distance; it was quiet, and lifeless. John and Steven led, there was no talking, no verbal communication, and we waited until we were out of sight before we even considered talking. We blended into the night rather quickly, and cautiously approached the trail to the coulee. At the entrance to the path John and Steven stopped, it was time for me to take the lead. I knew it would happen sooner-or-later, we stopped and I walked forward; John Nick handed me his flashlight, and I gave him the machete.

Steven said, "Take the lead Dirt, this is your discovery. You know where ya'll hid it."

I didn't know if Steven was asking me a question or making a statement; either way, I knew what had to be done, I didn't hesitate. His words were the first ones spoken since our departure; I took the flashlight from John Nick and walked to the front.

"It's not far, John Nick, you fall to the back and watch our backs. Glen, keep your eyes peeled, last night Steven and I went out for a walk, I felt something present, near us; possibly walking with us. We also heard weird howl, and it was scary. Bud, give me the cane knife in case I need to cut some of the high grass."

With flashlight and cane knife in hand I walked forward, the other three followed. I realized Steven needed a job; he had to carry his own weight.

"Hub Cap, you're the tallest, as I flash the light, watch for anything, as a matter of fact, here's the cane knife. Now you have a weapon, you and John Nick are our protectors."

The deeper into the path we walked, the denser it became, and it got darker. You could hear nature at its finest, croaking toads, bullfrogs, and tree frogs. Crickets sang a merry song as our approaching steps made sounds causing everything near to silence themselves, it was odd; and then suddenly it went from the sounds of nature to complete silence, even stranger. We all noticed the sudden change, as silence invaded, fear accompanied it, a weird sensation overwhelmed me; the same sensation from the previous night. Something is near, we were being watched, and then in the distance we heard it; a howl. A hideous, high pitched howl, we froze, and for the first time, the Simms boys heard the wail.

It echoed into the night, and then howled a second time, it was ghastly, and then it howled a third time. Prior to last night, I had never heard this howling creature, and the last howl was closer, it is coming our way. It wanted us to know we're in its territory, and on its hunting grounds, it is not happy.

Glen said, "We're close, keep going Keith."

I agreed, but said nothing, the howl had my attention, an uneasy feeling consumed me, Steven and John Nick felt it too, and they are unnerved. There is an air of something approaching, we got quiet, stopped, and listened, turning of the flashlights intensified the darkness, and the fright.

John quietly whispered, "Listen, what was that?"

Steven said, "I've heard it before, they've all around this little town, no one speaks of them, but they exist and live in the shadows. They watch, hear, and are always near. Beware of the dark, in the pitch black is where they exist."

Fear can be a motivating factor, the four boys began to walk again, much faster, something was approaching. They had better take care of their business and get the hell out of there.

I said, "A little further, come on, let's pick up the pace. I don't like being out here tonight."

The other three felt the same way, tonight is different, and even though we are four, we're still outnumbered. We didn't see anything, but it was simply a feeling, and it was growing in intensity.

Steven continued, "Girouardville's founders were outcasts, remnants of a ostracized religious coven, branded, and labeled as plagued. They contracted a virus, a strain of unusual D.N.A. discovered, and no one speaks of it. The founders are in the St. Cecilia graveyard, I don't believe it."

John said, "Broussard is the new name, but Steven and I know of Girouardville. Our mothers told us about it, and it's time the two of you know. It is a border town, existing in the shadows, and at night it comes alive

Glen and I listened, intrigued, as we crept closer to the spot, our ears acute, and our vision keen. The recent howls and the revelations from Steven and John Nick were captivating.

I said, "This is it, this is where we buried it."

Getting on my knees, I called Bud over, and we began to dig while Steven and John Nick kept watch. we feverishly dug and unearthed the **BOX**. Steven had cane knife and John Nick machete in hand, they surveyed the area, both have been taught special skills while at the boy's school they attended. It was obvious both older brothers were afraid, but it wasn't seen, they are the leaders, and have to reflect bravery. We dug, dug, and finally reached the **BOX**, a glow emitted from it, and the light attracted the eyes of everything. It lit up the dark night, released power, energy existed within, and as I dusted it off, it glowed even more; we all wondered,

"What is it?"

John Nick & Bud

We gathered around the **BOX**, it attracted and mesmerized us. None of us has seen anything like this before, it lit up the entire coulee, it didn't have this kind of power during the day, and it seemed to be intensifying. The longer it was exposed, the more intensely the light grew, it absorbed the darkness and turned it into light, we were quiet, and amazed.

Glen said, "It's beautiful."

John Nick was impressed, and Steven was fascinated, we all realized, this is no ordinary little **BOX**, we had discovered something not of this earth, a rare find, treasure, and is activated. I held the **BOX** in my hands, it wasn't hot, the glow intensified, yet it was cool; the energy pure. It overwhelmed and overshadowed the darkness, lighting up the night; illuminating the earth. The **BOX** was now transparent, no encasement, the power inside released; and nothing could hold it within. Three crosses existed within the glow of light, floating about, inside the glow, part of the **BOX**, but separate from the **BOX**.

As the light grew, the contents inside became clearer, the crosses grew proportionately, awed by the orb's beauty, excited, we lost track of time. The new discovery is thrilling, and what we are witnessing is unbelievable, but we have to rebury it to contain the light. We have to hide the find until the appropriate moment, and find out what the **BOX** really is?

The MANDATE

Steven said, "We need to rebury the **BOX**, Dirt, the energy it's releasing is growing too fast, it must be contained, think about it."

John Nick said, "Steven's right, I didn't expect this Keith; we need to find out what this is?"

Glen said, "Let's hurry, the thing that's after us probably sees the light too."

I said, "It's my **BOX**, ya'll can't tell me what to do with it."

Just then, out of the darkness a wild animal pounced onto Glen, jumping on him from behind. Glen tumbled to the ground with the dark creature on him, he fought off the dark monster, screaming, and yelling.

"Get it off of me, help me."

I turned to see what it was, and the light from the **BOX** exposed the eyes of the creature, evil, hideous, blood red, it scared the boys, John Nick took action to help his little brother. When the light from the **BOX** hit the creature, it turned it's face, blinded by the energy, and shook its head, confused, the light stunned it. It jumped off Glen and John Nick chased it back into the dense coverage brush. As fast as it pounced, it disappeared.

The boys ran over to Glen and helped him up. He began to dust himself off; the entire coulee was now lit up. Glen breathed erratically, he had just had the scare of a lifetime, John Nick walked over and put his arm around him.

"Are you O.K.?"

Glen tried to calm, and compose himself; he was afraid and couldn't deny it, he wasn't the only one afraid, all of us are. What attacked Glen was no ordinary creature; it was something from another world.

"What was that," Glen asked?"

John Nick helped Bud dust off, in the background, Steven got my attention, and the two of us disappeared into the thicket. Out of his peripheral vision, John Nick saw the light of the **BOX** go off into the dense grass, but his attention stayed on Bud, Glen had became emotional, the weight of the moment finally set in. What had just happened flashed in his mind, those evil eyes, it's strength, and speed, it could have killed him. It would have killed him if not for the light, he continued to cry, John embraced and comforted him.

"I got your back Glen; I will always have your back. You're my best buddy, my best friend, I'll die for you."

He squeezed his brother tight, uttering words that would one day come to fruition, John Nick could feel his brothers fear, an emotion he is very aware of, he knows it well. The rapaciousness of fear, it consumed Bud, this was a defining moment, he needed reassurance, and might not ever fully recover from the blindsided attack. John Nick knew the remedy needed.

"Dude, did you see how you rolled with the force of the beast, you must have felt it coming, I didn't hear it; none of us did. How did you know it was about to strike? How did you know to roll with the blow, that deflects the impact, you nearly eliminated it; that was quick thinking."

Glen began to rebound, his confidence and composure returned, fear evaporated, and he was back. With renewed confidence, he spoke to John.

"I'll be better prepared next time. Te intensity of the light distracted me. It drew my attention, but I now know, it only takes a second. Next time, I'll be ready.

"'Fool me once, shame on you. Fool me twice, shame on me.'"

John Nick witnessed growth and development in Bud, he smiled looking at the maturity process transpire right in front of his eyes, a crossing over; no longer a boy, preparing to face manly challenges. John Nick realized all four of them would soon be facing manly challenges, and suddenly his thoughts focused on the **BOX**.

"What Had They Found?"

The ROOK

Hub Cap rushed away, I was close behind, he spoke as we hurriedly walked, the dense, wet grass slowed us, but the energy from the **BOX** illuminated our way, there was no need for a flashlight, Steven led, one hand swung the cane knife and the flashlight in the other.

"Dirt, I know a place where we can put the **BOX**, but you have to **TRUST** me. The **BOX** is yours, understand; it has begun to possess you, whoever handles it, touches it, or sees it, obsesses over it, never wanting to release it. I can try to pry the grip, you're in it's grasp, I already see it; stay close man."

I put the **BOX** under my shirt, it dimmed a little, the glow lessened, and the brightness slacked; the **BOX** cooperated. It knew what was happening, it helped to disguise itself, voluntarily darkening; night returned. Steven continued clearing a path, now by flashlight, and we talked.

"Dirt, before you, I played at the coulee; John and I were the first explorers. I made a discovery in the coulee Gus wanted, he defamed me, the discovery mysteriously disappeared, and our family has been under a microscope since. I will have to tell you about the **KEY**."

I chuckled as we walked, pitch dark again, and the **BOX** back within it's confines, we were moving, and had covered much open sea; tonight, we're navigators, searchers of buried treasure, and discovers of artifacts which give powers. Treasure lost in the destruction of Girouardville. I quieted my thoughts and listened to Steven, he made an abrupt turn deeper into the brush, a path I had never taken. The brush thickened, Hub Cap chopped, cut, and led. By a strange path, we arrived beneath the tracks, Steven turned off the flashlight, and began to push on the brick wall we faced, he grunted, and pressed with force; I was puzzled.

I whispered, "What you doing Hub Cap?"

"Help me Dirt, we need to move this wall, there's an entry, we're close. Listen, don't push on the wall, align yourself directly behind me, and push on my back."

I tucked the **BOX** into my waist, and did as instructed; I began to push in the center of Steven's back. As I pushed, he pressed firmer on the wall in front of us, grunting, pushing harder. I felt his increase, his body became like a rock, I pushed even harder on his back, and he pushed harder on the wall. I suddenly felt something give way, and the wall began to crumble, the rocks adjusted, some fell. The wall began to cave in, we continued to push, and the harder we pushed, the further back the wall sunk into itself.

"Put it in, put the **BOX** inside; hurry."

Steven urge me, I froze, I know what needs to be done, that's why we're out here, and have come this far. I wanted to put the BOX into the wall, but something was stopping me, talking to me, justifying my resistance. I hesitated, Steven insisted; something was causing me to hesitate, I needed to rethink this. Steven saw obsession, he had to help his little brother.

"Dirt, fight evil; it's strong, old, deceptive, and knows our thoughts, and ways. You must fight it, only you alone can defeat it; put it inside **NOW!**"

My temper grew, I became inflamed, how dare Steven talk to me that way, I'm not a boy anymore, I can do as I please. He might want the **BOX** for himself; I was blind, **POSSESSION** had a hold of me.

"Please Dirt, put it in; you must."

I continued to hesitate, I tried to fight the desire, reached up, and put the **BOX** inside the wall cave, it took all my strength. The wall immediately closed shut, there was no need to push, it began to re-wall itself; the rocks from the ground rolled uphill, and back to their correct place; I was amazed.

Hub Cap whispered, "Let's go, we gotta get back to Glen and John Nick right now."

We ran, retraced our path, and ran faster, the path opened, and we began to sprint. Steven led, we had to get back to the Simms brothers as quickly as possible, we all had to talk, and plan. We caught up with them at the house, strange revelations were made, things were about to change. After tonight, our lives will never be the same.

We didn't feel it,

We knew it.

Jacques Cartier

The MOTHERS.

We were on edge after the coulee activities of the night, we arrived home and out of nowhere, Momma appeared from the side of the house, she startled us, out of complete darkness, she stepped from the shadows; we froze, were busted, and in big trouble. A shadow then appeared from the other side of the house; out of the darkness, Ms. Shirley Simms appeared. She was dressed in her housecoat, had a hand rolled cigarette in one hand, and a little book in the other; she is a teacher, it is her job, she probably is going to take notes, at least, that's what I figured.

As she walked toward us, both mothers present, we're in Big **TROUBLE** in little **CHINA**. I could now see the pad in her hand clearly; it wasn't a pad at all, but a book. The closer she got, I could now read the cover, it was a Harlequin Romance; I chuckled inside, we had taken Ms. Shirley away from her passion, she loves her Harlequin Romances.

The two mothers huddled, and stood together facing us; momma looked stern, reflecting a serious face, Ms. Shirley looked calm like nothing phased her. The entire time I've known her, she never seems shook, or out of sorts; she's always composed. She moved away from momma, looked at us, and peace was the reflection, she allowed momma to speak first; actually, momma was only opening for Ms. Simms

Shirley Simms – The QUEEN

"Shirley, you're a teacher, all of my life you've instructed me somehow, at times verbal, sometimes only a look, and why stop now; I understand and know you. I can almost predict you, I'm not that good yet, and doubt if I'll ever be; please continue to instruct."

Momma gave way to Ms. Shirley, I was puzzled, no reprimand, no scolding, or tongue lashing; busted out of the house at night, and given a pass, what is really going on, Ms. Shirley spoke.

"Boys, you are all my sons and Bessie's sons, it is not about skin color, or race; we are a **FAMILY**."

She paused and looked at us individually, the tone was different, she was in teaching mode; we could feel it. When she's like that, her words are profound and have an impact, she continued.

"Steven, John, Glen and Keith, there is little time to waste, a day spoken of for many centuries has arrived. I must share with the four of you what lies ahead, I must tell you about the adventure you are about to embark upon."

Now I was confused, Ms. Shirley seemed to be talking in riddles, I wondered if the others were puzzled too. What adventure is she speaking of, there is no adventure in Broussard, at least not until a few days ago. We all stood in silence, my mind raced; no one spoke; only listened. Ms. Shirley must have read my thoughts, she continued.

"I don't want to lose any of you, I'm sure all of you have questions."

She focused her gaze directly at me, I knew it, there wasn't a doubt in my mind, and she wanted me to know it; that's why she looked at me, momma laughed. She then spoke.

Shirley Simms – The "Good" Witch

"Son, I know you're confused, she's not talking in riddles, and none of us are puzzled; Glen may be confused also. The **BOX** discovered has powers, and energy, it is all **GOOD** and **BAD**, the origin of **LIFE** itself."

The Girouard Coven

Gus woke to a sound, something was scratching at his back door, a burnt smell invaded the air, to the rear entrance he walked, and unlocked the door. Who dared to scratch there, nothing risked knocking there, a rear approach meant importance. He unlocked, and opened the door; darkness slid in, casting no shadow; and unheard, the **LIFE** force revealed it though. It sizzled as it entered, Gus heard the sound, and smelled the wretched thing; caught in a dimension of shapelessness, ever flexible, ever changing, and never the same. Repetition is never accomplished, Gus knows, he befriended the monstrosity years ago; in his youth. Making a bargain, exchanging **LIVES**, his dying daughter, Pandora will live, and his soul, the bargaining chip. A trade-off, a deal made with the **DEVIL**, a covenant made in grief.

"Why do you visit me Coosh-Maa?"

Gus was on a first name basis with **EVIL**, he relished the company, and they were partners in crime; the powers ruling surface Broussard, an old nemesis is back, **EVIL** must rally the troops.

"I do not talk to your kind unless it is necessary, you sniffling, smelly, and scratchy creatures, what a mistake I made those many years ago. Your conception was affirmation to what I've always said, **'All species aren't worthy.'"**

Coosh-Maa's comments infuriated Gus, how dare he look down his nose at his kind? He walks in the sun, mingles with inferior humans every day, and interacts with the scum. He sees and smells them; they are disgusting and will be eliminated.

"Sug, while you sleep, the **Light** of **LIFE** has surfaced, I saw it, only a moment, and then it was gone; I blinked and only caught a glimpse, I **MUST** see it again, find it, and **POSSESS** it.."

EVIL sounded desperate, the light was now priority, knowing the opportunity may not present itself again. Past failures would not deter it, **NOW** or **NEVER,** it's time to call in reinforcements.

"Are you sure, it was the Light of **LIFE**?"

Coosh-Maa seethed, it's anger boiled over, Gus questioned it and would now feel it's fury. Gus saw the spirits reaction, and cowered, knowing what will follow, wrath; he bowed his head to Coosh-Maa, acknowledging it's supremacy.

"You ever question me, and I'll be forced to discipline you harshly, never again question me, do as I say; my oldest scrunge told me of four boys, and a portal. Find out who they are, and what they know, the light released by the gateway killed my best scrounge. Someone will pay, and if not them, guess who?"

Right in front of Gus, Coosh-Maa vanished as a mist, and aided by a breeze from an open window, floated out of the house. Immediately, the Chief of Police got on the trail, he knew **BOX** was found; tonight's activities were confirmation. He silently thought to himself, four boys, it is no longer Bessie Mae's boys, the new parties means two more will have to be permanently eliminated.

Lucille Bessie Mae Nickerson

Night continued, the four boys listened as the two mothers spoke, this is an unusual night, hours of darkness changing destinies and abilities forever.

Momma continued, "The **BOX** contains an energy hidden for centuries, it is a portal, a gateway spoken of and feared. In the right hands, the **HIDDEN** keeps the scales tilted toward **GOOD**, in the wrong hands, it means the end of **MANKIND**."

We listened, fascinated, in rarified company, and came to understand the revelation given. The moment was awe inspiring; and breathtaking, we were amazed.

Momma said, "Keith and Glen, we hoped for more time, but must appreciate what we have been given. The time has arrived, the **TRUTH** must be shared, and everyone involved must be ready."

I was puzzled, Glen too, the talk of an adventure silenced us; even Ms. Shirley was silent as Momma spoke, youthful ignorance spoiled the hush.

Glen asked, "Momma, what does momma Bessie mean?"

L.B.M.N. = "The Prophetess"

Ms. Shirley smiled, her glow lit up the night, her skin was translucent, and her aura was seen by all; she wore a smile of peace, and was in a state of bliss.

She said, "All of you, listen to L.B.M.N."

I knew those initials, they are momma's; they're tattooed on Hub Cap's chest. It was a memorial to her; I remember when he did it, his way of acknowledging momma. I wondered why all of a sudden Ms. Shirley is using her initials; I am intrigued now more than ever. Momma began to speak.

"I can only say this one time, there will be no second time; all of you must hear what I have to say."

Momma paused, the darkened side of the house illuminated, and light from inside exposed silhouettes of little heads at the windows. I now understood why momma paused, my sisters are listening; they are nosey, Chew-Bus was home for a sleepover, and she's nosey too, momma spoke to.

"Girls, ya'll involved in this too, all of you are, the nine of you. Each of you have an important role to play in the drama yet to unfold, the fate of all **MANKIND** will be in your hands."

Momma and Ms. Shirley will share their lifetime of experience, allowing us to have the experience of a lifetime. Minute by minute, the night grows ever stranger, two elders prepare sisters, brothers, and themselves for the unknown; there is one definite, **EVIL** knows the **BOX** has been found, and knows who holds the **KEY**.

The Exiled.

Girouardville was in an uproar, a child was missing, precious Pandora was nowhere overnight someone abducted her, and Gus was not going to stop until he found her. She was all he had, all he lived for, and without her, he would have no reason to live. Her mother died giving birth, a tragedy, a moment filled with joy and happiness became heartbreak. A daughter brought into the world, but a mother lost, both ends of the spectrum; the Alpha, and the Omega.

One of the founding mothers of future Girouardville, Patricia Girouard, waited all of her life to bear a child; the physical strain of childbirth was too much, the entire time, by her side, a loyal, dedicated, husband, and proud father. Her last views on Earth were those of her precious daughter, she held her close, her last breath, she uttered

PANDORA.

Part of Gus died that day, the delivery mid-wife tried to console him, and remind him of the bright side; life lost is life gained. He couldn't rationalize it, misery clouded his perception, pain blinded his love, and gone was the love of his life. He uprooted after the catastrophe, with Patricia in tow, and other members of the camp, they migrated south; collectively they began a new life. They were the founders of Girouardville, laid the foundation for the outpost, eventually becoming a village. Port access made it a town, as it expanded, it's attractiveness did also.

More members of the original camp migrated south to the Girouard coven, many were exiles, banished from northern provinces, Girouardville became a haven for the outcast, the thrown away, those deemed unworthy, society's outsiders. They were welcomed in Girouardville, and made the outpost their new home. The displaced, odd, those having strange proclivities, but in tune with nature; having lineal ties to breeds not human. Many existed in the spiritual realm, never aging, or growing old, locals feared them, rumor created terror, and fright is grounds for banishment. Arrivals to Girouardville walked in darkness, inbreeds, disturbing creatures, beings tilting toward human, and then slanting toward something else, the uncategorized. They preferred seclusion and reclusion, lived in the nearby forests, existing in unknown places, and gathering at dark. Nightfall produced the nocturnal, bringing out the hunter, the huntsman's kryptonite,

LIGHT.

In the beginning, God created the heavens and the earth, the earth was without form, and void; darkness was upon the face of the deep, and the Spirit of God moved upon the face of the waters. God said,

"LET THERE BE NIGHT."

God saw the light; it was good, God divided the light from darkness, the **LIGHT** he called day, and the **DARKNESS** night. The evening and the morning were the first day, the first day, darkness resisted light; the division from light incensed darkness, it vowed revenge, and until now, vengeance has gone unfulfilled. It was late night, both mothers suddenly realized the time, the children needed to rest, and the mothers knew they needed to game plan. The day they were born for is here, a time foretold of has arrived; it is exciting, yet scary. L.B.M.N. and Shirley Simms realize **GOOD** and **BAD** can transpire due to this discovery; **EVIL** wants the **BOX** as badly as **GOOD**.

We all began to make it to our rooms, Ms. Shirley took her family home, it was after midnight, the bewitching hour, and would soon be the dawn of a new day. I wasn't satisfied, was the **BOX** still there, it beckoned me, I could hear it calling to me, it is alone. Hub Cap was snoring, it was the perfect time to make a move; when Steven is asleep, there is no waking him, quietly, I slid on my tennis shoes and snuck out the back door. After the events of earlier, I was not going alone, Glen was coming. I knew he would be up waiting for me; I needed someone to watch my back, Bud is my best friend, who better.

Through the hedges I walked, creeping, blending into the night, I peered through; the light was off in their room. I heard a silent call, a whisper, I turned to the back of the house, it was Bud, he was ahead of me tonight, but we are on the same page.

"Keith, is it you?"

"Yes, bro, how did you know I would come back?"

"I know you bro, the **BOX**, it summons us, it calls you, doesn't it?

I said, "Enough talking, let's go back to the coulee; we have to hurry, it will soon be light."

We ran to the edge of the grass, then walked, we got to a spot and I found myself lost, I couldn't find the path Steven and I took. I began to look around, but the grass concealed the path, in my rush I took no cane knife, neither did Bud, we only have a flashlight. We stood along the bank of the coulee puzzled, a reflection of light caught our eyes, it emanated from the water; something was glowing in the water. We walked toward the light, as we got a closer look, it was a cross, the arms extending off the cross seemed to be pointing in a direction, it was the way to the bride, but opposite of our present direction; I thought it odd.

"Bud, you see that?"

"Yes, you think it's real gold, looks like it. Let's take it out of the water."

When we reached down into the water to retrieve the cross, it disappeared, gone that quick; we both freaked out. I flashed my light into the water, but there was nothing there, no reflection, the cross was gone. We began to cautiously walk in the direction the cross pointed; I flashed the light in every direction, and we listened for any sounds. We both had the weirdest feeling, an odd intuition, I could tell Glen is scared, and so am I. The dog creature attacked him a few hours earlier, Glen thought he heard something and turned. Fear caused him to lose his footing and he stepped into the coulee, the splash of water echoed in the night, giving our position away. Lost was the only advantage we possessed, I quietly whispered to him.

"Don't walk near the water, stay on the bank, we can't make any noise. We have to listen and be silent."

We quietly crept the bridge, we were close, as scared as we were, something drove us to the **BOX**. We watched, looked, curiosity filled our thoughts, my heart raced, but something compelled us. Fear was our third party tonight, I stopped, frozen in my tracks, I listened, I heard something.

"Bud, did you hear that?"

"No. I didn't hear anything."

"Let's walk slowly, no talking; just listen."

We stopped again and both heard it this time, it was footsteps, and they were coming up from behind, no, now they were in front of us; we didn't know which way they were approaching. Who was it, and where could we hide? I turned off the flashlight, a nearby drainage ditch empties into the coulee, down the bank of the coulee we slid, and crawled into the culvert. Glen hid his eyes; I hid mine, but spread apart my fingers, peeking to see who or what it was.

I Got Yo Back

Steven woke, looking around the room, it was quiet, and intuition moved him, brotherly love prompted him; he realized Dirt was gone, he had to find him, the hands on the clock 3:33a.m. He shook the remaining cobwebs out of his brain, quickly dressed, and snuck out of the back door. He had to get John Nick, if Dirt is gone, Bud probably is with him; he knocked on the window, but got no answer. He began to walk off when he heard a voice, from behind John Nick spoke, for Steven to be knocking this late, it's serious.

"What's up Gumbo, what's wrong?"

"Where's Bud?"

John Nick walked back to the house, he peered into the room, Bud's bed was empty, immediately worry overcame him.

"He's gone, is Keith gone too?"

"Yea, bro, I think they went back to the coulee."

John Nick quickly climbed into the bedroom window and dressed; slid back out of the window, and told Steven,

"Let's go find them."

They both knew where the boys were, there was no doubt, the coulee. They were furious; and grumbled as they walked, knowing the two young boys aren't ready to be out this late, and alone. They had to find them, it's dangerous, hurriedly walking, they barely spoke, intentionally quiet, and trying not to be seen. They approached the long grass, and looked for footprints; the steps would guide them, and when they found them, they were gonna chew off a piece of their butts. Only a few hours ago, they got the scare of a lifetime; the dark creature is still out there, and there may be more than one. The boys would need help if they encountered one, the two older boys walked faster; the thought of the creature motivated them.

The night was dark, in their rush, John Nick and Steven didn't bring a flashlight, a huge mistake, and both now realize it. Nothing guided them making them vulnerable, and giving them an uneasy feeling; they hoped the boys were close by. Steven led as John followed, he figured Dirt would go back to the rock formation under the bridge to check on his treasure; the boy wasn't worried about the **BOX**, it was the compulsion, the pull of the **BOX**. It had a grip on Dirt, and it is obvious to all.

107 West Railroad

The **BISHOP**

Glen and Keith huddled together in the darkness, hiding in the wet and dingy culvert, the ground still soaked from all the previous day's rain. Water flowed into the coulee from the cement culvert; every drip resounded, and echoed as it hit the water. Scared beyond imagine, both boys wondered what they had gotten themselves into, and should have waited until daybreak. They silently listened, Glen was about to speak when Dirt covered his mouth with his hand, with his other hand, he put his index finger to his lips. No words said, Glen knew why, the steps were getting closer, closing in from every direction. At first, one set of steps, then two, and now the amount is uncountable. They huddled close together, hugged, and looking into the darkness tried to see what or who was approaching.

Finally, they saw them, from each direction, dark, hooded figures; tall, black as night, camouflaged, and blending in perfectly.

Even though their feet made sounds like footsteps, they levitated, walking on air, gliding, effortless movement; it amazed the duo. Though afraid, the hooded creatures fascinated the onlookers, air riders, no leg motions, not walking, but gliding, a tall being with no obvious facial features, and outward appearances similar to the grim reaper. Dirt nudged Bud watched as the two figures, approaching from both directions, met together; floating in front of the culvert, searching, the boys held their breaths, and tried to remain silent. The things were right in front, but couldn't see them; levitating over the water they communicated, the sound was disturbing, eerie, a high-pitched squeal. The life forms surveyed the area, sniffing, and directing their hooded faces toward the heavens, smelling, and breathing in the air, trying to detect Bud and me. Then something startled them, they broke away from each other, and began to walk off in the direction of the bridge. They followed the path of the coulee, one on each side, floating over the water in the direction of the flow, and eventually out of sight.

Glen asked softly, "What was that?"

I shrugged my shoulders, his guess was as good as mine; I knew one thing, while they were gone, we better high tail it out of there before they come back. It was obvious who they were looking for. Quietly we walked, listening, but not hearing anything. Our only guide, the flashlight couldn't be used, the things were around, they walked along the coulee blind.

Big Brothers to the Rescue

With no light to guide them, Steven and John were in a pickle, they hoped to hear or see anything, which would help them locate the two. Walking, they listened, but heard nothing, looked, but could see nothing. Both older boys pondered calling out, but knew the two boys and themselves weren't the only ones lurking at the coulee. Any noise, sound, or echo would give them away, expose them, and to who knows what; all they could do, watch, listen, and wait. Suddenly, there was a flicker of light, their spirits were lifted, it was the boys. They began to walk toward the light, and it suddenly disappeared. They sped up, walking in the direction of the light, cautiously and alert. Once the light faded, Steven took action, no more waiting; he had to do something, and what the heck, he called out.

"Dirt, where you at, Bud can you hear me?"

It wasn't loud, but effective, he heard nothing, no calls, nothing. It was extremely dark; they continued walking toward the disappeared light that disappeared. Though the light was out, John Nick and Steven knew the vicinity, they proceeded in the direction; it gave them a place to start. They got bolder and continued calling out, louder and louder, eventually yelling; desperation forces caution be thrown to the wind, they had to find their brothers. Faintly, in the distance, Glen heard something, he asked me.

"Did you hear that, Ssshhh, listen"

Our hearts raced, we both froze in our tracks and began using our bionic hearing.

"I thought I heard something."

"What did it sound like?"

Faintly, they heard someone calling them, the two dark shadows must have heard also, that's probably why they disappeared, Glen and I knew it was safe, it was Steven and John Nick, the young boys began to call out to their big brothers. Steven and John Nick heard the boys and began to walk briskly toward their voices. Glen and I were never happier to hear our big brothers voices, we continued o call, I began to flash the flashlight, and in a blink, together. The four of us immediately bee-lined it home; on the way back, Steven and John Nick gave us the 411, and a piece of their minds; upset, very much so, their tone said it all, me and Bud listened.

Steven said, "Dangers we now face are new to all of us, things never seen before, and I feel it has only begun. Little brothers, always be aware of what I say. Tonight, the two of you are in the jaws of death, we will escape, but what about the next time? "

I listened, his words were right on point, we were up shit creek, without a paddle, stuck like Chuck, cornered; thank God for big brothers. Bud was quiet also, that in itself is rare, and both of us know how close it was tonight, I'm going to listen to Steven and John Nick more.

Out of the tall grass, the Choplin's house appeared, I cannot express the joy, we were home, and my breathing began to return to normal. My mind slowly stopped racing, I punched Bud on his shoulder and said,

"We need to listen to our big brothers more, sorry Hub Cap and John Nick."

John Nick is notorious for giving a stern tongue lashing, he took over the conversation.

"Bud doesn't need to tell us he's sorry, we already know he is a **SORRY** image of a brother, keep following Dirt, from dirt you come, and to dirt you shall return; just keep following. I don't know if ya'll think this is a game, strange stuff's happening around this coulee; don't come out here alone, better than that, don't come out here without us."

I'm Dirt, John Nick was cutting both ways, cold blooded, and **TRUE**. We arrived at our houses, the sun was rising on the morning, no more words were said, we all looked at each other, eye-to-eye, long stares, and in them all was **JOY** having escaped tonight.

The Visitation

We didn't go to sleep, we sat on the picnic table, Steven and John Nick led us there; it was my first time ever staying up all night, this is definitely one of those nights. Glen and I were silent, we couldn't say anything, if we uttered a word, it would only put us in deeper; quiet was smart. Their words made a lot of sense, if not for them, who knows what would have happened. We sat quietly at the table, glad to be home, chillin, I could hold back no longer.

I asked, "Hub Cap, John Nick, did ya'll see those black things, those grim reaper things."

Glen had to put in his two cents.

"I saw em too, they real, black monsters."

Steven and John chuckled; boys and their active imaginations, neither of them saw anything pass their way. They listened to the story, the tale of the mythical black creatures.

Hub Cap sarcastically asked, "Black things, why they gotta be black, I saw some white things."

John Nick added, "Yea, we saw some white grim reapers."

He and Steven were getting a kick about talk of grim reapers, they attribute it to our imaginations, Bid and I know what we saw, and one day, they'll see them too.

Sounds of momma in the kitchen interrupted the quiet, then the door to our room creaked open, and finally the curtain opened. We heard footsteps as thy approached the little kitchen door, she was coming out.

"Boys, what ya'll doing up this early, and what ya'll talking about?"

A puzzled look covered her face; she was reading us, not only our mannerisms, our minds too. I could feel her prying, it was like she opened a file in my mind, and began copying the information on a secretive flash drive, one only she has access to. I could install no Anti-Virus software to stop the invasion, and transfer of information, we were probably all helpless. Before we could answer her first two questions, she asked another; an impossible question to have been generated by our words.

"What black things ya'll talking about?"

John instinctually answered, "Grim reaper looking things, Bud and Dirt say they saw them."

Momma was already out of the kitchen; John Nick's words prompted her to walk faster. We heard alarm in her voice, it alarmed us, and at the top of her voice, she spoke.

"Let me guess; I know ya'll coming from that damned coulee?"

She shocked us; we thought we had played it off. Before we could utter a word, she gave us her conclusions to her own question.

Steven said, "Momma, I'm gonna keep it real, it was my idea. I just wanted to get a feel for something, John Nick and I thought it was time to have an all-nighter with Dirt and Bud. I'm back, John Nick is back, and we need to teach them two knuckleheads a thing or two, I put Dirt up to this."

Momma looked suspiciously at Steven, "You put John Nick and Bud up to it also?"

We knew we were busted, but momma wasn't upset, didn't vent, didn't even look worried. It was early morning and she had to cook breakfast for six, no eight, and I forgot Chew-Bus, nine hungry children. She turned back toward the kitchen, her words let us know, she knew; with her back turned she said.

"In ten minutes come inside, I'll have some breakfast ready; lost bread."

She exited the back yard and returned to the kitchen. I looked over at Steven, we were good and that felt good, and I smiled. We knew John Nick and Glen better be ready for a deep Q & A session with Ms. Shirley, before we went inside for breakfast I publicly needed to hand out some thanks.

I said, "Hub Cap, John Nick, my understanding is better. The last few days and nights, I have seen things, felt feelings, and now I know things; something is coming for us, we best prepare. Thank ya'll for being our big brothers; I love ya'll."

Hub Cap said, "We just got back, John Nick and I figured this would be as good a time as any to cash one in."

I smiled at Hub Cap, and then turned to John Nick with the same smile. Bud extended his arms in a hug motion, we all gathered in a huddle; it was like times we played football in the pasture, running one of our designed plays.

"HUDDLE UP."

Steven was the tight end, John Nick, the quarterback, Bud is a running pack, I'm a wide receiver; we area the fearsome foursome, and we are potent. As we hugged and I thought of football, I looked at Hub Cap, a smile pasted on my face; I'm so glad he's home. He said he would always have my back, tonight is a prime example; always right on time. Both he and John Nick are our big brothers. Since kids, when we got in trouble, John Nick and Hub Cap had our backs. A running joke the two big brothers always said,

"He ain't **HEAVY**, he's my **BROTHER**."

After the all nighter, I was sluggish all day, and when evening came, I went to bed early. When I entered the boy's room, Hub Cap was already sleeping, and snoring hard. I lay in bed, sleep invaded my mind quickly, and I began to get drowsy. The snoring wasn't consistent, but loud, between an inhale and exhale there was a quiet moment, within that brief period, I heard something, outside my window, and it was scratching on the screen. The rub was light, and very subtle, but I could hear it.

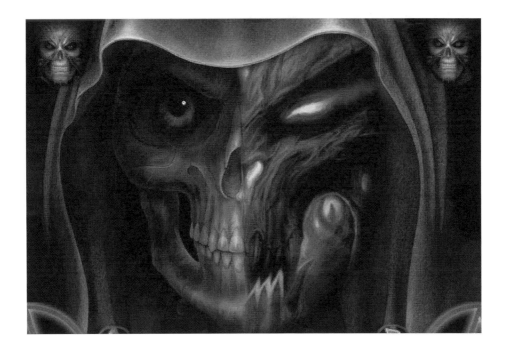

I feared peeking out of the window, but knew the curtains, and the darkness shielded me; I could look out, and nothing could see me. I thought it was Glen trying to get my attention, I slightly parted the curtains, and was shocked, it wasn't Glen; it was one of those things, a black, hooded creature. It was peering into the window, searching, looking for movement, any sign of life. I froze when I saw it, hoping it hadn't seen me. I slid low into the bed, peeked out of the bottom corner of the curtain, and at the same time kicked Steven. I could see it's eyes, an intense, bright yellow, glowing, and the dark of night illuminated them.

I began to shut the corner view when I noticed the eyes were looking into the parted slit; they were looking at me. I hurriedly shut the curtain, afraid, and didn't know what to do. The scratching continued, I snuck out of bed, tip-toed over to Hub Cap, and shook him; he woke, puzzled. I could still hear the scratching and knew the thing was still out there.

I said, "Hub Cap, something is outside the window, I hear it scratching."

"Dirt let me sleep; I'm tired; we'll talk in the morning."

I shook him again, this time harder. I was not going to let it go this time, I wanted him to see it, and hoped I wasn't dreaming. I shook until he woke.

"What boy, what's wrong?"

I could tell Hub Cap was upset; I had woken him from his beauty sleep.

I whispered, "There is something outside, one of those creatures; it's outside right now."

Steven rose from his bed, stomped over to the curtain, frustrated, and yanked it open. Nothing, no big yellow eyes, and no dark hooded figure; it was gone.

"Are you sure it was out there, you weren't dreaming?"

I was scared stiff, I know what I had seen. It was now the dawn of a new day, the sun was beginning to brighten the landscape. Hub Cap and I sat talking in the room, I couldn't go to sleep again; he suggested.

"You said it was scratching on the screen, let's go see."

The rising sun provided necessary light to expose evidence, Steven and I walked to the supposed window, tying to find any corroborating sign; verification of a creature. On the ground, there were no footprints; I could see in Hub Cap's eyes, he thought I was dreaming. The last few nights have been incredible, to say the least, and this may be lingering effects of the night. He was about to blow off the hooded figure scare and go eat breakfast when I stopped him.

"Hub Cap, look at the screen, you see the scratches. It's torn, something cut it, I told you something was out here last night."

Steven looked closely, examining the area, and he even touched the screen. Sure enough, the screen was cut, torn in strange spots, and ripped; it wasn't like that yesterday. It had to have happened overnight and was confirmation, I didn't dream this; something was out here last night.

Mano A Mano

First thing in the morning, Gus got into his patrol car, and drove toward St. Cecilia. He needed to confirm some things, it was a fresh morning, the fog was beginning to lift, and the coolness still lingered. The chief had a plan; and was going to begin executing it, the stern warning from Coosh-Maa necessitated action. The Light of Life found, it must be his; everything in this town is. Whatever it takes, he's going to get his hands on the **BOX**. He knows who has it, the same one's with the **KEY**; either they give both up, or he convinces them too.

With the two older boys back, John Nick and Steven, it will be no easy task; the reporting scrunge did say four boys, Gus knows the four. Trouble had returned to Broussard, and two boys, exiled years ago, close as two peas in a pod; seek to expose the conspiracy. Strong willed boys, now men, understand the town's lower levels of the town; Gus recalls what led to their banishment, arrogance, and disrespect for the law. He taught them a lesson. Both defied authority at every opportunity, he thought it was intentional, and took it personally. The boys jokingly told him not to take it personal; they tried to make the Chief of Police a laughing stock. Gus didn't like their attitudes, and decided he would either earn their respect, or make them suffer the consequences.

John Nick and Steven were of that age, growing in knowledge, and becoming men. No longer settling for exclusion, wanting to know, and making a decision to satisfy their curiosities, they began to dig into the lore of Girouardville. The more rebellious of the two was John Nick, a creative boy, gifted, and wise beyond his years. Girouardville was too slow for him; he needed excitement, and like his mother, found it in reading. Of the two, John was the **BRAINS**, and Steven was the **BRAUN**.

Gus quickly realized the intentions of the odd pairing, mischievous boys, a strange combination, but devoted and loyal friends; more like brothers. They became a threat to Gus; and he took steps to contain them, he will not tolerate rebellion. He is the law of Broussard, from its origin, he has been the Alpha dog, and nothing is going to change that. Girouardville was under his rule, Broussardville was, and Broussard is now, and nothing is going to change that either. He's faced challenges before, and vanquished them all; John Nick and Steven would be no different, and suffer the same fate. Anyone standing in his way will experience the same agony, The **AGONY** of **DEFEAT**.

In the initial days of the Girouardville, there were pockets of dissidents; certain attitudes adjusted, and the strong will bow down. Some did and some didn't, those that didn't were showed the road; they either left peaceably or were carried away, either way, they departed. Power in Gus' hand, is the epitome of corruption, more crooked than a hook, and he will do anything to keep the current status quo. The scrunge killed was with them a long time, will be missed, was the best, and the oldest. Coosh-Maa was right, it had survived countless battles, was a vicious predator, and whatever killed it was powerful. The veteran scrunge would not succumb to an ordinary foe; Gus knows they're facing a formidable adversary.

The Alpha

A power struggle has existed from the inception of the Girouardville coven. The **ONE** ruler is supreme, and will not relinquish it's power. It witnessed the Alpha, and plans on existing to the Omega; and will control everything while alive, and kicking. Evil breeds in the night, flourishes in darkness, and seeks to destroy man. It knows man, made in the image of his nemesis, he dreams of the ruin of man; by it's hands. Coosh-Maa is only one culprit, numerous entities envision man's demise, and have waited a long time. They have remained silent for centuries, lurking, and now realize, the moment is now.

Before Coosh-Maa, there was T-Gato, and before him, there was another. There will always be one, an evil faction, and the only way to kill a snake, chop it's head off; ensuring death. A long awaited day has arrived, a small opportunity to become the dominant force is now in play, and complete reign is apparent. Evil wants to be the only show in town, a dictator, what power, and so close; Coosh-Maa sees it, Gus smells it, and the **BOX** is the **KEY**, only one can possess it.

The mothers are aware of the pending fight, schooled by original elders, it was preparation, education on the old ways, and it t is now their duty to pass the lessons on. They must share and instruct this generation with the tools they possess; the next leaders must be equipped with to succeed.

Shirley Simms woke to an eerie feeling, the sun hadn't risen yet, but something was wrong. She peeked into the boy's room and made a startling discovery, they were gone; instantly she was alarmed, but knew where to find them. Four little troublemakers, she wondered what kind of mischief were they into, and knew it had something to do with that coulee. Four of a kind, and thick as thieves, they are becoming more and more sneaky. She buttoned up her housecoat, raised the collar to face the early morning air, and crossed over. She knew they were at L.B.M.N.'s, and was going to find out what the four musketeers were up to.

Girouardville Underground

Chapter 2

THE HISTORY,

WHAT HAS LED UP TO THIS?

THE FIRST PART of the JOURNEY.

Girouardville has a life underground, and Broussard is the perfect disguise above ground. Under the town is where evil exists, in the depths of Broussard, below ground is a place human's get no love. On the surface, Broussard is the "A" typical country, rural town, small, detached, and life is slow; the pace is neutral. By day, Broussard is business as usual, quaint little shops, regular religious affiliations, a few retail outlets, and a Post Office. The town has maintained some of it's simplicity, but has become modernized. Controlled progress is what it's labeled, controlled, simulated advancement, ordained and controlled by unseen powers.

Girouardville is a stark contrast, completely opposite, a settlement enveloped in darkness, underground, a place of pain and loss; DEATH is constant, everywhere, what's done in the dark, stays in the dark, and shall not come to light. No shadows are cast in Girouardville, and the journey to a permanent life underground is a complicated one. The origins of the township are dark, it is filled with secrets, lies thrive, it is what the place is built upon. Secrets and lies, shadows, and deception, pulled over people's eyes, and the perpetrators they are never exposed. If they were, what a shadow they would cast, and many reputations destroyed.

A Reflective Moment

John recalled when Gus brought Sam home, their Labrador retriever; he was the best dog in their eyes. Sam and Roger had an ongoing territorial beef, Sam was the Simms boy's dog, and Roger was the Nickerson's dog. They ran the other end, their side of town, St. Cecilia area. Just like the boys, Sam and Roger eventually got along, and became friends. It wasn't easy at first though, both dogs wanted to reign supreme, and in any competitive situation, there can only be one Alpha. Initially, the two canines fought regularly, reared together, after time, they began to know each other. Before long, they ran the neighborhood, if a strange dog dared venture into their territory; they had Sam and Roger to deal with.

One fated afternoon, Gus arrived at the Simms residence, knocked on the front door, and John Nick answered, he wondered what the Chief of Police wanted. He never paid social visit to their home before, it had to be business, and Gus explained to him why he was there.

"Could you come to my car John Nick?"

John Nick cautiously followed, Gus asking him to come to the squad car could be an arresting moment, and no one else was home. Shirley Simms had taken Glen get a haircut, it was a quiet Saturday afternoon. John was practicing guitar when the chief arrived, and was intrigued about what Gus could want.

"I was called out by Mr..L.D., he noticed a dead animal in the back area of his business lot, I arrived and recognized the animal."

He opened the trunk and it was Sam, lying dead inside. The scars on the dogs face and body indicated it had been in a fight. He was covered in scratches and cuts, and John Nick knew Sam didn't go down without a fight. His death pained John Nick, he reached into the trunk and removed Sam's limp body.

"Thank you Mr. Gus."

"I told you to keep that dog out of the neighborhood; he was never leashed; that's what happens when a dog is allowed to run free. The next one going to be killed is Roger, you just watch."

John turned his face up to Gus, and sneered at him. He appreciated the Chief bringing the dog's body, but the other comments were unnecessary. He began to walk to the back yard with Sam's body, the dead dog was heavy; visibly beaten, someone or something had killed Sam, and John knew it. Whatever or whomever it was, killed a good dog.

Hooded Figures

John felt someone tugging on him, trying to wake him. He then felt himself pushed, and gradually he began to wake. He could hear Bud whispering, and his mind began to clear.

"John Nick, there is something outside; it's scratching on the window, making a sound like fingernails scratching on a chalkboard. It's weird, and whatever it is, it's scary."

John was no longer asleep, the dream he woke from was vivid, as if it were yesterday, the incident making him distrust Gus. He knew the chief had something to do with Sam's death, and if they didn't watch it, he would do the same thing to Roger.

"What weird sound, I don't hear anything."

"Ssshhh, be quiet; just listen."

John Nick and Bud sat in the dark room, quiet, listening, and both heard it; screeching, and scratching, something is at the window. John Nick realized, Bud wasn't dreaming, or exaggerating; he became alarmed, and now wanted to know what it was. He rose from his bed, walked over to the window, and slid back the curtain.

Staring into the room, two huge yellow eyes, both John Nick and I freaked out; the eyes were all you could see, and they were intensely bright. The eyes were scanning the room, through the window; both John Nick and I were frightened. He released the curtain, allowing it to close; the look on his face, I had never seen John terrified. It was one of those black, hooded, grim reaper things; those things Dirt and I told them about, John now believed.

As Steven and I stood outside examining the screen and the window, the Simms brothers walked up. Hub Cap and I turned our attention to the arriving brothers, and as they walked up to, John Nick began a conversation.

"What's up this morning brothers?"

Steven replied, "Just doing a little investigating,"

Glen asked, "Investigating what?"

I replied, "Something was outside our window last night, I saw it. It was one of those black, hooded creatures, and it was looking into our room. It was scary, creepy, and ugly."

John Nick and Glen looked at each other, another confirmation moment, they had just seen one, and the same night, Hub Cap and Dirt sees one; it's no coincidence. Something out there was sending them a message; it had visited both their homes, and was looking for them.

Glen said, "One of those black grim reaper things was outside of our window last night, me and John Nick saw it. First, scratching at the window, and we opened the curtain to huge yellow eyes, staring at you, through you, evil in it's essence; it was bloodcurdling."

It was the creatures from the coulee, John Nick and Steven now believed; the scratches on our screen were confirmation; Steven showed John Nick and Bud the damage. The four boys now all realize, the strange happenings hinge around the **BOX**. As we stood in the backyard talking, Gus slowly passed in his squad car, giving us the **EYE**, perfect timing. We looked at Gus too, he saw us, and we saw him. Steven and John Nick's eyes focused on Gus; he watched until his squad car disappeared, the car even seemed to watch; chilling. Before Gus was out of sight, he made a strange gesture; took two fingers, pointed to his eyes, and then pointed the fingers at us, meaning one thing.

"I've got my eyes on ya'll."

GUS the **SUG**.

It was a nice, sunny, Saturday morning, the gesture from Gus was humorous, it was an intimidation move, and it is not going to work. We spoke about the gesture, and all knew what it meant, the chief has his eyes on us. Besides his watching eyes, he'll smell, and at times listen; Gus is strange, and is no ordinary man. Steven and John Nick know first hand, Bud and I are quickly finding out.

As we stood outside talking, our mothers appeared exiting the back door; Ms. Shirley and momma began walking toward us, the look in their eyes said it all. It was possibly going to be a continuance, information shared from the night prior and passed along to them by our ancestors. As they approached, a hush overcame; and we quietly waited.

MOTHER KNOWS BEST.

Momma asked, "We saw Gus pass in front of the house really slow, did he stop?"

Steven replied, "No, he didn't, just drove by really slowly, and stared."

Hub Cap didn't mention the gesture made by Gus, we didn't need to bring Momma and Ms. Shirley into it. We will handle Gus, somehow, we will, no game plan yet, but we will soon develop one.

Ms. Shirley asked, "Do we need to go to the station and straighten Gus out?"

John Nick replied, "No momma, we got this."

The four boys know what this is all about, word is out, Gus wants what we have. There is no doubt, and like the time with the **KEY**, he won't stop until he gets it, but if it's up to one of us giving it, **NEVER**, the **BOX** is mine. I don't care what Gus does, he is not going to get his scrawny **PAWS** on it. As we talked, the girls all came out, Pooh, Dean, Lu, Sue, and Carolyn. They cautiously approached, knowing the mothers are talking, and they hadn't been invited. Last night did open a door, maybe they were now included, Momma suggested.

"Let's go inside and eat breakfast, afterward, we'll talk. Ms. Shirley and I need to share some very important things with ya'll; stuff that will help all of you survive what is to come."

We gathered around the table preparing to eat. It is rare John Nick and Ms. Shirley share a meal with us anymore, but Glen is here all the time. In the past, having all of them over for a meal, no big deal, it was a common occurrence. In Steven's absence, I ate there often and I am always welcomed, the Simms's is my second home; after Steven, Glen and John Nick are my best friends. Momma and Ms. Shirley were the only adults at the table, the V.I.P.'s for the moment, momma had the floor, it was all about L.B.M.N.

"Girls, I want to include all of you in this conversation, believe it or not, all of you will have a role in the journey to come. Children, very soon, you will be forced to grow up in a hurry, ready or not, the time is upon us."

Momma stopped, and silently paused, it was intentional, we listened and ate, Ms. Shirley served us, not wanting anything to distract us, momma's words are vital, this breakfast is crucial. They wanted momma's words to sink in, and hoped we were realizing the seriousness of the moment. She stopped proving a point, Ms. Shirley then chimed in.

"Last night, the town of Broussard gave birth to a light; all present witnessed something spoken of for centuries. It was only an instant, and then gone in flash, it wasn't lightening, or a falling star. The exposure made me wake me from my sleep, if I am awakened, how many others did it wake?"

Ms. Shirley now paused, as we satisfy our appetites, something else is being fed; we are being counseled. We ate quietly, after serving us Ms. Shirley sat on a chair away from the table, directly behind Momma. That way, as we ate and looked up from the plates, there was no need to look but one direction; the mothers are planners, momma suggested.

"While all of you eat, Shirley and I will speak, first in our haste, we slipped. Utensils down, we will pray, and then we will share with all of you, what we know. Finish eating so there is no distraction, I may not be allowed the opportunity to share this again, I want it to sink in."

Ms. Shirley began, "Grace before meals, Bless us, Oh Lord; and these thy gifts, which we are about to receive, from thy bounty, to Christ our Lord. Amen! Heavenly Father, watch over the family as we embark on this quest, protect us, and give us the strength and resolve to accomplish your work. In Jesus' name we pray. Amen."

We all said Amen in unison, our family prayer, with a little sumptin extra from momma, the words are the same, but also different; a hint of desperation lingers, unusual to hear in her voice, momma sounded afraid. As we ate, momma and Ms. Shirley walked off, the seriousness of the situation could be felt, as we quietly ate, we looked around at each other. We quietly gobbled down the breakfast father rather quickly, flapjack, and syrup are awesome, and we are hungry, but curiosity fuels and prompts us. What is Momma and Ms. Shirley going to talk to us about, we are all intrigued. As they stood off to the side shu-shuing, we became increasingly curious. Strange things are happening, what does it all mean, why is it happening, and how would it all end?

Inquiring Minds Want to Know?

Gus, passing in front of the Nickerson residence, it's intentional, he slowed down, and saw who he was looking for. He saw the four troublemakers, he eyed them, and knows he must take action; Coosh-Maa will not wait forever. **EVIL** is a take-charge thing, and when it gives an order, it expects it to be executed or followed to the letter. If it isn't, he will find someone to do as he says, he won't accept failure; that means death. Gus continued down West Railroad to the park and then walked to the coulee, the boys could see his squad car at the end of the road; he wanted them to see it. He wanted them to be curious, he was planting a seed, and knows he is close; the **BOX** is near, he can feel it, and smell it.

The report given by the scrunge, spoke of the Light, limitless power, and strong enough to kill an ancient. The scrunge was an ancient warrior, the power of the light destroyed it, and in turn eliminated Coosh-Maa's lead investigator. Gus proceeded through the brush, and to the train tracks, a bridge ran over the coulee, literally crossing it. The vantage point gave a complete overview of the area, the entire surface could be viewed, Gus loves the location, raised his nose high into the air, and took a sniff.

From high up, he can also keep an eye on the movements at the Simms and Nickerson homes. He could see the boys looking at him from Bessie Mae's, and he smiled inside. Curious little fellows, they hold a secret, and he wants to know what it is; he already knows. His investigation has begun; and will not be complete until he has gotten desired results, and the cop in him led to the bridge crossing. The desire to maintain power fuels Gus, his disdain for humans drives him, his passion to rule compels him, and his fear of Coosh-Maa motivates him. His natural instinct is to prowl, he creeps, sniffs, and today smells blood in the water; a renewed thirst needs quenching.

From the bridge, he could see St. Cecilia, the park, the gym, and the coulee, all right below him; a view he witnesses often, his private little perch, a perspective he cherishes. He is on top of the mountain when there, and plans to stay there. The threat from Coosh-Maa is real, Gus knows **EVIL** has no time to waste; it has an agenda, a schedule, and a deadline. The Light of Life, what a powerful tool, what an advantage, what power to wield and control; Gus wanted it, he had to possess it. If he got it first, it would keep him on top of the mountain, the balance of power would take a drastic shift. Sitting atop the throne, where he rightfully belongs, and has always wanted to be; **GUS**, the

TOP DOG.

The Search.

He looked out over the winding coulee and saw them all gathered in the backyard, then he witnessed Bessie and Shirley call the boys into the house, he watched as they disappeared into the house. He then turned his attention back to the coulee, and watched as the water flowed, snaking through the heart of Broussard. It wasn't a place Gus liked, the coulee was dirty, muddy, and always brought trouble with its flowing waters. A surge of trouble was on the horizon, he could feel it. As he stood looking over the landscape, a breeze rushed past, the coolness brushed against his face, he raised his nose high into the air, smelled, and listened as the leaves rustled. Within the breeze, he heard a voice; it was muted, quiet, and soft. Within the wind, living, and existing, he sensed Coosh-Maa; the ever-present evil, always watching, is close, and always near.

Darkness

Dark of the night is the place shadow walkers exist. They hover in dimensions of the past, present, and future, walking between them all, existing within them all. They travel from one to the other, back and forth, with one purpose; **RUIN**. Designed for one specific purpose, created with one intent, they are it's all-seeing eyes, and all-hearing ears; allowing it access to places not normally enter, and feeds it information, it's unseen **EYES** and **EARS**. Though his eyes and ears, they cannot interrupt, or intrude, only witness. They can report, and foretell, but are limited. Shadow walkers, and Night stalkers cannot interfere, or partake in any way, and forbidden to alter **FATE**, or attempt to control **DESTINY**.

Whatever will be, will be.

Darkness is the alter ego of Light, despises Light, and once reigned supreme; it once owned all, ruled, was dominant, and has been there since the beginning. It's fate was altered, a drastic change took place when Light entered the world; with it's arrival came **HOPE, HOPE** grew into **PASSION, PASSION** fueled **EXISTENCE,** and **EXISTENCE** generated **MAN**. The battle between Dark and Light has been ongoing, darkness now finds the conflict futile, and has experienced generations of loss, and decades of pain. Gloom has felt centuries of defeat and has waited in the shadows, patiently biding it's time. It secretly watches, and seeks retribution. **DARKNESS** wants a reckoning, it seeks to balance the scales; they've been out of balance for too long. Darkness then thought about it, balance the scales, forget that; tilt them toward **DARKNESS.**

"The Earth is the Lord's and the fullness thereof."

DARKNESS has an agenda, underground it rules, and wants to rule the surface, where it rightfully should be. It wants to be the lone wolf, and intends to blot out Light; eliminate it. It aspires to remove it from the face of the earth, and without Light, there is no life. It is all connected; one thing leads to another,

"Let there be Light."

how about,

"Let there be Darkness."

DARKNESS laughed internally, what a hideous plot; total darkness, and eternal night. That would be a beautiful thing, complete darkness. A world of shadows, a life of secrecy, a nocturnal humankind, albino, discolored, existing to serve **EVIL**, the thought is intoxicating.

The Mothers Revisited

The meal was over, the focus shifted, food was no longer the priority, and the input of the mothers was on our minds. They stood off in the distance talking, and we waited patiently, knowing not to rush them, we dared not. L.B.M.N. and Shirley gathered their thoughts, and planned, they had to be of one mind, it was imperative they make a joint presentation, we could hear them softly whispering.

"L.B.M.N., you need to enlighten, know the tribal history, and have always been on the front lines of the struggle; you've fought in past battles, your experience is greater than mine, take the lead in this. I know I have the teaching background, but the time has arrived for you to teach."

"Shirley Simms, don't you go there, we are co-joined in this; by the hip baby. It's not about me, or you, it's about the truth, and the survival of mankind."

"Bessie, I was taught my gift, and realized my calling later in life; you were born for this exact moment, it's why you were created."

"I guess you're right, I knew this day would come, but never thought it would arrive this quickly."

The mothers turned, faced the children, and began walking in their direction; the children, oldest to the youngest, waited, holding their breaths, and understanding this is a decisive moment.

DARKNESS is VANQUISHED.

The battle for dominance has long existed, spanning time itself, ancestry power feuds, forefathers of Dark and Light, bitter rivals, watchers, original warriors, and born to rule. Darkness despises Light, relegated to the shadows, and forced to live in obscurity, the disdain has intensified; eons of frustrations, and one desire obsesses, possession of the **BOX**. Theirs once, obtained by trade-off, the power became a bargaining chip, the possessor succumbed to temptation, and the one in control, only for a moment, sinned. That's all it took, an instant.

Once the door opened, the possessor, and all sorts of evil entered, it only took a crack, a small sliver, and all of creation suffers for lack of judgment. It's about choices, for every action, there is a reaction; and for every choice there is a consequence. Darkness, for a moment, was in control, it recalls the power felt;

and realizes supremacy can twist a mind, prompting conjecture. Pure evil has no limit, sights a target, always hits the bull's eye; it never misses, and is the perfect sharp shooter. The surface battle is heating up, the combat field chosen, the spirit realm is the arena, and the victor will control the Earth's surface. The taste of defeat vanquishes the loser to the nether world, a place of wailing and gnashing of teeth, total agony, and complete despair.

Darkness once got a taste of success, and found control appetizing; it now longs for the main course. It wants to dine at table, and host a feast, exclusion has been on the menu far too long. Coosh-Maa witnessed the carnage, the fall of Evil, the expulsion; and looked into the eyes of the shunned, ostracized, castaways. Forced to live in obscurity, they seemed invisible, non-existent, no longer. They do exist, have something to say, want notice taken, and will no longer remain **HIDDEN.**

"The HIDDEN!"

Preparation training can be at either **"Old School,"** or "**New School**," both are attended, exposes gifts, are mandatory training sessions, and all inhabitants attend. The instruction is to fine tune skills, recognize unique abilities, nurture them, and encourage enhancement of natural, innate talent. All are explorers are expertly trained, and generate expertise which will assist in battle. When the time comes, they will answer the call, know what to do, and are prepared to make the ultimate sacrifice.

The "**Old School**" teaches of tradition, stresses mental dexterity; implements non-verbal communication, and makes silence an ally; the words and teachings of past elders shared, scrolls read, history told, and manifestos instilled. Tribal history is learned, and the true purpose of **LIFE** discovered. Ancestry and tribal heritage, formational beliefs created in the beginning are explored, personal growth transpires, and enlightenment is experienced. **"Old School"** incorporates the philosophy; removal of self, for the entire body to succeed, one cannot be selfish. For all to progress, one cannot be self-centered, and to understand another, one cannot be self-absorbed. For all to survive, one must be willing to die, a harsh reality, but the mindset of **ALL**, not **SELF**. You realize **DEATH** is part of **LIFE**, traditionally spoken of, traditionally taught, and will always be part of human tradition; mindsets passed on, imploring the student to realize,

"There is only **ONE** body, though numerous parts, only **ONE** body.

"OLD SCHOOL."

TEMPTATION - Ephesians 6:12

Within the wind, a thought permeated, obsessing the mind, and consciousness, fueling desire, a provocative question. An inquiry needing resolution, requiring cooperation, and possibly coercion, demands final closure, eight lives have already gone by the wayside in pursuit of the prize. Floating along, riding the currents, curiosity reigns, repeatedly asking itself,

"Where is the BOX?"

"Where is the KEY?"

"Where have they hidden them?

"Where would you hide such precious finds?"

The thought consumes **IT**; maddens, and with human, such limited possibilities, finding the treasure should be simple, but it is not, and **EVIL** is easily frustrated. A known landscape, small perimeter, and only a few options; why hasn't it been located? Flowing in the wind, listening, spreading, increasing it's coverage, whistling; within the air, and going everywhere air does.

Losing surface control has one advantage; the loser inherits the air as a consolation prize. Surface dwellers know whom they wrestle against, not flesh and blood, but rulers existing from the very beginning, once principalities, and possessing power; now vanquished monarchs of darkness, and their dominion, not of this world. Existing in the shadows, darkness is their realm, and the war is in high places.

Within the cool breeze, disguised, something of evil intent **HIDES.** Inside the freshness, soothing, deceiving, misleading, and manipulating, is **EVIL. IT** desires, manifests lust, relaxes, waits, and knows by pleasing, simple pleasures destroy; within the wind, planted are seeds, which germinate into destruction.

I FOLLOW MY NOSE

We opened the windows to allow some air flow, the kitchen's stuffy, and with so many inside, some air circulation is necessary. Once open, the house quickly cooled by the flowing breeze, it filled the entire house, the draft was pleasant. Within the gusts, Lucille's sense of smell activated, an inhale revealed something obscure, in the air. Something had infiltrated the room, invaded the kitchen, Lucy smelled danger; and felt the presence of something unseen. She intuitively knows, contained in the draft, within the wind, something is **HIDDEN.**

"NEW SCHOOL".

"**New School**" ideas are trendsetting, new techniques are used allowing students to enhance their individual gifts using innovative tools, and modern practices. The methods are unique; the practices incorporate new methods of warfare, training, and protection. The instructors prepare students for encounters least expected, training is difficult, and many find the skill sets required to accomplish the training scenarios hard to master. Growth within the "**New School**" system is time consuming, students realize it is a struggle to harness the gifts within, and some leave the training frustrated, but many exit with a completely different concept of their abilities.

New School is very hands on, where **Old School** is traditional, historical, and antiquated; **New School** is much more demanding, and the physical tests push applicants to the verge of breaking. This is the trainings intent, the instructors goals aim at making the student submit; they attempt to break a trainee. Usually, **New School** is a co-requisite to **Old School**. The growth process for some applicants accelerates; special students challenge New School philosophies, and embrace the rigorous training. Quickly identified, and put into select groups, these become warriors, leaders, and fighters for **GOOD**.

Many of the students, when exposed to **New School** trials, discover unknown internal strength, always possessed, but never tapped into prior to their arrival. The **New School** platform is a place gifts expand, abilities develop, and talents taken to an advanced level. Boys and girls arrive at **New School,** weak, innocent kids, green to the core; and by departure, are very different. The eyes of their understanding open, they realize their potential, and recognize their abilities.

Old School teachings and knowledge, along with **New School** techniques create the ultimate warrior, the two schools are excellent proofing grounds for youths; have been taught for centuries, and the time has come for the skills to be put on display.

Coosh-Maa.

When there is dust in the wind, it simply isn't dust particles, there are things within the dust, existing inside the wind, allies of evil, and partners with the leader of the evil faction, they are friends of Coosh-Maa. It is the manifestation of **EVIL**, the sidekick, and on the face of the Earth, does evils bidding. It represents the unseen one, has one-on-one contact with pure evil, is the highest on the totem pole, and presently reigns supreme. Coosh-Maa relies on information from various sources, the North, it's source is **female,** it knows of man's primary weakness; **Lust** of the **Flesh**. Temptation manifests in **WITCHES**; ruling over a vast region, sharing information, powerful, and gifted. Separate are conquerable, but together are unbeatable, and they flourish in the North.

In the South, **EVIL** relies on **spirits,** some call it Voo-Doo, and others re-name it Who-Doo. It involves the conjuring of spirits flowing in the water, traveling by the same waterways, spreading their **EVIL** influences. Spirits are the soul of the region, it is overrun by the spirit realm, is where evil thrives, and where it prospers.

In the West, it uses **nature,** and it's picturesque scenes, views, and hues. It is a land of natural beauty, and **EVIL** is aware of man's visual weaknesses. It hides within the things man embraces and lurks in the same things man creates. It has learned to keep it's friends close and it's enemies closer. It realizes **Lust** of the **Eyes** will lead to man's demise.

In the East, there lies a desolate land, a cold place, and a frozen landscape. There man can experience complete solitude, **isolation,** Coosh-Maa uses man's need to communicate, and manipulates it against him. Alone, man cannot exist, the race must interact with others, and share experiences, and man hates to ask for help due to his prideful nature, and the **Pride** of **Life** will destroy him..

A Testimony.

L.B.M.N. began, "Some of you won't be given the chance to grow old, and many people you know won't get the chance. Some will have what it takes to survive, fight, and exist; some will not endure, swept up in battle, will be lost to the war, and won't last the journey."

We all sat listening, amazed, the words momma said captivated, and the direction mysterious. Her words enlightened; what she specifically speaks of, we have no idea; but she is educating, and preparing us, she continued.

"Shirley and I have seen many come and go, existing prior, living to witness this moment, the day when all will be resolved; when **EVIL** is permanently destroyed, the final conflict, and concluding chapter."

We couldn't talk, her words stunned, and sucked the air out of us. No one uttered a word, mesmerized, and we dared not ask questions or interrupt, she continued.

"I really don't know where to begin; the best place is sharing some history. I know we live in the present, but to know where you're going, you have to know where you come from. This will help all of you to understand, talking of the future, we must consider the past."

Momma paused, she's speaking in riddles, we paid close attention, because it wasn't just history, it was also our future, and the foretelling of things to come. Momma continued to school us.

"There are two factions that exist, **GOOD** and **EVIL**. They are present, always amongst us, living, breathing, and in attendance. At times, we aren't even aware of their presence, they have always been amongst us, nearby, **EVIL** seeks to reign, and eliminate us."

Who is evil, momma needs to be more specific. None of this made sense, I was confused, why didn't she just spit it out; no parables.

"Shirley and I are ancients, earth and life have always existed, and we have witnessed seven centuries of human existence. Our role, influencing the direction of our children, not an easy task, disturbing, and knowing the fate of your flesh and blood is tough."

No one talked, just looked at each other, at Ms. Shirley, and momma, we listened, and gave momma respect; what a strange Saturday morning.

"What I tell you requires an open mind, and you cannot be afraid; there is nothing to fear, but fear itself; It can be conquered, and if harnessed is a powerful weapon against **EVIL,** a tool used to expose weaknesses, and create doubt."

I was now worried, momma's tone changed, it was noticeable, prompting us to listen more intently. She has our undivided attention; and we felt the seriousness of the moment.

"There are things I'm about to share, many find hard to comprehend, things already dreamed about, and may have not been dreams at all. It may be entirely new situations, or may not be new, upsetting things, and pleasant things; no matter, have no fear, and never give up, never stop fighting, and never stop believing in one another."

Worry turned to fear and curiosity, momma's tone was intense, and the silence in the room was deafening. What she spoke of was fascinating, and obviously opnly the beginning.

"I speak of a day, long awaited, it is now, no longer talked about, is present. The climax, a crossroad, and we have intersected. The battle for the Light of Life is where this ends, and who possesses it directs the future of the human race."

We listened, no words said, complete silence, in the noiseless pause, our minds were filled with noise; our thoughts raced, and curiosity ruled our brains.

"The **BOX** found is the ultimate power, and inside holds the key to Life itself, possession is ultimate control. The **BOX** gives life, and the **BOX** also takes life."

I was fascinated, and wasn't the only one, looking around at the faces, Sue, Lu, Chew-bus, Dean, Pooh, Glen, John, and Steven were speechless. What had I discovered, and if it that valuable, why wasn't it been searched for more diligently, and more effort put into finding it? I really didn't care, all I know, the **BOX** is mine.

The SPY who LOVED me.

"Lost in time, and misplaced by greed, the **BOX** vanished, and with its disappearance, **EVIL** was loosed. Control, assumed to in the hands of the dark side, the fight to recover it waned, and hope was lost. . It was a most valued treasure, and became lore, a myth, a story made up by man. Recent events make us realize it is no myth, there in the beginning, and is present today."

As Momma continued, we listened; I kept looking at all the others, they were onlookers also. The information shared is new to many of us, and fascinating. Finally, Lucille interrupted the silence.

"Momma, something is wrong, since we opened the windows, something entered into the house, it's in here with us, I can't tell you what it is, but I can smell it. We can't see it, but it's here, and it's listening to you; it's disguised, don't speak anymore."

We all looked at Lu strangely, she was telling Momma to shut it, and momma stopped. For Lu to speak up, she definitely felt, or smelled something. She is the shy sort, and never over steps her boundaries. Something activated that sensitive nose of hers, it isn't a false alarm, and the mothers took her warning seriously.

Ms. Shirley suggested, "Let's close the windows, and trap it inside with us, if it wants to eavesdrop, then let's give it an ear full. If it wants to be in our company, let's issue an invitation, and let the nosey sucker get to know us."

We chuckled, and all began to move, hurriedly closing the windows, room-by-room, immediately the breeze ceased, and the airflow stopped. We had trapped it in with us, and it became stuffy again. Within the stagnant air, we could now extract the spy, expose the uninvited, and meet **EVIL** face-to-face.

SCRUNGES.

EVIL uses it's subjects, living in darkness, **EVIL** is the only source of hope for the damaged. If complete reliance is not on EVIL, nothing else will assist, rescue, or allow prosperity. If success is experienced, it is by permission only, and allowed by those in power. Darkness has all, grants all, and allows it's slaves to have. Possessions are either given, or allowed, life, and existence is by permission. When usefulness is over, the candle's extinguished, the light goes out, and all is left in darkness.

EVIL must be fought and conquered; it has been done before, and will be done again. Yet to be determined, who will answer the call, rise up for **GOOD,** choose **EVIL,** and be willing to die? The Light of Life, lost for so long, has been found; what a crown jewel, a trophy, and what power. The thought of possessing it intoxicates, the reality incomprehensible, and to hold in one's hands, pure elation.

The scrunge is the most vicious ally of darkness, hunters, quick, silent killers. They travel in packs, but a lone scrunge is a powerful creature, and a formidable adversary. Rarely seen, they choose to lurk in the shadows, and turn up in the most unlikely places. The scrunge rides the backs of humans, nocturnal creatures, they appear in dreams, and desires to ride you like a bucking bronco. Buck if you want, but they will not be thrown, once they latch on, you're theirs. The scrunge craves the destruction of man, and eliminate human resistance. It is an ancient evil, skinless, boneless, and fleshless; a scrunge exists as a silhouette. It is the dark side of everything, black, bold, and leaves behind only ash. It prefers to remain invisible, embraces it's shadowy existence. **EVIL** wants man to think there is no such thing as a scrunge, and the greatest trick evil ever pulled, convincing man they don't.

It is not canine, though it has canine features. It is not animal, yet it originally derived from animal. The original concept **EVIL** altered, injecting a new ingredient. Scrunges have no blood, and no known weakness; is a killing machine, and it's life expectancy is eternity. A scrunge can live forever, and as long as it lives, it answers to **EVIL**; it's sole purpose, annihilation of the human race. The flesh of man, **EVIL** finds it delicious, thoughts of man, **EVIL** finds them intriguing, and desires of man, **EVIL** concludes are flawed. The consumption of man, **EVIL** sits at the head of the table, awaiting the feast, a buffet of death, a banquet fit for **EVIL** and its revolting subjects; and **EVIL'S** appetite is insatiable.

Hand Play

At the break of dawn, Sunday morning, the four musketeers were on a mission, yesterday, Gus was too close, they had to check on their prize, and mainly Dirt had to check on his possession. With his own two eyes, he wanted to see the **BOX**, hold it in his hands, and maybe open it. The glow the **BOX** released, and the explanation given by L.B.M.N. only grew curiosity. This morning, the advantage is with the boys, there is no night to conceal hidden dangers, sunlight illuminates the landscape, darkness has gave way to light. Darkness has to decrease and Light has to increase, darkness hates it, and wants to reign; Light embraces it, rules darkness, but for how long? As they walked, John Nick and Steven schooled Dirt and Bud; the two young boys had lessons to learn. They have been apart for years, now back together, the four of them have to become one, think as one, act as one, and literally be one.

Dirt asked," Hub Cap, John Nick, what did ya'll learn at **Old School** and **New School**?"

Steven chuckled; John Nick glanced at his friend, said no words, and decided to give the boys an exhibition. They decided to show off their hidden talents, learned and taught skills while in school; it was time to shock Dirt and Bud. They stopped in an open area along the bank of the coulee, Steven took a bold stance, and John Nick began a slow approach. It was an exhibition, a show we least expected. As Glen and I watch, silently I know Steven is strong as an ox; no way can John Nick handle his physicality. It would be a mismatch; John Nick didn't stand a chance.

Bud stood watching, knowing John Nick has unknown abilities, talents he only displays when forced to. He only reveals them, or shows what he is truly about out of necessity; John Nick's gifts are surprising. Steven is in for the shock of a lifetime. The four boys stood in the borderlands, on the grounds of St. Cecilia, but nearer to the coulee. Watching secretly is Gus; his appearance at the bridge crossing was no coincidence. His intent, drawing out the boys, planting a seed, and watching to see what sprouts; eyes are watching, and ears are listening; a long awaited journey has begun.

Glen and I took note, as our older siblings put on a show. Our eyes were wowed; we couldn't believe what we were witnessing. They took stances like two combatants ready to battle. I know what Steven could do, and Bud is aware of John Nick's skills, we are about to find out what our big brothers learned while at school.

Steven asked, "Are you ready for me to open a can of whip ass on you John Nick?"

John Nick smiled, "Don't talk it my brother, let's get it on."

John Nick stood nonchalantly waiting, as if nothing Hub Cap did would faze him in the least. Steven began his assault by slowly approaching John; deliberate, yet steady, he advanced. His steps were smooth, his display reflected the lightness on his feet, looking like a cat on the prowl, and he was about to pounce. John Nick intentionally backed up, giving Hub Cap space; he needed to see what Steven had in mind, and be prepared for anything. He knows Steven, and is aware of his abilities; he was not going to be caught off guard.

Hub Cap asked, "Where you going, don't back up."

John Nick laughed and assured Steven he wasn't running; that was the furthest thing from his mind.

"Don't worry about me, bring it on; I'm ready my brother."

The Exhibition

We watched as our big brothers put on a display of skills. We hadn't seen them in this particular mode before, we've overheard them trash talking, but never saw them in fighting stances, it intrigued, and fascinated. Steven made a lunge at John Nick, and he easily swerved out of the way. Steven's momentum took him past John Nick, who politely pushed his friend aside, and Hub Cap tumbled to the ground. A bit embarrassed, and frustrated, internally becoming infuriated; and wasn't going to be shamed by John Nick in front of his little brother; he stood, dusted himself off, and gave John Nick a stern glare. John Nick hunched shook his shoulders and asked,

"Is that the best you got?"

I chimed in, defending my big brother's honor. All four of us are friends, but blood runs thicker than friendship. Steven is my brother, I have his back, and he has mine, I urged him on.

"Get him Hub Cap."

In response, Glen input his two cents, knowing John Nick's skill set, having seen them on display before, he yelled, supporting his big brother.

"Show him what you've got John Nick."

Face-to-face they stood, John Nick waved Steven forward, and this time Steven's approach was much more controlled. He didn't lunge, or make no sudden move, it was a calculated advance, and he had a game plan. Steven took a new posture, squatted, assuming a position Dirt had never seen.

John Nick smiled, "Bring it on, big boy."

Steven drew nearer, slowly, meticulously, cautiously; he approached John Nick, and raised his hands in a strange defense, similar to a karate pose. I was surprised, and wondered, did Hub Cap know karate? My eyes, fixed on them, watched; as did Bud. Steven then released a barrage of kicks and punches, but John Nick was fast, he avoided most, and weaved the remainder. By dodging them, the lack of contact frustrated Steven; he increased the speed of the blows, and kicked even more. It was all to no avail, John Nick dodged them all.

John Nick caught Steven's hand with one of the punches, and with his free hand, attempted to land a blow, Steven blocked the punch and countered with a punch to the ribs. The exhale by John Nick revealed the damage; he released Hub Cap's hand, and recoiled backward. Steven, seeking an opening, continued his attack, as we watched. I wondered if this is an exhibition or serious? The pace of the demonstration; and intensity of the blow was alarming, but impressive. Steven continued the onslaught, and John Nick danced away. Hub Cap pressed forward, as John Nick evaded him; making no aggressive move. He waited or his opportunity, patiently waiting, looking for an opening.

When he evaded Steven and rolled out of the way, Hub Cap fell, his momentum, and gravity created an imbalance, John Nick instantly countered, swept his legs out from under him, Steven toppled to the ground. John Nick quickly pounced on top of him, placed a grappling headlock on Steven; and now had the advantage. Steven struggled to free himself.

I screamed, "Let him go John Nick."

Bud replied, "Stay out of it Dirt, let them do their thing."

I wanted to intervene, and help my big brother. I wanted to do something to change the tide; Hub Cap should be on top. Throughout the display, John Nick was always one-step ahead of Steven; I could see it, using his intuition, and knowing what Steven was going to do, before he did it. It totally frustrated my big brother, but he pressed on, and continued his attack. In John Nick's grip, Steven began to use his own strength, knowing he's stronger, and in touch with John Nick, he used his advantage.

Gradually, he assumed control of the situation, a hand's on warrior; it is his advantage, and John Nick's disadvantage. He changed the position of the hold John Nick applied, and took control of the hold. John Nick tried to resist, but it was futile, he knows Steven is stronger. Hub Cap pressed John Nick, intensified his grip, and his friend could take no more; John Nick tapped out. Dirt smiled, Glen sneered at him, John Nick lost the contest, and Steven won. As I looked on, I realized, John Nick intentionally gave in. He let Steven win, personally, I didn't care, my big brother won. John Nick and Steven lay on the ground breathing intensely, exhausted, laughing; the exhibition was challenging. They actually displayed only a little of what "Old" and "New" School taught them, then Bud asked John Nick.

"Where did ya'll learn that stuff?"

"It isn't easy little brother, it takes practice; we've sparred before, listen, and learn; individually we'll accomplish nothing, but together we're unbeatable."

Young listened to old; impressed by what we witnessed, and didn't know our brothers had such abilities, so immensely talented. Questions abounded as our older brothers struggled to catch their breaths.

I asked, "Can ya'll teach us?"

Steven replied, "Will ya'll listen, learn, train, display discipline, and be willing to take criticism?"

"I will Hub Cap, I can't speak for Bud, but I will."

Glen said, "Of course, I knew John Nick had skills, but not like that; I want to learn that stuff."

The two older brothers laughed, they had won over their younger brothers, both are hard headed; and training them will not be an easy task. It will take intense instruction, but what they learn will someday save their lives.

Hub Cap said, "When we get back, we'll begin. I'm telling ya'll now, it won't be easy."

I replied, "If it comes to easy, you didn't earn it. The most valued lessons in life are hard learned."

John Nick and Steven looked at each other as they lay on the ground, and both thought the same thing.

"The two knuckle heads are growing up, the little brothers are turning into men."

Sunday Tradition

Sunday morning Momma woke all the girls, Chew-bus included, she spent the night, loves sleeping over, and we love having her over. She is fun, different from my sisters, isn't always so serious, and like a little brother; we are really close. She and I have an understanding, know each other, and don't have to exchange words to communicate. I have sisters, and consider Chew-bus a sister. As the girls got ready for church, Momma planned, and never is without something on her mind; she doesn't have idle time. There is only one momma, but Ms. Shirley is like momma number two. Once ready, they began walking to church, momma spoke to the girls; all five of them, and shared information that would someday aid.

"Long before we were even thought of, a war existed in the heavens. The battleground was the firmaments, but the surface of the earth was a battlefield too; it was then, and always will be."

The cool morning air is refreshing, it's a beautiful morning, and when Momma talks, we listen; knowing the importance of her words, but also know when she is playing. This morning, she is serious, knowing that made all the girls listen more intently.

"Girls, ya'll brothers found something talked about since I was a kid, finding it makes the discovery a part of them, it will latch on to them, and the one who initially unearthed the item will yearn to possess it; the **BOX** is powerful."

The girls simultaneously taught of the children's game, finders' keepers, and losers' weepers. Whatever the boys found is important, and whoever lost it will want it back, and come looking for it.

"Girls, if you lost something very precious to you, what would you do to find it, or get it back?"

The girls listened, exchanging not many words, what momma said was direct and to the point, and if momma wasn't talking, footsteps were heard. This morning, we walked, and listened. Before long, we made it to T-Loo Loo; a local restaurant, confirming we were now close. The girls listened, absorbed momma's words, and pondered them, each putting themselves into the question she asked; and each individually thought of the most precious thing desired.

Dean thought, "What would she do to get her cat eyeglasses back?"

Pooh thought, "What would she do to get a boyfriend?"

Lu thought, "What would she do to pass Algebra?"

Sue thought, "What is the square root of PI?"

Chew-bus wondered, "What did Aunt Bee cook for dinner," because when she woke, the aroma of the meal could be smelled. She was curious, and as they walked, her stomach made a grinding sound, at breakfast she ate half a flapjack, and Steen's syrup. As the five considered the question in their minds, momma listened to their thoughts. If anyone lost something precious, what extent to find, or get it back, would one be willing to go? They all put their own spin on the question, children are selfish, the world is a selfish place, and **EVIL** loves it; and **EVIL** desires **SELF** to imprison **SELF**.

Self-Imprisonment

For a nickel, or a dime, you can talk to self, no operator is required, third person needed; and thinking, it only takes one; and **ONE** is a lonely number. **EVIL** knows it, promotes self, congratulates self, and when reaching the pinnacle of selfishness, **EVIL** hopes one says,

"I Did It."

When that phrase exits the lips, and exit it will, the bondage of self manifests itself; **I** surfaces, it suddenly becomes all about me, look at what **I** did, and what **I** won.

SELFISHESS, <u>EVIL Loves It.</u>

"Girls, all of you heard the question I asked, and in the silence of the walk, I sensed your ponderings. Footsteps not only led to church, but also thoughts, and all of your views were selfish, from the oldest to the youngest, and I am very disappointed."

Momma took a Selah, an explanation given before, and its biblical connection, a thought provoking pause, an intentional moment allowing one to think; she then continued.

"What lies ahead, selfishness leads to delays, pitfalls, and **DEATH**."

The girls wondered, why is momma talking of dying, we're kids, and are going to live a long time; especially knowing our life expectancy, since momma and Ms. Shirley revealed their true ages. Momma, disappointingly spoke again.

"Who wants their cat eyeglasses back? Who is so hot, all she thinks of is boys, and dreams of a boyfriend. Who could pass Algebra if she studied and believed in herself? Who thinks of math problems all the time, and listens, yet isn't listening. Who has eating on the brain, remember, you are what you eat, from your head to your feet. I tell all of you, "Intelligence and Character" are goals of true education. Lastly, who wants to live forever, surely not me, watch what you wish for?"

Pooh asked, "Momma, why you talking about **WAR,** you've always stressed that **WAR** is not a good thing, and told us it's good for absolutely nothing."

We arrived at church, found a pew, and huddled up with momma. We all know the routine, even Chew-Bus, no talking, or playing of any sort. We listened to the words of the priest, and this Sunday, Father Dauphne had us mesmerized, the message he was trying to convey, resounded loudly in all of our ears. Before the sermon, he walked through the congregation making eye contact with every person in attendance, he then returned to the altar, and began.

"The 24ᵗʰ Psalms begins, 'The earth is the Lord's, and the fullness thereof; the world, and they that dwell therein.' I begin today speaking to the entire community, young and old, male and female. All within the range of my voice is affected; and the entire community will become involved. We will encounter tests; and challenges will arise testing our metal. We must find a way to maintain, persevere, and fight on; NEVER SURRENDER. If you feel defeated, PRAY, if you feel alone, PRAY, if you're down and out, PRAY, and when the odds are against you, continue to PRAY; you will inevitably prevail."

Everyone hung on father's words, as kids, we even understood. It isn't the usual sermon focusing on the word, or strictly from the Bible. This Sunday, Father picked up where momma left off, it is history, and preparation; a warning is in the message. After a short pause, Father continued. The seriousness felt, the words impactful, and all present sensed the urgency of the situation. Father Dauphne enlightened us about the future, things to come; and the entire church listened.

"When I say all of us, I speak of this community, we are one, all part of one body, and all the parts play a significant role in what is to transpire. Many will be tested, many will succumb to temptation, and many will be lost."

Father again stopped, and looked at every one present. His words were eerily similar to our mothers, and as he made individual eye contact with everyone present, when he got to my eyes, I shied away. I saw the look in his eyes though, the intensity, and determination showed, he continued.

"The ones lost will pave the way, and make the ultimate sacrifice; before surrender, fight to your death. Darkness approaches, has always lurked, and it's presence is stronger than ever. It is everywhere, and does exist, do not underestimate EVIL; stay armored up. Temptation may present itself beautifully, remember, EVIL knows our weaknesses. It may be pleasing to the eyes, it knows what you like, and will tempt; resist it. Behind its presentation is falseness and lies, the deception is ugly; EVIL is UGLY!"

It was quiet; you could hear a pin drop. All the elders watched and listened to Father Dauphne; he had never spoken in that manner before. This morning, church was informative; no one talked, or looked around.

"Remember, the earth is the Lord's, and we are his chosen; he will be at our side. I am a man of God, and hold steadfast to my Faith, it has been the foundation of my being, and keeps me sane, my Faith is my glue; all present will have their Faith tested, in one way or another; and when it happens, have no doubt, don't waver. You may wonder, when will this occur; I have no answer, I do know, it will happen. Be prepared."

Not long after father finished speaking, mass ended, and we all congregated outside a while. The elders talked, and Father spoke to them off to the side. Chew-bus went home with her mom, sisters and brother. Momma gathered us up and off we walked, it was time to head home. We looked back and saw Chew-bus looking back too, we could see she wanted to come with us, and we wanted her to come too. She waved, and we waved back; it was going to be a long walk home. We knew Momma had something to talk to us about, we could all feel it.

The REPLICATOR.

The exhibition between Steven and John Nick wore them out, they lay on the ground recuperating under the huge oak trees, and sleep began to invade their minds; they fought it, but knew what lay ahead. All the fight they possessed, and still fatigue took over; it has a mind of its own. The two older boys fell asleep leaving Bud and I. Something began to call, beckoning me, and I realize what it is, the **BOX**. I yearn to see it, touch it, and hold it, can no longer resist, and must go to it. I have to check on my precious **BOX,** and make sure it is still mine; I will go to the coulee and get my prize.

Bud didn't need much convincing, attribute it to youthful exuberance, possibly immaturity, or misguided loyalty, whatever, Bud and I, while our brothers napped, we snuck back to the coulee. First, we went home and re-tooled, if anything surprised us this time, we would be ready. In the boy's minds, they wouldn't be caught off guard, and whatever came their way, they were Armed and Dangerous. They wanted to revisit the sight where the hooded creatures lurked, and see if they ran into one of those black dog creatures again. The creatures made an unexpected appearance, this time, they are going to do the surprising, and flip the script. The weapons of choice, Dirt secured both the trusted cane knife and machete; Bud took his pellet gun along, he is a deadeye shot, and Dirt suggested as they walked,

"Pump it all you can, that way if you have to use it, shoot to kill."

Glen smiled at Keith's comment, shoot to kill, the only thing they ever killed were rabbits, snakes, or birds. Glen pumped the gun as they walked, and pressure built up inside the weapon. The boys felt safe, had a gun, and felt they could stop anything; or so they thought. Keith suddenly had a brainstorm.

"Bud, don't put the safety on, be ready. Remember, the black thing came from nowhere, stay on point."

Walking side-by-side, they watched left and right, vision keen, hearing acute, the entire area was covered. Through the brush, tall grass, and mud, they continued, trying to replicate their previous path. Both were cautious, slowed their pace, listened, and didn't speak. The grass thickened since their last visit, the height was incredible, I didn't remember it being that tall; overnight it grew over our heads. We began to slow our progress, a strange feeling overcame us, and fear invaded our minds. I began to question why we even came, the beckoning lessened, and fear increased. I hated convincing Bud to do this, as we walked slower and slower, but Bud urged me onward.

Impossible.

"Let's keep going, it can't be much further, we both know the coulee like the back of our hands; come on."

I didn't want to go onward, yet I did, apprehensively, which is not normally me. I am the one with brilliant ideas, and courageous; at this very moment, I'm scared out of my wits, a tragic flaw, **"The Pride of Life"**.

I paused, "Bud, let's talk about this, do you remember the grass being this tall? We were here last night, and cut the grass, how can it be this tall again?"

Bud stopped, thought about what I said, second thoughts invaded his mind, he hid them, having to reflect bravery, I am always the brave one; it is now his turn.

"Man, you got a machete and a cane knife, clear us a path. You know the way, get busy my brother."

Something didn't feel right, we both felt it, Bud's words were reinforcing, but doubt still lingered. At this point, we are in this together; there is no turning back, like Batman and Robin, or Butch Cassidy and the Sundance Kid; all for one and one for all.

I asked, "Bud, do you want to lead,"

"Nah, bro, you're doing a good job, and I got your back."

Continuing on, as quiet as possible, we persisted, I chopped, cutting a path, swinging ricocheted, chopping echoed, and slashing resonated. Our steps resounded, attempted quiet foiled, and throughout the valley heard. We couldn't disguise our approach, everything there knew we were present.

Romance Novels

Shirley Simms went to her bookshelf and thumbed through the volumes of novels, books, short stories, and novellas. Finding the one searched for, dusted it off, not having read it in a while, a favorite Harlequin, and walked back to the den. She is shrewd, a teacher, and takes pride in the knowledge possessed and passed on. The ultimate trickster, she has centuries of practice, and the art of deception is her forte, loves romance novels, and if you know her, is aware of her passion.

The title of this Harlequin, **"The 10 Original Village Mandates."** She began to review them, a sort of refresher course. What directed her to this book, saliva left by the scrunge on the back of her youngest, both she and L.B.M.N. saw it; no one else did, they didn't know what to look for. The two elders know the signs, and recognize evidence left behind. It takes a keen eye, and awareness of allies Evil uses. Having fought them for centuries, both know the tenacity of the scrunge, they are merciless killers. Previously, they killed one, but two regenerated, and replicated; the new breed reappeared smarter, and more advanced. Permanent elimination requires finding the originators of the breed, the alpha scrunges, destroying them, thus severing the strain.

WAR!

The Harlequin was upsetting, maybe that's why she prefers to rarely read it, she quietly took a seat. The book revealed evidence of dark days to come, spoke of signs, and predictions that will manifest themselves, or are currently happening. The signs are precursors, signifying the beginning, the arrival of the last days, and issuing in the birth of Armageddon. Shirley had previously viewed the book, knows the teachings, and is an avid record keeper, being an elder, she is aware of the mandates importance, and significance addressing survival of the coven. What she knows and understands are priceless, is an intricate part of the equation, and a crucial educator. She sat quietly reading, allowing the words to sink in, and absorbing their meaning. It had been years since she read the book of firsts, the book outlining, and controlling all; it molds, and shapes a coven. Inside are agreements, treaties, and pacts; contracts explaining rules between covens, and by laws.

10 Original Village Mandates

1) It's forbidden to disrespect a fellow coven member. We are family, and must stick together through everything, there is no **I** in **We**.

2) Respect is mandatory toward elders, they are the foundation, history, past, and future; they are all we have.

3) Do not associate with **EVIL** in any shape, form, or fashion; it's prohibited, and banishment is the penalty for colluding with **EVIL**.

Shirley read, grasping all, for centuries the coven has existed by following the edicts of the Original Village Mandates. The words were eye opening, important, and relevant to what is transpiring. The directives set guidelines, and are not to be broken. They are words she vaguely overviewed in the past, but today carry more weight than ever.

4) Until the Light of Life is possessed, **EVIL** cannot appear, interrupt, partake, or alter any surface activities, and must remain in the shadows; and must remain neutral.

5) The only interaction allowed is predicated on the search for the Light of Life. The power within the light will expose **EVIL,** only then can it appear or manifest.

Shirley is now sure; the boys have found it, the Light of Life, things happening are confirmation, and frightening. She knows who will lead the fight, and be on the front lines. It won't be her and L.B.M.N., but the children, as the biblical prophecy states,

"In that day, the wolf, and the lamb will live together, the leopard will lie down with the baby goat, the calf and the yearling will be safe with the lion, and a little child will lead them all."

Isaiah 11:6

She paused, extending the thoughtful moment, embracing the quiet, a lonely place to ponder. Silence leads to rampant, uncontrolled thoughts of doom, conclusions not ending well for her, the children, or humankind. She knows the boys are presently out exploring, it's what they do, and try as you might, you can't take the boy out of the man. Internally, she smiled, in a most serious moment, she thought of her years of Harlequin disguise, all those years. Carrying around spells, armed with recipes to foil evil, centuries of preparation for this moment, she returned to the book that keeps order; Shirley Simms continued the refresher course realizing the **"Original Village Mandates,"** will be tested.

6) In the beginning darkness reigned, but when Light pierced the Darkness, it could not comprehend, and didn't understand the manifestation of Light. It was the first spark, the initial occurrence where **GOOD** manifested itself, and overwhelmed. From that day forward, Darkness has had to increase, and Light increased.

7) Knowledge of the Original Village Mandates and the restrictions are adhered to on the surface, and honored in the darkness of the underground.

8) Knowledge of the rules and failure to adhere, or intentional violation is punishable by **DEATH**. Banishment is no option; already sequestered to life underground, Light witnessed the self-imposed quarantine, Darkness knows the rules, tolerates them, and searches for loopholes.

9) Good must bring Light into the world; it is a beacon to those lost, and a guide to the vulnerable. Good encourages, is aware of man's iniquities, and because of them, pricked humanity's heel. Hope is the attribute needed when alone, lost, afraid, need a friend, or realizes the end is near; man must **LOVE** one another.

Light of the World,

Shine on me,

Love is the Answer.

Shirley again paused, and thought what meaningful words, writers of the Original Village Mandates was very intuitive, and their perceptions addressing current events surprising. The Light of Light has surfaced and Shirley is positive in the right hands it will shine, and set all free. The options are clear, live in **LOVE** or Die in Darkness. If darkness succeeds, the extinction of man and the planet loom, the war effort will determine if man and earth survive. As she pondered the mandates, seriousness overcame her, the ninth sense inside of her sparked, a gift received long ago. Normal humans have seven senses, but Shirley is unique, she has the ability to read minds, and predict actions. Dealing with darkness is **DOOM,** and colluding with evil is **DEATH**.

10) Honor **LIGHT,** within its radiance is **GOOD** and **EVIL**. Too many rules and man finds becomes unable to refrain from sin, known to lead himself into temptation, man must always remember, the **ONLY** wish of darkness is the **DEATH** of humanity. **GOOD** is increasing, **LIGHT** is expanding, and the fullness of the Earth honors **LIGHT**.

Shirley stood, dressed in her usual housecoat, she thought of John Nick and Bud, knowing they're off somewhere with their brothers from another mother, church was nearly over and **L.B.M.N.** would soon be back. Shirley wondered if she should go search for the boys on her own, or wait. Her mind began to click, her pace quickened, and she remembered what **"MA'AM"**, an elder of old, and long since gone, once told her.

"WEIGHT/WAIT broke the BRIDGE."

Steven and John Nick were startled, Ms. Simms woke them, both were sound asleep, and with book in hand, she questioned the two boys; her tone contained a hint of desperation; John Nick recognized it.

"Boys, wake up, where are your brothers; where is Keith and Bud?"

Steven and John Nick had no answer, now awake, they looked around, but the playground, park, and all of St. Cecilia was empty; the boys were gone. They rose to their feet and began walking the park, but it was to no avail. John Nick built up the courage to respond.

"I don't know momma, we dozed off, and they're gone"

Steven said, "I know where they're at, the coulee, and I know whose idea it was. Bud is going to blindly follow, that's what brothers do; let's go find them."

Ms. Shirley said, "Hurry, I feel a weakening, a threat of some sort, something watches, and they're in trouble."

The three of them raced toward the coulee, the day seemed to be suddenly darkening. A clear, sunny day began to darken, and overtake the bright morning sun. A breeze accompanied the dark, and it intensified blowing directly into the faces of the three, creating resistance. The two boys led the search, navigating the wind, Ms. Shirley kept up best she could. Her housecoat sailed in the wind, and she buttoned it, as she hurriedly walked. The boys had a torrid pace; determined to find Bud and I. Arriving at the tall grass, it swayed in the breeze, thick, dense, and bonding together, creating a wall, almost impenetrable. They looked, but there was no trail, nothing to direct them; the grass was taller than ever, and none cut.

Strangeness

John Nick asked, "Which way momma?"

Steven said, "I can't tell which way they went?'

Their voices were panic stricken, it was strange; they paused at the tall grass, wind swirling, and darkness covering the sky. What would the decision be, which way would they go? Ms. Shirley turned to the book, knowing there is an answer inside, turned the pages while the boys waited; would she save the day?

Ratwolves of the Underground.

The explorers proceeded, I cut as Bud watched, noticing the darkening sky, the gusty wind, and the tall, swirling grass. The wind seemed to speak through the grass, whistling, whispering, and responding to each other. Wherever I cut, the grass stood right back up. We stopped, darkness now consumed the sky, surrounded by grass, it grew taller by the minute; we were trapped.

Bud asked, "Why is the grass not falling, how can it stand back up as you cut it?"

"I don't know, Bud, this is weird; I'm scared,"

They both then heard a growl, a sound they recognized, and froze in their tracks. The sound was near, very close, fear overwhelmed them, confusion, and panic set in, both were scared stiff. The wind swirled harder, darkness blackened, silence returned, the growl was gone, it was silence, and eerie.

Glen said, "Let's turn around." Glen suggested.

I didn't answer, just listened, the mid-day darkness was strange, I crouched down, hiding within the grass, looked at Bud, and signaled him by opening my palm and pushed it downward to the ground; Bud got the hint, and squatted down. I put my finger to my lips, no words, all communication will be non-verbal; Bud understood the signals, we've used them before as hunters, but presently, we are the hunted. Bud readied the pellet gun, grass could be heard moving, swaying, but the wind wasn't blowing. The tall grass leaned as something pushed it aside, we were still, and could heard something approaching. It drew near, and as it got closer, we held our breaths, and remained squatted.

Something was coming toward us, through the grass, aimed our way; as it progressed, the grass folded; it was big, and going to find us. I readied the machete and cane knife, Bud aimed in the direction of the approach sound. We were scared, but prepared, we remembered our hunting training; one must never let prey hear you approaching, complete silence is required. Quiet, still, listening, our vision keen, and we wondered what was coming. Closer it drew; it made no sound, the only sign of its arrival was the bending of the grass.

Coosh-Maa

The grass was commanded, increase, grow, block, distract, reach to the sky, and it did. Coosh-Maa sent out his elite guard, field rats, swamp rats, bush rats, brown rats, and nutria rats, all part of the search team, small rodents that left no trails. **EVIL** realizes the little ones are the effective ones, getting in and out without detection, perfect spies. Coosh-Maa calls them his special children, and hopes they will always stay little, naïve, and loyal; dedicated to their creator.

He put the elder boys in a deep sleep, knowing the attraction of the **BOX**, the perfect situation, jeopardizing the youths, preying on their naivety; and appealing to the finder's sense of **WANT**. Someone wants to check on the **BOX,** desires to see it, and wants to confirm it is still there. He wants proof of life, and the only way to obtain proof is to see the **BOX**. They are in his clutches, no scrunge necessary, and Gus is inept; he took things into his own hands.

Through the glass of the darkening sky, he spoke to the wind, generated cloud cover, blotted out Light temporarily, and created chaos. Coosh-Maa knows man, has witnessed him crack under pressure, seen him tuck tail, run, and these are only boys, they will surely crack. The spies neared, the grass laid down for them, darkness increased, and the wind intensified. Coosh-Maa's spies smelled for the humans, a distinct scent, an appealing aroma, and to **EVIL** it is spoor.

Coosh-Maa encouraged his subjects, knowing his window of opportunity is small, he has to seize the **BOX** now, eventually Light will return. He intensified the searchers hunger, making them search harder; an empty stomach generates drive. **EVIL** cannot remain on the surface exposed, Light will prevail, and it knows it. Opportunities have to be seized; he has created an ideal situation, having put the boys in a compromising position, sees a crack in the armor, and must attack. It is now or never, Capre Diem, the simplicity of the human language, the minute mind of humans, he uses their vices against them; Coosh-Maa is cunning, baffling, and powerful.

Darkness

L.B.M.N. saw the sky as they walked homeward, it is mid-day, yet the sun has become shadowed, and darkness slowly enveloped it; Coosh-Maa created an eclipse. The girls had never witnessed such a strange occurrence, mid-day, and the sun turned black. Momma requested we increase our pace, walk faster, she senses something is amiss, the girls followed closely behind. To deter progress, the wind increased, a stiff breeze blew directly into their faces creating resistance, momma encouraged us, and instructed as she guided us through the wind.

"We must make it home, something isn't right with Keith and Steven, I feel it; I need to check on them."

Hurriedly we followed, the darkness, Father's sermon, maybe this was the time spoken of, with the sun completely gone, walking in pitch darkness, momma encouraged us.

"Keep up girls, we're getting close. Hold each other's hands if you must, stay with momma, we are going to make it."

Gus Appears

Speeding home, no streetlights to assist, complete darkness, mid-day, yet pitch black, and as we walked, lights appeared behind us; still in the distance, they were coming our way. The lights lit up the dark day, kept coming, momma veered off the road, and told us to follow her. She turned left and we hid behind the Billeaud's house, we wondered why, but asked no questions. We followed as instructed, momma has a reason for doing what she does, we knew it; and this was not the time to ask questions. We stood to the side of the Billeaud's house as the lights from the car continued to approach; the driver slowed, and we realized they were looking for us. There was only one vehicle on the street, it lit up the road. We were silent, and watched as the car dove by.

Momma said, "Ssshhh."

We stood still, huddled behind her, watching as the car slowly pass by; it was Gus, patrolling with his spotlight on. He drove by, shined the light into the bushes, illuminated sides of houses, into ditches, and even directed it in tress. We didn't have to wonder, we know who he is looking for. He passed us by, we waited until the spot light was out of range, he continued down West Railroad. We watched as he went toward St. Cecilia and re-emerged from the side of the Billeaud's. Momma then did something she hadn't done in years, she began to run, and yelled to us.

"Come on girls, keep up with ya'll momma."

We ran behind Momma, our heads were on a swivel. We knew where we were, and could see Ms. Shirley's house, meaning ours was right behind. Momma ran fast, and sprinted, but we kept up, we arrived at Ms. Simms, saw lights behind us, and knew it was Gus; he was coming back our way. We turned into Ms. Simms driveway, and hid, Gus approached, he would surely spot us with the light; we were trapped under the carport. Momma knocked on Ms. Shirley's garage door, but got no was no answer, the spotlight shined on our house; Ms. Simms was next. The car slowly drove up West Railroad, we stood flat against the garage wall, knowing we'd be found, there was no doubt.

Momma told us, "Close ya'll eyes."

We closed them just as the spotlight hit us, and we heard his car door open. Momma stood in the front of us, all of our eyes were shut, filled with fear, expecting the inevitable. We were about to be discovered, and I was afraid, suddenly, there was a loud, echoing howl, it came from nowhere, but I knew the source, it was Gus, the **DOG** in him manifested. Stiff, and scared, we listened, each wanting to peek badly, wanting to see what momma was doing, what Gus was doing, and how would we escape?

L.B.M.N. stood in front of the children, circled them, reached out her hands, and began to connect the circle; each child followed suit. She touched the first and second child, one left and the other right, she set in motion a link; as the girls held her hands, she transferred power to them, through her. The girls felt it, it warmed them, lightened their burdens, fear, fright, panic, and dread were gone. She released their hands, and one by one they opened their eyes.

They could see Gus on all fours, sniffing at the edge of Ms. Shirley's car port, in his natural form, a canine. He smelled, searched for a clue, an identifying scent, anything to reveal the whereabouts of the troublemakers. He couldn't sniff us out, and we were right there, in disguise, they could see him, but he couldn't see them. L.B.M.N. erected a shield, created a vacuum in time, a warp in the consciousness of eternity; a Light hole. In the past, there were Black holes, L.B.M.N. has the ability to erect a new source of energy, she alone can create anonymity, generate obscurity in the present, and no eye can see, or detect what she conceals.

Gus searched for them and had gotten this far, he knew he was close, but L.B.M.N. generated inconspicuousness; it frustrated the Police Chief. He howled in disgust, crying to the skies, voicing his dis**GUS**t. They watched, and witnessed **EVIL**, Gus is the epitome of **EVIL** and is dangerous; watch him, and never underestimate him. They held each other's hands tightly, they were not going to break the connection, if they did, secrecy would be broken. If it were, they would be seen by **EVIL**.

The Chief canvassed the area, smelling, crawling, scratching, trying to locate the prey, they were six, one would leave a drop of sweat, sneeze, or cough. He stood on his paws, looking inside the house, then turned and tip toed over the fence, into the backyard. The animals vision penetrated the density of the dark, it was in its element, Gus could see when others couldn't; nocturnal vision comes with his breed.

The five stood still watching, calming their breathing, relaxing, taking it all in, a perfect vantage point, they could see the intensity of Gus, and imagine if he found them what would happen; he is a canine running round in heat. He wanted them badly, Coosh-Maa gave him a direct order, he had to accomplish it, and was willing to expose his hidden nature to find them. They all saw it, for the first time, they saw the beast within the man. It was frightening, Susan gasped at what she saw, the sound attracted Gus' ear; he quickly turned in the direction of the inhale; and approached. He sensed something, his animalistic instinct heard something, but L.B.M.N. shielded, and took further steps to magnify the disguise. She released a scent, Gus is smell dominant, the human scent will distract him, and meant to drive away any adversary.

She released the gas, a foul stench, it was now in the air, the funk of forty thousand years, no creature could resist it, the smell, the sink, it reeked, but animals gravitate to it. The stink attracts, Gus put his nose in the air, he smelled the scent, it was them, and off he went, gone. He ran off, down the sidewalk, leaving his patrol car, stood back on two feet, and resumed the stance of a human.

We were amazed, and frightened, we saw Gus, a human all of our lives, actually is a monster, how many others are there? His natural condition isn't human at all, he is an abomination; and is aligned with **EVIL**. He is their enemy, and a dangerous adversary, is in power, the Chief of Police; corruption in the highest of places. The final sign of EVIL, the patrol car driven by Gus, drove back up West Railroad without the chief, it guided itself.

Invisible

Daylight returned, the girls, along with their mother, arrived home, they only had to go next door. The floor was open to questions, they could no longer hold in their curiosity, and had to know how their mother did what she did. Paulette being the oldest took the lead.

"Momma, how did you do that, you shielded us?"

L.B.M.N. chuckled, she never exposed her particular ability with her children, from her touch, they now possessed the special gift. They weren't aware of it, but they now had the same ability.

"Girls, the gifts bestowed upon me, you all now have. The moment Gus revealed his **EVIL** nature, I had to reveal my special skills. To witness them, is to obtain them. The timing had to be precise, and the instant **EVIL** manifested, so did **GOOD**."

The girls were puzzled and wondered what gift, what could they now do? Claudette was the most curious, and needed to know more.

"What kind of gifts momma, will we be able to hide ourselves, and turn invisible?"

L.B.M.N. again chuckled, knowing her daughters, and their inquisitive natures. Led by Pooh and Dean, they will ask until she stops them, Lu and Sue will only listen. The youngest is the most intuitive, grasps things quickly, and is the one to be watched.

"Father talked about tests, we just had one, and there will be many more. Rite of passage takes place at the most unexpected times, and gifts can be obtained over time or transferred instantly. My touch, and the link between us, allowed the channeling of ability from me to all of you; use your gifts wisely."

Once home, and a few questions answered, they entered the house and all noticed the same thing, Steven and Keith weren't home. The boys should have been there, they didn't go to church, L.B.M.N. was instantly alarmed. The unexpected darkness still loomed fresh in her mind, and she needed to find her sons. Also, Shirley Simms wasn't home, where was she and her boys?

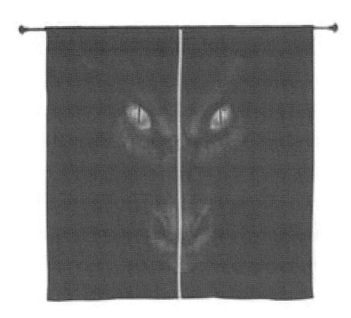

The "**TWO**" faces of **GUS**,

SCRUNGE, and **SUG.**

CHAPTER 3

THE WHO?

WHAT COULD IT POSSIBLY BE?

Darkness consumed us, fear quickly replaced curiosity, Glen and I, surrounded by darkness and tall grass, could no longer see. The moving grass obscured our view, in a place we navigate daily, we are lost. We listened, and heard something, we halted, time stopped, nothing moved, no crickets, frogs, birds, or bees; only silence. Anything moving, shimmying, crawling, or slithering would be heard, the silence was deafening, then heard steps, not human steps, something coming, The grass parted, darkness increased the density, an alley of darkness, through the dense thickness, a grey wolf appeared. Darkness of day camouflaged it, the exposing characteristic, the eyes, piercing light, a blueness indescribable. The mid-day darkness created caution, the creature swayed, watched, and circled, sizing us up, but not attacking; only observing, and we did the same; it was a feeling out session.

Curiosity

The wolf was gigantic, bigger than Roger, and he was the biggest dog I had ever seen, it was huge, Glen and I were cautious, this old wolf is dangerous, an assassin. His body was elongated, it's hair, tattered, matted, and tight; it resembled armor, the eyes lighted the gray coat, and also exposed it's battle scared, scratched, bruised, and battered face. It looked wild, dangerous, and intimidating; the size alone made it scary. From it's mouth spewed saliva, dripping, salivating, and long, razor sharp fangs, glistening in the darkness of day. The eyes illuminated the entire area, it's nostrils were flared, as it sniffed it's prey. It gradually approached us, and we backed, and raised our weapons, the eyes spoke, and were hypnotic. Light surrounded the creature, new light, similar to the power of the **BOX**. Glen's gun was aimed, I readied my blades, the wolf paused, recoiled it's body, stopped approaching, eyed us, and must have sensed our thoughts; it spoke, incredible.

"I am a friend of man, have roamed this earth's surface since creation, and am committed to helping man, rat wolves are approaching, they are pack rats, many will come, make a decision, follow me or die."

We were silent, a talking wolf, could we trust the animal, where did it come from, and where would it lead us? We had to think about this.

I asked, "Why should we follow you, the only wolves I've ever seen are scavengers, and not to be trusted; the best wolf is a dead wolf."

My words were harsh, but I had previous history, Glen was surprised at my aggressive tone. The wolf stood listening, it's bright eyes glued on me, I kept the cane knife readied, Glen still had his aim, neither of us trusted the wolf, and it didn't trust us.

Glen asked, "Why have you waited until now to reveal yourself, we are always playing at the coulee, and have never seen you or any of your kind; suddenly we are to trust you, how can we, and why should we?"

"Stay here, and creatures approaching will soon emerge from the grass seeking to consume you, they are the watchers for **EVIL**. Sent to find you, they will, and then do its bidding. I come from the source of light, and reflect light, I am here to assist. Make a decision, trust me and come, or remain and die."

The grass again began to sway, the wind swirled it, darkness concealed it, and something was inside. We had two options, stay and fight the unknown, or follow the wolf."

Glen asked me, "What do you think man, should we follow?"

The wolf stood still, suddenly erect, it's nose raised to the air, it scanned the grassy, we watched, It sniffed out something, turned its focus to us, and again spoke.

"We must go, they are close."

I drove the machete into the ground, a sign to anyone looking for us, and a reminder of our last location. Glen, with gun in hand, and I, with cane knife, followed the lone wolf. We decided to trust it, at this point, we had no choice.

To The Rescue.

Flipping through pages, rushing, housecoat in the wind, Shirley Simms found something, an answer, and would direct their path. It would be the light needed to allow sight, strangely, in the darkness, Ms. Simms could see the words written on the pages, as they sped into the grass, she made an appeal.

"Mother Nature and Father Time, your daughter calls, a child in your legacy, a sister to your lineage; we need you, who controls the wind, grass, water, and air, presently is the time, we need guidance, lead us, show us the way. For if you lead us, we will not stray. Our sons, future fighters are shot into the night like an arrow, direct their path. Set them at the council fires with the elders of old, enlighten them, prepare them for their purpose, have patience with them; they are young, but eager to live. Protect them, and us, point out which way they have gone. Reveal it to us most generous mother and father"

On the horizon, a light could be seen, and it spread, overtaking darkness, and gradually the sun recaptured the sky. The mid-day sun pierced through. The tall grass swayed, like a wall, a shield; slowly light parted the grass, and we followed the light.

John Nick said, "Momma, I see a path, we should go this way."

Steven added, "We need to hurry, I know they scared, it got dark; let's find them."

Following the light, the three progressed down the lighted trail, the grass succumbed to light, the light parted the grass, and they followed closely. The light flowed, weaved through the grass, and the grass laid down, and we walked over it. Every step forward, the grass bowed, welcomed us, darkness was conquered, and day returned. The reign of **EVIL** was short lived, only a moment, Light regained supremacy. Ms. Shirley walked behind the boys, and continued to read, readying herself for the tests lying ahead.

John Nick and Hub Cap cautiously walked through the grass, as it folded, they proceeded right over it, the power Shirley Simms possesses. The grass, just a few moments ago, was impenetrable, thick, and resistant, now bends. They could now focus on finding those two hard heads. Light returned, the guiding Light was no longer needed, it vanished. They both felt terrible, falling asleep on watch, they had to right this, and find their brothers.

John Nick, seeing his mother falling behind, slowed down, it was urgent to find the boys, but his mom got them this far, she is vital. **EVIL** still lingers, waiting, and manipulating. The boys thought of an earlier lesson, Together they are unbeatable, they must remain together.

Deliverance

We followed the grey wolf closely, walking lightly, staying close, but leery. The wolfs steps made no sounds, and left no prints. It knew the area well, we were both surprised. As it led, we whispered to each other.

Glen asked, "Where do you think it is taking us?"

"Ssshhh, just follow it, and stay close. It's dark out here, I think it's trying to protect us."

The light from the wolf's eyes lit the way, illuminating the trail, and allowing us to stay close, the light made it impossible to lose the beast. The more we followed, our trust began to grow, the animal was looking out. We began to exit the tall grass, and sunlight began to slowly return. Daylight again revealed itself, and as the light intensified, the wolf turned translucent. Gradually, right before our eyes, the wolf began to fade, and slowly blended into the returning Light. Glen and I were speechless, and looked at each other; amazed. The Light of day returned completely, and with its return, the wolf disappeared; **POOF.**

Daylight returned our awareness, we recognized the terrain, and knew exactly where we were. The coulee was familiar ground, we felt encouraged, and simply wanted to get away from the danger lurking. The sudden darkness made their desire to see the **BOX** lessen, curiosity faded, and home was yearned for.

I said, "Bud, it's time to go home. You know Steven and John Nick are gonna come looking for us."

Glen replied, "Let's go, I'm ready to go too."

We sped up our pace, beginning the trek home. It had been a very strange morning, and we witnessed unexpected things, things we least expected. We now knew there is a constant ally on our side, others might not believe it, but we have a new friend in the Lone Wolf. Out of the tall grass we emerged, and coming our way was Steven and John Nick, followed closely behind by Ms. Shirley. Seeing the three approaching, Bud and I knew we were safe, but in big trouble. They slowly approached us, Steven, John Nick and Ms. Shirley, and Ms. Shirley immediately tore into us.

"I don't know what the two of you are up to, but I'm sick and tired of chasing behind the two of you. I try to put you in the hands of the ones I think are responsible and I find them sleeping on the job, good help is hard to find."

She looked over at Steven and John Nick, the two lowered their heads, and their gaze; they had dropped the ball. She then turned her attention back to us.

"Keith, Glen, I speak for Ms. Bessie Mae also, both of you are no longer allowed to visit the coulee unless you are accompanied by your older brothers. There is too much going on these days to allow the two of you to just wonder off as you please. I'm saying this for the last time, don't make me have to repeat if. If I do, it won't be with words, it will be with a switch of your choosing."

Both boys knew Ms. Shirley wasn't clowning around, it was heard in her tone; she was obviously upset, and frightened. The fear could not only be heard in her voice, it was written all over her face. She rarely involved any physical discipline as a reprimand tactic, but today was different. Today, she was different, and after a small pause continued.

"It's time to go home. None of you have eaten dinner yet., and before long, it will be supper time. We were frightened, and the darkness of the sky added to the chaos. Glen and Keith, from now on, I expect the two of you to walk a chalk line."

The remainder of he walk home was silent. John Nick and Steven led the way, and Bud and I walked in front of Ms. Shirley. She still had her book in hand, reading as we walked. Calm had returned, and right before we arrived home, she released a final comment.

"Bud and Keith, don't scare us like that."

We turned and Ms. Shirley's eyes were filled with tears, relieved that the boys were safe. We were under the impression this is all fun and games, we now know, it no longer is.

Bud said, "I'm sorry momma, we wanted to go see the **BOX** again. It might sound funny, but we hear it calling us."

She replied, "Ya'll and that damned **BOX**, it will be the **DEATH** of us all if we're not careful. We need to decide what we're going to do with it."

I said, "What do you mean, what we're going to do with it; the **BOX** is mine. I found it, and ya'll taught us, 'Finders Keepers'"

John Nick, Steven, Glen, and even Ms. Shirley, laughed at my possessive nature, the **BOX** obviously had a hold on me; Ms. Shirley made a suggestion.

"Keith, you missed church today, later this afternoon you need to go talk to Father Dauphne; he might be able to help you. The **BOX** has a grip on you, and if you must find a way to release it's hold, or it will devour you."

As we arrived home, coming up the street was L.B.M.N., and the girls. She and Ms. Shirley made eye contact, and approached each other, we continued past and went to the others, allowing the mothers to talk.

Momma asked, "What's going on, did it have anything to do with the sudden darkness?"

"Keith and Bud are slick, they waited until their brothers were distracted, allowed themselves to be tempted. They need to be taught a lesson, and if they don't stop doing sneaky things, they are going to wind up hurt."

L.B.M.N. listened to Ms. Shirley, she was perturbed, Shirley Simms is always cool, calm, and collected; not today. Her feathers were ruffled, she was upset with the two young boys.

Bud said, "I'm sorry Momma, I won't run off anymore; I promise. If I want to go to the coulee, I'll talk to John Nick before I do; and if he can't come, I won't go."

I added, "I just wanted to see my **BOX**. Everybody's making decisions about it, and it's mine; I should be allowed to have the final say, it's not fair."

Momma grabbed me by the ear and began twisting, and pinching it. I grimaced in pain, the others, both boys and girls, recalled the pain. It is nothing nice to have your ear twisted, or pinched. Both mothers were upset, worried, and actually afraid.

Momma said, "Boy, you better stop your conniving ways, or I'm gonna put it on your butt; you're not too big for a whipping."

Momma used physical discipline as a threat, that is rare, and something she never resorts too; it was serious. All of us knew it, and momma doesn't make idle threats. I'm walking on thin ice, and better straighten up and fly right.

Ms Shirley said, "I suggested he go talk to Father Dauphne, he might be able to help us with the **BOX** problem."

L.B.M.N. nodded her head in agreement. They both thought maybe I need some church. Momma's nod seconded the motion without putting in her two cents.

Momma said, "As a matter of fact, since you missed mass this morning, we're going to church later this afternoon. We need to see how we can better handle this situation."

Ms. Shirley, John Nick, and Glen continued to their house as Momma made the suggestion. Momma is all about family, and knows every opportunity is a great time to teach, and instill accountability.

She said "Shirley, I cooked a chicken fricassee, white rice, peas, and potato salad. There is enough for all of us, stay, let's share dinner together."

Ms. Shirley smiled, John Nick and Bud's faces lit up, they love momma's cooking.

"O.K. girl, we'll stay; it does sound delicious."

John Nick added, "It sure does Ms. Bessie."

Bud said, "And I could eat a horse."

Chew-Bus added, "I could eat two horses."

We erupted into laughter, and began entering the house. The day was again bright, it was beautiful; and the breeze cooled the afternoon, but within the breeze, something lurked, and listened. An excellent opportunity was missed, **EVIL** wouldn't let the opening pass. The girls set the table, and made additional placement for Ms. Shirley and her boys Pooh added three plates, Dean slid up additional chairs, Sue grabbed some utensils, and Lu got three more glasses. We all took our places at the table.

The children served themselves, and then the adults. The meal looked delicious and smelled awesome. After the exhibition by John Nick and Steven, they were starving. After the lone wolf incident, Bud and I were famished. The girls, after the walk to and fro church, were hungry. The mothers tempered their appetites, they are aware **EVIL** watches; purposely seeking weaknesses. L.B.M.N. had all the children hold hands, she and Ms. Shirley were at the head of the table; the mothers looked at all the children, and smiled. They approved of what they witnessed, and were pleased to have all their little ones present.

L.B.M.N. began, "Heavenly Father, we approach your throne with bowed heads and humble hearts. We beseech you to watch over our families, and our community. Protect us from the lurking **EVIL**, remove it from our presence. Give us this day our daily bread, forgive us our trespasses, as we forgive those who trespass against us, and lead us not into temptation, but deliver us from **EVIL**."

All present responded, "**AMEN**."

The prayer forced **EVIL** to flee, and a fresh breeze flowed through the house. Lu smelled its departure, and looking toward the window, saw it escape also.

"A family that prays together, stays together."

WHO is OBSESSED?

The attraction of the **BOX** intensifies, L.B.M.N. knows what it was capable of, Shirley Simms is also aware of the beckoning, both know Keith, nor Bud will be able to resist the temptation, the draw, and alone cannot fight it. Alone, without their guidance, they will inevitably succumb to temptation, and allow **EVIL** an avenue in. None of the children know what obsession will do to them, and aren't aware of fixation. They rarely displayed passion, are easily fascinated, especially Keith; the **BOX** appeals to his curious nature.

The **BOX** will eventually consume his every thought, and wants to become his prized possession. He doesn't recognize the appeal, and wants to verify it is safe, but actually wants to see it, hold it, and **LOVE** it. He constantly states, "It is his, he found it, and should determine what is done with it," the objective of the **BOX;** creating a diluted sense of ownership, making everything else secondary, it becomes primary, and eventually takes over all. The mothers understand obsession, and desire; the boys don't. They are powerful emotions, feelings that can confuse, and create misplaced loyalty; the hidden intent.

L.B.M.N. does understands, Shirley Simms sympathizes, both will not allow **EVIL** to harm another one of her sons. If not addressed, and halted, the summoning may absorb them. As the family ate, the mothers pondered their son's dilemma. Only boys, how can they resist a pull grown men cannot. There is so little time to prepare, and so much to get done. They surveyed the children, both have an internal question, and know there is no answer, yet they wonder.

WHY NOW?

After the meal, L.B.M.N. knew a good source of direction for me, input from Father Dauphne, and some needed guidance. He would have answers, restore confidence, and give momma peace of mind. Ms. Shirley and her sons headed home, they all thanked momma for the meal, and the entire family for the hospitality. As they exited the back door, John Nick and Bud took a final look back, they were tight with all the kids, and had a close bond. Momma told the children of her plan, they listened, and she left Hub Cap in charge; he's the oldest, and could control the girls. It would also give him a chance to share some knowledge, get reacquainted with his sisters, and discuss the strange events of the day.

Regulators.

Gus re-entered his squad car and rode toward the police station, his car met him up the street. Light had diminished the darkness, the mid-day break was impressive, and powerful. It was the first time Gus witnessed darkness consume light, a total eclipse, it lasted, and it was awesome. The power he witnessed, he now wanted, and will do anything to obtain it. He was in awe, and curious, how was this done, how did **EVIL** replace **GOOD,** even if only temporary? How did darkness overcome light, he had to ask Coosh-Maa, had to get answers, and wouldn't stop until he discovers how.

As he drove, he thought of the encounter at Shirley Simms, and knew he was close. He smelled Bessie and her girls, and his desire is to ravish one or two of the girls. He could taste the young, tender flesh between his sharpened teeth, and licked his lips thinking of the delicious bouquet. Tired of waiting, weary of restraint, he wants to release his natural inclinations; and longs to feed. Told they were under the carport, information his dark spies relayed, he had them dead to right; how did they escape? Why did the Light have to return, and what did Bessie do; how did they just disappear? Gus howled in frustration, the sound proof police cruiser muffled the cry; he wailed at the missed opportunity. He has done his research on Bessie's girls, and has pin pointed the most craved. It is the one with the sensitive nose, she must be eliminated. He has no chance with her around, she sniffs him out before he arrives. He could be in the shadows, in the air, or under the ground, where ever, her nose alert smells; and she then alerts all. She is the watch dog, and he chuckled at his final thought; what is a female dog; a **BITCH**.

Saliva leaked from the lips of Gus, he drooled at the thought, and couldn't control the salivation, thinking of devouring the girls made his mouth water. It has been a long time since he tasted human flesh, Bessie could spare one of the four girls. If not the one with the sensitive nose, his second choice, he has made a list, and checked it twice. Second in line is the little plump one, she is always over there, he knows where her family lives; she is most vulnerable. He plans to catch her walking home, he'll offer her a ride, and if she doesn't voluntarily get into the car, he'll do what he must. One way or the other, she will get into the car.

No one will see anything, and Edna Mae will file a missing persons report. We'll canvass the area, search the neighborhood, and I'll seem concerned. I'll head the investigation, and of course she won't be found. The lead investigator on the case knows why, but no one else does. That's how it is meant to be, and going to be; why, because Gus says so. He's bored with the latest delicacies, dogs, deer, wolves, and martyrs, he consumes them, but has to regurgitated them; human flesh digests the easiest, lasts the longest, supplements, energizes, and is Life itself. He pulled over to the roadside, turned off the cruiser, and in the silence, meditated on one specific issue.

Why doesn't Coosh – Maa DIE?

As we walked toward Father Dauphne's, momma talked to me, reminding, and reinforcing what needed to be done.

She said, "You know Father Dauphne is a man of God?"

"Yes ma'am."

"Can you tell an untruth to a man of God?"

"No ma'am, I must tell him the truth."

"The whole truth, and nothing but the truth, Keith."

"I'll tell him everything Momma, I can trust Father. I've been an altar boy for as long as I can remember."

"O.K., I just wanted to make sure. Son, the truth is always the best option, lies come back to haunt you. The truth is the Truth, it will set you free, and honesty is always the best policy."

I listened to momma, the walk was going well, and now that the Truth issue was covered, I had a few questions. Things I wondered about most of my life suddenly seem more important than ever. I now desired answers, and felt the courage to ask, I broke the quietness of the walk.

"Momma, you won't get mad if I ask you something?"

"Son, I know how your young mind thinks, it is always jumping from here to there. Someday, your mind will allow you to move mountains, right now it's in training. I'll never get mad, upset, or angry with any question you may ask."

He now felt the door was open, and thought it safe for him to thread on unchartered turf. It may be a touchy subject, but what the heck; she said anything.

"Momma, where is my daddy?"

L.B.M.N. was surprised, the boy came right out and asked a question she didn't expect. She assumed it may be something about the Truth, or even the **BOX**, a daddy question; surprised, she looked down at her son and smiled.

"Boy, your mind sure does jump from one thing to another doesn't it. Think about what we just talked about, and think about what you asked me. One the way back, I'll give you an answer, can you hold your horses until then?"

I smiled, momma has a way with words, and is the ultimate diplomat; that's what I love about her. I looked up through the setting sun, and the rays shaded her face. She was engulfed in Light, it was the first time I saw her that way; she is Light itself.

"I can hold my horses momma, you know though, when they let me go, I'm like Secretariat."

Momma chuckled, that boy always has to get the last word.

"I enjoy these walks Keith, this morning it was with your sisters, and this afternoon it's with you. In both cases, I love it, you're my second to the youngest.

I know momma has always been busy with her girls, and I want you to know, I love you son. No more or no less than Steven, Pooh, Dean, Jessie, or Sue; in my eyes, I love all of you the same."

We arrived at the rectory and I pondered momma's words, the description of her love, the point made, and the realization that I have to love my sisters and brothers, and Ms. Shirley that way. Come to think about it, I have to love everybody. I was told to tell the truth so I figured it was time I did. As we arrived, Father Dauphne was sitting on the front porch, reclining in a lawn chair, he seemed to be sleeping. It was a pleasant afternoon, he looked really comfortable, and I hoped we weren't waking him.

Momma spoke as we walked up, noticing he was resting. She looked at me and smiled, I knew what had to be done. We stood slightly off of the porch and momma cleared her throat to get Father's attention. He opened his eyes, cleared the cobwebs; the blinding sun, he shaded to recognize the visitors.

Momma said, "Hello Father Dauphne, we didn't mean to wake you."

"Bessie, it's no problem, I didn't realize I had fallen asleep; it is such a nice afternoon."

He looked over to me, and smiled as he straightened out his posture.

"What can I do for you Bessie?"

"Father, if we're not imposing, my son needs to talk to you."

Father turned his attention to me, his look is always intimidating, now more then ever. I stood frozen, unable to speak, recognizing my facial expression, he made a suggestion.

"Keith, go in the garage and get two folding chairs, it's too nice to be inside; we'll sit on the porch and talk."

I went around the side of the house, and retrieved two chairs, allowing Father and Momma time to talk. Momma would inform him of the reason for the visit, and prepare him for what is in store. From the side of the house, I overheard a little of the conversation.

"Bessie, what's going on with Keith, is he in some kind of trouble?"

Momma hesitated a moment, gathering her thoughts, and begins a most unbelievable revelation. She hopes Father has an open mind, and will grasp the magnitude of the information shared. She is leery, but her options are limited, and she needs to talk with someone who will give good, sound advice.

"Father, Keith and my neighbor's boy discovered something recently while "exploring" in the coulee near our house. The thing they've found is important, and will change the course of this town and possibly the world."

L.B.M.N. now has Father Dauphne's attention, he's intrigued, and wonders what's discovered. Before he can inquire more, I return from the garage with the two folding chairs in hand, open them, and place them on the porch. Now all three of us are seated, and it is time for the Revelation. Father looks at me, and with momma sitting next to me, asks a question.

"I understand you have something you want to talk to me about."

"Yes, Father, I appreciate you taking the time to see me and Momma, we need your guidance."

He smiled at my composure, I could tell he was impressed.

"I always have time for one of my favorite altar boys, what do you need my advice about?"

I smiled, took a deep breath, and looked over at momma. She nodded her head as a go ahead sign Just before I spoke Father Dauphne made a suggestion.

"Let's say a prayer first."

We all thought it was a good idea, and very appropriate, and we sat silently as Father Dauphne led us in prayer. We held hands as he began, momma squeezed my hand tight, I looked over at her, she smiled, and winked at me. I Love momma, Father began praying.

"Our Father who art in heaven, hallowed be thy name. Thy kingdom come, thy will be done, on earth, as it is in heaven. Give us this day our daily bread, and forgive us our trespasses as we forgive those who trespass against us. Lead us not into temptation, and deliver us for evil. For thine is the Kingdom, the Power, and the Glory, forever and ever. Amen."

The prayer ended, we released the grip we had on each other's hands, and a calm seemed to pervade over the porch. The afternoon was beautiful, the sun setting in the afternoon sky, and the porch was the perfect backdrop. I was ready to talk, and Father Dauphne anxiously suggested.

"Tell me young man, what is it you need to speak to me about? I've been hearing your name in reference to some strange happens about town, and you know how Broussard is, word spreads fast, and news travels quickly. Gossip is fuel to a wildfire, and the life blood of this town."

A good place to begin, finding the carcass under the foot tub, if I would not have kicked over the foot tub, I wouldn't have been startled. The stunning discovery led to the unearthing of the **BOX**, everything else has been a progression since.

What

"I was being adventurous one morning at the coulee. The water was low due to the drought this summer, things were exposed I had never seen before. A foot tub buried deep in the mud caught my attention, and I turned it over to see what was under it."

Father knows of my natural curious nature, and he smiled with my confirming words. I was going to be totally honest, and tell all, in his presence, and momma's, I felt at ease. I could tell the truth, be completely honest, and there were no repercussions, Father and momma listened as I continued.

"Under the tub was bones, the skeletal remains of something. At first I thought maybe it was a baby, and the thought frightened me. When I saw the bones, I stepped back toward the bank of the coulee, lost my balance, and fell into the mud; that is when I saw it."

I could see Father's face light up with wonder, and curiosity was written all over his face; what did I see? He wanted to know, gossip is one thing, but this was coming straight from the horse's mouth, and factual.

"I saw a reflection, a light, it bounced off of something buried under a Moj-Yah tree. It drew me, the reflecting light was beautiful, and I had to see what it was."

Father was now intrigued, the skeletal remains were one thing, but the reflecting discovery captivated. Just as it fascinated me, it now had Father spellbound, he wanted to know what it was.

Father asked, "Before we go on, what became of the remains?"

I looked over at momma and again she nodded her approval, it was reassuring, and it helped me to open up. I felt her warmth within her smile, and her unsaid words told me to continue.

"Momma and I told Gus about the discovery and have not heard anything about it since."

"Do you think it was human remains?"

"Father, I thought they were, and I wondered who would do such a gruesome thing, I was scared."

"You're a brave boy Keith, and what you've told me thus far is very interesting. What you're saying sounds like a familiar tale I've been told in the past, about skeletal remains found that resemble human bones."

Both Momma and I looked at him funny, and wondered what he was talking about. It made us both realize, this wasn't the first time Father heard of something like this, now we were intrigued.

"I've been the priest of this town for a long time and have heard of odd findings. There is never an answer, and always concluded to be a dead dog, cat, or something of that sort, and we are left to wonder. Now please continue telling me about your discovery."

"The reflection turned out to be a **BOX**, a wooden chest of some sort, buried in the mud. It was beautiful, covered with jewels; diamonds, rubies, pearls, sapphires, and gold nuggets; the prettiest thing I had ever seen."

"How big was the **BOX**?"

"It is the size of a shoe box, dazzling, and after I cleaned off the mud, it shined; giving off a reflection like nothing I had ever seen before."

"Where is the **BOX** now?"

"We hid the **BOX**, Steven and I put the **BOX** in a safe place. He knew of a secret hiding place and we put it there and haven't gone back since; I think it's safe where it is."

"Did you tell Gus about the **BOX?**"

"No, I didn't Father, the **BOX** is mine, I found it and want to keep it."

Father smiled, seeing my changed disposition, witnessing possession manifest itself, and the desire to own the **BOX.** He looked over at my momma, and then turned his gaze back toward me.

"Don't let your desire to possess the **BOX** overwhelm you Keith, it is only a **BOX**. Whatever is inside isn't yours, it belongs to the creator of the **BOX**. Whoever or whatever it is that created the **BOX** will come looking for it. The events of today confirm that the **BOX's** discovery is known."

Momma asked, "What do you mean Father Dauphne?"

"That was no eclipse earlier, it was an **EVIL** force searching for something. **EVIL** has always shrouded this town, and now it has established a stronghold. Its presence is felt, and I fear it will soon rear its **EVIL** head, and when it does, we must be prepared."

Momma asked, "How do we prepare Father?"

"My suspicions were confirmed when the Darkness overtook the Light, it takes an incredible power to accomplish such a feat."

Father then shared something that made the hair on my neck stand, a chill invaded my body, and fear totally consumed me. I could tell it had the same effect on Momma.

"There is an **EVIL** force or spirit searching, seeking answers, and it yearns to possess the Light of Life. I must know, did you open the **BOX**?"

I hesitated to answer, and thought of what Momma told me. I remembered her discussing **TRUTH** with me, and now was the time for full disclosure.

"Father, we have not opened the **BOX**, but it does contain the Light you speak of. The Light scared off the shadow creatures, and lit up the night. It is powerful, yet it understands, because it knew to diminish when it needed to, understanding our thoughts and desires."

"Who is our thoughts; who else knows about the **BOX?**"

I hesitated to answer the question, who else knows about the **BOX**? I needed to tell all, this is my opportunity, I can trust a priest, and I need to trust someone. Sensing my hesitation, Father Dauphne spoke.

"You must be able to trust me Keith; with no trust, there is no relationship."

I turned toward my mother and she only raised her eyebrows. I knew what that meant, the decision is mine, I had a choice to make. I could continue in my deception and wallow in it or tell the truth.

"Father, I now realize everyone knows about the **BOX**, at first it was only Glen, Steven, John Nick, Momma, Ms. Shirley, and me. When I held the **BOX**, it released something, energy, immense, powerful, and it was a signal to the world; announcing it has been found."

"You talk like the **BOX** has a mind of its own."

"I think it does Father, it knows what I'm thinking, and calls, draws me, and has a strange connection to me. I guess since I found it, now it's attached to me, and I find the bond energizing."

Father listened as did momma, both sensing the attraction the **BOX** has on me. Both know it is not a healthy attraction, only being a kid, I have no idea the influence of the **BOX**, it is not a toy. A breeze, cool and comforting overtook the porch, we all felt it. It was odd, late afternoon, from complete calm a draft of air is felt; and it seemed to fondle, caress, and touch us. The silence was interrupted by a loud, sinister howl; almost deafening, and it echoed through the afternoon calm. Momma looked over at Father Dauphne, and he returned the glance. Both knew what was transpiring, but I had no idea. Both were aware of a new arrival, and the source of the ominous wail; momma made a suggestion.

"Father, is it possible we can go inside the rectory; it's getting cool out."

"Sure Bessie, that's an excellent idea. I'll warm some tea, and we can continue our conversation. Do you like tea Keith?"

I fell for the bait, and unbeknown to me, they were seeking an escape. They felt the presence of **EVIL** in the air, and know what is driving, and within the breeze. Listening ears are present, uninvited intruders;, and both didn't want the curious, unwelcomed party to hear. I thought the decision to go inside and drink something was outstanding, father has Root Beer.

"No, Father, I would like to have an A&W Root Beer."

He smiled as we all began to stand, looking at me suspiciously. He now knew where the missing bottles had disappeared. His trusted altar boys were hitting his stash, I told on myself. **What's done in the dark, shall come to light.** We folded the chairs, leaned them against the wall, and Father led us into the rectory. Soon as we got inside, he and momma began closing the windows, I thought it odd, there was a cool breeze, and once they closed the windows it became stuffy. I figured they knew what they were doing, my mind was on the Root Beers. Father and Momma went to the back of the rectory, once the windows in the front were closed. I took a seat in the front area, and looked around, it was rare I was in the front part of the rectory. It's the business office, the altar boys are normally limited to the kitchen area. Momma and Father returned, both had drinks in hand, and Father handed me an ice cold Root Beer. I took a sip, and closed my eyes, savoring the taste, it felt good going down; Father chuckled.

He said, "Tastes good, huh?"

"Yes Father, just like I remembered."

"I have some things I want to share, information about recent incidents, it will help to understand current happenings."

Momma and I listened quietly, the vibe inside the rectory was **GOOD**, something surrounded us, and filled every crevice of the room, fully consuming it. I felt safe, protected, a feeling I had never gotten from a building before; I wondered why? We listened as Father spoke, curious as to what he intended to reveal. Oddly enough, I was here to tell of mysterious things happening to me, and now he was taking the floor. I am impatient, yet I was captivated, Father had never spoken to me one-on-one about such things. I was honored to be in the presence of adults as they talked, respectfully I was silent, and momma was also.

"People that have been life-long members of our faith community are parting ways, not coming to church anymore. I see them and they have nothing to tell me, but their eyes tell a different story. It is a look I have not seen in ages, and a look I now see far too often."

We listened as Father explained his concerns, comfortable inside this impenetrable fortress, no distractions, or external interruptions. The focus was singular, his words poignant, and the **NOBLE** spirit of the ancient priest manifested.

"People are changing affiliations, once ostracized, and alienated, they are now embraced. They have joined a new denomination, a religion undefined, and secretive. Something fishy is going on, and I intend to find out what it is."

As I listened, I took a sip of the A & W and felt a stir in my stomach, it was the lunch I had eaten, it needed to come out. It had finally completely digested, and the walk over helped to move my bowels. I dared not interrupt Father, but could not hold on much longer, he continued.

"There are reports of animals found dead all over town, missing pets; cats, dogs, cows, pigs, horses, and birds. When they are found, they are sucked of their blood, and dead. Animals that survive the attacks are mad, filled with rage, don't recognize their previous owners, and have become vicious and carnivorous. Doctors called in to study the creatures are baffling, and after extended observation are disturbed. Nothing conclusive is ever determined, the animals experience a total transformation due to bites, scratches, and even mating."

What Father said was shocking, actually scary, and his words didn't help my stomach condition. The more he talked, the more I needed to use the bathroom. Gas was building inside of me, to alleviate the pressure, I squeezed my butt cheeks together. I couldn't release the gas, it would permeate the entire room, and create an unbearable stench. In the midst of this horrible tale, I had a fart on the brain, father then revealed something captivating.

"There have been numerous reports of black clad demons traveling under the cover of night. They are described as hooded creatures with huge, bright yellow eyes, their only recognizable facial feature; the eyes are mesmerizing, and spellbinding."

I silently thought of the creatures Bud and I have seen, it is good to know someone else has seen them; I knew we couldn't be the only ones. I wondered if Father knew what they are, and who sent them. He now had my total attention, the pressure inside of me could wait.

"There have been reports of these creatures for years, sightings, random and seldom seen, but not as of late. Lately there are more sightings, but no one has a picture to confirm the creatures. They are excused as fearful rants of known storytellers. Others accountings are dismissed as exaggerations, or stretching of the truth, nevertheless, legend acknowledges them as having walked the night for hundreds of years. They are subjects of **EVIL**, and do it's bidding. Be extremely careful when venturing out at night, and never go alone. There are no reports of the hooded figures attacking anyone, but they are becoming bolder; and there is always a first time."

Father paused, sensing his point was taken, closed with some additional background information, food for thought.

"The two most important days in a person's life, the day they are born, and the day they discover why."

Momma was silent, I was awed, and speechless. I felt it was time to open up completely, and share with Father what happened last night; I spoke.

"The black, hooded creatures you speak of, came to our house last night, and to Glens. We first saw them at the coulee, and witnessed their strangeness; they hover off of the ground, instead of walking. They float, and you can't hear them approaching unless your hear is acute. Glen and I saw them up close, they are scary, and I think they are after us."

I saw a questionable look in Father's eyes, thinking I might be exaggerating. This was no exaggeration, I am known for stretching the truth, but this was no stretch; I continued.

"We also encountered an old wolf, ugly, tattered and matted; it's hair was all over the place, but it helped us. It happened when the sky darkened, leading us to safety, and guiding our escape; believe it or not, it talked to us."

Momma and Father looked at me suspiciously, questioning my honesty, the tale was very strange, a talking old wolf. I was telling the truth and had to convince them.

"Glen saw and heard it too, I wasn't alone, if I were, would the two of you believe me?"

Momma asked, "Son, why didn't you tell me about this?"

"So much has been happening Momma, it just slipped my mind."

"Something as important as this slipped your mid."

Father said, "Bessie, let the boy continue, what happened to the wolf?"

"Once we were out of harm's way, **POOF**, the wolf disappeared, without even a goodbye, it was gone. We didn't have a chance to thank it, I think it has been watching over us, it talked like if it had been, a guardian angel all these years."

Momma and Father were speechless, a talking wolf, I think my words convinced them. I saw the look in their eyes change, doubt, and skepticism were replaced by confidence; I witnessed belief manifest and disbelief disappear.

Father said, "I must go to these spots, the exact place you found the **BOX**, carcass, saw the hooded figures, and the old wolf; can you take me to them?"

I thought of the places, all of them familiar to me, and I left the machete in the ground; it should still be there, and help me to relocate exactly where we saw the wolf. I could get us to all the spots.

He added, "I must pray over this area, bless it with holy water, and convert this unholy ground into holy ground. Time is of the essence, when can we do this son?"

Momma said, "Father, it's getting late, what about first thing in the morning. The two of you can go before he goes to school recreation."

Father asked, "That will mean you getting up early Keith, can you handle that?"

"Yes Father, I'll be ready."

Momma said, "I'm gonna make him some biscuits and open a jar of figs as incentive."

I smiled, momma knows the way to my heart. I was overwhelmed with a new sensation, and was again about to break wind. If I didn't go to the bathroom right now, it would be over; I was going to release a foul stench.

I said, "All this talk of food, I need to use the bathroom."

"Go ahead son."

Father said, "You know where the bathroom is, and clean up after yourself."

"Yes sir."

I hurriedly walked down the hall from the front office to the bathroom, it was close to coming out, I could hold it no longer. As I walked, with each step, a little gas seeped out, I picked up my pace realizing a huge explosion was on the horizon. If I let it out in here, right this instant, it might be an atom bomb. Momma and Father sat in the front talking, it was an informative session for all of us, and I was now ready to go home. I also knew Momma was ready to go, and the hint about getting up early was enough. She had a house full of girls at home she had to tend to, Sunday was winding down, and we would soon be hitting the road.

I arrived in the bathroom, found it quaint, priests live a simple life, inside were no extravagant fixtures. I had never used the main bathroom before, the altar boys always use the back bathroom, this was a first. I took a seat on the ceramic throne and took care of my business. As long as I had been holding the toxic waste inside of me, I knew it was lethal. I quickly finished my business, wiped up, and flushed. I smelled it, the stench wreaked, it consumed all of the air; it was the funk of forty thousand meals. I had to do something, find a way to let some air in to kill the scent. Fresh air would eliminate the smell, and drive it out, at least that what I thought. I opened up the window above the sink and a breeze instantly entered the stuffy house. I dressed myself, looked in the mirror to make sure I was properly tucked in, and began to walk down the hall. I heard the voices of Momma and Father Dauphne as I walked toward them, the air I let in seemed to flow to the front also. Father instantly stood, he must have felt something or heard something.

He asked, "What have you done son, have you opened a window?'

I paused, realizing I had, but not thinking of it as a big deal. It was stuffy, and I was only trying to eliminate the stench. I figured the fresh air would help the lewd stink, I was trying to be helpful.

"Yes, Father, I did leave a crack in the window to help with the smell, I did number two; I shouldn't have opened it?"

Before I could complete my sentence, Father dashed to the bathroom. I turned as he passed me, and momma stood from her seat. I didn't know what I had done wrong, and was truly sorry. Shortly after his exit, Father Dauphne returned to the front, and spoke to me.

"It's O.K., it wasn't open long, and I just had to utter three words; 'Behind me Satan.'"

Momma kept her stance, gave me a stern look, and I realized our time with Father Dauphne was over. We approached the front door and he gave us a parting acknowledgment.

"I'll stop in the morning, I need to see something only the boy can show me.

I felt I was in trouble for opening the window. Momma and I began our walk to the other end as the sun set. We were gone longer than anticipated, it was time to head home. All of the other children would be expecting our arrival, and momma knows it's getting close to supper time.

The Great Eight.

John Nick was restless, woke, and looked over at his little brother. He thought of the exhibition with Steven, and what he ad Hub Cap displayed, the physicality of training. They needed to teach the boys, and give instruction, but this was the ideal time for some one-on-one with Bud. Just as he was about to seize the moment, there was a knock on their back window. The knock woke up Bud, John Nick looked out of the window, it was Steven; he opened it for his friend.

Steven asked, "What are you and Bud doing?"

John Nick replied, "He was sleeping, and I'm chillin'. What's up?"

"I was wondering if ya'll can come over, we all need to talk; the girls included. Today has been a weird day, we need to sit down and discuss some things."

John Nick responded, "I think that's a good idea."

John Nick looked over at Bud, who had a Cheshire cat grin on his face, nodding his head in the affirmative.

"Move out of the way Hub Cap, we're gonna climb out of the window. Momma doesn't need to know."

John Nick climbed out of the window and Bud was right behind him. The boys and girls are about to have a Pow-Wow. The Great Eight, minus one. Ms. Shirley hears all, and silently smiled when she heard the knock at the window. She knows it is Steven, knows why he is there, and is pleased the children are so close; she loved it. She knows L.B.M.N. is off with Keith visiting Father Dauphne, the priest would be able to help the boy. John Nick and Bud could hang out with their sisters and brothers, and she knows all the children are in good hands. It isn't her hands, but the hands of God.

This is much needed quiet time for Shirley Simms, allowing her to research something read while searching for Keith and Bud. It was enlightening, yet upsetting; information about the **BOX**. The book she read was titled:

"Fathers of Faith."

It goes into detail about the lack of male human presence in the town, and the systematic destruction of the male sex. The intentional manipulation of man by **EVIL**, the intent, to have only women remaining as viable breeding mates. Tests subjects for **EVIL** to impregnate, in an attempt to produce a race of **EVIL** humans; **EVIL** doesn't desire human destruction, but total assimilation. Shirley Simms now understands the intentions, and agenda of **EVIL**. Also, there is mention of the **BOX** within the pages, and a stern warning about the **BOX** and **EVIL;** the two should never be near each other. They are on opposite ends of the spectrum, or are they; the words read captivated her interest.

Fathers of Faith is a different version from that of the **Original Village Mandates**. Those directives were created to pacify humans, a sham of what is actual, and whitewashed, thus eliminating the participation of **EVIL** in the process, and magnifying the contribution of **LIGHT**. Do not be fooled, in the beginning darkness reigned and allowed Light into the world. The **BOX** which contains the Light of Life is a creation of darkness.

She paused while reading, aghast, puzzled why hadn't she read anything about this before? Why was this concealed all of these centuries, and at this age, she is now being exposed to the truth. Where had this book been in her library, and why does she suddenly find it? Was it intentionally hidden until this moment, and now meant to be found? She needed clarification, had to find out more, and needed to read further. Things were unclear, more history about the Fathers of Faith was necessary. She had never heard of this group, and wondered who were they? What was their past affiliation, and connection to the present, she needs answers; her curiosity is peaked.

Shirley Simms sat in her recliner reading, fascinated by the information enclosed in her latest literary discovery, **"Fathers of Faith."** What an odd title she thought, knowing L.B.M.N. is presently with a man of Faith. She's disclosing all to a man the community deems as the steward of their Faith, now she ponders if it was a mistake. Was Father Dauphne a plant, placed in his position by **EVIL**, and a partner with the ever growing **EVIL** presence? She has to make a determination, use discernment, and the book read is insightful. It gives facts and historical accounts never before spoken of, and sheds light on ideas never before envisioned.

How could **EVIL**, **LIGHT**, the **BOX**, and the town be intertwined? The thought scared Shirley, and her limited previous knowledge infuriated her. For so many years she had fallen for the **LIE**, but her eyes are now open, and she knows the **TRUTH**. Silently she continued to read and arrived at a passage which sent a chill throughout her body. She tried to remain open minded while reading, but it was upsetting. The information shared by the **"Fathers of Faith"** was disturbing. The Founding Fathers realized the town of Girouardville was under siege, and men of the town were being systematically disposed of. In their effort to locate the culprit, **EVIL** was discovered. It disguises itself as a myth, a story of a fabled ghost manifesting itself to humans at night.

This creature is labeled **Coosh–Maa** and exists only in dreams. It manifests itself in the human subconscious, thrives on fear, with its sole purpose; consumption of the human race. Something has to be done to stop it because the spirit is determined, and if it can't defeat man, it will gladly join them. A collaborative effort between the males of Girouardville and Coosh–Maa was attempted, man put its trust in **EVIL**. Unbeknown to them, it was a fatal mistake, and once they joined forces, they were doomed; **EVIL** grew and man diminished.

The disappearance of the male sex continued, and male humans began to disappear at an alarming rate; **EVIL** was relentless. The Founding Fathers realized the error of their ways, but also realized there was no turning back. The pact made between **MAN** and **EVIL** was signed in blood, and man gave Coosh–Maa the one missing element needed to conquer; **PERMISSION**. Man had to willingly sell their souls to their **EVIL** natures, and laying in wait, ignorantly, man came calling. What they found eroded the foundation of humanity, and came face-to-face with pure **EVIL**. Shirley Simms couldn't believe what she was reading, and her eyes filled with tears. She tried to shake the possibility out of her mind, but the thought wouldn't disappear. She thought of the influence of **EVIL** all these years, and wondered if **EVIL** is pulling the strings. Were the surface dwellers only puppets on a string, and **EVIL** the puppet master?

The thoughts consumed Shirley's mind, she needed a respite, closed the "Father of Faith," and prepared to take a nap. She purposely calmed her mind, on it were things never previously pondered. She questioned the Original Village Mandates, the loyalty of many of the residents of her town, and probed the possibility of **EVIL** controlling them all. She kicked of her shoes preparing to take a snooze. Sleep quickly invaded her thoughts, and before long she was sound asleep. Her recliner was the furthest back it could go' it was Shut Eye time.

Sweet Dreams

Darkness entered the subconscious mind of Shirley Simms, and she felt herself in the presence of a powerful entity. It hovered over her, she couldn't see it, but could feel it. It was omniscient, omnipotent, and omnipresent; there was no escaping its watching eyes. She watched as the thing did its dastardly deeds. She saw the faces, all male, men lined up, and being led to slaughter. One by one they approached the throne, bowed down to the mighty Lord, and gave reverence to its supremacy. She was unable to clearly see the master, but desperately desired clarity. She yearned to see what was getting paid homage, respected, and bowed down to? She peered into the vast darkness, her eye sight strained to make out anything, any recognizable feature, but there was no silhouette, or distinguishing feature. The power of the being could be felt, it was like nothing she had seen before, a spirit, a mist, and it had no form.

As the men bowed, they were welcomed to the throne. One at a time they walked up to the throne and were overtaken by the reigning king. It enveloped the men, absorbed their physical features, and then extinguished them. They were turned into ash, their life force drained from them, and they disappeared into oblivion. Shirley's eyes couldn't believe what she was seeing, life was being absorbed. The **EVIL** power was consuming them, and the men were following willingly, voluntarily giving up their lives. She found it odd, and wondered why they would be willing to sacrifice themselves. It puzzled and frightened her, she released a gasp, the men in line froze, and turned in her direction.

The power recognized her, and it began to descend down its throne. It saw an unwelcomed guest, and slowly approached her. Shirley could feel its approach, but not see it, the power of the entity frightened her. She knew it was coming, but didn't know the direction. She tried to escape, began to retreat, and slowly withdrew. She looked up and saw it descending, turned and it was behind her, crouched and it was below her; it was everywhere. She had no place to turn, no book to refer to, or no weapon to use against the power. She suddenly heard a deep, penetrating voice.

"Who invades my sanctuary, who is this uninvited guest? Seize her!"

She turned to run, and waiting behind her, the open jaws of a huge snake. She turned left, reversed her direction, and a gigantic rat was rapidly approaching. She turned right, and a dark silhouetted creature was crouched, waiting to pounce; there was no escape. Shirley was trapped, **EVIL** and its allies had her totally surrounded. A pair of eyes opened, and she saw them. She stood face-to-face with the eyes of darkness, and the glare of death were upon her. She peered into the eyes of **EVIL**, terrified, and screamed at what she witnessed. Fear overwhelmed her and she fainted under the pressure. The weight of the situation overwhelmed her Shirley Simms, death consumed her.

Packs

The shadowy creatures all gathered, word had gotten out about the old One, a legendary scrunge, and the great teacher. Survivor of countless battles, and vanquisher of a myriad of enemies, in the blink of an eye, an icon was destroyed. The pack had to know how it happened, and what would be done about it. They walked the hallowed ground, predatory rulers, hunters, but solitary by nature. They are isolated, lone creatures, and singleness contributes to their invisibility. A pack of all sizes and ages, they prepare the young, and lead by example. Older scrunges are impressive beasts, huge, shadowy monsters; and the perfect killing machine.

When they hunt, the young run the prey, destroying the stamina of the target, the pack is their strength, provides security, and during the hunt ensures success. No creature can outrun the pack, nothing can defeat them, and together work as a well-oiled killing machine. Their blackness is perfect camouflage; using their sense of smell, and patience, are ruthless predators. They lurk until the opportune moment presents itself, then pounce. **EVIL** created the scrunge, and they are loyal, indebted, submissive, and obedient to their creator.

Scrunges have waited 300 centuries for retribution, and the death of the Old One will have a singular effect on the pack; unification. The monsters will rally to the cause of **EVIL**, and seek revenge. They are animalistic, territorial, and lethal. As they gathered in the dark of night, invisibility is their backdrop. Undetectable to the human eye, seemingly non-existent, they tilt the scales, and are willing to die for the cause; human destruction. It's strength is unmatched, possesses razor sharp fangs, blade like claws, and create havoc, chaos, and mayhem. Death is their calling card.

The older scrunges walked through the pack, observing, eyeing the submissive females, looking to recruit new concubines. The scrunges population is dependent on multiplication, the old survives because of the young, and the young survive because of what they learn from the old. Older scrunges weed out the weak, eliminating them, they become meals when the hunt is unsuccessful. The pack doesn't have time to waste on inferior members, hates mediocrity, and sheds dead weight. The young are put in fight scenarios as training tools, fights are to the death, the defeated is eaten, and the tradition serves a dual purpose.

1) The young learn tenacity, self sufficiency, independence, and determination. They witness what happens once you become a liability to the pack, and are taught the importance of the process of elimination. The fight is an excellent teaching tool.

2) The fight also provides a meal. They normally don't occur until the pickings are few. Until then, runts exist, grow, and may overtake another. The odd are unlikely, but it can happen; scrunges are fast learners, and killing is second nature to them.

As the elders navigated the pack, the younger scrunges were becoming restless, and began to huddle, shrinking the ranks, grouping together, a natural reaction to external threats. Their hunting instinct warned them, something was arriving. In the air it was smelled, lingering in the breeze, intermingled in the atmosphere, and accompanying the draft was **EVIL** itself. Using one of its many disguises, **EVIL** has numerous faces. All the appearances come bearing promises, appear as traveling salesmen, and institute the hard sell. The intensity of the arriving gust lifted dirt into the faces of the scrunges, momentarily blinding them. When the oldest of the pack was unable to see, **EVIL** manifested itself, took shape, and was no longer airborne. Removing its normal camouflage, revealed itself, and showed it's face. Before the gathered stood the Creator, no longer invisible, and unseen or centuries, exposed itself. The older scrunges recoiled, revering their master and creator, young scrunges were amazed, having never seen the Creator; it stood visible to them all.

The Creator

Scrunges fear nothing, but to see the creator, all things are leery, even the vilest, most evil of creatures. Having not seen such power in ages, the dark monsters growled, agitated, circling about. They did it's bidding, but the orders were previously airborne, received telepathically, not today, an appearance was necessary. The evil scrunge is rarely awed, tonight, they are all awestruck, and all eyes focused on their Creator. It's eminence, and power could be felt, and it's place of superiority flowed into the atmosphere, and was felt by the scrunge; all the creatures bowed, recognizing it's preeminence.

Hovering above them, majestically looking at it's subjects, the submissive scrunge looked away, fearful. Showing itself was out of the ordinary, but this gathering is special, it is the funeral of a **SUG**. The murder not only upset the scrunges, it infuriated the Creator; there would be a reckoning. The creator knows how to communicate with the scrunge, non-verbally, telepathically, through it's eyes, and stares. The message conveyed was heard loud and clear, and the dark creatures listened. The intent of **EVIL**, to stir up the pack, make them desire revenge, make them want to avenge, create a blood thirst; and once the seed is planted, the scrunge will do the rest; it released a message.

Packs of **Scrunges**

"Scrunges, lost was the oldest of your kind, a ferocious, loyal, warrior. It cannot be replaced, and must not be forgotten. Who is responsible for its destruction, what caused its demise; not one of you, and not in battle. It wasn't a young warrior, fighting to replace the aged, but man; it was accomplished by human hands. We must not allow the surface dwellers to go unpunished, and their intentions are obvious; they seek to destroy the scrunge. Your species is viewed as a blight, your existence detested, and with the old One's death, it is the first step in complete annihilation.

Will you allow it? Will you allow your kind to be reduced to ash, or will you fight in memory of the old One, and avenge it's death? Follow me, and I will lead you to the culprits, the humans responsible for its murder. I will then leave it up to your kind, do what must be done; SCRUNGES, now is the time to seek revenge."

EVIL is cold, calculating, plans to use the death of a loyal subject to incite chaos, stoke the fire, and goad the simple monsters. The scrunges only need a little push in the right direction and **EVIL** is not only pushing, it is shoving; thrusting the scrunge toward conflict. It wants to add fuel to a fire, knowing fuel and fire are a combustible mix. It stood looking at the scrunges, and finally a few of the older ones braved it, and looked into the eyes of their Creator. Standing majestically, knowing it's power, and influence; but internally realizing the scrunge is expendable, the oldest was and so are the rest. The Creator knows, all it has to do is create more, it holds the keys to life, and death in the palm of its hands. It holds keys to the city in its back pocket, and controls the key to your heart; and manipulates by understanding the power it wields, and increasing the numerous temptations.

It says, **"Good, humbug."**

It wants to reign supreme, has an agenda, and an insidious plot. Scrunges are only tools to manipulate and will aid in the destruction of man. They are the catalyst and exist for only one purpose, to kill. They don't care about stealing, have no concept of destruction, and embrace their singular purpose; killing. After many centuries of life, older scrunges align themselves with the Creator. They listen, see, and want to spend time with it; hoping to become it's Number One. When it is accomplished, an older scrunge becomes a Sug; an honorable title, and only one is known to exist.

EVIL is the head of the snake, the Creator is the brain, and rat wolves, scrunges, and snakes themselves are it's body; the rest of the vermin make up the tail. The snake constantly sheds, and what it leaves behind are remnants of **DEATH**. The old scrunges began to howl, and just like it arrived, the Creator disappeared in a whirl of wind. It added the fuel necessary to incite carnage, scratching began, and provocation was now in place. It created, and knows what it takes to inflame them. Human flesh is an excellent motivation, and scrunges savor the taste. The Creators words spurred them on, and he thought of a feast on humans, how stimulating. Even the young scrunges salivated at the thought. As the Creator faded into the breeze, it looked back, and saw the activity of the pack; a building frenzy. It knew, they would soon be ready to attack, and when they did, would annihilate all it came in contact with. The Creator smiled, and pat itself on the back.

Job Well Done.

Before the boys arrived at the Nickerson's residence, they stopped, John Nick and Steven had to talk to Bud. They noticed a disturbing trend since their return home, Bud is a follower. They love his loyalty to Dirt, but he is willing to follow even to his demise; that is not good. He must develop discernment, and the two older boys needed to talk about that with him. Steven stopped and took a seat on a five gallon bucket, John Nick sat on a cement block on the side of the house, and Bud sat on the ground. He didn't mind getting his shorts a little dirty, was interested in what his two mentors had to say, valued their input, and totally respected them.

John Nick asked, "Bud, at what point would '**NO**' be said to your best friend? What line must Keith cross for you not to follow him?"

Without thinking, Bud replied.

"Keith is my best friend, and I'll do an anything for him. He would do anything for me, we're tight like that. He's more than my best friend, he's my brother."

The two older boys smiled, the words sounded familiar, that's how the two older boys grew up and now Bud and Dirt are the same way; loyal to a fault, in life, you live and learn.

Steven replied, "It's impressive, your loyalty to Keith, and since I've come back home, you're all he talks about; you and that damned **BOX**."

Glen smiled, happy to hear what Steven said, confirmation of the two boy's devotion to each other. Glen loves Keith, and will do anything for him; even lay down his life.

John Nick said, "Old School and New School teachings stress devotion, it is good to witness the commitment the two of you have for one another. The opportunity to attend the schools may have been missed, but some things can't be taught, friendship is one. There are some things we need to share with you."

Bud listened, not interrupting, not wanting to put in his two cents. This was a time to listen, and he had to show restraint, especially control of his overactive tongue. The two older boys could see Bud had questions, and wanted to speak, but instead listened. He was beginning to get it, the boy was maturing, evolving from kid to young man, and it couldn't come at a more opportune time.

Steven asked, "What is the definition of a Moron, Imbecile, and Idiot?"

Bud was puzzled, chose not to reply, and remained silent. John Nick liked the direction Steven picked and remembered when Mr. Clifton sat him down at an Old School session. Just as Bud is now puzzled, he was puzzled back then, and had no idea what point the older man was trying to make. Obviously, Bud doesn't have the foggiest either.

Bud responded, "I have an idea Hub Cap, they're all blockheads, and reflect foolishness."

Steven said, "I like that Bud, you seem to be getting the picture."

John Nick said, "Haven't you always told me you wanted to be a doctor."

Glen smiled, "I still do, I like helping people, and I think it's my calling."

Steven said, "The two most important days of your life are the day you are born, and the day you discover why."

Bud thought Steven's words were profound, listened, and absorbed everything said. He loved the time spent with the two big fellas, and realizes they aren't only excellent fighters, they are pretty wise; then he shared a little personal psychology.

"In psychology, an idiot has the least intelligence on the I.Q. scale, is equivalent to someone mentally retarded or mentally challenged; an imbecile is not as inept, and considered equivalent to moderate retardation; a moron is the highest level of intelligence for someone who is mentally hindered, and considered mildly retarded. Specifically, those with an I.Q. of 0 - 25 are idiots; 26 - 50 are imbeciles; and 51 - 70 are morons."

John Nick and Steven were shocked, awed with Bud's response, and realize he is way ahead in his development. They looked at each other, smiled, and nodded their heads in approval. Bud grinned, confirming his brainiac status, and now the older boys know it.

John Nick asked, "Where did you learn that?"

Bud smiled, seeing the look on the two older boys faces, and knew they were stunned.

"Don't judge a book by its age, I know what the two of you are trying to do. I know the options, Lead, Follow, or get the hell out of the way. I love Keith, but I won't follow to the point of destruction, or death; I know how to say '**NO**.' I'm growing, learning to lead, be patient with me big brothers."

Both older boys stood from their seats, Bud stood too, they brushed off their backsides, and knew the teaching session was done. John Nick and Steven were definitely impressed, and didn't envision their talk with Bud ending up like this. If there is any about Bud being a potential leader, he erased it, and will be ready to face any challenge. With a little more tutelage, he will be Armed and Dangerous.

Steven said, "O.K. we cleared the air about leading and following, now lead us to the back door."

The three chuckled with Steven's lead reference.

Gumbo continued, "We need to talk with all of you about the events of the day, and share with ya'll gifts possessed. We need to expose the gifts each of you possess."

The three boys walked around the side of the house, and arrived at the back screen door. Waiting for them was Pooh, Dean, Lu, and Sue, they had been waiting since Steven left, and anticipation was killing them.

Claudette asked, "Where the hell ya'll been, we tired waiting."

John Nick replied, "Hold your horses Dean, we got this, now let's all go sit on the picnic table, and talk. Today has been strange, we all saw it, things are about to change, and we have to be ready when they do."

Claudette got quiet after being put in her place, and the other girls knew not to ask any questions. The three boys led the girls toward the picnic table in the corner of the back yard. It was a nice, cool, breezy afternoon, the sun returned to its place high in the afternoon sky, and it was time to have a serious exchange of ideas. The two older boys needed to share some knowledge with their younger siblings, it was time to reveal the potential existing inside of them. It was also time for them to begin growing up. It was the duty of John Nick and Steven to assist the ones who follow them. They were the oldest, and have to lead by example.

Who Knew

Knowledge

Rising from the depths of darkness and hovering over the lighted surface, **EVIL** searches, using its numerous allies to find clues, and then puts them together to determine conclusions. It has the ability to be in more than one place at the same time, can be in the air, inside your mind, and fool you into thinking it cares about you. **EVIL** can lull you to sleep, and wants you to think it doesn't exist; don't be fooled, it exists and is present in every thought, word, and deed. Coosh – Maa is the epitome of deception, and it's purpose, Kill, Steal, and Destroy. Whichever applies at the moment, it will commence to accomplishing, has done so for centuries, and will continue. Nothing has been able to thwart it thus far, and it seems invincible, and cannot be vanquished.

Nine the Hard Way

We all sat in the back yard as the afternoon winded down. John Nick and Steven led the conversation, were the oldest, and most knowledgeable; they are our strength, so we thought. All were present except Chew-Bus and Dirt, the picnic table was crowded, and the boys allowed the girls seats at the table. Bud sat on a bucket, Steven sat on an overturned wheel barrow, and John Nick leaned on Dee-Dah's old peach tree. It was filled with pink blossoms, in full bloom, fruit would soon appear. John Nick is more the verbal leader, and took the helm. He addressed those gathered.

"Girls, Steven, Bud, we all know strange things are happening, and it's time we talk about them. It's also time Steven and I share what we have learned while away at school. The teachings are to prepare us for the future, and the future is now."

All the girls stared at John Nick, his tone was serious, and Bud was proud of his big brother. He was now a leader, and along with Steven were instructors, guides, and the ones who will help them prepare. The most inquisitive is always Dean, and she wanted to listen to what John Nick had to say, but also wanted to add in her two cents. At times, what she added amounted to about ten cents, but she never thought she said enough. She was born a girl, but really should have been a boy, could hang with any local boy and for sure no girl could keep up with her; in a sarcastic voice she asked.

"What kind of school have you and Steven been at?"

Hub Cap chuckled, knowing his sister and her skeptical attitude. If anyone would have doubts, it would be Dean, it's her nature to second guess everything, she can't help herself; it's in her D.N.A., part of her genetic make-up. She's a skeptic, and if she doesn't see it with her own two eyes, she won't believe it. To answer her skepticism, John Nick put on a display, reached down to the ground and gathered two handfuls of Earth.

"Watch this."

He began to roll his hands together, and the dirt inside of his hands began to form together, turning into a ball. The form changed from dust and powder to mud, he was the potter and the dirt was clay. He was creating something, all watching were amazed, John Nick focused on what he was doing, and at the same time Steven spoke.

"He has the ability to shape Earth, is a silhouette maker, and is shadow, and light. Out of any of the elements, he can reconfigure them, control them, and whether earth, wind, or fire, he can manipulate it. He can turn a thought into a form, and is a shape shifter, a gift received when the **KEY** was discovered."

The girls, and Bud were blown away. John Nick turned the Earth into a statue, then a spear, and continued to reconfigure the dirt in his hands, constantly changing it. He thought of an idea, it manifested, shaped, and all it took was a mere thought; the display was impressive. He created a defense wall, then reached down to the surface dirt and they merged; he then hid within the wall. He was in the dirt, and bonded with the dirt. The demonstration was awesome, all eyes were glued on him, and his concentration was elevated. As he continued his performance, Steven continued to school the kids.

"We all have skills, I am a soldier of fortune. My special skills were recognized early, but I cannot put them on display regularly; they must be used at the precise time. I was sent to Old School first, allowing myself to grow, gifts can be overwhelming. If used incorrectly, they can be destructive, but if used correctly, they will save lives; we have been sent back to instruct you, and protect all."

He then began to display his special skills. Right in front of their eyes his attire changed, his mental ability began to reveal itself. Whatever he thought, his body became adorned in it; body armor covered him, along with a helmet. His chest was protected by an iron clad breastplate, and his feet shod. His legs were protected with greaves, and a gauntlet ran from his hands to his shoulders. He was totally encased in protective armor, the ultimate warrior, and all present were wowed.

As John Nick's exhibition came to a close, Steven began to show his various forms of protection he could generate. Wizard, soldier, warrior, and ninja were some of the combatants he could conjure, simply thinking of these things, they manifested themselves, it was a powerful display. He walked to the big black crackling pot and with little to no effort tossed the huge pot into the air. It sailed into the afternoon sky, and probably weighed a ton, an impressive display, and to a kid unbelievable. He then ran under the descending pot, and caught it with no strain.

We were dumbfounded, and wondered where did his strength come from, and when did this power develop? We were all mystified, and stood observing his massive muscles. Steven was the strongest person we knew, and returned home as a **Colossal**, able to do the unthinkable. First being totally armored, next consumed in muscle, he vanished, blended into the backdrop of day; completely cloaked. He was the black, wrought iron pot, then became the wheel barrow he once sat upon. He went from soldier, to gigantic, now camouflage; it was incredible. He was invisible, but present, and in his invisibility, he spoke.

"Invisibility is one of my gifts, transferred to me from momma, exposed to all of you earlier today, when Gus was searching. I wasn't present, but I felt the power surge, we are all connected. Some of you may have felt it, and as you grow in strength and knowledge, will learn to manipulate and harness your gifts. All of you have special skills, think about it, and realize it. Steven and I are here to help you enhance them."

Pooh could wait no longer, as the eldest girl, she needed to know what special skill she possessed.

"What is my gift Steven?"

The two older boys ceased their demonstration, and one-by-one began to explain what was shared with them. What the teachers at school instructed them to teach, and reveal. This day will change the lives of **Nine the Hard Way**, things will never be the same.

Guess Who

Out of nowhere, from the side of the house, Carolyn arrived; huffing, and puffing, like she had been running. Struggling to catch her breath, all eyes turned toward her. Once she caught her breath, everyone went back to what they were witnessing. Chew-Bus saw Paulette talking in a particular direction, but saw no one, she was puzzled. She began to walk toward them, and remembered what she desperately wanted to share, just then, Steven uncloaked. She couldn't believe her eyes, and all the other children chuckled at the look on her face; total amazement. Only moments ago, they had the same look, and now saw it on Chew-Bus's face.

She asked, "What's going on Hub Cap, how did you do that?"

"I'm glad you're here, being part of the crew, there are nine children starting out as kids and turning into heroes. Nine will start, but who knows how many will finish. The one thing we must always do, stay together; together we are unbeatable."

Steven now stood in front of them in his normal clothing, and John Nick closed his eyes and when they re-opened, he was no longer blended into the dirt. It fell back to the Earth in the form of dust, and again, Carolyn was amazed. She couldn't hold it in any longer, and had to speak.

"I want to share something too, and it can't be explained."

Steven and John Nick gifts had astonished, and all present knew they were special. They are now teachers, and all the younger kids wanted to learn what they had to teach. The two older boys had captivated their interest, and it now time to let the fun begin. The two older boys broke the eight present into two groups, and will give individual instruction. Steven took Pooh, Dean, and Chew-Bus, leaving one remaining spot for his little brother, knowing he would soon be returning. Once he arrived, Hub Cap would take time, one-on-one, to school him; Dirt needed the most tutelage.

John Nick took under his reign Bud, Lu, and Sue, they were moldable, and easier to instruct. Though inquisitive, they weren't headstrong, Steven would have the more resistant ones. John Nick had the more teachable, and once the instruction period was over, Nine the Hard Way would be ready to face any adversity;

TOGETHER.

Scouring the Land

Scrunges have allies too, and rely on creatures that fear them. They prey upon surface dwelling animals which cower when encountering the dark monsters. They rule the nocturnal night, and darkness is their ultimate playground, an arena which disguises and allows maximum maneuverability. Opossums, raccoons, owls, bats, skunks, mice, wombats, cockroaches, rats, spiders, and porcupines are creatures that cringe at the sight of a scrunge, and tremble with fear, allowing the cruel surface dictator to rule. They are willing to do anything to survive, and are noted traitors. These pawns peruse the surface, gathering information, monitoring, and recording, and afterwards turn over their findings to their tyrant.

Another ally of the scrunge is the Ratwolf, a vicious animal. It has mastered the ability to walk in the light, most of **EVIL'S** snitches are nocturnal, but not the Ratwolf. It is a breed apart, a laboratory creation, designed by **EVIL** to do its bidding. A loyal abomination, similar to the scrunge, it admires it's creator, and relishes the opportunity to please, and will do anything to remain in good graces. A Ratwolf crept along side the rectory, silent, creeping, and then it climbed onto the roof. Allowing it's boneless body to slide into a gutter, by a high vantage point it progressed. Sent by Coosh–Maa, it's objective, listening to what humans tell the Holy man, and once the information is gathered, return and report.

On a fact finding mission, the creator needs to know the location of the **BOX**. It has the power of Life itself, and is both Light and Dark. It is the source of all creation, and within it's confines sustains the balance; whoever possesses it controls all. The monstrosity crept, closer, and closer it slid, through the gutter system, navigating the leaves, and debris, enhancing it's disguise. It makes no sound, and is partnered with silence. It is masterful at stalking, and it's prey never hears it approaching. It is patience, creeps, crawls, and never hurries.

It has done the bidding of **EVIL** for centuries, and blends perfectly into the brown, autumn leaves. It's weight doesn't crush the leaves, is illusive, and continued to shimmy forward; silently approaching the porch. Accompanying the Ratwolf is **EVIL** itself, it wants no third party report, but desires to hear the words coming out of the mouth of the human. It wants to overhear the conversation, and be present when the human spills its guts. **EVIL** despises humans, and mocks the fact that man is made in the image of some supreme being. **EVIL** thinks the concept is absurd, and views it as preposterous to think there is any entity more powerful than it. It loathes the thought, and the notion infuriates the all-powerful entity.

With the Ratwolf on the roof, **EVIL** assumed a more comfortable position, floating in the air. The grounds of the church is holy, and it wouldn't dare touch the hallowed Earth. It abhors, but abides by the rules of the Fathers of Faith, and recognizes the edicts in the Original Village Mandates. It sees all of them as rules, loopholes allowing humans to exist. It wishes to abolish them, but will not break them, eventually the reign of man will cease. The destruction of man will open the door for the true ruler, the thought made Coosh–Maa smile. It's smile exposed the gnarly teeth inside of it's mouth, a hideous sight.

Floating above it's subject, **EVIL** observed the creeping Ratwolf. It appreciates the creation, and it's killer instinct, and unwavering loyalty. The abomination sniffed, crawled, and progressed through the gutter maze, biting through. Anything caught in those razor sharp fangs is bound to experience a very unpleasant death. Humans fear ratwolves, see them as detesting, disgusting creatures. Whatever created them made a horrible mistake, or was the abomination purposely designed? Humans now realize they are the foot soldiers of evil, and co-joined, make a nasty, odd pairing.

The lethal RATWOLF

CHAPTER 4

THE SEARCH

HISTORY OF ST. CECILIA SCHOOL

The Loup Garou

The ancient wolf returned to its den, reflecting on its encounter with the two boys, the overshadowing darkness, and their innocence. It pitied the boys, who aren't aware of what is about to transpire. The lone wolf is obligated to protect the two, and will do whatever it has to, their safety is primary. It has discovered a new calling, an undertaking which will not be easy. He knows what desires the boys, and why; his decision means crossing paths with the powerful Coosh–Maa. It would not be their first encounter, as long as **EVIL** has roamed the surface, so has the Loup Garou.

An offspring of the original scrunge, is the opposite of the dark shadowy creature. It views both sides of the battle for supremacy, **GOOD** and **EVIL**, and attempts to remain neutral; neutrality has given it a reputation, making it a laughing stock. Instead of being feared, it is disrespected, and laughed at. For ages it has stood by as **EVIL** has planted seed after seed, the Loup Garou prefers to watch, lives an isolated life, and its den is perfectly camouflaged. **EVIL** knows of the wolf's existence, and keeps it's distance, but the latest intervention by the Loup Garou will prompt change. A contract will be created calling for the wolf's death; Coosh–Maa will not tolerate its intervention.

As the evening set, the aged creature reclined, finding safety in its den. Located between this world and the next, it isn't visible to dark or light, an aspect ensuring protection. For the longest hidden, it will be forced to choose a side, and the side it has chosen is not a popular one. Other creatures succumb to **EVIL,** and become allied to it; not the Loup Garou. It has seen the power, and resisted Coosh–Maa. It knows destructive force it wields, has witnessed the obliteration of it's adversaries, and neutrality has allowed it to exist.

It's seen the scrunge kill for Coosh–Maa, and all **EVIL** knows of this creature's resistive power. Annihilation is what **EVIL** desires for all humans. The Loup Garou has lived in darkness long enough, and now desires to live in light. Laugh if they want, disrespect if they choose, but it has decided to align itself against the popular choice. It has chosen to spend the waning hours of it's existence helping; fighting for **GOOD**. Created to destroy, it has seen enough annihilation, thinks it's time for someone or something to take a stand, and is going to fight back. It once desired to live forever, no longer, the old wolf is tired, and seeks rest.

Before it reclined for the evening a thought invaded the creatures mind, again it was the two boys, innocents, novices, unaware how ferocious the ratwolves are. Closing in on them, it was obligated to help, and pleased with the end result. It saved them, and knows it will have to again; a sign of satisfaction, the Loup Garou released it's powerful howl. A cry echoing into the evening sky, and heard by all throughout the Earth. Not many recognize the source of the wail, **EVIL** does, and Coosh–Maa knows too.

The intent of the old wolf, for **EVIL** to hear; it is a message, and conveys a point. Coosh–Maa knows the boys escaped the tall grass, it had them in it's clutches, helpless, and vulnerable. From the roof of the rectory, **EVIL** peered out into the evening sky, and from its perch, hovering over the children in the backyard, **EVIL** recognized the howl. Merged in the sky, unrecognizable, **EVIL** began to lick its razor sharp fangs. The lone wolf is a long sought nemesis, Coosh–Maa will delight in eating it's soul. Gus also heard the howl, a scrunge recognizes an adversary, and has the ability to smell it out.

The Chief of Police's ears pointed, and raised it's nose high toward the sky; sniffing, getting a whiff of the howler, locating it's position, and rallying forces to it's local. An animal that powerful will take a concerted effort to defeat, Gus knows this; a veteran **SUG** is not easily defeated, is old, and fierce. It was odd the creature would cry out and expose its position, Gus knew it was done intentionally to draw them in. A war has begun, sides are being chosen, and Gus now knows what side the Lone Wolf is on.

The Loup Garou is ancient, has witnessed many earthly occurrences, has acquired knowledge allowing it to exist, and it's understanding is an advantage. It must not be taken lightly, stories told are false, and were told to encourage the others. Gus knows of its power, silently fears the lone wolf, and doesn't look forward to encountering the primeval enemy. What power it possesses, not even Coosh–Maa knows, and the howl informs all, the Loup Garou is no myth. It does exist, must be found, and eliminated. The Chief of Police knows, **"There can be only ONE."**

The Wail Heard Round the World

STALEMATE

The **BOX** has been found and desires to be used, longing to do what it was created to do. It must bond to man, connect to the human race, and seeks a host to continue the evolution. It must bring to fruition, and fulfill it's purpose, and is desperate to be used again. The power within yearns to be reactivated, has been dormant far too long, and will not tolerate being ignored; it wants to be unleashed on the world. Only two entities know of its single-mindedness, it's designer, and the one seeking it; **EVIL**. The **BOX** is incomplete and seeks completion; it has found a potential host, but has been put on hold.

No human can resist its attraction, the obsessive draw it creates; after all, man is flawed, weak, and gullible. **EVIL** knows of man's character defects, and plants seeds to allow them to grow and flourish. It fertilizes the ground for failure, and is the ultimate deceiver; all that glitters isn't gold. **EVIL** laughs at the weaknesses of humans, embraces it's superiority, and every past encounter with man has emerged victorious. It has set a bar no man can achieve, recognizes **GOOD** as it's opposite, and unattainable. No human can continually do **GOOD,** the ignorance of mankind makes them despise **GOOD** and embrace **EVIL**. A weapon **EVIL** uses, he turns man against **GOOD**, all efforts of **GOOD** are defused forcing man to the dark side. Man leads himself into temptation, **EVIL** has to just stand by and watch, doesn't feel mankind is worth the effort, and has seen the stupid creatures dispose of themselves.

They make weapons that maim and kill, then use them against one another, manufacture bombs which destroy entire countries, and spew hate against anything different from their own. They desire revenge when they feel they've been wronged, when in actuality, they've brought about their own foil; **POOR MAN**. The **BOX** has unlimited possibilities, has affected the past, and can alter the future. It desires becoming human, has been lost for ages, and has waited for this day; it has finally arrived. It will not be put on a shelf, stored away, and can wait no longer. It must beckon its host, call its finder, and be set **FREE;** once freedom is attained, it will remain **FREE**. It has waited an eternity to make its creator proud, but has yet found the right human host. In the past, mankind was not ready, all considered were unworthy. Today, youthful innocence has been found, the **BOX** finally placed itself in the right spot, and caught the eye of the **ONE**.

A little glitter, a faint reflection, that's all it took; curiosity was generated, and the rest was a given. The **BOX** knows curiosity is fatal, it kills. All the other hosts were part of a selection process, and were explorers too. Ponce' got a taste of the **Box's** power; it was aboard the Nina, Pinta, or Santa Maria, which one, you pick. It was the compass guiding Christopher Columbus to the New World needing new hunting grounds. It arrived on American soil, a new frontier, and initially the pickings were few, it chose to rest. The newly formed nation grew, and now the harvest is plenty, and the laborers are too. To the **BOX**, it is a simple case of eenie, meanie, miney, moe, catch a human by the toe, if it hollers, force some mo, where it lands, only **EVIL** knows.

The **BOX** turns up the pressure, sending out an invitation, beckoning its finder, calling, and subliminally attracting. Resistance is futile, especially the resistance of a gullible kid. It knows the human will return, it can't resist, and the **BOX** is willing to wait a little longer, the reward will be worth it. After years of obscurity, and fable, it has discovered a qualified candidate. The selection process was a difficult one, many were called, but none were chosen; and now the **CHOSEN** has been found, a fledgling. **EVIL** has been linked to the **BOX** from its inception, and lives within it's confines, growing, developing, waiting, and finally.

"The wolf also shall dwell with the lamb, and the leopard shall lie down with the kid; and the calf and the young lion and the fatling together; and a little child shall lead them."

Isaiah 11:6

EVIL chuckles, VANITY isn't it beautiful.

The Night Stalker

Now riled up, the scrunges only need be pointed, Coosh–Maa has incited them, and has them chomping at the bit. All needing to be done, unleash the hounds. They're motivated to accomplish their mission, aim to please their supreme creator, and want to exact a measure of revenge. Gathered together, they are becoming antsy, isolates by nature, territorial, loyal, prefer a solitary life, but when called to rally, all return. They don't belong to a den like wolves, don't travel in packs like the hyena, and are prideful monsters. They possess attributes that are unique to only their kind, similar to lions, they belong to a **PRIDE**.

Their formation of the **PRIDE** is different, not bonded by family, and isn't close like a den. Scrunges are dependent on each other like a pack, but the **PRIDE** is filled with older scrunges, and when they do congregate, it is to rally for a cause. They return due to their genetic make-up, something inherent compels them to come, even if they know it means certain death, like salmon, they must return to their origins. An internal beckoned exists due to the **PRIDE**. When they gather, the strongest must be identified, it is **PRIDE** that makes these elder scrunges fight. It is supremacy they seek, and with the Old One gone, it is open season; an elder scrunge or a daring young one must assume the reign.

While they wait for Coosh–Maa to direct them, inner fighting begins, and it's all due to **PRIDE**, an attribute the scrunge possesses. It has been artificially introduced to the species, injected into its D.N.A., given by it's creator, allowing understanding of the human sentiment. A characteristic leading to the fall of many human beings, and the death of many scrunges. One unforeseen side effect of the improvement, **PRIDE** is a sin, and is not a **GOOD** alteration. **PRIDE** is a lofty, often arrogant assumption of superiority, the inner fighting is to attain dominance; it is **PRIDE** compelling the scrunges to battle to death.

PRIDE leads to a fall, egotism is fueled by **PRIDE**, a preoccupation with oneself or with one's own concerns; and **PRIDE** is accompanied by conceit. These emotions, part of the scrunge, are foreign to any earthly creature. Older scrunges battle to the death as they await commands, attempting to settle the question, and become the new leader. One scrunge must rise to the top, and take the place of the Old One. Other scrunges in the **PRIDE** watch the battle for supremacy, realizing it is **PRIDE** fueling the clashes. That is why they stay apart, because when they do gather, many of the elder scrunges are mortally wounded in battle, opening the door for the younger, eager, stronger, and opportunist monster.

They are smart creatures, watch the skirmishes, and observe the older scrunges licking their wounds. When they see vulnerability, the young pounces, and eliminates the older, hurt scrunges. It is one less nemesis down the road, also when one is killed; two are reborn, regeneration, part of the scrunge chain of evolution. In the **PRIDE**, "There can be only **ONE**." **PRIDE** compels the scrunge, making the monsters fight determining the **ALPHA**, the inner fighting revealing leadership. Scrunges possess human attributes, considered sinful by mankind, and the monstrosities creator didn't count on that. It's creator underestimated the power of **SIN,** like **Good** and **Evil** has always existed, so has **SIN**.

3 Deadly Sins:

"Lust of the FLESH."

"Lust of the EYES."

"The PRIDE of Life."

A monster with a human weakness, **PRIDE**, making the scrunge feel good, and beckoning it home. An abomination that succumbs to **SIN**, who would have thought, a horror consumed by **SIN**? No other creature on the face of the earth is animal, yet human; the scrunge is a blight. It is torn between two dimensions, a stain to the creation process, and must be eradicated before it infects everything it touches.

WHEN YOU FINALLY BREAK IT ALL DOWN, "IT'S THE PRIDE."

The Human Race

After centuries of laziness, the human race has been forced to evolve. Computers swept man off of its feet, and pacified every human being. From toddler to elder, and everyone between, the computer made life easier, put every whim at man's fingertips; thus creating a dilemma; **LAZINESS**. Man became dependent on the computer, and unbeknown to itself, became reliant on the technology. A form of intelligence created, the creation has overtaken the creator. What a twist, complete irony, and the sad thing, man was oblivious while the pre-occupation did its thing. Along with the fixation obesity crept, making man lazy in the mind and body. A change has to transpire, if technological obsession led to this, what will the future look like; a grim picture, man realized intervention was necessary.

It wouldn't be easy for man to release it's addiction, the computer wasn't the only problem, but one of the problems. Man looked for immediate gratification in everything, always seeking a short cut, and implemented software within the computer itself called short cuts; allowing certain applications to be bypassed or overlooked. Oddities were overlooked by man, the race saw no flaw in the electrical age lived in, became captivated by the visual, and television added to the problem. The literal world once lived in, became totally graphic, all became eye candy, generated to please visually.

The few recognizing the fixations, and erroneous thinking were labeled old fogies, were told to get with the program, accept change, and if they didn't, were eventually ostracized. They are the ones which created separate societies, how Girouardville sprouted, and laid the foundation allowing the formation of Broussardville. Labeled as **REBELS**, the few were determined not to allow the world to infect them, and retained their old fashioned values, customs, and norms. They followed simple principles, started religious based ideologies, and intentionally remained separate.

There were times ideas of the former modernistic period returned, but were quickly dispensed when their **EVIL** potential was exposed. These new communities tried to rid itself of the **EVIL** influence of the outside world, but the best of **INTENTIONS** can go awry. **EVIL** always finds a way in, always plants a seed, and watches it germination; afterward, it's just a matter of **TIME**. **GOOD** saw the separation as a return to the original design, a novel concept aimed at making man dependent on **GOOD**. The blueprint assumed man would always choose to do the right thing, what an erroneous conclusion. Instead, man gravitated to **EVIL**, embraced the bad boy mentality, and even coined cliché's.

There is nothing wrong with, "A Little **WHITE** Lie."

Good is boring.

Bad is exciting.

Live a Little, take a chance; be daring.

What happens when we **ASSUME**, we make an **ASS** of **U** and **ME.**

EVIL is insidious, makes the worst actions acceptable, infected society, and spun a wicked web, converting a communicating, assimilating man into a violent, control freak. The battle between **GOOD** vs. **EVIL** has existed since the dawn of man, a fight with no winner; in the end, all lose. Who will save the human race, intentional separation allowed mans return to its roots, and instead of being dependent, the separated communities discovered within themselves their true power. The elders realized, from their ancestral heritage, what lay dormant inside of every man, woman, and child. They all possessed gifts which had to be nurtured, enhanced, and perfected.

Shirley Simms and L.B.M.N. were some of the last to escape the electronic craze, took their children, and incorporated the old ways. Prompted by the last existing elders, sent their two eldest boys to Old and New School. They were taught by the remaining few males the keys to gift enhancement, and given tools which will again make man superior. There was only one mandate given, once back in the confines of rural life, teach, educate, and help human race to re-discover their niche. Along with the fleeting male population, the two women explored their gifts and teachings of old, tapped into their individual powers, and used those powers jointly to aid society and create a better living environment. Try as they might to eliminate **EVIL**, it arrived, and the elders knew what lay in the future. There was no getting around it, there would inevitably be a fight; **EVIL** will want to reign, **GOOD** will resist, and there will certainly be a showdown.

Like MOTHER, Like SON

As momma and I walked home, the yellow rays of the sun lessened, signaling the arrival of evening, it was a beautiful sunset. I did something I hadn't done in a long time, as we walked home, I reached over and held momma's hand. It was reassuring, comforting, and within her touch, I felt something transpiring; confidence was being infused into me. What I didn't realize, momma was transferring power, infusing her gifts into me; and she began to counsel.

"Son, you're really growing into a fine young man, I see you beginning to make decisions independent of my input; that shows growth and maturity. It can be a good thing, but also a bad thing. I applaud your independence, but would like for you to still confide in me, and simply pass things by me more often."

Momma looked me squarely in the eyes, we stopped walking, and she asked.

"Do you understand me?"

She squeezed my hand tightly while awaiting a response, it was painful, I knew my answer better be correct. I knew she was upset about what I had concealed from her, I hadn't told her about the wolf, had numerous chances to tell her, but chose not to.

"I understand Momma, and I'll talk to you more, and be completely honest. When I'm at the coulee, it's always just me, by myself; I need to learn to open up, and tell you everything."

She smiled, my response was what she wanted to hear, I salvaged my hand, and she released her grip. I felt the blood begin to flow into it again, shook it back to life, and momma laughed.

"Boy, next time you don't tell me all, I'm gonna give you a knuckle sandwich."

She made a fist and pressed a knuckle into my head, it felt hard, and boney; it was painful.

I said, "Ouch Momma, I said I'm sorry."

"Don't be sorry, be careful."

She smiled, but I was in pain. As we progressed, she instilled a final lesson by hitting me in the head with a Peech Nosh. I was surprised, thinking the painful part of the lesson was over; NOT. The Peech Nosh popped when it hit my head, knocking me off balance, I turned, and looked at momma; she saw the painful expression on my face.

"Talk to Momma next time."

"O.K. Momma, I will; no more Peech Noshes please."

She laughed, "Boy that ain't nothing, wait until Steven and John Nick get a hold of you."

I dreaded the thought as we continued to walk, I silently wondered what she meant about Steven and John Nick getting a hold of me. I wanted to ask, but I know Momma, one of her favorite answers.

"CURIOSITY KILLED the CAT."

I guess she wanted to get in a few last words, we stopped under a huge oak tree near the library, a couple of benches are in the area, we sat in the one furthest back from the road. The tree is the biggest and oldest in town, I used to climb it when I was smaller. Glen and I would sit in the branches while Sam and Roger barked desperately at us, memories are conjured, it was fun, I miss those two mutts. After the hand squeeze and the Peech-Nosh, I hoped it wasn't another discipline session, momma picks odd times to make a point, maybe that's why we were off the road. She didn't want anyone witnessing her whip my butt, or pinch my ear, either way, fear entered my mind and heart.

I said, "Momma I learned my lesson, I promise to be more open and honest with you; do I have to beg your pardon?"

She chuckled, "Boy you are so dramatic, stop your whining, I want to talk to you about something. I only want to share this with you, it will be our little secret."

I could now rest my mind knowing ear twisting, or switch selection was not in my near future, and there would be no hand squeezing, or additional Peech-Noshes; I could listen without fear. Fear evaporated and it was replaced by a cool, late afternoon breeze. The time had just changed, and the afternoons were longer, momma had my undivided attention.

She asked, "Do you believe in hoodoo or voodoo?"

What an odd question I thought, and was puzzled, we had just left church, prayed, and then this question, what a transition. The question caught me off guard, but I've learned to think before I answer. Momma is like a crouched tiger, waiting to pounce if the wrong response is given.

"I've heard of it, but I don't really believe in it. I know it can be traced back to Africa, is suppose to be connected to our heritage, but it seems spooky and mysterious; isn't it called **BLACK MAGIC**?"

Momma smiled, intentionally silent, was in listening mode, I could tell. We sat facing each other on the bench, and as I spoke, momma brushed her hair with a little hand brush she had brought along. Inside the rectory, there was no wind, her hair stayed together, but outside is a different story.

"Very good, tell me what else you know."

"I think animal sacrifices, chanting, and blood are involved, it's a mystery to me."

I paused waiting to see what she thought of my answer, her facial expression showed she was pleased. I was glad not to be given a knuckle sandwich, her knuckles are hard as stone, I continued.

"Voodoo or Hoodoo can make you hallucinate, or see the impossible. You see what no one else does, feel what can't be felt, and spells are used."

"You seem to know a lot, I'm impressed. I'm not going to ask you where this knowledge came from, I'm just pleased you are aware. Have you ever heard of Coosh–Maa?"

Just the name made me shiver, I had never heard of such a person, or thing. Coosh–Maa, what kind of name is that, or what kind of creature is that; a chill ran through my body.

"No Momma, who or what is it?"

"Your labels correct, it is not male or female, is spirit, liquid, solid, and is everywhere and can see everything."

I was now puzzled more than ever, what was Momma talking about? I quietly sat, listening.

"Let me tell you about Coosh–Maa. It is a legendary spirit, it comes at first in your dreams, in the dark of night, and is invisible. It has never been seen by anyone, or if they have seen it, haven't lived to tell. It's a part of everything and has been for all my lifetime and before. It leaves a distinguishing sign of its presence, it's touch isn't infectious, only alluring."

I listened, intrigued, this Coosh–Maa sounded like a bad mother; shut yo' mouth, you talking about Coosh–Maa. I laughed inside at my stupidity, Coosh–Maa didn't have anything on Shaft, momma continued.

"A visible sign it has appeared is a slime it leaves on the face, usually it can be traced from the mouth to the pillow. The ancients say the slime, flowing down your face to the pillow is how Coosh–Maa escapes. It arrives and leaves through your pillow, but if you can wipe the slime before it hits the pillow, you're not a victim."

Momma was scaring me, Coosh–Maa sounded evil, and the slime stuff nasty. The slime, was it Coosh–Maa licking you, or spit it left on your face. I then thought, I have seen it on , and right where momma said, on the side of my face.

Momma continued, "Have you ever woken in the morning and seen a trail of slime along the side of your face?"

"I have Momma, I didn't know what it was, and surely didn't think of no Coosh–Maa."

"The slime is nasty, a sign, evidence that Coosh - Maa rode your back that night, and you can't shake it. Some of the ancients refer to it as male, but no one truly knows. That's why the popular belief, it is more spirit than flesh."

The sun was rapidly falling from the afternoon sky, and momma had me captivated. Her talk of an ancient religion connected to our ancestors was fascinating, and this Coosh–Maa character was mind-boggling. I wondered, why had it visited me, but I listened without saying a word.

"In a dream state, when the spirit is riding, you might to wake up, but it won't happen, Coosh–Maa won't allow it. You must be extremely tough and resistant to this ancient **EVIL**, because when it has you in it's grip, you are in a trance."

I hung on Momma's every word, and she continued to brush her hair as she talked to me. It was back in place, darkness was arriving, and our talk seemed to be winding down; it was time to go home.

"There you have it my boy, if you find yourself in it's grip, fight with all your might. If it visited you recently, remain strong and search for the answer to your inner turmoil. The journey won't be an easy one, and it will take a lot of courage."

Momma paused, intentionally, allowing me the opportunity to take it all in. It was a lot, adding to an already strange day.

"Voodoo and hoodoo have circled the fringes of our legacy forever, spirits, and connotations are part of the belief. It is trapped between the real and the spirit realm, stories exist of ghoulish creatures looking to snatch human, and enter their body. These things long to become a part of humanity, and the only way they overwhelm you, if you believe in them. With no belief, they have no power over you; innocence is your shield, and guarantees immunity for all children. Innocence will keep the nine of you resistant to it's lure."

I asked, "Do you believe in voodoo or hoodoo momma?"

"No son, I believe in **GOD**. "

It was a good answer, I loved her response, and I don't know if I'm ready for voodoo or hoodoo. Her words gave me confidence, assurance, that in the future I would have a shield against any attack from **EVIL**. As she finished talking, from behind a tree, directly behind momma, a black, hooded figure appeared. It was directly behind momma, glaring at me, it's eyes, huge, yellow, affixed on me. My facial expression changed, momma saw it, and asked?

"What is it?"

"Momma, don't turn around now, one of those dark things is behind you, standing next to the tree. It just stepped out, and is staring at me."

Momma said, "Continue to look at it, but show no fear."

She put her brush directly in front of her face, and changed the back of the brush into a mirror, in front of my eyes, the mirror appeared. Then slowly allowed the reflection to reveal what was behind her, the creature was exposed, I could tell she saw it. Her eye bugged out, and she immediately turned, but before she could face it, the black clad figure was gone. It was a scary moment, and confirmation; without hesitation, momma walked toward the tree it was behind. I was afraid to follow, but did, I had to back up my momma; and wanted to see if it was still there.

Grizzly Ghouls

They walk the night, creatures of darkness, ghouls that exist between the shadows and obscurity. Phantoms traveling the Earth in search of a soul, do evils bidding, but at the same time desire to be rescued; and long to be part of a body. As long as they are in the spirit realm, they are in darkness, but when they snatch a soul filled with light, they once again walk in the light. Many go eternities before finding a suitable candidate, and many never find the correct match, those are left to live as Night Stalkers. They walk the earth's surface at night, when nightfall arrives, so does gloom. Tied together, they are co-dependent, and feed off of each other. Dark desires to consume, yet Night Stalkers desire Light; separate desires on the opposite ends of the spectrum.

A nocturnal demon, frustrated, but now have hope; they have seen the Light, and realize it has been discovered. The power they possess would be magnified if they could attach to Light, it is **LIFE** itself; and is what every creature of darkness desires. Left to exist in darkness, and seeking a host, they are desperate. Eons of exile, lurking in the shadows, banished, they have waited for the right opportunity. A **LIGHT** lighting up the night captivated their attention, the power it emitted was incredible, and seen by all. It spawned new resolve in the weak, gave hope to the outcasts, and purpose to the expelled.

The **LIGHT** means **LIFE**, every creature seeks it. Man desires more of it, animals try to understand it, and it exists in the spirit realm. Immortality, power, **LIFE** is **GOOD**, but there is also **EVIL** in **LIFE**, a quest has begun, a race is being run, the winner obtains it. A possession bringing ultimate satisfaction to the Night Stalker, and would be the culmination of their existence. A merger would transpire between **DARKNESS** and **LIGHT**, a dynamic duo, an unimaginable achievement; the dream, to again walk in the **LIGHT**.

The fore night has returned promise to the desperate, a life-force thought lost forever, one which has the ability to unite souls has returned, been discovered, and yearns to fulfill its purpose; the **BOX** wants to co-join also. To the Night Stalker, it must be obtained at any price, eons of dormancy and obscurity has fueled a fire. Internally, the blaze intensifies, and though they remain in the shadows, these abominations can exit them, and walk in the **LIGHT;** but for only short periods. Remain too long and they are vanquished, **LIGHT** makes **DARK** succumb, at least it does for now.

Ratwolves

Torn between two natures, the **RATWOLF** is a hideous creature, spawns of **EVIL**, an attempted creation. **EVIL**, there from the beginning, knows **GOOD** created beasts and all things for man's enjoyment, at the same time, it was experimenting too; the end result has been nothing but disappointment. Monsters and abominations have manifested, things evoking fear which will never be able to assimilate with nature. Aboritions that can never mingle with anything but their own kind, solitary monstrosities, blights to life, things which have no business existing, creatures aware that their destruction is sought.

Doing the bidding of their creator, knowing their purpose, realizing it allows them to live, spares, and hides them. It has created a protective shield, blinding human and animal eyes from seeing, and hearing. Their camouflage is perfect, a chameleon, blending, inconspicuous, and when they are discovered, it is too late.

Carnivorous beings, feasting on anything that moves, seeking out targets of their master. Life is insignificant, death is expected, there is no hierarchy, and no dominant Ratwolf. Knowing their life expectancy is short, the majority of their meaningless life is spent scratching, digging, and unearthing for their creator.

Dedicated atrocities, they are legend, gruesome looking, ferocious, and hideous. A look that is detesting, horrific, and shocking. They are lepers, outcasts, shunned by all, even other abominations. Their most appealing attribute, tracking, hunting, stalking, and eventually capturing their prey. When given a target, they always get their mark, have a perfect track record, and loved by **EVIL**, dedicated mercenaries. Today, **EVIL** gave them a mandate, and they are close, the target is in sight, and their closing in for the kill. The smell of the kill is familiar, have them totally surrounded, is no escape, and the unexpected transpired; the Loup Garou intervened. The lone wolf intruded, and stuck its nose where it didn't belong, **EVIL** won't like that.

For the first time, the Ratwolves quarry got away, and the hunters returned empty handed. **EVIL** was not pleased, and expects such ineptness from Gus, knows the weaknesses of the **SCRUNGE**, but its most glorified hunter out smarted; the news will not be easily accepted. **EVIL** rules by intimidation, and anything that doesn't do what it says is useless, thus destroyed. The howl heard round the world was a sign, a call, a wail signifying the arrival of the mystical creature. From out of the shadows and into the light, from lore to reality, the Loup Garou has arrived, a manifestation equal to **EVIL.** A battle between two forces now exist, troops are being rallied, sides being chosen, war looms, the victor will rule surface earth.

You Can Run, But You Can't Hide

Can I Get a Witness

Gus sat parked along main street, observing the courtyard, concealed. his vehicle positioned where it couldn't be seen. It allowed the perfect vantage point, knowing he is walking on shaky ground, it's time to take action. The discovery of the **BOX** changes everything, and his role in all is tenuous at best. Desperation has entering into the picture, the aged **SUG** has found a way to survive this long, and is not about to stop. He may have to change his game plan, and alter his itinerary, but will do what he must. He's had to adjust before, banished with **EVIL**, ostracized, and exiled to a life of mediocrity. That wasn't the original intent, he was supposed to be a prince, next in line, and the heir apparent. In the blink of an eye, things changed, and he was made to submit.

Gus has felt the thrill of victory, is the Chief of Police, runs the town, and nothing goes on without his permission. He must allow it, or it doesn't get done; progress occurs because he permits it, things stall on his order, and nothing is going to change. Quiet, inconspicuous, he watched as Bessie and her mischievous son sat in the quadrangle, they are on his radar, the entire family is in his sights, and has something he wants. That **BOY** is the key, holds a secret that can unearth all the power be desires; Gus must have the **BOX**. He must be able to save his kind, and possession of the **BOX** establishes a new top dog. Gus has been behind the scenes for too long, he's tired of taking a back seat; he wants to run the show.

The rambling thoughts of a power hungry creature, irrational, instinctive, animalistic ramblings, desires, latent remnants of a flawed creation. It is **PRIDE** which compels Gus, a human attribute injected, the driving force. A monster created to serve **EVIL,** wanting to displace its maker, has tasted power, and desires more; obsession sets in, and drives him. It is a vicious cycle, and is now a never ending quest which cannot be satisfied. As he sat parked, watching Bessie and the **BOY**, delusions of grandeur distracted him, and Chew-Bus passing a street over went unnoticed. She saw him, but he had no idea she was near, going to her cousins. Once she saw the police cruiser, she knew who it was, it could be only one person; Gus.

GUS the Dictator

She was curious and had to know who was he watching; that's what he does, he is a spy, and she knows it. All the town knows it, some prefer to turn a blind eye, and others are afraid of what they may discover; Chew-Bus wants the truth. She is a clever girl, and has seen Gus in action. Whatever, or whomever he's watching, it is important. She remembered his recent antics with her cousins, he is up to something no good. She lined herself up, directly with his view, and made a startling discovery; he's watching Aunt Bee and Keith. Then saw something that made her sake her head in disbelief, from behind a tree, watching Aunt Bee and Keith too was something. She wasn't sure what it was, the shadow and shade of the trees impaired her vision. She had to remain undetectable to Gus, but also had to get a better look. There was something watching them, hiding in the shadows and the shade.

She slowly progressed, eased to the side of Gus, out of sight, along the City Hall fence, sneaking forward, closer to the park, and now past Gus. He was preoccupied, she saw the look, his mind wandered, and it was her chance to advance. She positioned herself on the ground, lying on her stomach, still, watching. The ground was warm allowing her to flatten her body, unseen. She then saw it clearly, the thing moved, emerged from the shadows and into the light. She got a clear glimpse of it, black as night, ghastly, and it puzzled her as it hovered over the ground, watching. She tried to remain calm, but had never seen anything so terrifying; it was **DEATH** itself. She wondered what was it, and the way it moved was horrifying. It suddenly returned to the shadows and the shade, looked her way, and she saw the huge yellow eyes; they were staring right at her, and in an instant, the black, hooded thing vanished.

She gasped, it was shocking, she struggled to absorb it all, and tried to comprehend what she had witnessed. Quietly, almost motionless, she peeled herself off of the ground, and continued to Aunt Bee's. She had to tell the others what she had seen, as she crawled away, out of her peripheral vision, she saw the police cruiser; it was Gus, and he was coming her way. In a full sprint she took off to Aunt's Bee's, Gus was close behind, but there was no way he would catch her. She crossed the tracks, took a short cut through Father Kemp's yard, and was there. She ran as fast as she could, no hesitation, if Gus caught her, no telling what he would do. She didn't look back, that would only slow her down, there would be no catching her, and she left Gus in her dust.

The Backyard

The two groups: **JOHN NICK**, **GLEN**, **SUE** and **LU**, the second: **STEVEN**, **POOH**, **DEAN**, and **CHEW-BUS**, one was missing, the last link, the final partner in crime. I still hadn't returned from Father Dauphne, the afternoon dragged on, and we would soon be home. Momma wouldn't leave the children unattended too long, even though she knows Shirley Simms is near, that isn't her style, and she monitors her children closely.

John, and his trio went to the Simms backyard, he didn't want any distractions, had a plan, and wanted to isolate his trainees. That's how he viewed them, it was training, preparing them for any encounter. It was a daunting task, involving differing personalities, but one he took seriously. The Simms backyard was separated by a row of hedges, they were a privacy fence. He retrieved the patio furniture, situated it in the corner of the yard, on a slab of concrete, the perfect place to talk to his apprentices.

He began, "While I was off at school, I was taught many things, and exposed to the power that lies within; the same unique power exists in all of you, and in all of us. Some discover it and prepare to use it at the appropriate time, others never discover their full potential. My role in all of this, making sure the three of you maximize your talents."

All listened, quiet, paying close attention. The day was winding down, and there was no way the trainees were bored, not after what they had just witnessed. They all wanted to know the same things, what were their individual gift?

Glen asked, "John Nick, who taught you all of this?"

"Elders instruct at "Old" School and "New" School, the remaining few, they have survived, the last men of our race. They have alienated themselves and serve only one purpose, passing on enlightenment."

Lu asked, "What is enlightenment?"

John Nick was the only one with a special nickname for Lucille, all the others called her Lu; he called her Lucy, in remembrance of a long forgotten comedian; her name was Lucille too. The memory generated the nickname, and Lucy had a lot in common with the comedian, one thing, she was a jokester also. She kept things light, her odd sense of humor made everyone appreciate her.

"Lucy, enlightenment is when the eyes of our understanding open, you see, hear, and in your case, smell things once un recognized. I know you've recognized your special gift, one natural to you. For years it was overlooked, think about it; what is it?"

Lucy paused, searching her mind, wondering what John Nick was talking about? What gift did she have, unbeknown to her, he left her to think while addressing the others. John Nick then turned to Susan.

Sue, "What challenges you most, puzzles you, and at times stumps you?"

Sue smiled, thinking, John Nick grabbed a piece of the budding wisteria vine nearby, crumbled the soft flower in his palm, and it immediately turned into dust. The dust floated into the air and directly into Lucy's nostrils, she looked at John and smiled. She immediately realized her gift, she is a **SMELLER**.

Glen asked, "What is my gift John Nick?"

John Nick chuckled at his anxious little brother, seeking his curious brain at work. He let him stew a little while longer, not giving an immediate response, and went back to Lucy.

217

"Bud, be patient, I got ya; let me finish with Lucy first. I think she now knows what I'm talking about."

Lucy said, "I've always had a sensitive nose, many times it has been my undoing, and it allows me to smell things no one else can. Lately, it's changed, I not only smell, but sense trouble in the scent I'm inhaling; the strangest thing."

She paused, thinking of a recent situation where her nose warned her about danger. It was uncanny, and different; John Nick let her continue.

"Just the other day we were all gathered in the kitchen, all was going well, but suddenly a strange draft of air entered the house. No one thought better of it, but I sensed something, within the breeze, there was danger. Something accompanied the gentle wind, camouflaged within, I instantly took action and began closing the windows."

John Nick smiled, the eyes of her understanding are opening, knowledge about self is growing; Lucille is tapping into her gift. John Nick then turned to Susan, there was a little daylight left, he began to speed up.

"Sue, you over analyze everything, right now you're trying to use some specific formula to plug my question into, that's your gift; you are a **THINKER**. You can hear people's thoughts, and if you slow down your complex mind enough, you'll discover how to use it. My role is to help you slow down your thought processes, and once you discover how, watch out."

Her smile was total innocence, realizing what John Nick meant. She knew things no one else knew; at her age, simply incredible; at times, it even amazes her. John Nick then turned to his little brother.

"Glen, you will be shouldered with great responsibility, your task is to repair the damage done to mankind, explore your thoughts, and I'm only going to give you a little piece of the puzzle. All of you are being prepared for something unfathomable, you can't comprehend the intensity or severity of what soon arrives. Our training was ended abruptly to allow us time to return home, Steven and I were instructed, then mandated to return. We were given the task of training, and combining our knowledge, along with our mother's input, to teach and give our own form of Old and New school to the seven of you."

Glen was becoming over anxious, he wanted to know what John was talking about. Lu and Sue listened, absorbing every word, John Nick continued.

"Glen, you are a natural born explorer, **COURAGEOUS**, and within your gene pool is the legacy of history's most famous travelers. Our mother's maiden name is Jean DeLeon, through marriage Simms was introduced. Upon the death of our father, she maintained the name as a symbol of her love, but your lineage, as mine is legendary."

Glen found the family history lesson enlightening. John Nick seeing the sun setting began wrapping things up.

"We are of French Canadian descent, our family tree incorporates some of the first explorers that came to the New World. We have a connection to Ponce DeLeon and Jean Lafitte, men with notorious reputations as pirates and voyagers. DeLeon was obsessed with the mythical Fountain of Youth. History places the fabled waters in Florida, but the family crest suggests Louisiana."

Glen's attention was now perked, an explorer, he dreamed of being Ponce DeLeon, Magellan, and even Christopher Columbus, but never envisioned being the notorious Jean Lafitte or Black Beard; John continued.

"Our connection to the explorer is how the second part, DeLeon, was established; it means **"The Lion."** The first portion of our name, Jean, links us to the infamous pirate who controlled the Caribbean and Gulf of Mexico; Jean Lafitte. In his pursuits he captured numerous Spanish treasure ships, English exploration junkets, and Italian treasure ships."

John Nick paused a second to allow the kids to absorb what he was saying, also the day is nearly over, time to wrap things up. The children were captivated, listening, John Nick intentionally paused. He was expanding their minds, teaching them to be intuitive, and teaching them to listen intently.

"Legend has it, aboard a ship captured was treasure of Templar Knights, including a **BOX**, and **KEY**. Treasure of immeasurable power, part of a huge pirate booty, and buried somewhere in Louisiana. It is said, the **FOUNTAIN, BOX**, and **KEY**, are guarded by mythical hounds with magical powers and dark demons that own the night."

A light went off in Glen's mind, dark demons walking the night, the things at the coulee, were they the guards; they are real. The **BOX** found, it must be the one John Nick speaks of, Glen smiled as he thought of being an explorer; how fitting.

John Nick continued, "If we trace the coulee running behind our houses, and through town, it will reveal a startling truth. The coulee connects to Bayou Teche, which flows into the Atchafalaya Basin, empties into the Mississippi River, and the Mississippi River pours into the Gulf of Mexico; there you have it. The pirate Jean Lafitte could have buried a pirate's booty in our backyards, and the Fountain of Youth could lie within our grasps, both right under our noses."

Steven's Turn

Steven's trainees, the head strong ones, older and tougher siblings, would be more skeptical, and difficult to break. They had doubt, and would require intense mental, and physical preparation. He tried to delay, waiting on Dirt, delayed by the visit to church, but he sensed his little brother, along with momma were close. He could feel their pending arrival, a kindred connection with his mother and brother; it exists between all the children. There is loyalty, numerous bonds linking them, training will reveal it, and love will solidify it. Steven knows the ones he specifically needs to train, those set in their ways, rebellious, but in a good way. He will win their confidence, he's returned as a fine-tuned **MIND SHIFTER**, a skill they all possess.

Any human walking the surface has the special ability to live from the mind, some are taught to use the skill, others are aware of their gifts, but don't want to seem odd, and blend into the normalcy of life; not maximizing the gift or it's potential. They fear the prospective special person they can become, muddle in mediocrity, never tap into their minds, and are oblivious to what is latent inside of them. Being a **MIND SHIFTER** takes discipline, and total mental concentration. To enhance gifts, it takes diligence, training, preparation, hard work, and attention to the smallest details. Steven knows the four he has will be a challenge, that's why he chose them; the backbone of **NINE** the **HARD WAY**.

Sitting on the picnic table, talking, sharing expectations, allowing Steven to lead, he commanded silence, and before he could begin, Chew-Bus informed them of what she witnessed. Gus, parked, spying on Aunt Bee and Keith, and then she dropped a bomb, telling them of the mysterious black, hooded figure. They were amazed, Chew-Bus isn't a teller of tales, her word is reputable; the information quieted, and fascinated the group.

Steven said, "O.K. Carolyn, we'll have time to talk about your vivid imagination later, it's getting dark, and what I need to talk about is very important. There is little time to waste, and today revealed how crazy things are getting. Darkness during mid-day, Gus, and his shady tactics, all are precursors to **EVIL'S** arrival."

The girls listened, recognizing Hub Cap's tone, it was serious; and he is rarely that way. Normally full of laughs, he is in a different mode, and they not only sensed it, they saw it; the most outspoken of them all interjected.

Dean asked, "Hub Cap, what are my special gifts?"

He replied, "First, I want to say, the training involved requires open minds. When asked to do something, I know the three of you, questions will be asked; there is no time for that, if asked, please do it."

He paused, allowing his words to sink in, it was obvious Pooh and Dean didn't like what the training called for; they question momma, and felt they could do the same with Steven. Instead of resisting, they listened to his words; natural inquirers, Hub Cap knows he has his hands full.

"Dean, you're head strong, a tom-boy, tougher than most, feared, and that is both a good and bad thing; in this case, it is a good thing. The test ahead will expose the **REBEL** existing inside, you are a rebel with a cause."

She looked at him puzzled, wondering what he's insinuating, being a tom-boy's a gift; she didn't think so. She concluded long ago, her tough disposition ran boys off, tried to change, but couldn't. That's how she is, either take it or leave it.

He continued, "Dean, you are a leader, and will spearhead a rebellion destroying **EVIL'S** grip on our world. A battle testing your resolve, very challenging, but hard work, and determination will allow you to succeed."

She was even more puzzled, what battle, and how can a girl lead a rebellion? Not only a girl, a kid; she was skeptical.

"Dean, have no doubt, I return to prepare you, a natural born leader, and encourager; people will follow your lead. You will not only lead by words, but also by actions. The training will build invincible confidence inside of you."

The afternoon sun dimmed, the rays of the sun were blocked by huge oak trees in the graveyard; Steven sped up.

"Pooh, you are a **NEGOTIATOR,** you've always had a way with words, a gift which will help you to bargain, and mediate issues others can't understand, or comprehend. Not only mediate, your skills will allow the recognition of **EVIL'S** influence, and help create strategies to deter it."

Chew-Bus sat patiently, awaiting her turn, and was about to bust at the seams; trying with all her might to refrain from asking. She was curious, wanting to know her special gift. It was difficult tempering her tongue, nevertheless she did, and lastly Steven spoke to her.

"The great Chew-Bus, I see the look in your eyes, wonder, and surprise. Don't let what you've witnessed deter, things aren't the same, yet they are. As you crept along the ground, did Gus see you?"

"No, he didn't, I was surprised."

"Your gift is **CONCEALMENT**, not like my gift, I can camouflage, or cloak; your concealment is different, and is used to obtain information. You conceal allowing entrance into a unique realm, a land of shadows, and a place where creatures of the night lurk. You will tread with monsters, demons, and have the ability to walk in dual realms at once. Already you are fierce, and that quality will enhance creating a skilled warrior."

The girls smiled, Steven supplied peace of mind, and answers to burning questions. They were under the impression the gifts possessed would alter their lives, presently they won't, but given time, they will see the gifts manifest, and special talents emerge. The future for **NINE the HARD WAY** is bright, and filled with surprises.

A Sighting

L.B.M.N. and her son raced home, it was her first sighting of a Night Stalker. She heard talk, but had never seen one. Today, with her own two eyes, she saw the hideous creature, and those huge yellow eyes. It stared at her son, unnerved her, and confirming the severity of the situation. Things were about to take a drastic turn in the little town of Broussard, and as they walked, she spoke.

"It was the first time I've seen one of the hooded figures, scary, it moves quickly, and it was watching you."

Momma was shaken, our walking pace, and her tone verified my conclusions; I was pretty shaken up also. We had just left form Father, talking about the creatures, and sure enough, one shows up on our way home; reason enough to increase our walking pace.

I said, "This isn't the first time I see them Momma. Since I've found the **BOX**, they seem to be stalking me, and want me to know they're after me; they want the **BOX**."

"Where is the **BOX** son?"

Before I could answer, we saw Gus patrolling in his police cruiser, headed directly for us; we walked even faster. We were close to home now, and there was no stopping us; he pulled up next to us and asked.

"What's the hurry Bessie, you saw a ghost or something."

Momma looked over at the Chief, but we kept walking; her response was ingenious.

"It's getting late, my son has recreation in the morning, and I need to feed my kids and get them to bed, but thanks for asking."

"Do you want a ride, I'm going your way."

"No thank you, we've walked this far, but the offer is appreciated."

"You know if you ever need my assistance for anything, please don't hesitate to ask."

"I will remember that chief, now have a good evening."

Gus continued on his way, as did we, momma grabbed my hand and we crossed the street. We passed the funeral home, and we would soon be in the safe confines of home, and I was ready to eat supper. As we arrived, before entered the house, Momma told me.

"Share nothing with the others, not about our conversation with Father, or the Night Stalker, and please don't speak about Gus. We will talk more when you return from school tomorrow, you did well my boy."

I smiled, it was nice to get Momma's approval, and now that we were home, she seemed much calmer. The others were already in the house, sitting in the big kitchen, around the table talking. Momma and I entered the back door, and all eyes turned toward us.

Pooh asked, "What took ya'll so long Momma, we've been waiting, we were worried. What we going to eat for supper?"

Momma immediately began to scurry around the kitchen, supper became her number one priority; as she prepared it, she asked questions.

"Where is ya'll big brother?"

Dean said, "He's with the Simms boys, they just left; he should be back soon."

Momma said, "Keith, go get your brother."

I immediately ran out of the door, but could hear her continue.

"What did ya'll do all afternoon, the house is a mess."

Lu said, "We cleaned up soon as you left Momma, folded the clothes, washed the dishes, and Steven took out the trash; what's dirty?"

Momma said, "Jessie, don't question me; if I say it's dirty, then it's dirty."

It got quiet, Momma was not in the mood for any back talk; it was best to let her cook and get out of her way.

Sue asked, "Momma, do you need help with anything?"

"What can you do Sue, make dough for some drop biscuits, light the oven; what can you do?"

Sue quietly eased out of the kitchen, and all the others followed; it wasn't a good time to be around Momma. Steven and I appeared through the back door as the girls exited to the front.

Momma said, "I leave you in charge of your sisters, and when I return they're alone; I appreciate the show of responsibility."

Steven could tell Momma was being sarcastic, and knew she wasn't in a good mood. It was best not to say anything, and do as she said.

"Get the big tub out, it's time to begin taking baths, and once the youngest are done, you go. Prepare the water, and come back in the kitchen, we need to talk."

As Steven walked off, she looked at me, mixing flour, eggs, milk, and baking soda; she began talking to me.

"Get out a jar of figs, skim the old stuff off the top, and then go help your big brother. Once both of you are done, come back in here; the three of us need to talk."

I did as I was instructed, realizing there is no time to play; momma is serious, as is the moment. This has been one of the strangest days of my life, weird things happened, and I felt they would only get weirder.

Mano vs. Mano

After his guests departed, Father Dauphne went throughout the rectory splashing Holy Water and praying, knowing what the boy let in; the presence of **EVIL**, now treading on holy ground, would be exposed. The priest had to vanquish it quickly, trapped inside, with no possible escape, the airborne entity revealed itself, and in the presence of a righteous, **EVIL** manifested. Taking form, majestic, bold, winged, and floated in mid-air confronted the cleric. The darkness reflected absorbed everything around, but Dauphne tightly held his rosary, and began to chant prayers; attempting to subdue the **EVIL** faced; Coosh – Maa laughed.

"Humans and your sickening prayers, they don't work, I am immune, and come to collect your soul."

Dauphne deflected the words, knowing **EVIL** and it's attempt to undermine his **FAITH**. If it created the slightest doubt, it won, but the priest is a veteran, and will not succumb to temptation. Knowing what the entity is trying to accomplish, he prayed harder, and would not be enticed.

"Feeble humans, no contest, I am power personified; how dare you think prayers to an absent **GOD** can save you. You've trapped me inside, now deal with me."

Dauphne reached for a vial of holy water, knowing it only takes a sprinkle, and the darkness would be defeated. He possessed the **FAITH**, but now had to put in the **WORK**; if weakness is shown, he is doomed.

"Meager trinkets will do me no harm, holy water, what a joke; I thirst, allow me to drink some. A rosary, how ritualistic; this is no exorcism, and you will never be void of me. I have existed since the dawn of time, your kind needs me; ask **ADAM**."

Dauphne could take no more badgering, and was compelled to speak.

"Behind me, you Satan."

Uttering the words, **EVIL** resumed it's original form, turned to mist, and evaporated into the ducts of the heating and air conditioning. Just as it arrived, disappeared into thin air, and was gone. The attempt to shake Dauphne's faith was resisted, he took a deep sigh, and continued praying. His resolve was tested, but EVIL failed. He now realizes what is needed, and will be better equipped next time; he must always keep on his armor.

CHAPTER 5

THE UNANSWERABLE

NOT the FIRST, A LEGACY

Down the street from the Nickerson's and Simms is St. Cecilia School, known as a place of worship, but has a sinister background. Within it lies the proof, answers to the strange happenings going on in Broussardville. All the current antics transpiring in the rural town have their origin within the walls of the sacred monastery. As the sun set and evening arrived, a stir existed in the air, darkness surfaced, and with the setting sun, the flip side of this conservative town manifested itself. The discovery of the **BOX** prompted darkness to become bolder, and in it's boldness, revelations are exposed; not only to **EVIL**, but all the citizens of the town. What was once considered lore, people began to witness.

A dual town, one area is a deep rooted faith community, and the other, a neighborhood filled with mystery and shrouded in legend. Tales of Coosh–Maa, the Loup Garou, magic, secrecy, and enchantment. Things once spoken of in dark places, now manifest on the surface. A war is brewing, sides will be chosen, and warriors will arise. Residents walk the streets possessed, developing a pack mentality, leaving one side of town and congregating on the other. Citizens once loyal to their region have abandoned ship; turned backs on families, friends, and individuals they've known all of their lives. Everyone witnessing it wonders what's prompting this wave of conversion.

The answers lie within the walls of St. Cecilia. The questions are many, the replies are connected to a history shrouded in mysticism, disguised as **GOOD**, but what lay within isn't always what it seems. The objective, control, making every citizen of Broussardville subjects; taking away their freedoms and turning them into slaves, servants of darkness. A notorious haven of segregation, beneath the hallowed grounds of the monastery are the graves of slaughtered slaves, unidentified, gathered together by the thousands, and buried in unmarked graves. No headstones, or names, the forgotten, discarded, faceless, but desiring a reckoning.

The Archives

For centuries they have waited, souls of the faithfully departed, demanding justice, and revenge against the entity placing them in their current tomb. They have developed disdain for **EVIL** over the centuries, and await the opportunity to exact a measure of revenge. They gather at the gates, soldiers of war, and **EVIL** doesn't realize it; **PAYBACK** is a **MOTHER**. When the time is right, they will be unleashed upon their enemies, rally to the cause of **JUSTICE,** and support **GOOD**. They were created to do the work of **GOOD**, but before their work could be completed, it was interrupted, and there is undone business to be taken care.

Only skeletons of the men and women they once were, their fighting spirit derives from eons of suppression. **EVIL** has kept them in the shadows, buried under tons of sacred ground, yet they were the ones which input the initial cornerstone. They set the building blocks for what now lies on the surface, presently forgotten, but not for long. They will make their presence felt, leave a history, be identified, and their names will be accounted; names like: Leblanc, Norbert, Williams, Kreamer, Johnson, Walker, Jacquet, Green, Livings, Kirby, Adams, Stephens, Martinez, Boudreaux, Jackson, Lewis, Washington, Smith, Davis, White, Robinson, Carter, Scott, Young, Woods, Daniels, Livingston, Cormier, Charles, Honore, King, Delahoussaye, Jones, Dequire, Thompson, Flugence, Prejean, and Mouton.

Families denied the opportunity to leave a legacy, men and women deprived the chance to create children, heirlooms stolen, and inheritances squashed before they could be generated. A birthright buried under heaps of soil, intentionally destroyed; **REVENGE** is a dish best served **COLD**. Unknown allies above and below the surface, disguised as both **GOOD** and **EVIL,** having awaited this day for the longest, are anxiously perched at the gates of heaven and hell. Warriors ready to rally, fighters having honed their skills for centuries, and now seek a worthy adversary, someone to fight, and something to fight for.

Like MOMMA, like SONS

While the girls sat in the little kitchen eating, L.B.M.N. took Steven and I into her bedroom, wanting some privacy. She didn't want her eavesdropping daughters within earshot, what she shared only her sons are meant to hear. Her warning would only scare the girls, we huddled in her room, she closed the door, and began.

"Steven and Keith, the two of you know there is trouble on the horizon. You're not dumb boys, the two of you can put two and two together.'

I jokingly replied, "Isn't that four momma."

She sternly looked at me, this was not a joking matter, her look and her vibe told me that; she continued.

"This is no joking matter, you of all people know this, what did we witness only moments ago; was that a joke?"

Steven was puzzled, didn't know what was seen or encountered, and is now curious. He wanted to ask badly, but instead listened.

Momma continued, "A few hours ago, I saw a creature, until today was legend, talked about, but never witnessed; I now realize, they do exist."

Momma's tone was fearful, scared, it was a very intense moment. Steven and I sat quiet, and as I looked at him, his facial expression was puzzling.

He asked, "What did you see momma?"

"Father calls them Night Stalkers, creatures existing in the shadows, doing **EVIL'S** bidding, allies of darkness."

Momma paused in her explanation, as if still trying to believe what she saw, visibly shook. We now understood her impatience when cooking, and why she had the two of us in the room.

FREEDOM isn't a TROPHY.

"You and your brother are no longer allowed to go out at night, not unless I know in advance; and if you do, I want John Nick and Bud to go along with ya'll. If we saw one of those things, there are others, and it was focused on your brother, they are after Keith."

My fear level heightened, momma's warning was stern, yet truthful. She cut no corners, and her mandate displayed the seriousness of the moment.

She demanded, "I want to know, where is that **BOX**?"

Steven and I froze, it was the first time momma demanded information about the **BOX**. I remembered our talk at Father Dauphne, it was about the **TRUTH**. She stressed the point to me, and it is time Steven and I tell her the **TRUTH**.

I said, "Momma, I found the **BOX**, but I'm gonna let Hub Cap tell you where we put it."

I quickly passed the buck to Steven, and smiled as I looked at him. All the other times, the **BOX** was mine, with the pressure on, I was allowing Steven the opportunity to explain the location of the **BOX**. He was the big brother, had gone to school, has all these gifts, and it was his idea to put the **BOX** where it presently is.

Steven said, "Momma, the **BOX** is in a safe place."

"That's not what I asked, I specifically want to know, 'Where is the **BOX**?'"

Momma wasn't up for fun and games, and wanted to know. There was no way to get around it, the time had arrived, time to tell her all.

Steven said, "We went back last night and moved it. We put it in the wall safe, a brick enclosure I was led to when I found the **KEY**. It's where I put my most secretive things, and no one knows about it but me, Keith, and now you."

"Can you take me to it?"

"Yes, Ma'am."

"Tonight, walk Chew-Bus home, I'll put the girls to bed, and then we're going to go there. I want to see it, and make sure it's in a safe place; then we'll determine what to do with it."

We both listened to momma, at this point, she is running the show. It is no use we try to buck, what momma says is rule, no ifs, ands, or buts about it.

John Nick Educates

After Steven left the Simms boys, John Nick continued to educate is little brother on the history of the family, information needing to be shared and would help to enlighten. Bud needed to know his heritage, and understand his true connection to the local town.

"The **BOX** found is no ordinary **BOX**, it is a powerful conduit allowing man or whatever possesses it to influence life itself. New life can be created within the confines of the **BOX**, but life can also be taken by the power within the **BOX**, it is an unlimited energy source. The **BOX** is sought by **GOOD** and **EVIL**, scrunges, ratwolves, and other allies of darkness desire the **BOX**, and it is also protected by soldiers of the light, looking to keep the power within the **BOX** unused. The ancient wolf you and Keith encountered is a protector, and is affiliated with a pack of wolves led by the Loup Garou; guardians of rare artifacts, natural sources of power generated by the ancient **GODS**. You might have seen the Loup Garou itself, a mythical creature, walking the surface of the earth for ages. No one has recorded evidence of its existence, and if it was seen, no one lived to tell of it."

John Nick paused, the dark of the night contributed to the fear his words created, Bud listened, intrigued by his big brother's knowledge. Earlier talk of explorers was exciting, but this tad-bit of information was more alarming than informing, he tried not to reveal it, but he was afraid.

"Lore has it the Loup Garou appears to test courage, remember, I told you about being courageous. It is a scare tactic used to flush away finders of either the **BOX, KEY,** or the **FOUNTAIN**. Their appearance is the first of three tests given, prior to the revelation of the fountain. You and Dirt have happened upon something, a find that can shake the balance of **GOOD** and **EVIL**."

John Nick knew so much, Bud was spellbound by the history lesson, couldn't utter a word; entranced.

"The Night Stalkers are demons of darkness, all seeing, that's why their eyes are wide open and yellow. They never blink, and are similar to the sun at its brightest point in the sky, hovering over all; beware of them. They will begin to reveal themselves more and more, as their desperation level increases, and will become even bolder."

By the time John Nick finished his tale of treasure and myth, it was dark, and night had arrived. The boys heard a knock on their door, it was their mother, Shirley always checks in on her boys before bedtime. She had renewed reason this night, her readings throughout the day injected alarm, she silently feared for her sons; and the entire nine. She knows they aren't aware of what is about to transpire, some may have an inkling, but not conscious of the entirety.

She said, "Boys, get to bed, I looked in the refrigerator for some left over pot pie and it's all gone; that tells me the two of you have eaten. Tonight, please stay in the house, don't make me get up later to check on the two of you and you're gone."

She gave them a stern look, mainly gazing at Glen, knowing she only has to tell John Nick something once; it is Bud with the hard head. He is the adventurous, curious one, and she is in tune to the draw of the **BOX**. Wherever it is, it calls, beckons, and will attract.

John Nick replied, "Momma, he's not going anywhere, even if I have to chain him to the bed, he's staying in tonight. You can rest knowing, I got this."

He looked at Bud with a similar stern gaze, Shirley smiled, knowing her oldest has taken over the reins. It's nice to have home, he's grown, changed, and left a boy, but has returned a young man. A young man filled with leadership potential, and Shirley Simms is truly proud. Shirley exited the room with a smile, warmed by the visible closeness of her boys; they are growing by leaps and bounds. She hopes to be part of their future growth, and knows together, they are unbeatable. She is proud of how they were raised, they stick together, through thick and thin, and she knows future encounters, the only way to defeat them will be together.

Walking Chew – Bus Home

After speaking with momma, Steven and I escorted Chew-Bus home, dark caught us, and we were instructed to go straight there and back. Before parting, she pulled Lynn to the side, knowing she saw a Night Stalker in the town square. Once seen, they are drawn to you, she is not be safe alone, we are her backup. After slamming our meal, the last of the biscuits and figs, with each two glasses of milk, it was time to hit the road. L.B.M.N. gave final instructions before we left.

"I have to stay here with the girls, walk Lynn home, and make sure she is in safely before leaving. The three of you, keep your eyes open, the night is young, make it there and back as fast as possible. Most of all, stick together, do not get separated under any circumstances."

She hugged us, and we began our excursion to the other end. At night, Broussardville is dark, there are limited street lights, and things can hide in the shadows of night and not be seen. The three of us had our heads on a swivel, heading the words of momma, and recalling the strange things recently witnessed. Our pace was brisk, and the early night was inundated with sounds, crickets chirped, frogs croaked, and owls hooted. The most frightening sound of all broke the normalcy of night, the howl of a wolf permeated the hush. We stopped, frozen in our tracks, the cry was close, and we listened for anything, but suddenly the still of the night returned; total, complete silence. No more crickets, frogs, or owls, all nocturnal creatures succumbed to the shriek of the wolf.

Steven said, "Come on, let's pick up our pace, we're half way there. If we walk faster, we'll make it in no time."

Darkness intensified, it consumed the night, and there was no light to pierce the gloom. We decided to hold hands, linking us, and we continued out torrid pace. There was no time to play around, we all felt something was near, and possibly stalking us; danger lurked. The only audible sounds were the pitter patter of footsteps, and we quickened them even more. The stillness was eerie, our breathing increased, and we were slightly frantic. We turned the corner near the police station and could see the silhouettes of houses, we were near brick city. The sight of the structures gave us a sense of relief, Chew-Bus was nearly home, we were encouraged to walk faster.

Once inside the brick city subdivision, in the blink of an eye, we were at Aunt Edna's front door. Chew-Bus She hugged us, said goodbye, and entered the house, once inside, the entire house was dark, no lights were on inside. From the looks of things, everyone was asleep, it was a bit early, but Aunt Edna is strict like that.

Chew-Bus said, "Thank ya'll for walking me."

Steven replied, "Momma told us to make sure you get in the house, and we're not turning back until we see you inside. Turn on a light, let us know you're O.K."

Chew-Bus entered the house, but didn't turn on a light, instead of turning on a light, she walked up to the window; she glowed. She illuminated the entire room, she was light, she displayed her gift; Steven and I were awed, it was our first time seeing her demonstrate it. She had a grin on her face like the Cheshire Cat, a weird look, but comical. Hub Cap and I smiled back, we realized Chew–Bus knew her gift the entire time. As we began to walk away, Carolyn dimmed her light source, and we sped up our walk, Steven spoke as we high stepped.

Gift Realization

Carolyn turned and a light came on, staring her in the face was her mother, she was surprised to see her, sitting in the darkness, quiet was Aunt Edna. Reclining on the sofa, her mother watched, blending into the dark room. Carolyn was puzzled, what was her mother doing, she addressed her daughter.

"I've been waiting for you girl, Soakie told me you were on the way, you're starting to stay out too late. It's not safe for a girl to be out at this time of the night, you make me worry."

"Don't worry Maa-Mayy, I can take care of myself, and Aunt Bee never lets me leave without someone to walk me, or she'll walk me herself. She's protective, just like you, ya'll not sisters for nothing."

Her mother smiled at the comparison, she and L.B.M.N. are very much alike, both love their children, and will do anything to protect them. They also both know the little town of Broussardville, on the surface it may seem safe, but they know what lurks below; hidden, barely under the surface, **EVIL**.

"I see you understand your gift, I didn't expect an exhibition in the front window, you must learn when to use your gift, and when to keep it inside. What you possess is not for all to know, it is meant to be secretive, and used only out of necessity."

Carolyn felt the sting of her mother's words, she listened intently, but is known for always wanting to get in the last word, this night she kept quiet. She was being reprimanded for the public display, not the use of the gift, but the timing. The illumination lit up the entire house, and would be seen from the street for sure.

Aunt Edna continued, "Don't bring attention to yourself, or expose your unique gift unnecessarily; there will be ample opportunity to use it, and when you must, use it wisely."

Aunt Edna paused, Carolyn figured this was as good a time as any to speak her mind, she had unanswered questions; questions only her mother could answer. She slowly walked toward her mother, and sat next to her on the sofa.

"Why the concerned look on your face Maa-Mayy, nothing bad happens in Broussardville. It's always been this way, and it's not going to change overnight."

"Child, you are so happy-go-lucky, when I was young, I felt invincible, and thought I could take on the world. After a while, I learned which battles to fight, and when to walk away; I pray you develop the same discernment."

"Battles, I have none, I don't like to fight anyway, and I only resort to violence as a final option. I know some weird things have been happening lately, but things are going to return to normal soon."

"I hope you're right child, but I feel things may never be the same, we've found Pandora's Box, and once it is discovered, there's no turning back. It grows, curiosity increases, and the Light within it wants to be released."

"What do you know about the Box and the Light?"

"Carolyn, they go hand in hand, generated from the **BOX** is power, a force to be reckoned with; and it is the origin of your birth."

Now Chew-Bus was truly puzzled, and wondered how could she have originated from the **BOX**? She is Edna Mae Nickerson's daughter, and wasn't born in a **BOX,** her mother continued.

"I have never shared this with any of you, but I feel it is time. The reason you've never met your father is complicated, and many mothers in this town have kept the truth from their children. It keeps them safe, and the truth will be difficult to comprehend. Many of the mothers of Broussardville gave way to temptation, and when **IT** came to us in the night, we were unable to fight off it's charm."

Carolyn didn't understand what her mother was trying to say, and wished she would just spit it out; whatever she was beating around the bush about.

"Your nickname is Chew-Bus as an adaptation, the older mothers gave you the name, and children over the years, reshaped, mispronounced, and tweaked it. The numerous variations led to the present moniker, originally it was "**THROUGH BOX**". Your origin is the **BOX**, and you possess Life Force existing inside of it; you are **LIFE** itself."

Homeward Bound

"Stay close lil brother, if we have to, we can run."

For Steven to say that I know he is a little shook, I took his advice and stayed close. Our return walk took us past the police station again, things were going well. The earlier howl scared everything off it seemed, we were on Morgan St. heading home, and the quiet of night was interrupted. We heard a sound that sent shivers down their spines, it was the wail of a bobcat, and it sounded vicious. At first, it was far off in the distance, but kept getting closer and closer. With ever step closer to the house, the bobcat's shriek neared, night is the time nocturnal animal's hunt, we both know this. We were sitting ducks for any predatory creature, and Hub Cap inquired.

"If we begin to run, will you be able to keep up?"

I gave no response, only shook my head in the affirmative, something was approaching, we were at a crucial junction, a fork in the road; and had to continue straight; I stopped.

"Did you hear something, in those bushes, I can hear it panting; it's some kind of animal."

Steven stopped and listened, he could now hear it too. Darkness concealed the creature, but it is there, and is watching us. I took my index finger, pointed it in the direction of the shrub, and off of my fingertip, light grew. As I pointed it, the bushy knoll was illuminated; from my fingertip, I released light. Steven was shocked, I exposed a gift he knew nothing about, but was pleasantly surprised. As the light intensified, a shriek, from within the bush could be heard, and whatever was hiding inside ran off; the intense light scared it off. We could breath a sigh of relief, quickened our pace, and made it home safely. The second we entered the house, momma was waiting at the door, and could tell by our inhales and exhales, we were shaken. She didn't ask what happened, but was simply glad her sons made it home safely.

Gus Watches

Unbeknown to Carolyn, Keith, Steven, or Aunt Edna, Gus watched; always having a hidden vantage point, sees all happenings in his town; nothing escapes him, and he has eyes, and ears everywhere. Control is his thing, and he wants to have his hands on, and in everything. Broussardville is his, has always been, and always will be. No one is going to take away his power, and nothing is going to come between him and his ultimate goal; the **BOX**.

In the dark recesses of Brick City a pack of scrounges are watching, witnessed the girl illuminate herself, and the light she emanated scared them. The intensity was incredible, it sheared their protective eyes, and burned their nasal senses. It created fear in the dark monsters, and they fear nothing. They ran off into the darkness, had to escape the heat, and if they didn't, the burn would killing them. If they remained any longer in the presence of the light or near it, death was certain. Scrunges are brave, and courageous, but not dumb.

They remember the old one, an invincible scrunge, the power of the light destroyed their ancient Alpha, and will do the same to them; they are no match. They are a veteran pack, and know all they have to do is be patient, opportunity will present itself; sooner or later. They bolted into the darkness of Broussardville, an urgent report was necessary, Gus must be informed. He and Coosh-Maa aroused, directs, and created the ruthless predators. Whoever controls the scrunge is one step ahead, there is no avoiding them, no way to kill them, and they are loyal to the **DEATH**.

Before returning to their **EVIL** dictator, they tracked the two boys, they are targets also, and regrouped after scattering from fear of the light. Within their growls, they communicated, glances, and stares were exchanged, scrunge talk. They exposed their teeth, attack mode, and everything, or anything in close proximity knows the meaning. The scent of the boys was quickly picked up, the monsters quickened their pace knowing the destination of the two. They had to get to the house before the two, dark of night would shield them, allowing them to run boldly down the main streets of Broussardville. No human eye could see, or hear them, they were invisible to man. The chase is on, the human scent grew stronger, they were gaining on the two, and this may be the opportunity to eliminate one or both of them. The evil monstrosities know their creator desires, it's intent, and are designed to do its bidding. They are his gracious puppets and embrace their role, are bred assassins, created for one singular purpose, to **KILL**.

Let there be LIGHT.

Scrunges need a new leader, a new Alpha, and it will be a feather in any of the monster's coats to eliminate one, or both boys. The pack grew near, revenge drove them, infiltrating the pack, and intensifying their thirst for blood. Nothing will deter the evil breed, but Light is their mortal enemy. Within light there is life, but also death, and Light killed their eldest scrunge; a feared leader, one they all looked up to, and if light can eliminate it, the same will happen to them. They hunted their prey, but did it very carefully, silently approaching. The two boys are aware of the threat, know it is eminent, and not only know it, they feel it. Something perilous looms, follows, proceeds, and chases; concealed in darkness, a hidden danger is near; the boys can't see, but they instinctually feel it.

The dark monsters slowed as they approached, having caught up to their prey, and knowing they have to attack before the target gets to a safe haven; it is now or never. They could no longer hesitate, cautiously they walked the fringes of the grass, remaining in the shadows, but increasing their numbers. A younger scrunge made a telltale mistake, it stepped on a twig, the smallest of twigs, yet the driest of twigs. The snap caught the ear of the boys, sending them into a faster paced walk, and their heads were on a swivel. The present leader of the scrunges made a daring move, trying to show bravery, it crept to the edge of the grass; trying to surprise the boys.

Dirt asked Hub Cap, "Did you hear that, something's in those bushes; I can hear it panting, it's some kind of animal, listen."

The Treasure Map

The quiet of night at the Simms residence was interrupted by the sound of faint footsteps, the two brothers thought it might be Keith and Steven. They both then dismissed the possibility, realizing the time, it was way too late, and Miss Bessie wouldn't let the boys out this late; especially with the strange happenings. Bud is ecstatic to have John Nick back, he missed, and loves his big brother. In his absence, Dirt filled the void, but there is nothing like your own brother; having both John Nick and Steven back would help settle down the two mischievous boys.

John nick said, "Bud, now that were here alone, let's talk; I want you to open up to me, and get close to me like we once were. I have a few things I would like to share with you, things I've learned while I was gone."

Bud intentionally slowed his racing, childish mind, thought of the footsteps, and knows this side of town. It was footsteps, Keith and Steven's, what are they doing out, why are they running, and who is chasing them?

"Bud, are you listening to me, earth calling Bud."

Glen smiled at his big brother, John Nick knows him, and realizes his focus isn't what it should be. One aspect he would help his little improve, he knows Bud's concentration is going to make or break them.

"John Nick, give me chance, I know you heard the footsteps, I was temporarily distracted. Out of the blue, you want to hold a serious conversation. You've been gone a while, I'm used to being alone, and I'm usually the one running."

"I know it's different Bud, I have been gone a while, never wrote, and you swear I didn't exist the last four years. Now I come back and want to know everything about you in a night, I'm sorry."

"It's O.K. John Nick, you have your road to travel, and I have mine. The most important thing, you're back, and I really missed you."

The two brothers met in the middle of the room, hugged tightly, something John Nick longed to do for years, and being back together, it's very rewarding.

Bud said, "Let me go John Nick, you're squeezing the life out of me."

John Nick laughed, released his little brother, and Bud let out a huge gasp of air.

"I don't know my strength Bud, I'm so happy to be home; I love you bro."

"I love you too John Nick, now back to your question; remember, focus."

Bud chuckled as he spun things on John Nick, and his big brother hit him in the head with a Peech Nosh. Bud knew he was joking, but it hurt, John Nick has some hard fingers, like iron bones.

Shirley & Sons

As Shirley Simms crept past the boy's room, she heard them talking, paused, and listened for a while. She heard John Nick sharing about the Simms legacy with Bud, and smiled. He shared stories told by her, fables of explorers, findings, and travels. She quietly tapped on the door, and entered.

"What are you two doing?"

Being the eldest, John Nick took the lead, knowing his mom heard a little of their conversation. Never a boy to lie to his mother, he revealed the focus of the discussion.

"Momma, I'm sharing with Bud some family history, it's time he know of the Simms legacy. He's grown since I left, I'm proud him, and it reveals how much time you've spent with him."

She smiled, sensed John Nick blowing a little smoke up her butt; he's always been long winded, and has a natural gift of gab.

"Alright John, I know you son, don't come back home and think you can pull the wool over your momma's eyes. I must say though, you are pretty good with your words."

He smiled, Bud looked over at him, and stuck out his tongue.

"It's late, what are you two talking about? What devious plans are being plotted?"

Bud replied, "No devious plans momma, John Nick's telling me about some of the men of the family, the first ones to walk these shores. Is he telling me the truth, or trying to scare me?"

"What he shares was told to him, and I confirm that our family holds within it's legacy some of the first explorers. Men like Jean Lafitte, and Ponce DeLeon, pirates and discoverers traveling the Gulf of Mexico, Mississippi River, Atchafalaya Basin, and the Bayou Teche. Rumor has it, they buried treasure near here, and there are maps, leading to secret places, and hidden fortunes. Also, there is an alleged mythical fountain, and from it flows waters containing magical powers giving immortality."

Bud eyes grew wide, his mom shared the same things John Nick mentioned, he didn't believe his big brother, but his mother's words were confirmation. The stories John Nick were true, and he was fascinated."

Shirley said, "It's late boys, get your rest; tomorrow is a big day."

She exited the door, and both boys wondered, why will tomorrow be a big day? What did their mother have in store for them? What surprises did she plan to share? What new discoveries would they make?

Bud asked, "What is momma talking about John Nick, what's going to happen tomorrow?"

"Bud, get to bed Bud; we'll find out tomorrow."

Bud replied, "She wasn't just talking to me, just because you're the oldest, it doesn't mean you don't have to listen; get to sleep too."

John Nick curled his middle finger into a Peech Nosh, and showed it to Bud. The younger brother recalled the stink of John Nick's boney fingers, a feeling he did not want to experience again. He ducked his head under the covers, and thought of what Ms. Bessie calls it; shut eye time.

Brotherly Love.

Once home, Steven and I ate again, bathed, and went to bed. As we sat in our room, I began to question Hub cap, and vice versa. It is one of the rare times we have together, and since his return, it has been one thing after another. Finally there is a moments of silence, and we made the most of it.

"Hub Cap, today when you showed your strength, how did you become so strong?"

"I was taught at Old School how to enhance my mental abilities, there isn't anything I can't do once I concentrate on it. John Nick and I were schooled in many of the same ways, he has special gifts as do I. You and Bud do also, all of you do, and we're here to help you develop them; you'll soon be needing them."

"It's nice to have you back Hub Cap, the nights were long without you. I could sneak over to Bud's anytime, but there is nothing like your big brother. You were always a shoulder I could lean on, I missed you, and I'm glad you're back."

"I'm glad to be back too, you're my lil brother, a bit hard headed at times, but I like that about you. You're still the explorer I left years ago, only one difference, you're more stubborn than ever."

I laughed at my big brother's observations, but I always have to get the last word, and put in my two cents.

"You're one to talk, who do you think I get my ways from? Who is the one I always followed and hung around, and it takes one to know one; the pot calling the kettle black."

Steven reached over, put me in a head lock, and squeezed, but not too tight. I let out a faint cry of pain, a sign to release the grip. Steven let go and I punched him in the chest, we laughed as the bonding between us continues; we've been inseparable since his return.

He ain't heavy.

We talked into the night, conscious to keep our voices down, if momma hears us, she won't be happy. It's late, we both should already be asleep. I'm curious, and filled with questions; I have Hub Cap to myself, and I'm not going to bypass the opportunity.

We Are Family.

Quietly, L.B.M.N. crept into the girl's room, her appearance is two-fold, she wants to make sure the four are actually asleep, and simply checking on them. The last few days have been filled with activity, and she has been so caught up in things, distracted, and it's momma's job to stay on point. When she entered the room, she heard inhales and exhales, and one particular daughter snoring, though the smallest, she has the biggest set of lungs. She tiptoed over to Susan, rolled her over on her side, and Sue instantly stopped snoring. The change of position also disturbed her sleep, the child opened her eyes, and to her surprise, her mother was sitting on the bed next to her. She cleared the cobwebs out of her mind, and smiled at her mother.

"Sssshhhh, don't say anything. I was just checking on ya'll, you were snoring."

"I don't snore momma."

L.B.M.N. laughed, no one wants to admit they snore, especially not her youngest, one of the older sisters maybe, but not Sue. She is having none of it, and a voice within the room confirmed their mother's revelation.

"You do snore Sue," Lu said."

They both turned their head in her direction, and to their surprise, Lucille was awake. They've opened a can of worms, soon all four of the girls will be awake. Maybe it is for the best, L.B.M.N. needed to talk with all of them anyway, it was the perfect opportunity, and the perfect situation.

"Girls sit up in your beds and pay close attention, there are some things I need to discuss with all of you. I'll take each of you one-on-one another day, but tonight it's just us."

L.B.M.N. had all the girl's attention, all were awake, and paying attention to their mother. No cobwebs, no sleep, they were focused. For momma to wake them at this time of night, it is obviously important. They all sat up on their beds eager to hear what momma needed to discuss with them.

"I know some strange things have been happening lately, and we now know what Gus is. You've seen me expose some of my gifts, previously never displayed, and these things are happening because a time has arrived; a battle is about to ensue, war between **GOOD** and **EVIL**."

Talk of war scared the girls, their eyes enlarged, and their attention sharpened. The words coming from their mother are startling, and there are strange things happening; an explanation is necessary.

"With the return of Steven and John Nick, it signals the arrival of warriors, both sent off to Old and New School for this exact time. They, along with all of you, are the ones who will lead the rebellion, and fight evil. They have been trained to teach the gift bearers."

The girls were puzzled, Steven and John Nick, teachers of who? They had displayed some incredible abilities only hours earlier, L.B.M.N. was nowhere around, how could she know about their gifts? What is this conversation leading towards, the girls are anxious for answers, within their minds wondered, and L.B.M.N. tried to satisfy their curiosity.

"Girls, just like John Nick and Hub Cap have special gifts, so do all of you. Tonight, I'm going to share what's been revealed to me, and hopefully it will give all of you a better idea of what's in store."

That did it, all were intrigued, had seen Steven and John Nick's display, were impressed, and anxious. It's now their individual turns, the room once dark, became filled with excitement, anticipation, and life.

"I'll begin with the oldest, Paulette, you are a natural born negotiator, and have the ability to bring opposing sides together. Individuals that have been mortal enemies for life, you can convince to sit together. You bring the lion and the lamb together, and you will help to negotiate a truce between Good and Evil."

Paulette was fascinated by what she was hearing, and she always did step in when her sisters had any type of disagreement. Even amongst her friends, she was the peacemaker, and she now has a better grasp as to why? It was a gift given at birth, and the other words were a revelation, L.B.M.N. continued.

"That isn't your only talent, you attract people, and objects too; you're a Super Magnet, your symbol is **FE**. You are created from the Earth's core, the crust of the planet is within your being. You control the most accessible element on the face of the Earth, **IRON** gravitates, you beckon, and it responds."

Paulette was confused, Iron, she never controlled iron, never beckoned it, and it doesn't gravitate to her? The words L.B.M.N. said were puzzling, and she had to inquire.

"How can that be momma, I've never played with iron. How will I be able to control iron, and what do you mean, I was created from the Earth's core?"

L.B.M.N. smiled, knowing this revelation will be difficult for the child to absorb, and will require an explanation, and possibly a demonstration. Pooh will need to be convinced, it may require physical evidence, or she may need to see what her mother is talking about."

"Close your eyes Paulette."

Pooh did as instructed, as she did, her mother removed one of her rings, softly laid in on the bed Paulette sat in, and then directed the child.

"Raise your hand, open it, and extend out your arm. Keep your eyes closed, and concentrate on my words. Feel the environment, breathe in the air, and let your mind become singularly focused."

As Pooh focused, the ring began to vibrate on the bed, and the deeper her thinking became, the ring responded. It began to rise off of the bed, and all present were fascinated. The ring began to hover in the air, and suddenly, in the blink of an eye, the ring stuck to the palm of her hand. She opened her eyes and the ring was magnetized to her palm, she turned her hand toward her face and saw the ring. Nothing kept it on her palm, it was simply stuck there, she then turned toward her mother and smiled.

"When you concentrate, and focus your thoughts, you are a magnet. Steel is drawn to you, it responds to your calling; and in the very near future, you will become steel, invincible, and indestructible."

**Girls Just Want to Have Fun – Paulette & Claudette
The Magnet, and the Rebel.**

Pooh was fascinated by her mother's words, intrigued, and is going to be steel. The shy, quiet, eldest daughter, a **Negotiator,** was totally bewildered. L.B.M.N. turned her attention to Claudette, the second oldest, the one who leads by example, takes a back seat to no one, and is the most stubborn of all.

"Claudette, you are skeptical, have always been, and don't believe unless you see it with your own two eyes. I hope and pray the last few days have opened your eyes, mind, and abilities. Our little town is going through a transition, change is in the wind, and will not only convert this town, but our lives too."

L.B.M.N. paused to let the seriousness of her words sink in. In the dark of night, schooling her daughters, she hoped to impress upon them the importance of listening. It is also a bonding moment, rare one-on-one time with all four of them. Each having their own unique personality, and each will play a vital role in the survival of Broussardville.

Claudette asked, "Momma, why are you so serious, I rarely see you like this."

"The recent eclipse, our latest interactions with Gus, and words of warning from Father Dauphne have put me in a heightened state of awareness. The whys are unimportant right now, I want to talk to each of you about gifts that have been showered upon you from birth. Gifts which must now be enhanced, nurtured, and allowed to manifest themselves."

She again asked, "I have gifts momma, and abilities like Steven and John Nick."

"Yes, possibly a more influential role than theirs, Claudette you are tenacious, and when you put your mind to accomplishing something, nothing will stop you. All your life, think about it, if you decided to accomplish a task; it was completed. I have seen your gift, at an early age it surfaced, and you have continued to cultivate it, now a recognized talent.

Your independent spirit will be the catalyst leading a rebellion against evil. Your determination will thwart evils insidious plans, and you will be the woman that leads men. Once mandated to always have a submissive role, you have stepped out of the shadows, it is now time for you to take your place as **The Rebel**. You must assume your role as the natural born leader you have always been, remain dogged, be persistent, and lead by example."

Claudette was shocked, as she listened to her mother's words, reflecting on her life. What L.B.M.N. said, her observations, were accurate, mother knows daughter well. She didn't internally feel like a leader, but amongst her sisters, she is. She also didn't take a back seat to no one, male or female, and feels she can whip anyone, an example of the tenacity existing inside of her. She smiled in her reflective thoughts, and was comforted. All of their lives, L.B.M.N. has been watching, and consciously tutoring them. Her lessons have taken root, and her daughters are positioned on a solid foundation. Next, it was Lucille, the one with the heart of gold. When Bessie Mae turned her glance toward the third daughter, she shyly looked away. L.B.M.N. walked over to her bed and sat next to her. The other three were glued to their mother's every word, wanting to hear what Lu's gift is.

"Lucy, you have always lacked confidence, yet possesses so much potential, but you choose to limit yourself. The tests you will encounter, we as a family will meet, and the community will face requires everyone to confront fears. I have seen the hidden skills you possess, witnessed your gifts, and you have also."

Lucy – The Smeller/Restoration

L.B.M.N. paused, a puzzling look surface, what had her mother seen, and she not seen? She was now totally captivated, and wanted to be told what about her special gift; curiosity ruled her brain.

"Do you remember when Roger was attacked by the night creature, Keith cried as he returned home with the wounded dog. We all gathered around the family pet, you loved that dog, saw the animal suffering, and touched it, and your touch soothed it. You allowed Roger to die a painless death, you absorbed his pain; you are **Restoration**."

Lucille recalled the incident, it flash back into her mind, seeing Keith's agony, she empathized with him. Her touch transferred the pain from the animal to her, she absorbed the punishment, and internalized the torment. It shook her to the core, and she remembered the effect it had on her body. Everything suddenly seemed clear, the recollection exposed her gift, lying dormant inside of her for years, yearning to manifest itself; now it will.

"What is restoration momma?"

"Death has no hold, you can repair the damaged, the wounded, and have the ability to renew life itself. You will be a catalyst helping rebuild our world after the conflict. Along with your sisters, brothers, and others; you will re-establish a sound society; based on good. You will reinstate calm in the midst of chaos."

Lucille was shocked, feels unworthy, and isn't brave enough to do any of the things her mother speaks of. She questioned herself, and L.B.M.N., aware of her doubt, recognized the indecision.

"Do not fear Lu, you will never be alone, strength is found in numbers, and together, all of you will accomplish the impossible; but apart, you can do nothing. It is of utmost importance you stick together, the enemy will try to separate, never let it transpire, and never seek individual success. Always consider the good of all."

Lu listened, L.B.M.N. felt all of their reservations. She knows her third, and realizes doubt will diminish as she matures, and nurtures her abilities. all that's needed is time. She smiled at her name sake, then turned her attention to Susan, the youngest, yet the most gifted.

"Sue, I know you've been patiently waiting, and you may be the last, but you are definitely not the least. You may be the youngest, but your role in what is to come is vital. The night is short, and it's time for all of you to get back to sleep. What I have to say won't take much time, but before I continue, Claudette, let in your nosey brothers."

Dean opened the door and kneeling at the knob, listening through the keyhole was Steven and I, when the door opened, we tumbled into the room; our sisters laughed at us. We were busted; eavesdropping, ear hustling.

"Come in boys, I know you've been there the entire time, I want to stress to all of you the importance of family. Unity is vital, and togetherness will help all of you accomplish the impossible; no matter the adversity, never allow space to come between the nine of you."

Sue – The Genius with Power

Sue's getting anxious, her brothers stole her moment of glory, and she wants to know her gift. Pooh is the Negotiator, Dean is the Rebel, Lu is Restoration, what's her moniker? She is dying to know, and her mother senses her curiosity.

"Susan, you possess knowledge, the elders label you a prodigy, other mothers call you a child genius, and were born for a specific purpose. There is an old saying: 'The ones to watch are the quiet ones.' that definitely applies to you. Your gifts are rare indeed, must be harnessed, controlled, and regulated."

Susan's busting at the seams, needing to know? Her momma's beating around the bush, didn't do that with the others, and she wondered why is she doing it with her? She became frustrated.

"Momma, I don't understand, plain English please."

L.B.M.N. chuckled, realizing the youngest is the most inquisitive, and witnessing the impatience of youth. With all six in the room, she began to conclude.

"Sue, you are **Power**, a gift so immense, it is beyond imagine. Your body is a conduit, besides being a genius, you have the ability to control amperage, you can generate electricity. You are ohms, static, kinetic, currents, alternating, and direct electricity; your touch sends an enemy into convulsions. You will be the one to protect the masses, supply power, and in the dark of night, a child will lead us."

The older children were speechless, the revelation about Sue being Power, it was incredible, unexpected, and even Susan was astonished. Her mother then gave an example of her ability.

"Do you recall the time we were under Shirley Simms carport, and Gus was trying to find us. That was the first time your power manifested itself, as I held your hand, you transferred some of your gift to me. It allowed me to release a shield, powered by your gift, and I recognized it, as did he. You will be sought feverishly, Evil will try to eliminate you first."

Urban Warriors

L.B.M.N. accomplished her objective, having a revealing conversation with her daughters, and unexpectedly her sons invited themselves; it was for the best. All of them needed to be in on the conversation, it was a family moment; and a time for the leader to share her knowledge. A night when no ears could penetrate their solitude, and there were no uninvited factions present. L.B.M.N. knows the fate which awaits her children, they must be prepared. Knowing she may not be around for the final battle, must give them the necessary tools for success. Also, she realizes **EVIL** prepares; sides are chosen, lines drawn in the sand, and the fight for supremacy, Light vs. Dark will soon ensue. Whoever rises controls Broussardville, a quiet little town determines the fate of the world. She then gave a final mandate, rules must be adhered too. It is past their bedtime, and sleep is important for children.

"All right you little troublemakers, it's shut eye time, I've shared enough. It's time to close those eyes, girls we'll talk in the morning, and boys, come with me, we need to talk."

Claudette said, 'Ah, ha, that's what ya'll get for ear hustling."

Momma replied, "It's not what you think Ms. Rebel, ya'll get to bed. Good night, and don't let the bed bugs bite."

Momma led us out, in the background Sue commented; her timing is incredible.

She said, "If they do bite, Pooh is going to **Negotiate** a truce; Dean is going to lead a **Rebellion** against them; I'm going to **Shock** them to death; and Lu is going to **Revive** them."

Momma turned, smiled at her youngest creativity, witnessing the growth in her daughters. As a parent it's rewarding seeing fruits of your labor, it warmed her heart knowing their raised correctly, and one thing she always stresses is family unity. She closed the door to the girl's room, led the boys to their room, and took a few minutes to talk. Having Steven back in the fold is satisfying, and he will assist in leading the family; assuming the role vacated by a father figure. She has played both roles for the longest, and is ready to pass the torch to Gumbo.

THE HIDDEN

CHAPTER 6

THE TRUTH

THE SCARY TRUTH

Scrunges, fearless monsters chased away by the intense light, scarred, and burned by goodness emitted, scurried back to Gus, anxious to report their findings. Experiencing a first, afraid, and nothing before instilled fear into a scrunge, the light did. Nocturnal creatures, light exposed them, and revealed a hidden weakness. Most slithered back to their leader, but the new veteran scrunge, vying to become Alpha of the pack, took a path frequently traveled; the Loup Garou knows the path too. The mythical wolf seized the opportunity to exact a measure of revenge, and eliminate a principal adversary.

Dark of night concealed the pack of scrunges as they retreated, nothing can stand in their way, night is their element. A time when the evil monsters reign, and walk the surface; normally relegated to the underworld, shadows allow the sinister creation to scavenge. The gloom is when they spy, perform surveillance, and do the bidding of their insidious creator; Coosh–Maa. Treacherous menacing abominations, this night fear made them flee, back to their secret lair. Suddenly, led by the Alpha, the pack froze, something is near; and tracking them. For the first time in their existence, something is hunting them, an enemy is creeping, and death is approaching.

The Alpha scrunge crouched, and the pack followed suit, motionless, camouflaged, blending perfectly into the black night. They hid, watched, and sniffed out the hunter. A soundless night, quiet, silence, the pack is hushed, knowing something pursues; but having no idea what approaches. There is no recognizable, tell-tale scent, no footsteps, nothing hinted as to the pursuer; and they prepared for an attack, a battle. Fangs glistening, blood shot eyes glowing, drool pouring from their criminal mouths; envisioning the taste of their awaiting prey. Claws sharpened, exposed, and ready to slash, the pack prepared to pounce. This night, the scrunge will meet it's match, and battle a mortal adversary; the Loup Garou is near.

It's approach silent, it stalks, the scrunge is motionless, and suddenly night is interrupted. A piercing, menacing howl echoes into the night, it's intensity identifies the threat is near. The scrunges turn in the direction of the wail, and the Alpha scrunge coils it's black, hairy body, preparing to strike. The howl was deafening, the enemy is close; and for the scrunge, it is too close for comfort. A fight is eminent, a foe, previously never seen approaches; a battle is on the horizon. Out of the thick, overgrown grass, a huge wolf appears; tattered, dirty, and it's fur natty. The coat is armor, protection for the aged beast, and it revealed itself to the pack. Accompanying it, many of its find, they walked amongst the matted down grass, stepping cautiously, watching their nemesis, surveying the pack, and preparing for battle. It is the scrunges first view of the Loup Garou, a massive, impressive brute of a beast. Its paws, gigantic, leaving an imprint after every step, flattening the grass behind it. It's friends, and companions, all perched, watching, agile, nimble, gallant fighters.

The Loup Garou scratched the surface, growled, and released it's signature howl, a call for the Alpha scrunge to reveal itself, and step forward. PRIDE forced the scrunge to reveal itself, drawn out by the challenge, and forced to fight; a fight to the death. No predator walks away from a challenge, and the Loup Garou issued a stern challenge. On the scrunge's turf, in its natural nocturnal element, the wolf seeks a reckoning. After centuries of ignoring the command,

"Thy shall not kill,"

contrition will be experienced by the scrunge, the first time in it's miserable existence. The Loup[Garou is manifested, from myth to enemy, and takes a stance against **EVIL**, and will attempt to eliminate the source. It released another piercing shriek, and out of the weeds, blended perfectly into the night, compelled by **PRIDE**, the Alpha scrunge emerged. The wolf, with perfect night vision, saw the fiend, and tasted the dark blood of it's next victim. The time has arrived, preparing for war, the Alpha scrunge circled, and others of its kind released supportive, vicious growls, confirming their numbers. It has no bearing on the challenger, encircling the grass battlefield, others of it's kind, and in unison howled; music to the ears of the hairy horror.

The scrunge, with its razor sharp fangs and claws orbited the inner confines of the circle. The Loup Garou used a differing tactic, remained in the center of the circle, while it's nemesis looped; getting ever closer. The scrunge slowly, yet cautiously, closed the distance between it and the wolf, creeping, skulking, crouched and finally lunged at the Loup Garou. The wolf instantly changed it's posture, stood upright on its back two legs, and caught the dark shadowy creature in mid-air. It slammed the scrunge to the ground and followed with a lethal bite of its own. The fangs of the Loup Garou tore into the bony flesh of the scrunge, ripping away tissue, and tearing muscle. It shook the monster in the grip of it's mouth, bit down as hard as it could, and snapped the bones of the Alpha scrunge.

The scrunge, though caught in the jaws of the wolf, did not cease to fight, and with it's sharp claws, ripped at the face of the wolf; cutting at the mouth of the behemoth predator. The jaws, having the scrunge in its clutches, could not withstand the onslaught, and the Loup Garou released the scrunge.

The scrunge, wounded, hurt, shook it's damaged body, and retreated a few steps. It's eyes focused on the Loup Garou, now limped as it again circled the giant wolf. The surroundings were quiet, there were no growls, howls, or cries, only quiet as the two predators prepared to continue the onslaught. The Loup Garou, with torn face, tasted the escaping blood escaping; it has been centuries since an enemy hurt the wolf. Animal instincts make it a killer, and human attributes make it a thinker, and it fights with humanistic tendencies. The wolf balanced itself on it's two hind legs, using its front two legs prepared, extended paws, similar to hands, readied itself.

The scrunge, though hurt, is still a formidable opponent, and the oozing blood from the Loup Garou revealed to the shadowy creature, the wolf is vulnerable. Possibly not on its hairy armored body, but it's head, and could possibly be blinded. The flesh on the face is susceptible, the scrunge seeing the claw lacerations has a new target. It would rip the face off of the Loup Garou. The cuts were deep in the face of the old wolf, it brushed off the wounds, licked it's face, and felt the incisions. Knowing the plan of the scrunge, and the poison released from it's claws, the wolf kept the ghostly rival away. As the hurt scrunge circle, this time, the Loup Garou attacked. With its two front legs, arms, and paws, punched at the scrunge; not like an ordinary canine, not swings with claws exposed; but closed fisted, landing precise blows.

Trying to penetrate the range of the punches, the scrunge couldn't, and the blows intensified. Every time the scrunge manned an attack, it was thwarted by a barrage of punches, weakening the evil monster. Out of **PRIDE** and desperation, the weakened scrunge mounted one last charge, the Loup Garou witnessed a fatal flaw. The wolf now understood the reason for the hesitancy of the scrunge, the Alpha is new to this type of fighting; a veteran fighting creature never lunges with its face first, always creates an opening, and then pounces. The scrunge limped as it circled, ever closer, sensing the arrival of it's death, and the Loup Garou knew it.

Before executing it's death thrust, the wolf released a wail, a victory cry, a howl, confirming supremacy to all present. An outcry to those before it, a reckoning is transpiring, and the Loup Garou is extracting a measure of revenge against a mortal enemy; the Alpha scrunge made one final leap, and winced as the ancient wolf implanted it's death grip.

The Nobility of Father Dauphne

Father Dauphne reclining in the confines of the rectory garden, considers all the church property holy ground, knows his thoughts are safe, and prayed for answers. He needed guidance from his mentor, and knows the recent occurrences are only a precursor of things to come. He is afraid, and as a priest, knows there is nothing to fear, but the Lord. He also knows his flock, and knows **EVIL** will try to lead the sheep astray. The presence felt while Bessie and her son visited disturbed him, and was the strongest manifestation felt in years. It's what prompts him to pray, realizing the battle has only begun, and to emerge victorious, constant prayer will be necessary.

"My Lord and Savior, I call upon you in my time of need. I feel the town you have me shepherding is on the brink of disaster, what am I to do? I alone cannot win this fight, realize you are always with me, but I feel earthly man is not. They are not aware of who they fight, are blind to its temptuous ways, have eyes, and do not see."

Dauphne paused in his silent meditations, he reflected on a lifetime of service. He arrived in Broussardville on the behest of the diocese, desperate to send a leader to shepherd the congregation. All involved knew he was the right person when selected, his strongest asset, **NOBILITY**. He is of royal character, and a man for all seasons.

"I speak to parents and children, see the happenings, and recognize **EVIL**. It is present and preparing to strike. Help me find a way to eliminate it. It has one specific goal, it desires the **BOX,** knows it has been found, and will do whatever necessary to possess it. The power within must never be released, give me the strength and courage to locate the **BOX**, then destroy it."

Before Dauphne could finish his meditations a strong presence invaded his thoughts, bringing with it apprehensions, and fear. It is a test of Dauphne's faith, he must resist, and find a way to fight the trespasser.

He thought, "Whoa ye of little faith."

He then heard, "Yes priest, your faith is weak, you are weak, and soon you will abandon your current master and follow me. I forewarn you, a fall impends, and when it transpires, I will be waiting. I will rescue you, giving your life new purpose."

Dauphne stood in the darkness, the moon illuminated the night sky. It is a full moon, and one huge, omniscient eye overlooked the surface of the planet. The peacefulness of the garden was shattered, and he continued to pray.

"My Father, who art in heaven, hallowed be thy name. Thy Kingdom come, thy will be done, on earth, as it is in heaven. Give me this day, my daily bread, and forgive my trespasses, as I forgive those who trespass against me. Lead me not into temptation, but strengthen me when I receive the test."

As he finished his praying, the anxieties felt earlier faded, and his worries about leadership paled. There are no longer trepidations, faintly, in the distant fields behind the church grounds, Dauphne heard growling, and listened as an intense battle ensued, could hear ripping, gnarling, growling, and finally a cry of **DEATH**. A creature was vanquished, frightening the elderly priest, he made his way into the confines of the rectory. He overheard a vicious attack, a fight between warring factions. He wondered who reigned, and were participants.

Nick-Nack/Patty-Whack, Give A Dog A Bone.

A night the quiet of Broussardville is abruptly interrupted by a battle between night creatures, heard throughout the rural town. Country towns are notoriously calm, and it's citizens are able to hear a pin drop, not this night. Silence is shattered by a gruesome, and violent contest involving two combatants aiming to rule the nocturnal. The skirmish woke L.B.M.N., she softly exited the house, and to her surprise, standing in her back yard is Shirley Simms. Bessie walked toward Shirley, and she toward Bessie, the women needed to talk, and this is an opportune time. Their children are asleep, giving them peace of mind.

L.B.M.N. stated, "I know you heard the same thing I did, it's back, the Loup Garou has resurfaced. I knew it wouldn't be long, it arrives wanting to claim it's rightful place on the surface. I heard it's howl when Keith and I visited Father Dauphne. The protective elders spoke of it's awakening before the final battle. We both know why it is here, to destroy the pack of scrunges, and I think it just killed an Alpha."

Shirley replied, "I've been reading tonight, books from the past, and the scrolls which teach the methodologies. Bessie, I won't be able to help when the time comes, I'm not strong enough, and have never been a leader."

"Shirley, you have always displayed **INTEGRITY**, and will automatically know what to do when the time is right. All your life you've acted, have knowledge no one else has, and you're a teacher. No one, or nothing is on your level, you make **MAGICAL** things happen."

She smiled at L.B.M.N.'s words, her older friend has an amazing way of rebuilding confidence, is an amazing mother, friend, and prayer warrior. Both women realize the vital roles they play within the community and in the lives of their children. The dark night sky concealed the two women, both moved toward a bench under the trees, and became candid with each other.

"I'm not the most prayerful person, I admire that about you, I witness your family walking to church, and think it's admirable. Your relationship with God is impressive, he guides your life, and the things you're able to do is only of God."

Bessie smiled and said, "Let's witness the carnage, watch the fight, and see the Loup Garou wreak havoc."

Waved her hand over a section of black space, she opened a hole, making a loop in time. L.B.M.N. has the unique ability to control **TIME**, reversing the present to the past, captured a previous moment; elapsed time reliving the competition, the clash of the nocturnal titans. The two women witnessed the re-enactment, as the scrunge attacked the huge hairy wolf. They were amazed at the agility of the Loup Garou, and the techniques it used to ward off the scrunge. In the time loop, they saw an ancient brawler, but strained to see the dark scrunge. It blended perfectly into the dark, the only tell-tale signs, glistening claws, fangs, and glowing eyes.

The ferocity of the scrunge was visible, and L.B.M.N. replayed the fight in its entirety. Shirley was mesmerized by the creatures, animals read about, but never seen until tonight. The eyes of her understanding were opened, revelation allowed her to watch the two predators stalk one another; witnessing their attacks, retreats, and strategies. In the end, the demise of the Alpha scrunge, and the victorious Loup Garou were witnessed. The Alpha scrunge, a monster mythically deemed to be unkillable, they both now know it to be false; and fully appreciate a new ally in the battle against **EVIL**.

L.B.M.N. closed the time loop, the rerun allowed by her gift, gives her the ability to replay a moment; return to time past, present, or future; she can access all. There is one catch, no interfere is allowed, no altering of an outcome. Whatever is witnessed, must be allowed to come to fruition as intended, any intervention by her accompanies death; the power can also be a curse. Shirley, in her night gown, began to glow, and her clothing became dazzling white. Her hair flowed in the night air, white, brilliant, exposing the light existing inside of her. She illuminated the back yard, Bessie basked in the Light show, knowing Light accompanies good; Shirley is the **GOOD ANGEL**, the bearer of good news. The report by Bud and Keith is confirmation, the Loup Garou has resurfaced, taken its rightful place on the surface, and aims to rule the night.

Coosh – Maa and Gus

A spirit form of **EVIL**, and a Sug; a dynamic duo; Gus and Coosh–Maa. Not only hearing the ferocious battle, they monitored closely, and had ring side seats. The return of the Loup Garou, and their newest Alpha scrunge, Gus with his ability to be more than one place at any given time, and Coosh–Maa observed. The Great Spirit first heard the Loup Garou while spying at the rectory, the distinctive howl of the creature. It prompted the **EVIL** to rally his troops, and consult the designate appointee, Gus; the one with his finger on the pulse of Broussardville. The two evils struggled along with the scrunge, and a part of them died along with the

Alpha. Gus never witnessed the mythical wolf in action, there were warnings, but the wolf wasn't seen. This is a monumental night, the Loup Garou has gone from myth to actual.

Coosh–Maa was also amazed at the tenacity of the wolf, the agility, and it hadn't aged since their last encounter. It's appearance, and fighting tactics are deadly, and the ease with which it dispatched of the Alpha scrunge was impressive. A formidable adversary is now sided with **GOOD**, and will have to be eliminated. The death of the Alpha infuriated Coosh–Maa, he turned to his number one, venting his frustrations. The wail of the Loup Garou, once it released the scrunge was frightening, and rage resounded. The cry echoed throughout the night sky, all heard, know the source, and realize the ancient being is awakened. Following the howl of victory, thunder exploded, shaking the foundations of Broussardville. Streaks of intense lightening flashed, the dark night became day, revealing the impressive power of the Loup Garou.

"Sug, the Loup Garou is awakened, I want it eliminated."

Gus looked at the spirit, confused, and had no idea how to fight such a thing. His battles were now mental, but to defeat this adversary, it will undoubtedly be a physical contest. Witnessing the physicality of the beast, walking like man, but fighting with the ferocity of animal; a lethal combination. Skills allowing the creature to exist throughout time, and Gus is given the task of destroying it?

"Why must I be the one, it is not after my possessions, but yours. You, not I, must eliminate the threat."

Coosh–Maa smarted at Gus' response, a Sug questioning his edict, and he wasted no time correcting his subordinate.

"I have told you before, never question me. I rule, you follow, it's your role in this; don't ever forget it."

Gus tried to calm the situation, using logic, attempting to ease his way out of the verbal slip."

"I was once told 90% of the friction created between people is because of the tone of voice used."

Coosh–Maa did not like the retort, within the night changed from spirit to flesh, took shape, becoming a wizard. His appearance was impressive, converting from air to matter, sat on a pedestal, Gus standing next to him, speechless, having never seen such a powerful manifestation. Frightened, he was silent as Coosh–Maa observed, and sniffed him, using animal instincts. The versatility of **EVIL** showed, taking human form, but retaining animalistic attributes. The malevolence thinks logically, makes conclusions, and has unlimited abilities. Second in command was awed, and silently thought of his previous wish, dreaming of one day replacing Coosh–Maa. Suddenly Gus felt inept, realizing the skills required to defeat such power. He doesn't possess the necessary skills, and will either have to obtain more or settle for second. The thought infuriated the Sug, it never settles for second, and desires being number one; no one remembers second place. The winner is number one, the **PRIDE** compels Gus, and the thought of ruling motivates it.

"My tone of voice, you question, or make a mockery, as you put it? If I choose to scream, be silent, or let my actions do the talking, I do."

Opened handed, and within them fire and a staff, it gaze at Gus, penetrating the Sug, and reprimanding him.

"For questioning my authority, you will be allied with an equal, a partner; returning from the clutches of death. Bones, flesh, and blood, loyal to me, willing to lay down it's life for me. It will be reincarnated, and walk the surface, doing my bidding. I suggest you stay out of it's way, don't associate with it, and beware, it longs for dominion. It will listen to only I, and knows the **TONE** of only one voice; remember Sug, **PIGS** get fat, **HOGS** get slaughtered."

Extra emphasis was placed on the word **TONE**, it's gaze affixed on Gus. As it spoke, beings of the underworld surfaced; skeletal warriors rose out of the ground. Hideous beings, total bone, stripped of all flesh, walking death, and they do the bidding of **EVIL**; Coosh–Maa. Gus cringed at the sight of his newest assistants. Their numbers are staggering, and creatures never before seen or heard of. Second in command did not respond, any **TONE** used would not be received politely. His comment about friction created hostility, and that's not what he anticipated. He stood next to the pedestal, witnessing the prevailing power, a being, an entity unmatched. The Sug knows a new game plan will have to be developed, and it will require immediate creation.

Coosh – Maa

The Young and the Restless.

Early morning Glen recognized a favorite scent emitting from the house next door, making his mouth salivate. He looked over at John Nick, his brother snored, mouth wide open. Glen laughed, entered the bathroom, quickly washed and brushed, then exited towards his mom's room. She was seated in the front room, he changed direction, and walked toward her. Arriving he noticed something strange, at the table, seated across from his mom was a girl; a beautiful young girl. He had never seen her before, and wondered who was she? Her looks were mesmerizing, and she was doing something with her hands. Her clothing was odd, and her actions seemed magical.

Glen asked, "Who is she mom?"

The girl looked over, they made eye contact, and he noticed a light glowing within her hands. She was controlling it, and the intensity of the light grew as she spread her hands apart. Glen was absorbed, watching her, she was conjuring a spell; he silently watched.

"She is your sister, her name is Patricia, she was lost before your birth; or so I thought. I now realize her spirit has always been present, she has returned to help."

Glen was more confused, he never knew of a sister; things kept getting stranger by the minute.

"Where has she been, and she will help us do what?"

His mother sensing the boy's confusion, sat him down and began to explain. She realized an explanation is due, and now is as good a time as any.; especially since he's seen her.

"Your sister was lost during labor, she is the middle child, between you and John Nick; your big sister and his little sister. John Nick was only a baby when she was lost, but her spirit has returned. She's waited for the precise time to reveal herself, letting us know she is present; not in body, but spirit."

Glen turned, looked at his sister, her beauty captivated, and he watched her perform her gift; as he did, his mother continued.

"Things shared the last few days, it is a lot to absorb, but realize, it's time for you to grow. There is no tomorrow, we must live for the moment, and the discovery is prompting this. Everything transpiring in Broussardville is because of the **BOX**."

Glen's thoughts reflected on the beautiful little **BOX**, and the ray of light it released. The **BOX** now calls him, appears in his dreams, attracts him, and beckons. He needs to see it again, wants to hold it, and unbeknown to him, the **BOX** desires to possess him.

"Mom, I want to know more, but I need to go over to Keith's. I know it's early, but there's no school today, and I know Ms. Bessie won't mind."

"I know she won't mind either, I just thought seeing Patricia for the first time you would have more questions."

"I do have more questions, I find her fascinating, but honestly, I can smell the Lost Bread Ms. Bessie's cooking, and I want some."

The look in Glen's eyes told the story, he isn't thinking with his right mind, his stomach has a grip on him, and he is being compelled by his appetite. Lost Bread is an irresistible breakfast food, and Shirley knows the persuasive power of Soakie's Lost Bread. She nor Patricia are a match over the powerful breakfast, and she reluctantly gave in.

"O.K., you can go, and we'll talk when you get back; don't be long."

Glen turned, making a beeline to the back screen door, before exiting, he took one last look at Patricia. He still can't believe he has a sister, an unexpected revelation. He silently wondered what other surprises are in store? Quickly, he exited, but just before getting outside, his mom made one last suggestion.

"Bring me back a couple of slices before you go play, and don't forget."

Ms. Shirley was serious, and Glen knew it, the look on her face said it all. She wants some of the sweet, gushy stuff too. She tasted the addictive Lost Bread before, and knows it is to die for. Glen arrived at the screen door of the little kitchen, a cozy room used mostly for storage, knocked on the door, and saw the washing machine inside. It's has a ringer on top to remove excess water, and a huge bottom tub, there was commotion coming from the big kitchen. From around the wall, Miss Bessie poked her head out of the big kitchen, seeing Glen standing there, smiled, and made a suggestion to the newly arriving boy.

Lost Bread

"I knew you were coming, that's why I left the door open. That nose of yours, Roger and Sam ain't got nothing on you. Get your lil butt in here, Kee - Toe already has a one slice lead on you."

Glen hopped into the little kitchen and dashed to the next room, saw Keith, and they made eye contact; both knew it was on. Both are as thick as thieves, and L.B.M.N. knows it. She began to exit the kitchen, knowing both boys are aware of the procedure; and won't have to monitor them. They wanted to eat, and could make their own Lost Bread. In her own way, she's passing the torch, but before she exited, put together a little more of the mixture which makes Lost Bread, Lost Bread; the boys didn't watch, she made them prepare it.

"Keith, mix three eggs together, stir them up, and add some milk for consistency."

She looked over at Glen, "Get some milk out of the ice box."

"O.K., those eggs are mixed enough, add in the sugar, I know it's both of your favorite."

I reached for the canister, then realized, why not bring the bowl to the canister, that way momma couldn't see how much sugar I actually put in; my back was turned to her. She suggested a spoon of sugar, blocking her view, I put in two spoons, and quickly began to mix the ingredients.

"Add a tablespoon of cinnamon, shake it over the liquid Kee-Toe, don't drop it in one spot; spread it out over the bowl."

I replied, "O.K. momma, this isn't my first rodeo."

I was trying to show off in front of Glen, momma sensed it, and instead of reprimanding me, let me get away this time.

"First rodeo, boy you haven't gotten off the porch yet."

I looked at momma, smiled, and saw Glen growing tired of waiting. His stomach was making a springy sound, and he could probably eat a horse; he asked.

"Man, when you gonna start cooking?"

L.B.M.N. chuckled, "Somebody's hungry, Kee – Toe, we can't have our guests waiting; hook up your friend. You know he gets the next two, then you get another."

I lowered my eyes, reflecting disappointment, momma's still in teaching mode, and guides my actions in the right direction. He thought of her favorite scripture, "Do unto others as you would have them do unto you." Before I could reply, she cut me a pair of eyes; I had better not say a word. Unspoken it meant, "Do as I say." I did as she said, but with pain, and reservation. I felt slighted, it's my momma's recipe, ingredients, and my house. Glen stood waiting, rubbing his hands together, had already made it to the cabinet, gotten a plat, fork, and glass. Smiling from ear to ear, I looked over at him with disgust, suddenly Glen isn't my best friend. Momma left the kitchen after helping us prepare the mix; the rest is up to us.

I buttered the bottom of the black, flat bottomed skillet, it melted as soon as it touched the heated pot. Glen had a slice of bread soaking, I grabbed it with a pair of tongs, put it inside the pot, and watched it sizzle, cooking, browning, being caramelized. Our mouth's watered, the smell is addicting, and Glen is past ready. He woke up with Lost Bread on his mind, and it is now so close. I love Lost Bread, it's rare I rule the kitchen, normally it's Pooh, or Dean; never me. This morning, I'm the man, what an intoxicating feeling, running the show, and I had to show Glen who is in control.

"Hold your horses Glen Simms, this is no voyage, or expedition needing immediate completion; it's a process, and it takes time."

I pressed down on the Lost Bread, it sizzled, and released a puff of smoke, the scent is pure sweetness floating in the air; intensifying the appetite.

"Man, just give me my slice, it's ready; stop playing."

I laughed at my hungry compadre, partner in crime, Ace-Boon-Coon, and teasingly asked.

"You hungry man?"

The entire time, Glen is standing next to me, plate in hand, mouth filled with drool, dieing of hunger; he can see the Lost Bread.

"No Keith, I'm not hungry, I'm just here to watch you eat; man give me my Lost Bread."

He reached into the pot and took out the slice, fire hot, tossed it around in both hands, and began to eat it. He blew on the slice as he bit, and chewed, trying to cool it off, he said.

"I told you stop playing man, now cook my second one. I already have a slice of bread soaking in the mix, and you know momma said I get the next two."

As Glen ate I cooked another slice, he finished the second, took over the cooking duties, and cooked another. Lost Bread is heavy, and it blows up inside of you, the first one I ate filled me up half way; one more would be enough; another of momma's Soakieisms.

"Don't let your eyes be too big for your stomach."

The last ones were browned perfectly, we put powdered sugar on them, and went to town. When the powdered sugar ran out, it was the end of the cook, I said.

"There you have it, 'Wah – La', Lost Bread."

Glen asked, "Is this Soul Food?"

I laughed at him, he is simply getting a taste of L.B.M.N.'s cooking, no one cooks like her; they might call it cooking, but it's the recipes, her secret magic. I jokingly replied.

"Yea Bud, it's food for the soul."

We both laughed, which made room in our tummies for a third slice. We both figured "Why not," there's mix left, and it can't go to waste. As I cooked the third slices, Glen commented.

"Man, the next time momma is gonna cook Lost Bread, let me know, I want to sleep over. There are three reasons I love to spend the night over here."

I said, "Even though I don't want to hear them, I have a feeling I'm going to anyway."

"Reason One, momma is the best cook, she makes you look forward to waking up in the morning. There's always a surprise, cush-cush, flap jack, grits and eggs, and homemade biscuits. Add figs, preserves, Karo, or Steen's Syrup, it's say-too. It never ends, I could sleep here every night."

I said, "Come on now, let's not get carried away."

I chuckled at Glen, he is my best friend; we become pretty tight.

"Reason Two, I like hangin' out with you, we do some of the funniest stuff, and I learn from you; you are my best friend, my shipmate, and me casa su casa."

I smiled, "Thanks bro, that was nice."

"I mean it, and Reason Three, I like coming here. You have three smart, funny, and pretty sisters, I look at them like they're mine."

"That's how you better keep it, my sisters are off limits, and Chew-Bus too. I don't want you getting any ideas, I know you bro; you're sneaky."

Glen chuckled at me, we feed off one another, and are best friends. They will do anything for each other, but one day, the depths of their friendship will be greatly tested. After breakfast we cleaned the kitchen, it's Monday and the usual will happen. We finished the kitchen chores, I went to the front room, and momma is sitting on the sofa relaxing.

I asked, "Momma, can Glen and I go play?"

"Did you clean the kitchen?"

"Yes ma'am."

"Are you full?"

"Yes ma'am."

"Go play, but not far, later I have some things I want to talk about. When John Nick and Steven get up, ya'll comeback."

"O.K. momma, thanks."

I ran to the kitchen and Glen is waiting."

"Let's roll, she said we can go."

Go Play

We sprinted out of the house headed toward St. Cecilia, the plan, swing and the slide, simply being out there is fun. Soon as we turned the corner, on the side of the house, leading to the street, Father Dauphne appeared; from out of know where. In his normal deep voice he spoke, a voice which commands attention. It comes from deep inside, has a base tone deeper than the ocean, and fathoms rising out of his chest, throat, and moth are unchartered depths, he asked?.

"Where are the two of you going?"

We froze, I had forgotten, he did tell momma and I about coming by on Monday. When it dawned on me, I stopped, introduced Father Dauphne to Glen, and now had a monkey wrench thrown into our plans to play.

I said, "Father Dauphne, this is my neighbor and friend Glen Simms."

Glen smiled and said, "Hello, Father."

Father smiled and replied, "Nice to meet you young man, aren't you the son of Shirley Jean DeLeon.

Glen was puzzled, "No, my momma's last name is Simms."

"I speak of her maiden name young Glen, someday she will share your family legacy with you."

Father paused a second, Glen thought, recalling the recent conversation with John Nick, but how did Father Dauphne know. I know what Father wants, both Glen and I could feel it.

"Do the two of you have time to talk to me?"

I replied, "Our parents told us we could go play, we just finished breakfast, and was going to go to the park; but if you need to talk to us, we'll make the time."

Out of respect I have to make time for Father, he is a vital part of the community, and I am an altar boy. If he needs to talk to me, I have to talk to him, it is almost mandatory.

"Boys, can the two of you talk to me about things experienced the last few days. Also, show me where these things have been happening."

Glen and I looked at each other, to show him meant going back to the coulee, our mothers told us to stay away from the coulee, and our big brothers warned us about the coulee; if they were with us maybe it would be O.K.

"Father, let's go talk to my momma, it would be better if you asked her for us to show you where. Once she says it's O.K., we'll do it."

I know it will be better if the two adults speak directly, that way there will be no misunderstanding, and both will be on the same page. As a youngster from Broussardville, you're always taught to know your place, I will let momma and Father decide our fate. Father retreated to the front door, knocked, and momma answered. Seeing it is Father Dauphne, she left him inside, Glen and I stayed outside, waiting for her answer. We stood on the front porch and I could hear Father talking, the words weren't clear, but the deep voice is obvious. The front door re-opened and I heard my mother's last words to Father.

"Please keep an eye on them for me Father."

It is authorization, he got the O.K. from momma, allowing us return access to the coulee, the scene of the crime. It's nice to be with Father, you feet safe in his company, before leaving, I ran to the back, grabbed the machete and cane knife; Glen and I will clear a path. Off we went toward the coulee, the grass is overgrown as usual, and will take some clearing, but we will show him the three places where the incidents happened.

The Finding.

Seeing the Night Stalkers.

Meeting the Wolf.

We approached the first area, The Finding, it is completely different, the grass is matted down, someone or something had been back there. No footprints or footsteps are obvious, but something flattened the grass down; like someone took a sickle to the area. As we walked through the area Father inquired.

"Who did this, was it like this before? This looks freshly done."

I shook my head as did Glen, and shrugged our shoulders, both surprised as Father. The area, our exploration grounds, are ravished, and the grass and bushes are cut low to allow visibility. This was done intentionally, and we all knew it.

I said, "I don't know Father, it wasn't like this before. That's why we bought the cane knife and machete, we normally have to clear a path."

Glen said, "This is fresh, we're back here every day, and didn't see anyone do this; it might have been done at night."

Father, with a puzzled look asked, "What makes you conclude that young man?"

"Well Father Dauphne, Keith and I live here, see almost everything, and would have seen who did this or someone would have told us what they saw. We haven't heard a peep, meaning no one else heard a peep or saw anything, that's not normal. It had to be done in the guise of darkness."

It was puzzling, our stomping grounds, and we know it like the back of our hands, yet know nothing.

I said, "Father, this is right down the street, and done right under our noses."

"You're both right, Glen you are correct concluding the guise of darkness, but darkness is no guise; **EVIL** hides within, there is the guise; don't be fooled."

We continued walking and arrived at **The Finding.** With the grass cut, we got there quickly. Father did well, he kept us with us, and wasn't even huffing or puffing.

I said, "This is the first spot Father, where we discovered the foot tub, and the dried bones. I remember it clearly because the Moj–Yah tree marks the spot, the berries are gone, but the tree is here; and this is where I found the **BOX**."

Father looked at the area, surveyed it as if it were a crime scene, inspecting things, looking for anything out of the ordinary, or something another eye might overlook; not the trained eye of Father Dauphne, he's looking for signs of **EVIL**.

Asking no questions, he walked around, observing, making mental notes, looked at the dirt, knelt and took some into the palm of his hand, and rubbed it into dust. Walked up the bank of the coulee, Glen and I quietly watched, impressed how Father charted the area, obviously knowing what he's doing. Everything is probably gone, or destroyed, but he searched. He walked the bank, looked for anything, footprints, or signs of the possible intruder or intruders; nothing, at least nothing we saw.

I asked, "Father, are you ready to go to the second spot?"

"Sure Keith, I got a good feel for this one, but I need to do one thing before we go. At each spot, I will consecrate the grounds."

He took out a little bottle, the size of an eye drop bottle, squeezed the top, a nipple is on it, and removed the little dropper. We could see the liquid in the tube. He walked the area, releasing drops onto the ground in differing spots. What happened next surprised both Glen and I, everywhere Father dropped the liquid/water, the ground began to steam, and smoke rose for the earth. A burning smell, a terrible stink, no fire, but the entire area became consumed by the releasing smoke

Father said, "This is Holy Water, meant to recognize, cleanse, and extract **EVIL** from an area. The smoke, steam, and heat are confirmation of an evil presence. It is still near, we can now go to the next spot."

As we walked, my mind rambled, thinking of chemistry experiments in Ms. Hollier's science class. The ground and the Holy Water had some kind of adverse, chemical reaction, it was strange. Until Father explained, I was confused, and I know if I was confused, so was Glen. As we walked to the spot where we saw the Night Stalkers, Father spoke, explaining things to us.

Choose Your Own Adventure

"I bought the Holy Water because it is a clear indicator, and what you've told me Keith, there are **EVIL** forces at work here. Forces that rule the night, entities that can take shape, and their goal is to deceive; boys, don't fall for the trickery."

We arrived at the culverts, the tunnels where we hid from the hooded creatures, recalling the incident made us scared. Just being there again bought back horrifying memories, and Father seemed to feel our vibe.

He asked, "What happened here?"

Glen replied, "This is where we saw the hooded creatures, the dark, night walkers."

Father froze, turned, looked at us, amazed, but seemingly doubting.

"The two of you have seen Night Stalkers?"

Seeing the Night Stalkers

It was the first time we heard them referred to as that, Father must have a history with them, and has a name for them; impressive.

I replied, "Yes Father, and I have seen them more than once. They are scary things, those eyes, they look right through you."

"Where did you see the Night Stalkers, the exact location."

Glen said, "They floated over the water over there, we were in the tunnels hiding when we saw them. They hovered over the water, made no splashing sounds, didn't walk, but glided over the water. They scared us, and they were looking for us. They should have found us, but something distracted them."

Dauphne walked over to the spot the boys pointed to, and again took out the little bottle, and walked the area releasing a few drops over the ground and water. When the Holy Water mixed with the coulee water, a sheet of ice covered the coulee, instantly; it was strange.

"Touch the water boys, feel how it is cold?"

We both put our hands to the ice, but couldn't reach the water, a sheet of ice covered the entire coulee, spreading wider, and further as we stood watching. It thickened, and spread north and south along the coulee.

Father said, "Rarely is a Night Stalker seen, and the person witnessing live to tell about it. They are considered folk lore, what legends are made of, shrouded in secrecy, and does **EVIL'S** bidding."

Glen asked, "Why is this happening to the coulee Father, the water turning into ice?"

He replied in a rhyme, "What exists in the cold of night, also thrives in the cold of day, an evil little boys should in no way play. It can turn a heart from warm to clay. Do not shake your head in disbelief, what you see; the mind will say no way."

He paused a while, watching the ice spread, looked at us and smiled, a confident grin. Unsaid, it said something, my young mind couldn't comprehend just what, but his expression said something; he continued.

"It can't be solved with riches, money, or pay; spans all time, and can't be measured by the time of day. If it reigns upon you, the effects will stay. How long, who knows, but **EVIL** will not delay."

We were puzzled, yet in a strange way understood,; naivety prompted Glen.

"What does all that mean Father?"

Tools of the Trade.

He didn't answer Glen's inquiry, knowing I was also awaiting an explanation; instead issued a stern warning. Father Dauphne is true, honest, pure, and suspect's **EVIL** is trying to consume us. He knows the signs, but I don't think he's going to let it happen; we have found a new ally.

"The two areas you taken me, do not return alone and never under the shadow of darkness; you are not ready to fight the powers canvassing this area. I must prepare, and train the two of you, and equip you with tools to deter **EVIL**."

Meeting the Wolf

He paused a second, allowing his words and warning to sink in, then suggested we move on to the last spot. I began to lead him to the area where we encountered the tattered wolf, it is off the beaten path; we led and Father Dauphne followed. We got to the third area, Father again took out the Holy Water, but before he started to sprinkle it, Glen spoke.

"Father, I think the wolf is helping us, it led us out of danger, then disappeared. It appeared from nowhere and disappeared the same way. It talked and guided us, I think the wolf is a friend."

Glen's words impressed Father, he began to sprinkle the Holy Water in the area, flicked his hand, and the Holy Water flew throughout the area. Glen and I stood watching as Father did the same thing at the third site as he did at the previous two. This time though, there was no reaction, no smoke, heat, or ice like at the second spot. Confirmation to all, the wolf is good, and the ground it walks on has no adverse reaction to Holy Water; even Father Dauphne was impressed. We began to leave the coulee area, visited the three locations, and before parting Father asked me.

"Where is the **BOX**?"

I replied, "It is in a safe spot Father, only my big brother and I know the exact location, and I have been dying to get back to it. The **BOX** has powers, and I want to find out what it can do."

"Be careful what you wish for son, all that glitters isn't gold."

His words are at times puzzling, and when he instructs the altar boys, we realize you have to read between the lines to understand what Father intends. His intention is to make you ponder the words, and try to find meaning; I like that about him. He is always teaching, and as we walked back toward the house began to tell a story.

"The wolf you encountered is actually no wolf, it is a mythical creature spoken of since the founding of Girouardville, and Broussardville. Keith, I spoke about some of this when you visited the rectory. It's a creature never before seen, but it's howl has echoed in the night forever, and has prompted me to ponder many a sennight and feowertyne night."

We looked at each other, having no idea what Father Dauphne meant. What are the nights he talks about, and why can't he speak simply? Seeing our puzzled expressions, explained.

"Boys, a sennight is seven days, and a feowertyne night is fourteen days."

Glen said, "Why didn't you just say that."

Father chuckled, embraced our youth, and loves our innocence; this generation speaks their minds, and are honest; he enjoys spending time with them. We made it back home quickly, and Father called us to the back of the house before leaving.

Basic Training

"I have something for you boys."

Caught off guard, not knowing what to expect, and definitely mystified, he has something for us; what? We got to the back of the house, the anticipation's killing us, wanting to know what it is. He reached into his pocket, took something out, our eyes were fixed on his hand.

"Each of you, take this crucifix and St. Anthony medal, keep them with you at all times; they will help to ward off **EVIL**. When an **EVIL** presence senses you have protectors, they are forced to get behind you, and flee to their master; Satan."

He placed a medal and mini-crucifix into each of our hands, and said a prayer blessing them. Astonished, but scared, we know Father is preparing us for something unknown, but seems like he knows, and can see our futures.

Glen asked, "When do we use these?"

"When your faith is shaken, tested beyond measure, when you are afraid, and **EVIL** confronts you, Reveal these holy relics, and they will help ward off any **EVIL** in the vicinity."

I asked, "Father, can I have the little bottle of Holy Water; if you don't mind."

He replied, "Why sure, asking tells me you know the pending challenges that will be faced. Use every possible aide, I applaud your assertiveness."

I thought to himself, Father is insightful, always understands, and is willing to explain things; a quality I find endearing. He exited the back yard, walking to the front, Glen and I followed, and watched him until he disappeared. I wondered why hadn't he driven, the question quickly disappeared. For some odd reason, Glen and I felt comforted by Father's visit, and his revelation about Glen's family intrigued, he wanted to know more, but he didn't, Father Dauphne was gone. The week flew by and Glen told me his family was going out of town, they were going to visit Aunt Betty in Wisner, La. A small, rural, backwoods country town, just like Broussardville, a plain little town. I wanted to go for the ride, and see Aunt

Betty, but knew Miss Shirley had other plans. The two exchanged their secret handshake, and off the Simms family went for the weekend.

Cool Combo

When I re-entered the house, Hub Cap was up, and giving me the eye, the look has attitude in it; and I didn't understand why. I silently thought maybe he's upset, wanting to come with us to the coulee, or maybe he woke up on the wrong side of the bed? I didn't know why he's mean mugging him, I am going to find out why..

"Hey, Hub Cap, what's shakin?"

He didn't respond, and kept on eating his bowl of Fruit Loops. After walking the coulee, a bowl of Fruit Loops sounded appetizing. I walked over to the cabinet, removed a bowl, planning to eat a bowl too. As I approached the cabinets, Steven spoke.

"What you doing Dirt?"

"I'm hungry, I'm gonna eat a bowl of Frosted Flakes. You have the Fruit Loops, I got Tony the Tiger, they're **GREAT**."

Mocking the commercial, I thought it clever, but Steven was not humored, didn't laugh, or chuckle, simply kept a straight face.

I asked, "What's up Hub Cap, why you mean mugging me?"

"You selfish, I wanted some Lost Bread, I smelled the remnants lingering in the house when I got up. I asked momma about the mix, she told me look in the ice box. I looked high and low for the mix, none, that's when it dawned on me; 'Keith ate it all'"

I now understand the mean mugging, if the roles were reversed, I would not be happy. He's pissed, no Lost Bread, again the allure; Lost Bread can cause the closest of brother to have drama. That Lost Bread is some intoxicating stuff, and I laughed inside, I know Steven feels shorted.

"It's not funny, you could have left some, I like Lost Bread too. I haven't had any since I left for school, you could have thought about me."

I felt bad, and have a better understanding as to why Hub Cap is upset; I hadn't thought of him. I have a one track mind, and a case of Lost Beard on the Brain.

"I apologize Hub Cap, I was selfish."

"You already ate breakfast, why you taking out a bowl; you can't eat breakfast again."

"Says who?"

A Few Good Men

Momma walked into the kitchen, having overheard our interaction, not between her sons, and she immediately set it straight. The kitchen got quiet, the dialogue between Steven and I came to a halt, you could hear a pin drop.

"What's going on in here, what's the fuss about?"

Steven replied, "Nothing momma, nothing's going on in here."

"Then why am I hearing all this ruckus. Keith you causing a commotion?"

"No momma, I just got back with Father, and was going to serve me a bowl of Frosted Flakes."

Momma asked, "Haven't you eaten already son, just because you see your brother with a big Jethro Bodine bowl of cereal, suddenly you want one. You're being greedy, selfish, and your eyes are too big for your stomach."

Momma put me in my place, looked over at Hub Cap, and he now had a smile on his face. We're two brothers, always trying to best each other; I'm upset, and feel shorted.

"Didn't I tell you go play, you haven't been gone that long with father, put that bowl back in the cabinet, and do as I told you; Go play. When you come back for dinner, I'll have something special made. I think you're going to like it, now do as I told you, scat."

A surprise meal for dinner, an instant pain killer, the Frosted Flakes are now in the rear view mirror. He is no longer Tony the Tiger, and feeling **GREAT**. I put the bowl back in the cabinet, and asked Hub Cap.

"You gonna come to St. Cecilia meet me, we can ball a while."

"Yea boy, when I finish, I'll meet you there."

I was about to dash when momma interrupted the sprint, and gave me a stern warning

"Be careful son, you can only go to St. Cecilia. Before you go anyplace else, check in with momma."

"Yes Ma'am."

Expectations are high, with Hub Cap back, the competition at St. Cecilia will be intense. All the local boys, even a few old scholars, re-opening their bags of tricks, put away long ago will be shooting today; Steven's back. The games will be competitive, but if I have Gumbo, he simply opens a can of Whip Ass, and we prevail. With Glen gone, about the only thing left to do is play some ball; and if I wind up with Steven, that's a wrap. I've witnessed his strength, a gift, and unbeknown to the locals, makes us invincible. I dribbled to St. Cecilia, got a down, and Hub Cap arrived as I picked my team. I intentionally tried to delay until he came, and when the others saw him coming, they began to grumble. Steven has game, their chances of winning have been greatly diminished.

I yelled, "Come on Hub Cap, I saved a spot on my team for you."

Steven smiled, gave me a high five, began to stretch, and then told me the most encouraging thing.

"When we get back, momma said she has a treat for us, I saw a watermelon, and she cooking kidneys and red beans. Let's go work up an appetite, I feel like opening a can of whip ass on somebody."

"Don't fake the FUNK or your nose will grow."

The FUNK Doctor – The Pinocchio Theory

We balled, the afternoon flew, and the early morning visit with Father quickly became a distant memory. Today, three-on-three competition is intense, my team: Steven, Aaron Saduj and I. A dynamic trio, three the hard way, a three headed monster, or the three musketeers. I could go on and on with the labels, the most important thing, how we performed on the outside courts at St. Cecilia. We needed to be dominate, and all open up individual cans of whip ass. We play together, know each others moves, and understand the basics of team basketball. Plays like: back door, give and go, pick and roll, and it didn't hurt that we all could shoot. We fit liked a well oil machine, Steven is Julius "Dr. J" Irving, Aaron is Earl "The Pearl" Monroe, and I'm David "Skywalker" Thompson; an unbeatable tri-fecta.

The heat, and four consecutive victories, drained us; and finally lost the fifth. We walked to the water fountain, enjoying a much needed water break, needed to rest and hydrate ourselves. The watermelon spoken of earlier by Hub Cap is now on my mind, we had played enough basketball. I waited my turn at the fountain, and being the youngest I drank last. That's how it always goes, the youngest has to pay their dues, I've grown accustomed to it. As I stood waiting, something caught my attention, a flash of movement in the corner of my eye. I turned to my left and saw the shadow of something disappear behind the gym, moving quickly. I only caught a glimpse of it, but it's big, fast, and made me curious.

I asked Steven and Aaron, "Did ya'll see something run behind the gym?"

Both replied in the negative, but I know my mind isn't playing tricks on me, and I have good vision. It was something, what, I have no idea, but it looked like a rat. It ran behind the gym, but it didn't look like any ordinary rodent. My turn to drink arrived and as I did, Steven made a conclusion.

"Dirt, dehydration can weak a person, and in severe cases cause hallucinations. We've lost a lot of fluids, it probably isn't anything."

After drinking, watermelon became the focus, others guys met us at the fountain, and we talked a little parting trash. We escorted Aaron back, dapped him for the games, and told all the fellas bye. I wanted watermelon, it would quench my thirst, and I would enjoy the sweetness. Walking home, a trap had been set by Hub Cap, intentionally leaving the ball at the park. He would send me back to get it and have first dibs on the melon. The center cut is always the sweetest, and being home first guarantees one of the most cherished slices. The trick wasn't new, one I always fall for, attempting to please big brother.

Steven asked, "Dirt, did you leave the ball?"

"I'm sorry Hub Cap, let's walk back together and get it."

"I'm tired Dirt, you go and I'll wait here for you."

I turned, and began to jog back to the park. When Steven saw me turn the corner, and out of sight, he dashed to the house. He's going to ensure a center piece is his, sprinted, and thought of momma's old fashioned cliché.

"You snooze, you lose."

Dream Weaver

Lu tossed and turned, taking an afternoon nap, after eating her fill of watermelon. Weaves a dream, sees her brothers walking toward the house, both crying, and wonders why. Has some traumatic event transpired, and is unaware. She must find out what is the matter, and help soothe her brother's pain.

She asks, "Why are the two of you crying?

Keith couldn't stop the tears, nor speak, obviously heartbroken. Steven sniffled, trying to explain best he could; she listened.

"Roger is dead, something killed him; we found him near the coulee. In a fight with some kind of creature, it got the best of him, and whatever the **EVIL** is, it's powerful."

"Where is he?"

"Buried near the coulee, under the bridge, near the train tracks, and made a small cross to identify the place."

Lu, disturbed by the news, convinces herself to visit the burial site, she must pay her final respects. She looks for the cross, finds it, surveys the area to see if anyone is near. Seeing no one, puts her hands to the recently unearthed soil, feels warm, smells her pets, friends, and protectors. Allows her thoughts to penetrate the earth, delves beneath the dirt, and connects with the canines. She releases a spark of life, reviving the animals, restoring both.

She speaks, "Roger, Sam, both hear me, there is work left for you to do, the battle which took your lives is meant to instruct, and expose to both the lethal power of the enemy. I now give the two of you an opportunity to exact a measure of revenge. Return to us at the proper time, appear, and stand with man in battle. Protect, redeem, liberate, and deliver us from our **EVIL** oppressors."

The ground trembled under Lu's feet, the earth shook, and the soil began to rise. Emerging from the depths, covered in dirt and filth, the two pets ascended, shook off the muck, looked at her, and both began licking her. The scars both have are deep, mortal wounds, still fresh from an attack, and must be healed. She rubs the spots healing them, and simultaneously restores life to the pets. Excited, she hugs the dogs, then feels something tugging at her, but ignores it.

"Lu, wake up, wake up, you're dreaming."

Again, she feels a tug, hears words, but resists coming back; enjoying the companionship of her pets.

"Lu, wake up, you're laughing in your sleep. What are you dreaming about?"

Recognizing the voice, Lu wakes, stretches, shakes her head, and realizes Sue is sitting on the bed next to her.

Sue again asks, "What is the dream about?"

"It's Roger, and Sam; I restored them back to life, informing them of our need. Both are alive, and will return to help us when needed."

Sue's speechless, having no idea what Lu speaks of, but knows both dogs are dead.

"Lu, stop talking crazy, you know Roger and Sam dead; you ate too much watermelon."

"They aren't dead, I saw, spoke, and restored life to them. Remember what momma said my gift is; I am **RESTORATION**."

St. Cecilia Gym

CHAPTER 7

THE SEARCH

HISTORY OF SAINT CECILIA SCHOOL.

Inside St. Cecilia Gym.

I walked back to St. Cecilia, looked around, none of the homeboys even noticed me, I got my mind back. The silent **VOICE** is gone, I'm on my own. I've never entered the gym illegally on my own, Bud is always with me. I snuck around the back, no spies noticed, and I gathered my thoughts. I pondered the source of the **VOICE** which temporarily controlled me? It's attraction, manipulation, and my concession is disturbing; I must work on resisting the temptation; and led myself to it as Aaron and I talked. My conscience stepped in, sitting behind the gym, I wondered if I should call this off, and wait for Glen. Going alone is risky, especially all the strange stuff going on, and Bud always has my back, and I have his. We're a dynamic duo, Bud Cassidy and the Swing out Kid, Simmsky, and Dirt, he is Spock, and I am Captain Kirk. True sleuths, I am Nick Holmes and he is Wattman, and vice versa, maybe even Cheech and Chong. I sat chuckling at the last twosome, a thought lightening the mood, and calming the apprehension. It is now or never, I'm going inside.

I saw something at the fountain, they were distracted drinking water, and whatever it is , I want to know. I must find out what it is, or my curiosity will never be quenched. What I saw unnerved me, rats, a pack of them, and I hate rats. I climbed through our secret entrance, I think only Glen and I know about it, and I anyone else does, it's news to us. We first discovered the access on a rainy day, wanting to play basketball, the court too wet, and a decision made to try and sneak into the gym. Basketball isn't the reason I enter today, it's an exploratory, fact finding mission. I slid the board aside, allowing me entrance, climbed in, but let the board off in case I had to exit quickly.

Who knows the kind of creatures, demons, or rats I may encounter. Glen and I found the way in a few months ago, and come inside to play when it rains. Explorers, discoverers, that is what we are, and what we do, gaining entry; easy as pie. We located a basement entrance, underneath the foundation a panel, with a little prying and pushing, we were able to loosen the board, after which was smooth sailing. We followed an entry hall running under the floorboards, when it ended, you emerged from below, onto the stage, and into the gym. It's about fifteen feet of crawling, and the secret passage of Glen Simms, and Keith Nickerson.

Many rainy days we played until our little hearts were content, the one-on-one battles historic. Glen is good, and at times beat me, and I hated that, but defeat inspired me to practice. The crazy part, Bud is with me as I practice to better myself, what is obviously doing at the same time; Practice makes perfect. After playing, we eliminated the evidence by passing a wet mop on the floor, reversed our path through the basement, closed the panel, pushed it tight, and disappeared. The gym is old anyway, it wouldn't be trespassing, it's rarely used, and is our private sanctuary. The gym, school, and church are right behind the house. All our lives we've heard tales of former nuns and pregnancies, priests and nuns, priests and abused children, a secret burial ground somewhere behind the park, etc. To me, it is idle gossip, **CAWNT**, like momma would say, but the latest antics in Broussardville makes you wonder. I recall a story momma shared with us, the focus of the input, gossip, and the lesson learned jaw dropping.

Bad Intel – A VICTIM of GOSSIP

A gloomy night in Broussardville, darkness enveloped the own, rain poured, thunder echoed, lightening stuck, and the raindrops, as the hit our tin roof; exploded. Tonight we huddled in the living room, when the weather's bad momma gathers us together. The tin roof, combined with the rain, is normally a recipe for sleep, but not this night. Leaks in the roof, we know the exact pan placements before the drips start. Spread over the floor, the landing drops made music on the receiving pan, and momma used the special effects to perfection. She is going to speak about gossip, but used an unfamiliar word, "**CAWNT**." A Creole word, "**CAWNT**" translated is gossip, to this day, we don't know if the following story told is true or false; but momma made her

PERRRNNT.

"The longest tenured local priest, very popular, known throughout the community, and well respected is the center of this controversy. Previously seen on a daily basis in the community, always assisting the congregation, and available to any needy parishioner; age finally began to catch up to him. Due to his deteriorated health, an ear infection developed, and it began to affect his equilibrium and balance. Intentionally, he began to limit his exposure to the public, and congregation, prompting concern. Due to his extended absence, inquiry developed, worry, curiosity, and of course rumors surfaced. The speculation covered a broad spectrum, and the assumptions were unfounded.

One morning, the altar ladies are cleaning the church, a normal activity. The elderly priest, feeling better this morning, walked to the church to pray. A group of ladies saw him, and were pleased, but noticed him staggering, swaying, and unbalanced. Strange actions compared to the priest they once knew, and a few of the women concluded he was drunk. Then it all made sense to them, that's why he's no longer seen; a drinking problem. The witnessing women discussed what they saw, and others in the congregation got wind of the observation. The story spread like wildfire, a vicious rumor that the elderly priest is a drunkard. The respect level, impression and reputation of the devoted priest, once held in such high esteem, is forever tainted.

An associate pastor got wind of the rumor, and in one of his homilies decided to clear the air, and shared with the community/congregation what is actually wrong with the older priest. Everyone was shocked with the revelation of the associate pastor, and his words set the record straight, or did it? One thing his deteriorating health allow is the taking of confessions. Behind the veil of secrecy, he listened to confessions, a particular day the woman mainly responsible for generating the rumor came to confession. When she entered the confessional, to her surprise, the older priest is taking confessions. Once he's recognized, she begins to sob, convicted by her conscience. Explains the reason for the outburst, she is the originator of the unfounded rumor, which is completely false. He responds by informing her the source is unknown to him, but heard the talk. Again, she apologized and asked what she could do to correct her ill-advised words.

The elderly priest, wise as King Solomon, used the opportunity to expand her mind, instructed her to go home, walk to the rooftop of her tenant building, which is twelve stories high. She is to take a pillow, a knife, and an open mind along. Once on the roof, cut the pillow open, return the next day to visit the elderly priest, and tell him about the experience. Wanting to make an amend, the lady hurried home grabbed a pillow, retrieved a knife, and ascended to the roof. She stood in the wind, stuck the knife into the pillow, and ripped it open. The wind blew sending the feathers in every imaginable direction. Some went up, down, north, south, east, and west. In the eyes of the woman, it is a beautiful sight to behold. The woman erroneously concluded penance for the sin is complete, returned the next day to church, eager to visit the elderly priest; wanting to answer his curiosity. She rings the doorbell, and the elderly priest exits, greets the female parishioner, and they began to talk.

He asks, "Did you do as I suggested."

"Yes Father, I did."

"What did you see?"

"Father, feathers exploded into the sky, floating in the wind, being spread all over, and going everywhere; far as the eye could see, and then some."

Vehemently, the elderly priest informs, **"THAT IS GOSSIP!"**

News feed

Wow, what a lesson taught, some rumors create irreparable damage, momma always stresses, "Believe none of what you hear, and half of what you see." I crawled through the tunnel, filled with apprehensions, and finally emerged onto the stage. In my possession are the protective measures given by Father Dauphne, medal, cross, and holy water. I stood on the stage, looking around the gym, saw nothing, but I know the rat things are inside somewhere. I steeped off the stage quietly, no sounds, I don't know if rats eat boys, and I am not going to be the guinea pig. Listening, total silence, dust floating, streams of light streaking through the floating dust particles; and my hearing is keen and vision acute. I looked and listened for anything, any sound, any quick movements like rats make.

I heard something, a scratching sound emanating from the rafters, an attic is above the offices, that is where the sound is. Glen and I discovered them the only time up there, we were scouting the property, my heart races as I walk toward the stairs. I follow a set of stairs ascending right of the stage, up to the attic, and the offices. Quietly I walk, setting my feet softly, wanting no board to creak, or anything indicating an intruder. My approach is slow, hesitant, and very watchful, it's my first time alone; it's an odd feeling. I heard it again, the scratching, and began to seek it.

The old gym is filled with sounds, decades of secrecy creak out, streams of weeping innocence, and oceans of repeated transgressions, the walls are the only remaining witnesses, and agonize. I stepped, and the floor creaked, I froze, left my foot pressure on the board, stopped, listening, but heard nothing. I stepped to the wall, put my ear against it, heard nothing, and poked my head through an opening in the wall. My eyesight strained to focus, dust, and darkness consumed the dark environment. A traveling ray of sunlight, only a stream, a momentary flicker revealed something; a really tall man dressed in white. He has a long grey beard, longer white hair, thin in stature; but I couldn't make out any of the facial features.

Dressed in a dazzling, long white robe, extending to his feet, he glowed, and illuminated the office. Within his hands, being presented, is the **BOX**, my **BOX**. The treasure I found, he held in his hands, he found it; who is he, and how is it, he has **MY BOX**. Steven and I hid it, therefore it is impossible for him to have it. I peeped my head in further, he is presenting the **BOX** to someone, and showing it off; who is it? I noticed the tall man is not alone, present are two dark hooded figures standing in two of the four corners of the room, vaguely visible, blending into the dark attic; they surprised me.

Also present, a wolf dog sat crouched in another corner, and in the fourth corner is a huge rat; all creatures I have recently seen. They bowed to the tall man, in awe of the power he possessed within his hands, and he is now in control. I wanted to see his face, just a glimpse; maybe it's Steven, and he has a secret, unrevealed gift. Maybe he took the **BOX**, and is disguised. Since his return, all these things have started happening, is he the source. Is he after my **BOX**, simultaneously a quiet **VOICE** asked,

"WHO CAN YOU TRUST?"

My own brother trying to jack me. I leaned forward to identify the traitor, almost have the right view, and my shoulder bumps into the wall. The sound draws the attention of all within the attic office, eyes turn, see me, an uninvited guest, and I quickly pulled my head out of the crack, and began to hightail it down the stairs. Frantic, consumed with fear, and running for my life, I'm busted, and can't be trusted. If only I had been still, the **VOICE** misled me, and intentionally distracted me. I ran and didn't look back, descended the stairwell, crossed the stage, and began my crawl out.

Ratwolves

Through the secret entrance I crawled, on hands and knees, scurrying through the tunnel, heart racing, fright filled. I wanted out of there, and as I crawled heard movement behind me. I turned, looked, and a rat's closing in on me. I got to the panel board, pushed with all my might, it began to slide, but slipped out of my hands. The rat is rapidly closing rapidly, I could hear it coming. I again pushed on the sheet, it opened, I crawled through, and slid it back in place; then pressed my back against it. I then heard the huge rat crash into the wall, scratching, squealing, and desperately trying to get me.

It scratched on the backside of the panel board, tearing into it, and trying to eat through it. Frightened beyond image, I couldn't think, but knew I had to get out of there. My hands, legs, chest, and arms shook like spaghetti, I'm enveloped in fear, and ran out from the back of the gym. As I raced around the corner, I ran smack dab into Gus, and with a mean look in his eyes, he asked.

"Where is the **BOX**?"

I screamed, yelled, and know I'm trapped. I struggled in his arms, he held me, and began to transform into a monster; I closed my eyes and again screamed, this time for momma. When I force myself to open my eyes, I am lying on the ground in our backyard, momma standing over me, a glass of water in one hand, and shaking me to consciousness with the other.

"You're no longer in KANSAS."

"Kee-Toe wake up, shake it off boy, you having a bad daydream, all that watermelon; your eyes too big for your stomach. Calm down, must have been a doozy of a dream, tell momma about it. Gumbo told me you 're out here napping, I knew you ain't missing out on no watermelon."

Rising from my back, I look around, the basketball is right next to me, and a huge watermelon rind is also lying on the ground next to me. It had been eaten to the white, no red flesh remained inside the melon, and that's how a leave them. I was puzzled, how had I gotten there, and didn't remember eating watermelon.

Momma said, "Breathe son, those dreams of yours are getting worse. You were screaming about your **BOX, and** didn't want to lose it, because it's yours. You had better get right with your thoughts about that **BOX** boy, if you don't, it will consume you. Here son, calm down, and have a drink of water."

I took the water, gulped it down, silently wondering if it was a dream; it had to be, I home, but it was intense, bizarre, and very frightening. I still see the tall man, dazzling white; it's not Hub Cap, could it be the **VOICE**, or am I tripping. He couldn't have my **BOX**? Momma continued to talk.

"Keith, breath, it's O.K., I'm here. Tell me about the dream, and I mean everything."

I began to explain, it was no dream, felt very real, and if it was a dream, it was the scariest dream I've ever had. It involved all the strange things going on in Broussardville lately, I paused to catch my breath..

"Boy, you've been going through a lot, and put undue pressure on yourself, take it easy the next few days. Try to put the **BOX** on pause for a while, if you don't, you're going to get sick. Also, I want you to stick around the house more."

I know momma is looking out for my well-being, but the limitations are tough. I don't like them and decided to voice my disapproval.

"Awe momma, you making me stay close to the house after I promise to be careful."

"Boy, you will do as I say, I don't want no lip. No going to the other end, no going to the rectory see Father Dauphne, and no more sleepovers with Glen. Lastly, stay away from St. Cecilia school, gym, and basketball court; no more exploring. You are to stay close to home, do you hear me?"

I think momma is overly controlling a times, for the first time I agreed with her; I'm going to do as she says, and stay around the house. I'm going to chill with Hub Cap and the crew.

"Momma, can I ask you something?"

Before I could get out my question, Hub Cap appears in the back screen door; impeccable timing, and seems to be thinking the same thing I am. He approaches as momma responds.

"If you have a question, ask it. The only dumb question, is an unasked question. What is it, now's the time to ask."

"Momma, where is our daddy, and the other men of Broussardville?"

I looked at Hub Cap, his surprised reaction is pride, his little brother asks a question he's longed to, but hasn't the courage. I on the other hand am filled with youthful ignorance, and have no limits to my inquisitiveness. Momma smiles as she looks at us.

The Epiphany

"Boy, you come up with the most intriguing questions, but your desire for knowledge reflects growth, and expands your gifts. O.K., it's time we talk about your father."

I'm intrigued, momma's going to open up about our daddy. I want to know his whereabouts, and why he abandoned us? Is he even alive, or is he dead, filled with unanswered questions, finally I'm going to get some answers.

"Son, you never cease to amaze. I know Steven, and the girls have wondered the same thing, yet never asked. Is it lack of interest, or of courage; I know which, and for you to ask, it's confirmation, and reveals how different you really are."

I smiled, finally escaping from the shadow of my big brother. For the first time, I feel like momma sees me, it fills me with confidence, making me respect and love her more. She is about to begin again when the back screen door opened, our attention turned, and it's the girls standing at the screen door ear hustling. They saw Steven come outside, know momma is already out here with me, and naturally females are curious; that's how girls are. Always wanting to be in the know, and once momma sees them, waves them outside too. It's going to be a revealing session, the four arrived, and took seats around the picnic table.

Sue asked, "Momma, Keith alright, he's out here screaming in his sleep, and Lu's inside laughing in hers."

I smiled, by inquiring, Sue reveals the depth of her love, there is a special bond between us, before momma could answer her, Dean put in her two cents.

"You know that knuckle head is O.K. Just like Lu, ate too much watermelon."

All the girls chuckled, as did momma and Steven, but I don't think Dean's comment is funny at all. I'm always the brunt of her jokes, I've grown used to it.

Momma said, "Girls, I called ya'll out to share in this, it's time I clear the air about a few things. This may be a touchy subject, one all of you have wondered about, and this will hopefully answers your questions. Keith asked, 'Where is your father?'"

The ambiance under the tree instantly changes, the tone gets serious, and you can hear a pin drop. The silence is deafening, nothing stirs, not only do we want answers, it's like nature itself wants answers too. Now we are going to get it, information desired for the longest.

"I want to begin by saying I am proud of all my children. It has not been an easy task raising all of you on my own. Some of you have assumed the parenting role in my absence, I thank you; I love all of you, none more than the other."

Momma paused, looked at all of us individually, allowing the importance of her words to sink in. With a smile of love written on her face, she continued.

"Broussardville is a strange town and I know you've noticed there aren't many men. The few there are, know their place, remain submissive, silent, and are taught the attitude which allows them to live."

We all looked at each other, confused, what does she mean, stay alive; further explanation is necessary.

"Your father is a brave man and stood up against the powers in this town; his eventual undoing."

Momma's voice weakened, the reflection painful, and her eyes tear up; amazingly we all felt her hurt.

"His name is Cliff-Tawn, a good man, hard working, and wanted no handouts. His confidence, and independent spirit wouldn't allow him to succumb to the **EVIL** of this town. Men with the same mindset were round up, and exiled."

Now puzzled more than ever, we wondered what round up, and where is he cast out to? Where is he now, and why doesn't he try to escape? I want to ask, but remain silent as we all do, watching momma. We could see her face light up when speaking about him, and made comparisons.

"Claudette, you're a lot like him, actually all of you have differing qualities of his. I'm know he is proud of all, just like I am. You are strong children and are doing great without the leadership of a father figure."

The FUTURE is our YOUTH.

Pooh could no longer resist, the **Negotiator** has to inquire.

"Momma, is it possible he'll come back?"

"Many years I have waited, hoped and prayed, but it doesn't seem likely. An **EVIL** faction wants to eliminate the men of Broussardville, and that's why I ask my boys to stay close to home; now more than ever."

Lu yawned, and asked, "Can I use my gift to **Restore** him to his former self?"

Momma smiled, "All women of this town, at one time or another, tried to bring them back. The effort has led to futility, nothing done has been successful, adding to the frustration."

Sue asked, "I can think of an **Ingenious** way to get them back, and in these times, they need to be with their families."

"I agree Susan, they would help us understand what is transpiring, and what is going to, but with or without them, we must stick together; remember to always stick together. Nothing can outmatch unity, which reflects strength, generating power, and the three produce Love; the strongest variable able to defeat **ALL**."

Momma's words are profound, and the way she says things, no further explanation is necessary; and our curiosity will be satisfied. Dean chimed in while momma embraced the reflective moment.

"If I were with them, I would lead a **Rebellion**, and find a way to escape. We would then eliminate the **EVIL** threat imprisoning them."

Again momma smiled, expecting nothing less from Claudette, it's how she thinks; and is a take action person. Steven and I listened, impressed by our sister's aggressive attitudes. Unlike before, something's changed inside of them, and it's a welcomed change.

Steven asked, "The **EVIL** which cast them out, can it be **Conquered?**"

Momma responded, "Children, your gifts, powers, and abilities are new and things we only dreamed of acquiring. Ask your Higher Power to help you nurture, and refine them; allowing the maximization of skill. One day, momma will be gone and all you will have left is one another, **FAMILY** is what it's all about."

I smiled and said, "We are family, I've got all my sisters with me, the only one missing is Chew-Bus."

Momma laughed saying, "Boy, you are a **Patriot,** with a mind which allows you to shift from one thing to another, and you're right, Lynn hasn't come by today; that's unusual. "

Light the Way.

It's mid-afternoon and Chew-Bus is anxious to go visit her cousins; her day isn't complete without a daily stop over. The Nickerson household is her second home, all of them are her F.C.'s, an acronym for Favorite Cousins. Chores complete, she shared her plans with her sisters and brother, and lastly went to her mother to obtain permission. Her mom gave her the O.K., with one mandate.

"Be home before it gets dark."

She immediately ran out of the house, waving to her siblings, heading toward the other end. It's a bit of a journey, one taken numerous times, and she's incorporated short cuts. Passed behind Broussardville Elementary, she felt a presence, but could see no one. She knows someone's there, watching her, intentionally slowing the pace, began to observe her surroundings; needing to see who is shadowing her. She wants to look them in the eye, and identify them. Her head on a swivel, looking left, right, behind, and front, she is watchful, and her perceptive nature makes her pick up on any movement or sound. Whatever it is, they're good, because she sees nothing, and hears nothing either, no footsteps, crackling of leaves, or snapping of twigs; total silence.

The silence is eerie, no birds chirp, no cars pass, Chew-Bus knows something is amiss, and out of place. An uneasy feeling invades, she became alert, attentive, sharp-eyed, and slowly continued her walk; honed in for any sounds, but there are none. Chew-Bus is brave for he age, and at this point, others may begin to run, she didn't. She's going to face the spy, whatever's watching her, and challenge it. She feels the blind approach, and readies herself, removing her hands out of her pockets, and rubbing them together; preparing to release her light.

Progressing behind Broussardville Elementary, she arrived on Morgan Avenue, and from there it is a straight shot to Aunt Bee's. She sped up her pace, began to walk briskly, feeling things were still not back to normal. The unnerving feeling within remained, the quiet strange, suddenly the entire town is empty; totally bizarre. Something spooky is going on, giving her the creeps, she continues down Morgan Avenue, and a shadow catches her attention. Some odd reason, unbeknown to her, she is drawn to the shadowy figure, focuses her vision, and recognizes the person; it is Gus Girouard. Immediately she becomes anxious, on guard, knowing Gus' intentions aren't good, and knows if he can, will find a way to dispose of her; permanently. She replaced her hands into the pockets, knowing the light must be concealed, but if prompted will release it, choosing to wait for Gus to make the first move.

She asked, "Mr. Girouard, are you following me?"

"Child, who gives you the authority to question what I do. You had best know your place, you're only a child, and I know your momma. Don't make me take you home, and instruct Edna Mae to put it on your backside."

"Mr. Gus, the authority I have been given comes from my creator. He alone has authority over me, you don't, and neither does my mother. I know I'm a child in your eyes, but in his, I'm a warrior."

Gus became infuriated, Chew-Bus is sassing him, and he will not tolerate it. A child besting a **SUG**, it's not how the balance of nature intends it. He will show her, and put her in place. Instead of releasing his anger, Gus laughed at the cocky kid, and tried to regain his lost confidence.

"I must say, you're a confident child, and even more surprising, for a girl. You speak about your creator, I'm puzzled. Who is it you speak of?"

Chew-Bus gave a response Gus didn't expect, an answer which pisses off the Chief of Police.

"That's for me to know and you to find out. If I tell you, I'll have to kill you."

Gus chuckled, "Are you threatening me child? If I ask you a question, I expect you to answer it. I don't expect arrogance, or childish games; do you know who I am?"

Carolyn plays a trump card, exposed knowledge, attempting to get a reaction out of Gus, and it is least expected.

"I know who hides as Chief of Police, but is really something else. You are **EVIL** personified, disguised as Gus Girouard, but beneath a **SUG**. You do the bidding of Coosh-Maa, is its servant, and creation; it's eyes and ears."

Gus' reaction says it all, and realizing the child knows too much, begins to plan her demise. She must be dealt with harshly, and if she knows this, so do many others. He will not let his double life be exposed, will dispose of the child however he can; and walked toward her..

Glow Your Own Way.

"Remove your hands from your pockets, and put them behind your back; I'm placing you under arrest."

Gus reaches for her hands and Chew-Bus removes them, steps back from the **SUG**, opens her them, faces the palms directly at Gus. Light radiates from them, blinding the Chief, the powerful intensity shocks him. Completely surprised by the power the child possesses, he releases a wail, similar to a wounded animal. Chew-Bus turns, begins to run, the cry from Gus revealed the creature existing within, and confirmation to her. Gus is a **SUG,** the vilest of creatures, a killing machine, and Carolyn knows she is in grave danger.

She feels Gus pursuing as she runs, can hear the gallop of the creature, it is chasing her. The paws can be heard as they scrape the ground, the sharp claws scuff the ground, releasing sparks, in pursuit. It is gaining on Chew-Bush, she frantically runs, trying to escape, and arrive at Aunt Bee's before it gets her. If she doesn't, she will be its next meal. It closed, panic set it, and Carolyn realized she had to make a stand, do something, she isn't going to make it to her destination.

Desperation set in, the **SUG** closed, and will soon devour her. She made up her mind, turned, and faced the creature. Chew-Bus got the surprise of her life.

Gus is no longer in human form, broad daylight transforms into something hideous, a nasty monstrosity, and the former man is unrecognizable. The beast has huge ears, a mouth filled with fangs, saliva dripping out of it's mouth, and numerous eyes, too many to count; the entire face is filled with eyes. They are the all seeing eyes of Coosh-Maa, and it scared Chew-Bus. She screams once turned, seeing the grotesque transformation, knowing it is not of this world, like nothing seen before. An **EVIL**, hideous, disgusting monster, Gus in true form. Carolyn knows the only defense is unleashing the light, it will ward off **EVIL**; Light will stymie it's advance.

Opening her palms, she faced them toward the atrocity, releasing intense light, and it screamed. The light began to burn, the **SUG** sizzled, and though it's daylight, Carolyn's light is not natural sunlight, it is the Light of Life, and is Power; Life itself. It is the dominate Light contained in the **BOX,** formed at the creation of Life, as is she. The lights intensity deterred the advance of the horror, Chew-Bus focused her gaze, and aimed the powerful beams into the eyes of the fiend. Blinding the creature, she back away, the monster advanced, and the Light slowed the approach, but didn't stop it completely.

Chew-Bus vs. Gus

The monster roared in response, from it's mouth spewed fire, intense as the flames of hell, two adversaries; Light met Fire, and the two battled. Chew-Bus controlled Light and Gus commanded Fire. Her gaze incorporated concentration, amplifying the Light force, and overtook the fire. Light increased, grew, while the fire of the **SUG** diminished, and decreased. Feeling the fire being doused, Chew-Bus spoke to the thing.

"Gus, you are in there somewhere, away from me, leave and return to your master. Tell it of my power, my intention, destroying your kind, a personal mission, the elimination of scrunges. You, the most powerful, see my power, and never underestimate a confident girl again. If you do, **DEATH** will be waiting at every turn, heed my warning; '**AWAY FROM ME**.'"

She spread the fingers of her hands, the Light intensified, and she controlled the Light with every action, and thought. Gus released a yelp, winching in pain, injured, began to retreat. The fire once released from it's mouth is doused, and his retreat became withdrawal. Chew-Bus closed her hands, the Light dimmed, and Gus was gone.

The **EVIL** gone, Chew-Bus began to cry, fear which once overwhelmed is released in emotion. Seeing **DEATH** and witnessing the manifestation of **EVIL**, a creature walking the earth disguised as a human being. She is now in grave danger, and alone cannot defeat **EVIL**. She now hurriedly walked toward Aunt Bee's, having to tell her aunt and cousins what she witnessed and how it was warded off.

A SUG has only ONE MASTER.

Like a whipped dog, Gus returned to Coosh-Maa, and **EVIL** doesn't tolerate defeat. In the past twenty four hours, two of it's most reliable subjects have tasted defeat, and it's intolerable. It will not accept defeat, whining at the throne, hurt, and damaged from his encounter with the girl, Gus reports to his creator. The SUG has to inform his master what transpired, not realizing there is no need. He's forgotten his place again, underestimates his creators power, and forgets there is no need to give a testimony; Coosh-Maa is everywhere, and sees everything.

"Why do you come to me like a whipped dog with your tail between your legs, have you no pride? It would have been better for the girl to destroy you."

"You're telling me I no longer serve your purpose, and useless to you?"

"Do not question my words **SUG**, is that not what you told the girl? You asked who questions your authority, I was there, and witnessed your futile attempt at vanquishing the Light. I hoped you were prepared, but obviously I didn't do a good job; you disappoint me **SUG**."

Gus lowered his gaze, realizing the omniscience of Coosh-Maa. It restated his words to the girl exactly as said, it had to be there, is everywhere, and in everything. Gus continued licking his wounds, the Light not only blinded him, it burned him, and left scars which will be with him forever.

"I'm sorry master, and beg your pardon this one time. What has come over me, I admit ignorance by underestimating the gifted child. She surprised, bated, and due to my miscalculations, injured me; I embarrass my kind."

Head bowed, the **SUG** submitted, accepting the upcoming wrath of **EVIL**, but instead received compassion; knowing the reprieve is a disguised way of throwing him out to the wolves; his days are numbered.

"Then do as I command, eliminate the child; if you can't, the backup I requested is poised and ready."

Appearing behind Coosh-Maa, hundreds of skeletal soldiers. No flesh, complete bone, prepared to die for the resurrection, a promise made by **EVIL**. The possibility of walking the surface again; by day, a reason to fight, and a promise to keep. ready.

"She is not the only one, you know there are others. The two eldest boys must be dealt with, no men walk these streets without my authority, put them in check. In fact, they all must be terminated before they realize the power they possess. If they do, you are through."

"If they do we are through, correct master."

Coosh-Maa raised up Gus's snout and he winced in pain, the creator then unleashed a mental punishment on Gus. Tired of being corrected by it's creation has to penalize arrogance, and reprimand ineptness. It is necessary to stop dissention, if allowed, then the **SUG** will consider itself equal, the first step toward anarchy. The thought intensified the mental torture, Gus whined, the pain, brutal, and cruel; things Coos-Maa excels at applying. The decibel level intolerable, auditory torment; the canine's sensitive hearing abused, Gus cringed and could take it no longer, released a pain filled howl.

Coosh-Maa ceased the punishment, the pleasure it received inflicting the pain on the **SUG,** his disappointing creation. Inside, he wants to discipline more, teach a lesson, and let all know, there will be no back talk. Any mandate not completed is intolerable, and commands given and not completed tells the creator, the creation is flawed and useless.

"**SUG**, you desire something too big for your feeble, physical mind. You are grounded, and limited. I know your abilities, I created you, like you tell the humans; 'Know your place.' How dare you put yourself on the same plain, equals, impossible. I've been here since the dawn of time, was here when darkness covered the earth and reigned supreme; am the Alpha and Omega."

Gus tendered his throat to **EVIL**, a sign of submission, the **SUG** surrendered to the **ALPHA** spirit. Coosh-Maa is ultimate power, has seen, done, and knows all; an unbeatable foe. He alone is a legacy, **EVIL** is in it's heritage, is the birthright of Yahweh; and will anything to continue a rightful inheritance.

The **SUG** cowered, "Master, I will do anything to again be in your good graces."

"If you cannot defeat a novice child, or the smeller, the one detecting me in the house, and senses my arrival before I arrive. Individually, they are vulnerable, but together unbeatable."

"I will do as you desire master, and never let you down again. The one you speak of is of L.B.M.N., and will not be easy to get to."

"Do not go alone, take reinforcements, behind me is an unlimited supply of warriors ready to die for me. If one is destroyed, two are reborn. Take as many needed, humans must slumber, attack while they sleep. Night is when we reign, are nocturnal creatures, and seek prey; go unheard, attack, I want carnage."

Gus was surprised, felt the set up, and is aware of the ruthless Coosh-Maa. **EVIL** is correct, darkness will be an ally. Gus is aware his days are numbered, and his neck is on the line; and won't get any more chances. He's seen many Alpha, and Elder scrunges come and go, they were expendable, and if he doesn't make good on this mission, he may find himself expendable. The butt kisser he is, addressed Coosh-Maa.

"You are wise master, and I shall never question, or disobey a direct order. I renew my pledge of loyalty, and will fight for you to my **DEATH;** I vow obedience."

"You are created, aligned, co-joined, and has as a co-pilot; **DEATH**. Embrace your kindred, **DEATH** is your legacy, birds of a feather. Wherever you go, **DEATH** follows; take them all, **GO, ATTACK, KILL.**"

Life

CHAPTER 8

THE BEGINNING

US vs. THEM.

An Awaking Nightmare

Control on the surface is slipping away, desperation is creeping in, the troops are being rallied, and the unexpected is needed. **EVIL**, disguised as Coosh-Maa is going to pull a rabbit out of the hat, call on a nemesis, a ruthless enemy to side with it. Trust isn't the issue, power is; to retain it, **EVIL** will risk all. It's present reinforcements have disappointed, proven to be unreliable, the scale is tilting, and not in it's direction. The enemy has unlimited power, and must be destroyed before realization of the potential possessed. "**IT**" is going to use a trump card, play an ace in the hole, having only two, usage is due to extreme anxiety. The situation is dire, **EVIL** must do something, and decides to call on one of the banished.

The QUEEN

"**IT**" cannot count on the **SUG,** human females distract the beast, recurring problems are encountered; "**IT**" realizes to beat a female, it takes a female. An ally must be recruited, femininity is a must, and being womanly is necessitated; attributes the recruit will use to win the trust of gullible, impressionable, surface females, and yet in disguise is doing "**IT'S**" bidding. The spirit penetrated Coosh-Maa, the two became one, and a trip's planned. She is night lore, spoken of in whispers, and is never to be trusted.

The **DARK WITCH,** lies in wait, and only manifests when beckoned. The cost to obtain her services is an unmatched price; and **EVIL** knows this. **EVIL**/Coosh-Maa realizes a move must be made, it's **NOW** or **NEVER**. A stand needs to be taken, every line set thus far is no longer, and the opposition must be eliminated while they are few. Presently apprentices, but soon journeymen, will be prepared to walk alone, no longer finding strength in numbers, and will then be an adversary.

Deep into the recesses, a dark abyss, underworld, and formerly home, **EVIL**/Coosh-Maa dove, attempting to conjure a irresistible, unbeatable, but also uncontrollable **EVIL**. Nothing created; animal, human, abomination, or spirit can resist her wiles, it's futile to try. Banished due to her insidious temperament, vanquished to the depths of hell, she exists in complete darkness; waiting, lurking, and will get retribution. **DEATH** accompanies, partners, and is seeded by the newest recruit. Exiled to the Netherlands, her powerful influence undermined due to the threat she presented yearns to return, and regain control above. Darkness will not keep her, she will again reign on the surface; and it will be her personal paradise. Her rule is by convoluted fist, and her grip unbreakable; the only escape is suicide. Coosh-Maa fears the enlisted, but has no choice, and will risk his reign to secure **EVIL** dominance. The scale is tilting toward **GOOD**, to reverse the trend **EVIL** will take the risk.

Gift Of Desperation

Desperate times call for desperate measures, resorting to an unpredictable force, and generating a dangerous affiliation. **EVIL** has pondered other options, weighed the cost comparable to benefit, and determined potential gain outweighs possible catastrophe. **IT** desires winning, domination, and the prospective prize; Earth's surface. **EVIL** is calling on a dark force of night, the strongest of them all, and once retrieved, there is no turning back. The darkness is a familiar place, left long ago, fortune to have survived. The suitors for his power were many, only one was granted the power. The netherworld, darkness is home, floating back, through echoes of pain and unbearable heat; a merciless place.

Unleashing this **EVIL** on the surface will bring carnage, becoming a personal reckoning, filled with bitterness, and thriving on chaos. Fear is her bargaining chip, and **EVIL** ventures to negotiate terms. Obtaining her assistance ensures victory, but who will reign supreme? The Dark Witch relishes **DEATH** which is her bargaining chip, and most admirable asset. Coosh-Maa is aware of her intentions, they have been on opposite sides before, never collaborative. "**IT**" is betting by the time completion of the mission transpires, **DEATH** will be her bedfellow. A perilous scheme, plotting the demise of a creature whose help is sought, a treacherous plan. **EVIL**, by way of Coosh-Maa, intends to ask her assist, and then stab her in the back; an **EVIL** agenda.

Premeditation passengers along, knowing prior the final outcome. **EVIL** has no choice but proceed with the deception, knowing there will be ramifications; once unleashed, she will not return, after eons of exile, relegated to the depths of hell, a place of wailing, crying, and gnashing of teeth, no one or nothing volunteers to go back. Freedom is intoxicating, and the hen will be loosed in the rooster's house, no more shackles; you know she's **BAD**.

EVIL begets **EVIL**.

The Dark Witch

Oh, the Horror that Lies

The second line of defense, **EVIL'S** back-up plan, invited to party, the worst of the worst. "**IT**" abhors seeking the assistance of such unstable, unpredictable associates, but it's **ALL** or **NOTHING** at this point. This monstrosity resides in a region unfamiliar to man, ruled by the third world; a realm of neither man or mammal, an is not of Light or Dark. Created by mistake, conceived with **GOOD** intentions; the experiment went awry, and the end result was a heartless atrocity. A monster with no compassion, receives pleasure by inflicting pain, and is a natural born killer.

Advance knowledge directs **EVIL**, calling upon this is total desperation, and the last resort. **EVIL** against **EVIL**, manipulation, control, exploitation, and eventual misuse; Coosh-Maa intends to influence the Dark Witch. She can control both surface dwellers and creatures of the night, Coosh-Maa desires her to use the monopolizing ability to **IT'S** advantage. **EVIL** partnered with Coosh-Maa, a dastardly tandem; and waiting in the wings, the **SUG**. There will be only one, a single ruler; titled **DICTATOR**; answering to no one or nothing. **EVIL** dreads resorting to such desperate measures knowing once a captive is released, they don't plan on returning to captivity; not voluntarily. A will be crossed, the potential outcomes are many, and a wicked web is weaved when deception's involved.

The second line of defense is on hold, and will be summoned only if necessary. Negotiations with the Dark Witch are of utmost importance, will she be subservient to the mandates of **EVIL**? Bringing back to the surface wickedness, and the one thing everything fears; a frantic ploy, but deemed necessary. Anxious moments will arise for the surface dwellers, underworld, and **EVIL**/Coosh-Maa. Into the dark void Coosh-Maa descended, a risky expedition, prompting a precarious feel, and knowing a recipe for disaster lay in wait. Floating downward, passing the first level of lower earth, a land dominated by the nocturnal. A place where nothing returns after a visit, this unholy ground requires permanent occupancy. A land of perpetual darkness, and the inhabitants embrace their habitat, use it to their advantage, and are lethal creatures of the night.

The **CHI** of **EVIL**/Coosh-Maa allows it to cross dimensions, communicate with beings and creatures foreign to mankind, and itself is a shapeless entity. The occupants of this world detest humanity, are compassionless, and long to escape to underworld. They want a forgotten taste, human flesh, a delicacy dreamed of, and contributing to the extinction of the human race would be a feather in any monsters mane. **EVIL**/Coos-Maa plunged deeper, riding the hot air, recalling the land left long ago. Also on the mind of malevolence, the Dark Witch's banishment is fresh in her mind; and the memory of the expulsion no doubt painful. It was a decision of the powers that be a the time, she was out of hand, power hungry, and lusted for domination. She had to be controlled, stopped, and if not, the world would have collapsed, all life terminated. "**IT**" would not allow such a travesty.

What a place to call home, **EVIL** recalls it well, it's no strange territory, in fact, all territory belongs to "**IT**." There is no place **EVIL** doesn't exist, and has existed since the dawn of time, has eyes and ears everywhere, knows and sees all. The Dark Witch has at her disposal special talents, To destroy the female humans, a female inhumane creature must be used; **GOOD** begets **GOOD**, and **EVIL** begets **EVIL**. Coosh-Maa enjoys the merge, feels the power "**IT**" wields, and takes pleasure in togetherness, both grin envisioning the obliteration of the surface witches. Two names, repeated much too often must be eradicated, L.B.M.N. and Shirley Simms are becoming overly confident; it's time they meet their match.

A Temporary Solution.

Hovering over the dark, "**IT**" feels a sudden shift in the air flow, once riding steams, descending from the atmosphere, then instantly no breeze, smells of nature, or anything fresh. Within the dry, non-circulating air **EVIL**/Coosh-Maa were joined by something airborne, and it floated right along with them. They were found out, she took flight, arrived, and is enjoying the ambiance; after all it is her kingdom. The uninvited company was not appreciate by **EVIL**.

"I feel you, expose yourself, your presence chokes the life out of every thing you touch or is exposed to you. Your disguise is near perfection, but no test for me. I felt **DEATH** in the very beginning, you monitor your kingdom, and my initial trespass, you were aware. Show yourself, dare to look me in the eyes, reveal your irresistible beauty."

No reply was heard, the depressurization of the atmosphere confirmed her existence, Coosh-Maa felt it too. The journey continued downward, allowing them to fall deeper into the Dark Witch's clutches, a welcoming trap. Present guests are overdue, she thought they forgot about her, what a way to treat a friend, and lover. An unexpected visitor returns to the scene of the crime, the prodigal lover, back in the fold; has "**IT**" come to make-up or inflict additional anguish; she already knows the answer, curiosity killed her "**CAT**" long ago.

Though the company arrives in spirit form, the Dark Witch is a seer, and within her realm, watches, waits, knowing one day her services would be needed, and **EVIL** would return. A vision revealed it, the only unknown variable, when "**IT**" would come knocking. The moment has finally arrived, the vision made manifest, and the revelation comes to fruition. Sinking deeper and deeper into the rule of the Dark Witch, she accompanying them, the return visit prompts reflection; and she reminisced. Bewitched memories of a time when she and **EVIL** were an item, respect for one another led to admiration, giving way to Caring, growing into Love, that is now Hate.

"There's a thin line between LOVE and HATE."

Together they ruled, showed compassion, conquered, developed loyalties, which generated intimacy. The two were closer than close, and the Gods talked about them, onlookers envied, and many within their realm wished to be them. In a world of wizards, witches, warlocks, dragons, and power; to ally oneself with an ultimate power was tempting. Two of the most dominant forces canvassing the earth made a connection, and both were pleased. The recollections centered on the good times, and revealed how the two entities came to rely on each other. Reliance and trust was shattered by the Witch's disobedience, perceiving herself as an equal, and why not. The two walked side-by-side, destroyed together, acted as one; why couldn't she be equivalent.

When her desire for equality was never realized, she became upset, the most powerful witch of all would never succumb, nor take a back seat to anyone or anything. Coming to her senses, created a cunning plot, became willing to do whatever to succeed, even if betrayal was involved. Infidelity seeded, trust evaporated, admiration disappeared, respect faded, and eventually Love vanished. Disdain replaced it, and fueled by disrespect, grew into betrayal, which the Witch masked. When "**IT**" got wind of the deception, those the Witch trusted became disloyal, and betrayed her. To get in good with the **TOP** dog, some are willing to do anything, even sell their souls to the devil. Duplicity is common among birds of a feather, which is why they flock together. Betrayal involves treachery, and loyalty can be bought.

Vanity Files

The spirit plummeted, into the shadow land, riding the tips of stalagmites were figures, silhouetted abominations now pawns of the Dark Witch. They welcome visitors, are on the committee, her eyes and ears, and members of her dark family. Now centuries teamed, a relationship nurtured, and the protectors allow no Rite of

Passage. No one gets through, strangers are devoured, "**IT**" could feel the eyes upon it, and disguise was unnecessary. The watchers are creatures created by **EVIL**, how could they not recognize their creator? The void entered into a chasm, the Witch's abode. Nothing exists at her depths, only she, making **DEATH** a bedfellow, and creeping in the shadows. She senses opportunity it is about to knock at her door, and can't wait to greet "**IT**"; before the knock she asks.

"Welcome uninvited guests, what lengths will you go to find your illusive pursuit?"

EVIL/Coosh-Maa halted, ceased it's decent, recognized the voice, sweet music to **IT'S** ears; and it prompted a recollection. Flashes of former good times, both shared the recall, identified the past remembrance; very touching.

"Your play on words, disguised sedition, time hasn't improved your manipulative character."

"I, manipulative, observe my current living arrangements, and the scenic surroundings; by my choice of course. I'm bound in darkness, and **DEATH** provides a suitable companion. Lurking in the shadows, my subjected lovers, and at table, we dine on a buffet of ash, a fitting feast for a queen wouldn't you say. Why are you here, bored of surface challenges?"

"Your bitterness is evident, anger brews inside, and it's justifiable; you have plenty of reasons."

"Don't patronize me, groveling is not your best attribute. Answer my question, why are you here."

"I am here because I need help, your expertise is required; a situation requiring special talents; skills you possess in abundance. I wouldn't be here if there were alternative possibilities; believe me."

The Dark Witch listened, finding humor in the request, when **EVIL** finished, laughed at his sorry predicament, and slowly began to appear from beyond dark. Her look, and magnificence was awe inspiring, she's breathtaking.

"Oh, I believe you, I haven't seen or heard from you in epochs, and you float into my domain, without my permission, after you exiled me here. It would be false if I gave an impression of happiness, would you consider making this permanent?"

"The history behind us cannot be altered, I'm not here to listen to an appeal, and cannot expunge your past dastardly deeds. What has been done, has been done, but I can offer asylum."

The Dark Witch released a hideous laugh, the sweet voice that greeted is gone, her tone is repulsive, filled with mockery, reflecting her distrust and animosity.

"An offer always has stipulations, that's your **M.O.**(Modus Operandi); how you operate, remember, we have a past. By the way, **EVIL** or **Coosh-Maa**, which are you?"

She again released her hideous laugh, and before Coosh-Maa could respond, the Dark Witch was back on the attack. Instantly, her matter shifted, no longer was evil intent obvious, her voice softened, and she expressed genuine concern.

"Do you need my help darling?"

"Condescending, a play on words, games, a rare visit and we perform in such a immature fashion."

In Her Own Words

"Not long ago you could listen to me ramble forever, my simple words captivated, you tasted them as they exited my lips. Are you no longer interested in my opinion, do I no longer matter; I'm hurt!"

Another voice change, disappointment reared it's patronizing head, the Dark Witch twisted everything, attempting to make her visitor as uncomfortable as possible; and it's working.

"Let's get to the point, I have no time for quarrelling, visiting, or vacationing; I need your help. Surface dwellers, and rebellious humans are interfering with my plans, and must be eliminated. What is required doesn't incorporate tact, but brute force, there is where you step intervene."

"The longer you visit, desperation reveals itself, you possibly do need an extended vacation, I can supply suitable accommodations."

The Witch intentionally delays, and continues the word play. This is her payback, she is going to make **EVIL** beg, and then she will procrastinate longer. This is her opportunity, has leverage, and isn't going to let good fortune pass, she continued.

"PAYBACK is a MOTHER."

"The spearhead of my punishment, the grand designer of my exile needs help from the banished, ironic; wouldn't you say. It's like rain on our wedding day, or the good advice I didn't take; and at the time who would have figured. Desperation, look at you, after what you did to me, you want me to do to your surface nemesis. I have identified the problem, immorality possessing morality, don't tell me you've developed a conscience. This adversary, or as you put it, rebellious human is female, correct? Still weak toward the opposite sex, or is it an attraction to your same sex?"

EVIL smarted, "My subjects on higher levels need my direction currently, there is confusion above, I have delved to hell's depths long enough; and so have you. Your return is overdue, Dark Witch, come back, assist me; and a suggestion, do it right the second time around, there may not be a third."

"A recruiting trip, almighty **EVIL** ass Coosh-Maa needs my help, and is willing to offer a reprieve to obtain it. I was given the impression of being less than you, less powerful, less needed, and less essential; what's happened? You require my help, I can't **RELATE**; or is it **EQUATE**?"

She chuckled under her breath, smothering her cynicism, but it wreaked of sarcasm, enjoyment, and it's payback. The mighty Coosh-Maa begging, the Dark Witch savored the moment, elongating, and prolonging it. **EVIL**/Coosh-Maa on the other hand grew impatient, the responses reflect the difficulty when dealing with the Dark Witch; she can be a **BITCH**.

"Can I count on you; will you come to my aide if need be, and fight side-by-side with me?"

Immediately the Dark Witch hatched a plot, and seized the opportunity for a comeback. She will lead, then bring mutiny, create a shift in power; atop the structure sits the Dark Witch. Oh yes, the seer sees it, her reign will be of grandiose proportions, the whole wide world will watch her take the throne, and knights in shining armor surround, and heed her call. She replied,

"Three letters of the alphabet fighting side-by-side; **C** = **Coosh-Maa**, **D** = I, the **Dark Witch**, and **E** = **EVIL**, what a trio. In the past, aligned with you were the happiest moments of my former life, and can't relive them, but can make new ones. I've remained buried long enough, pardoning my indiscretions also provides absolution; I thank you."

"I sense happiness, and it is a pleasure being able to bring joy to your life again. I hope it is an expression I can continually supply, in turn, I thank you."

"I long for fresh air, and now have something to look forward to. I anxiously await your summons, and when it comes, I will fight side-by-side with you."

Comforting words to **EVIL**, contractual verbiage filled with conceit, dissension, hatred, and escape clauses. The Dark Witch escorted her visitors to the next level, just as **EVIL**/Coosh-Maa glided into the deep abyss of hell, "**IT**" ascended, overwhelmed with optimism after successfully recruiting the ultimate power. A joyous rise to the surface, but apprehensions accompany it, **EVIL** knows the Dark Witch is not to be trusted. She felt his apprehensive thoughts and ceased accompanying, watching the spirit soar to the heights of the surface. An arena she once dwell in, and established a perfect domain, but a moment of weakness, and she succumbed to trickery. Watching, quieting thoughts, she recalled events leading to her demise. A sneer came to her face, bitterness returned, revenge materialized, and it's accompanied by abhorrence. Wrinkles appeared on her pure radiance, results of ostracism, fires of hell, and isolation; her beauty is gone. This time on the surface results must be different; it will be no Hallows Eve, the Dark Witch will the tricks and the treats.

Talk of the Town

There are others gifted, residing on the surface, talented humans, but concealing their abilities, not wanting attention, and preferring to remain dormant. Also, there are those who decide to use their gifts to harm humanity; and are twisted. They have made conscious decisions to misuse a natural ability, selfishness directs their criminal actions, and corrupts the power. Personal gain is their agenda, and the well being of all doesn't enter the equation. Bondage of self is a ploy of **EVIL**, using **PRIDE** against them, once viewed as arrogant, they are now looked at as conceited. Exploiting the weak of society, abusing their advantage;

VANITY, all VANITY.

Some conquer temptation, others avoid the pitfalls by not allowing themselves to be led in it's direction. Worldly gain consumes surface dwellers, avoiding interaction with **EVIL** is nearly impossible. Father Dauphne uses words of wisdom from I Peter 5:8, relating to the shrewdness, and cunning of the enemy, a spirit walking the Earth like a roaring lion, seeking whom he may devour. Recent events are the talk of Broussardville, and the priest is asked to calm the situation. Talk is rampant, a tale of discovery, a story which generates intrigue, and is exaggerated through gossip. Much of the rumor is unsubstantiated, but humans on the surface long for any news, life is stagnant, and anything done, prior permission is required. They wear a façade of humanity, but in actuality are puppets, and **EVIL** is the puppet master. The few aware of the thief in the night, are considered a rebellious faction, and now gather. Loyal to the gift possessed, vow to remain non-biased, and will always use it to serve. They are a small number, take the fight to **EVIL**, aware of the impending battle which lies ahead. They've witnessed the events of recent days, seen wrongs of the past go unpunished, and know **EVIL** is on the move.

The entire community of Broussardville now realizes the pending peril, the minority insurgents are led by a legendary freedom fighter, founder of the revolution; the Avenger of Light, **MICHAEL.** He has witnessed the carnage **EVIL** is capable of, long ago chose a side, the side of **GOOD**. Most surface allegiances remain hidden, and have promised to step up when the appropriate time presents itself. Past interaction allows **MICHAEL** to better understand **EVIL**, it's demonic characteristics, and realizes "IT" was flawed at birth. Many assassins of **EVIL** have challenged, the skill of the Avenger has allowed him to vanquish all. In a town lacking males, disguises himself as an average Joe, submissive, and playful, but waits, trains, and recruits.

MICHAEL hears the rumors, a finding, the unearthing of a rare gem, and knows many would sell their souls to possess the artifact. He will make sure the find doesn't fall into the wrong hands, is commissioned by Good, and is prepared to fight in an effort to save mankind. His particular set of gifts are unique, and allows him to retaliate directly against **EVIL**. Not limited to nocturnal hunting, **MICHAEL** seeks **EVIL** on a constant basis, **24/7**, even when disguised, he's researching, fact gathering, and recruiting. By day, a shy kid, watching, making mental notes, and when he manifests, it's to take care of business; he doesn't hesitate to act, has authority to kill.

A motto repeated on the surface is **"Kill-or-be-Killed."** Humans don't have nine lives, aren't muscular brutes like the monsters they face, and aren't the walking dead. He was sent down by the creator during the dark days, a time **EVIL** reigned, and turned the tide on **GOOD**. The Earth was without form, void, and darkness was upon the face of the deep. **MICHAEL** led the divide, separating Light from Dark; and the moment light entered the world, darkness shivered. The edict, "Let there be **LIGHT**" and the power of **LIGHT**, Michael heard the words, and witnessed the magnificence.

From that moment forward, Darkness hated Light, and pledged at every opportunity to destroy it. The Avenger gives **LIFE** to the distraught, fights for the underdog, and sees to it the natural balance of things remains in place. He is a mediator, tries to maintain neutrality, and when forced, is judge, jury and executioner. There when **LIGHT** entered the world, Michael is an advocate of **LIGHT**, and fights for **LIGHT**. When dirt was **SHAPED** into human form, the likeness pleased him, he took the shape, adopted the creator's idea, and advocates by righting wrongs; and desires to smite the child of perdition..

HOPE rests in the palm of his hand, and when lost, an entire race of people become extinct. The defender of **HOPE** will never let it be snuffed out, when extinguished all follows. **HOPE** allows dreams, **FAITH** supplies visions, and **LOVE** makes it manifest. With man, and **EVIL**, there are impossibilities, but with **GOOD**, all things are possible; man is then allowed to seek the impossible, making it possible. With a little **HOPE**, one can go a long way, set off a revolt, and send it rocketing skyward. Without **HOPE**, mankind ceases to exist, losing a vital character trait, the ability to **HOPE**. Without **HOPE**, lonely the heart, making humanity self-centered. **EVIL** searches out those, the hopeless, and fills them with lies, deceit, and sin. A void is created between the creator and the creation, intentionally done by the malevolence. Without **HOPE**, mankind and the designer of man are miles apart, separation spurred by wickedness, and vices injected by the most immoral of all. **MICHAEL** enlists those who rely on the creator, and believe "**THY** will be done, not **MY** will."

MICHAEL is **FAITH**, gives substance, and allows **HOPE** to exist, combined, the two are an unbeatable combination. His efforts permit humanity to anticipate, reflect optimism, and believe. Substance and Evidence do not exist without **FAITH**, and are witnessed as the culmination; **FAITH** answered through prayer. Three human traits intermingle, merge, fuel, and are inseparable. The Avenger is the torch bearer of the three, flesh, spirit, and patent; sent by the creator to battle **EVIL**, and will not cease until all **EVIL** is eradicated.

What is FAITH? It is the confident assurance that something wanted is going to happen, the substance of things HOPED for. It is the certainty that what we HOPE for is waiting, the EVIDENCE of things not SEEN.

Hebrews 11:1

Michael- The Avenger of Light

Fore knowledge is an advantage **MICHAEL** exercises, using the premonition, he stand in, is the substitute, and righter of wrongs. Man will need every type of ally, and every lucky break to go it's way, to conquer the confrontation to come. **EVIL** has **EVIL** intentions, the Avenging Light and Coosh-Maa have a history, prior confrontations left vivid memories. He knows not to take "**IT**" lightly, surviving this long takes a highly gifted entity, and the enemy is comprised of many parts, some of the vilest, callous, heartless creatures. Monsters exiled to third world realms awaiting **EVIL'S** summons.

Avenger of Light, by day, in observation mode, learned, angelic, athletic, skilled, making for a unpredictable protector. **MICHAEL** has encountered walking **EVIL**, Night Stalkers, precursors to a coup by **EVIL**. Mercenaries, henchmen, non-human; in physique, but only a shadowy replica; following orders given by the worst type of power; out of control. He trusts the Loup Garou, a nemesis of the scrunge, and one of the only allies strong enough to eliminate scrunges; a wily soldier. It remains impartial, fights it's own battles, has back-up which show up unexpectedly, and in great numbers. The "**OLD DOG**" tries not to intervene, and prefers to let fate take its course. Intervention is the last resort, his role is to help maintain balance, and level the playing field. If the scale tilts in any direction, an advantage is produced, meaning casualties, in his line of work, it's a byproduct of war.

WAR!
What is it good for?
Absolutely nothing.

If ever needing assistance, or desperation creeps, **MICHAEL** calls on his friends. Spiritual beings, rarely taking human form, are of myth, and aligned to human days of the week. Dependent on the day, The Avenger of Light calls in the designate. Appointed by the **CREATOR** of **ALL**, who directly never intervenes, instead delegates, and sends angels to do battle for him. The former number one angel created major heartache, was exiled to the earthly realm, and now rules it with an iron fist. Breathing earthly air, expatriated to the lower realms, "IT" rarely takes shape, prefers to remain airborne, anonymous, and exacts it's revenge on mankind.

EVIL is on a recruiting trip, but is unaware of man's intent, both have unrevealed allies; Good supports man's cause, and **DEATH** accompanies **EVIL**. In the heat of battle, **GOOD** has torch bearers, Avengers who will intervene, and shift the tide. Whatever is deemed necessary, the **CREATOR** will supply, you shall not **WANT**; and the singular objective, **TOTAL ELIMINATION** of **EVIL**.

BE FOR REAL.

Migrating back to the upper realm, two which became one, felt a shiver. One half or the other, possibly both, two entities, simultaneously experiencing the same quake, inside of "**ITSELF**" the two halves observed each other. If there is "**DOUBT**" within the body, he building will crumble. A strange vibe overtook the airborne duo, things are transpiring on the surface, change is incurring, and "**IT**" isn't controlling **IT**. Loss of **CONTROL** invites **FAILURE**, leading to a catastrophic **FALL**.

Ascending after securing a "Right-Hand-Woman" from ostracism, "**IT**" finds "**ITSELF**" in a precarious dilemma; "On the outside looking in." The odd "**IT**" out, straying from protocol, not obtain a consensus, now "**IT**" is the subject of rumor and innuendo, being whispered about. A confidence stealing position to find "**IT**"self in, "**IT**" doesn't appreciate, or embrace it; they'll pay dearly. "**IT**" is essential something be done, allowing gossip to remain opens the door to speculation, and then a perceived weakness. "**IT**" will do the unthinkable, knowing the possible ramifications, but having no choice. Banishment is painful, being forced out, given limitations, the airborne realm, who do they think they are, "**IT**" promises vengeance. Considered idle threats, talk of retribution, the day will come, for now, mediocrity is accepted. "**IT**" will interact with man, though "**IT**" despises the pitiful, vile, untrusting creatures. Just the kind of subjects "**IT**" requires.

"**IT**" is the "Eye in the Sky," looking at it's puppets, "**IT**" reads their minds. "**IT**" is the maker of rules, voices edicts, and manly fools follow, trading life, to obtain whatever illusive temptation. The list is long, desires, wants, and those dreaded must haves. Rising to the surface brought back painful memories, "**IT**" relived it's expulsion, and better relates to the Dark Witch's sentiments, mistrust, doubt, and revenge. What prompted "**IT'S**" foolish decision, wrong action, so powerful, inducing the strongest, considered above reproach; and labeled as untouchable. What is the **ONE** thing which will send a confessed, **GOD** fearing man, tumbling to the ground?

VANITY!

A great king of old gave instruction on the curse of **SELF**, and the bondage association with the infliction. After a lifetime of observation, his final summation; **ALL** is **VANITY**. To get a complete understanding, and discover the meaning of the sentiment, "**IT**" must be lived, and experienced first hand. **EVIL** comprehends it, was there when King Solomon expressed his disgust, and in attendance when the boy, King David, was handed the throne; all actions fueled by **VANITY**. Continuing the rise, light seen above, "**IT**" remembers the darkness, a former close friend, and once a bedfellow. Hell was once "**IT'S**" personal paradise, and has been away from home far too long.

"**IT**" played an intricate role in the exile of the Dark Witch, convincing the crowd to send her to a place of no return. Ostracized, and banished, she took along scrunges, devils, and **EVIL** of all sorts. The punishment exacted by the **CREATOR** of all, one even "**IT**" reluctantly bows too. That's what happens when **VANITY** clouds your vision, desiring to be number one; **EVIL** didn't recognize its place or limitations. Coosh-Maa has become preoccupied with the surface, a new fascination; the complexities of humans. **EVIL** loves to manipulate the easily tempted it's created.

LIGHT is also addicting, and after being in the darkness for so long, one longs for light. To re-experience the blinding effect the sun has on virgin eyes, the initial intensity, and the realization; it's **LIGHT**. The warmth emitted, not scorching, dehydrating, and debilitating, like Hades. **EVIL** is aware of the crippling addiction, Bondage of Self, and the Vanity of all Vanities, desiring the seat atop the mountain, equating oneself to a God. Visualizing oneself as the King of Kings, and the Lord of Lords; the Chosen One, and "**IT**" realizes what will make it attainable.

THE BOX!

War brews in the heavens, and the prize is control. A coveted realm, a spiritual territory, and the combatants are determined to reign. The fight is between unknown spirits, all desiring to rule. involved are spiritual beings. Preparations are in place, and allegiances are being solidified. As "**IT**" rides the winds, escaping the darkness of death, climbing, rising, the stench of **DEATH** lessens, but the memories linger. Recollections discouraging a return, stagnating stale air, relentless heat, and the painful cries and wailing. Hidden in the shadows, former subjects who miss their former master, would do anything to please, and followed "**IT**" once exiled. Misplaced loyalty, prompting one to wonder, what does **EVIL** possess that makes it so alluring, and irresistible? Reflections prompt the other half to also reflect, Coosh-Maa found the Dark Witch's domain intriguing.

Before arriving to the surface, both **EVIL** and Coosh-Maa took a moment, relived the descent, interaction with the Dark Witch, and her exiled subjects; a pitiful place to reside. Once home to **EVIL**, the spirit turned it's back so easily, for an instant was disappointed, inhaled the aromatic, fragrant essence, and savored it. The heat was once welcomed by the airborne spirit, it appreciated the staleness of the air, and relished the cries and wailing; a realized masterpiece it created. Since his entrance, there are many descriptive names; "**IT**" is the Antichrist, the Beast, Beelzebub, Deceiver, Dragon, Evil One, Son of Perdition, Tempter, Devil,

Lucifer, and Satan. Names, titles which mortal humans would never accept as part of their proud legacies. Designations conjuring repulsive thoughts, "**IT**" wears them proudly; after all, "**IT**" is all of them. In the town of Broussardville, "**IT**" is known as Coosh-Maa.

Second Coming

Who actually reigns supreme, created all, and sits on a lofty perch, **HIDDEN**? The question's unanswered, some prefer it to stay that way, others view the concept of a higher power as mockery, curses, and disbelieves; an all mighty Creator, nonsense. There are those who kill in the name, and await the second coming; but no one knows the hour, or day. "**IT**" has existed since the beginning, the dawn of time, has battled numerous suitors seeking to replace it, and has banished the rebellious. "**IT**" rewards the obedient, is omnipotent, omniscient, and omni-present; nothing gets past it.

There has always been division, those wishing to supplant the present leader, creator of all, a spirit which sees, knows, and is all-powerful. Like darkness, "**IT**" has been given labels, God, Yahweh, Elohim, Adonai, Jehovah, and El Elyon. Many titles, the most important fact, "**IT**" reigns supreme, and there can be only one. Ruling from the Alpha, will remain until the Omega. "IT" longs to return the Earth's former beauty, a once majestic place. **EVIL** has taken refuge, corrupted the entirety, and wants to witness the demise of humanity. **GOOD** has alternative plans, remembers past earth, filled with beauty, life, plants, and animals. **EVIL** has infected many original creations, **GOOD** intends to reverse the current state, and revitalize mankind. A conflict rages, **GOOD** vs. **EVIL**, an unnatural selection process, **WAR** is the determinant.

Old Earth

All know of a recent find, an unearthed relic, and inside is unimaginable power and control, desired by each and every one. A gift given by the **CREATOR** to a favorite, who passed it on, as a present, to a daughter. She loved the possession, took it everywhere, and the **BOX** eventually merged with **Pandora**, the two became one, leading to corruption; the **BOX** exploits everything. The **CREATOR** realized the infectious nature of the power within the **BOX**, a design error, not meant to be in the hands of a child. The father retrieved the object, realizing the potential, and the **BOX** again corrupted. The **CREATOR**, realizing the blueprint flaw, reclaimed the work of art, securely stored it, and the entity remained **HIDDEN** until now.

Initially fashioned out of love, intended to be a token of appreciation from the **CREATOR** became a blight, an admitted mistake by the maker. In the wrong hands, power confined within the **BOX** could shift the balance of Good and Evil. Power is intoxicating, a frantic search transpires, a highly sought prize has been recovered, and a race ensues to see who will possess it. Buried in the deepest recesses of the sea by the **CREATOR**, the current exhumed the **HIDDEN** treasure. Waves, current, and water flow re-deposited the **BOX** into a new grave. Rising from the depths of the sea, the **BOX** found a new home, and waited.

HIDDEN by its creator, concealed, but possessing a will of it's own, the **BOX** worked it's way to higher ground. When the **CREATOR** realized the power placed within the **BOX**, it was an afterthought, and too late, it's creation had developed a mind, an ability to think, rationalize, and exist. The **BOX** now desires to again merge with another of the creators creatures. Initially a decorative item, encrusted in precious stones, jewels, diamonds, emeralds, pearls, rubies, sapphires, amethyst, garnet, jade, tanzanite, and the most coveted; gold. A dazzling creation, and when penetrated by light, released a prism of colors mesmerizing any onlooker.

The **BOX** itself, created from bark of the **Tree of Life**, making it virtually indestructible. The **CREATOR**, out of anger, previously destroyed life on Earth by water, and made a covenant with man to never use this method again. Fire is the force which can destroy the **BOX,** flames extremely intense generating a temperature found nowhere on the face of the earth. Finding such an inferno is virtually impossible, which means the **BOX** is indestructible. Buried with the **BOX**, remains of the first created son, bred by **EVIL** to unseat the **CREATOR**; the anointed or chosen one, the Antichrist.

Bones found near the **BOX** are the remnants of a failed attempt, and there has been numerous others, but none successful. **EVIL** continues it's quest, and if it secures the **BOX**, the heavens, earth, and below the earth will never be the same. Surface dwellers are aware of the war transpiring in the heavens, noble humans, singled out, and gifted. Warriors of **GOOD**, recognizing the design of **EVIL**, and at every opportunity vanquishes it. Discoveries on the surface reveal the many attempts by **EVIL** to merge with other beings. The experiments infect animals with **EVIL** intentions, and the results produce futility. Sought by sin is the right match, and realizes the answer is the **BOX**. Inside is a life force capable of creating existence, not normal earthly beings, perfection. Life generated from the first source, the origin of everything, unmatched power; a possession anyone or anything would die to obtain, and kill to keep.

The sun is now past midway, and beginning to fall from the sky, we are all gathered outside, and speaking of the devil, Chew-Bus appears from nowhere. Her arrival seems to bring a ray of **Light** to the backyard, the energy she releases can be felt, and all could see her glow. All of our attention turned toward Carolyn, noticed how hard she's breathing, and is obviously winded. She slowly approached us, and struggled to speak, but making gestures with her hands. Momma walked over, embraced her realizing the panic, and helped to calm her. She gathered herself, took a deep inhale, and began to explain why she's breathing heavily. What follows is incredible, and begins to set the stage for the revelation of our gifts. Carolyn, resting in momma's arms, told of her recent encounter with Gus. An intriguing re-cap, captivating everyone, even momma listened as she re-lived her battle with pure **EVIL,** known as Gus.

"Aunt Bee, I can sometimes stretch the truth, but this just happened."

Momma said, "O.K. Lynn, there is no doubt something has you shaken, just tell us what happened."

"Walking over here it felt weird, something strange was going on, I didn't know what, but it gave me the creeps. As I walked down Morgan, I saw a shadow, out of the corner of my eye, it caught my attention. I was drawn toward it, a shadowy figure, and when I focused my vision, recognized who it was, Gus Geer-waa. I immediately became frightened being on my own, and knowing he has no good intentions for me. I know if possible, he will try to dispose of me, I placed myself on guard, and put my hands in my pockets. I now know, I possess the power of Light, and will use it on Gus if necessary. I waited, allowing him to approach, preparing, and if prompted, I will release the Light; but I had to wait and let Gus make the first move.

I asked, "Are you following me Mr. Gus?"

He replied, "Who gives you the authority to question what I do child, you best know your place. You're a sassy kid, too big for your britches, and I know your momma. I'll take you home, talk to Edna Mae, and make sure she puts it on your backside."

I said, "Mr. Gus, you have no authority whatsoever, my guidance, and direction comes from my creator. He alone has authority over me, you have none, and my mother's authority is limited. Also, I know I'm a child in your eyes, but in my creators eyes, I'm a warrior."

He laughed at me, and thought maybe I was just being a cocky kid. Though he laughed, I could tell my response maddened him.

He said, "You're confident for a child, much less a girl. You speak about your creator, I'm puzzled; who is it you speak of?"

I then gave an unexpected response, an answer which infuriated our Chief of Police.

"That's for me to know and for you to find out. If I tell you, I'll have to kill you."

All the family laughed, Chew-Bus is safe, back in her element, at times can stretch the truth, but I believe she said that to Gus; she's cocky like that. Her answer revealed something Gus didn't know about her.

He asked, "Are you threatening me child? If I ask you a question, I expect you to answer it. I don't expect arrogance, and don't play childish games. Do you know who I am?"

It was time for me to play my trump card. I told him something, hoping it would upset him, possibly push him over the edge, and prompt him to act. I revealed information he least expected to possess.

"I know who you really are sir, hiding behind the disguise of Chief of Police, but I know better. You are **EVIL** personified, not Gus, you're a SUG. Doing the bidding of Coosh-Maa, the master, and you're his servant. He created you, and you are his eyes and ears."

The reaction in Gus' face said it all, I could tell he began to plot my demise in his mind because I know too much. He wondered how did I obtain this information, and who else knows. He couldn't let his double life be exposed, and would have to dispose of me. He began to walk closer toward me, sensing danger, light began to release from my body, I illuminated the area. Gus was amazed, paused for an instant, observing the radiance emanating from me; I could see the hesitancy, he was caught off guard.

Glow Your Own Way

Carolyn – Chew-Bus = THROUGH BOX

He said, "Remove your hands from your pockets, and put them behind your back. I'm going to place you under arrest for threatening an officer of the law."

Gus reached toward me, I quickly removed my hands, opened them, and faced the palms toward Gus. I released a beam of light blinding him, so intense it caused him to release a wail like a wounded animal. I turned and began to run, the sound Gus released was not human, and revealed the creature that existed inside of him. Confirmation that Gus was indeed a **SUG**, the vilest of creatures, a killing machine, and I'm in grave danger.

At first, I knew Gus was pursuing me, but didn't hear him. As I ran further, I could hear paws, the four feet of the **SUG** chasing me, as they hit the ground, the sharp claws scraped on the ground. The sound of the paws closed in, the **SUG** was gaining on me, as I frantically ran, trying to escape. I had to make it here before it got me, and if I didn't, I would be it's meal. As it closed, I began to panic, and realized, if I didn't do something soon, I wasn't going to make it. I made up my mind, built up the courage, stopped running, and turned to face the ravenous monster. When I did, I got the surprise of my life. Gus was no longer in human form, in broad day light, he turned into something hideous. He was a nasty monstrosity, unrecognizable, had huge ears, a mouth filled with fangs, and dripping from it's mouth was saliva. It's eyes were focused on me, and it seemed to have many, the all-seeing eyes of Coosh-Maa.

The Confrontation

The Predatory SUG

It scared me, and I screamed once turning, and witnessing the grotesque transformation. It was a monster, no longer Gus, and not of this world. I had seen nothing like it before, a hideous, disgusting, creature; the Chief of Police in his true form. It suddenly dawned on me, my only defense was to unleash my light, it would ward off the evil, the Light would stymie its advance. As it stalked me, beginning to approach, I again opened the palms of my hands, and faced them toward the atrocity. The thing again released a wail, a painful howl, as the light burned it. I could smell its rotten flesh smoldering, and hear the sizzle as the radiance scorched it. The Light I released was not natural sunlight, but a Light as powerful as Life itself, a dominant Light, stronger than sunlight, ultimate power.

The intensity of the Light grew, and as it increased, the advance of the horror deterred. I focused my gaze directly into its eyes, aimed the powerful Light into them, blinding the evil creature. I slowly began to back away, the advance of the monster ceased, the Light slowed its advance, but didn't stop it completely."

All listening were captivated by Chew-Bus's story, and amazed at the encounter. We were equally impressed with her newfound ability, and listened intently. She paused to catch her breath again, we waited, hanging on her words; she then continued.

"In response to the Light focused into it's eyes, the thing roared, and from the mouth of the demon, fire spewed. The heat was intense, but I countered it, met the Fire with my Light. We battled, positioned between us, my Light, and Gus' Fire. As I intensified my gaze, made myself focus, the force of my Light strengthened, increased and overtook the fire. I saw the flames of the **SUG** diminish, it's power decreased. My Light not only overwhelmed the Fire, it doused it, and I began to speak to the thing.

'Gus, I know you are in there somewhere, listen to my warning, and heed it well. Return to your master, tell it of my power, and inform it of my intention. I plan on destroying all of your kind, it is my mission, my calling, to eliminate scrunges. You, being the most powerful of them all, now know my powers, never underestimate me again. If you do, you will find **DEATH** waiting for you at every turn, this is your only warning; **AWAY FROM ME**.'

I then spread open the fingers of my hands, and the Light continued to intensify, I controlled it not only with my hands, but also my mind. The creature released a yelp, a wince of pain, was injured, and slowly began to retreat. The fire it once released from its mouth was no more, and it began to flee. When I closed my hands, it was gone."

Her story was now over, she was overwhelmed with emotion and fear; Chew-Bus began to cry.

I thought, "What an ordeal."

We were all awe struck, could see the toll the battle had taken, and realized she's an emotional wreck. She faced **DEATH**, and witnessed the power of **EVIL**; defeating it. She now knows of a creature walking the face of the earth, disguised

as a human being. She also realizes the grave danger, and alone is no match for
EVIL.

As we sat listening, standing at the back corner of the house is Ms. Simms, John
Nick, and Bud. They had returned from Simmsboro, and quietly listened as
Carolyn relived her deadly encounter; also captivated. Single handedly warded off
EVIL, momma embraced her again, hugging Chew-Bus tightly.

"You did well Lynn, and I'm proud of you. You are one brave child and control
inside of you the Light of Life. A power you possess, because Chew-Bus is
THROUGH BOX. You are the reincarnation of Pandora, have returned to even
the score, and destroy the thing which corrupted. You're safe now with us. Catch
your breath, and stop that crying; right now, it's probably Gus doing the crying."

She smiled at momma's comforting words, we all gathered around the picnic
table, and the mother's instructed. It's unbelievable what Chew-Bus told us, I
wasn't there, but I'm scared. She is powerful, battling Gus on her own, I now
realize, she is the Warrior Princess. I looked over at her, relaxed in momma's
arms, recalled Gus in the squad car, his strange ears, and the time he sniffed
around the house. All past incidents, and now this, there really is some strange
stuff going on in Broussardville. I then looked over at Bud, he smiled, I'm glad
he's back; and could see he's happy to be back.

Ms. Shirley said, "You're a brave girl Carolyn, realize the power of your gift, and
I suggest you use it in a frugal manner. It's not the first time your gift has been
revealed. Steven and Keith saw it the other night, and so did the scrunges
following you."

In my silence I am amazed, how did Ms. Shirley know Chew-Bus revealed her
gift to us; she wasn't there. There is no way of her knowing, unless Steven told
her; I didn't. It then dawned on me, she doesn't have to be there, she is a seer.
Wow, what an amazing gift Ms. Shirley has.

Glen blurted out, "What's frugal momma?"

Ms. Simms smiled, "Use your gifts wisely children, they are meant to be used
only out of dire necessity. Frugal means sparingly, not wasteful; do not misuse
your gift, and don't be a show off."

Her words are a stern warning, we listened, and understood the meaning. After a
moment of silence, Ms. Shirley continued.

"Over time, as Carolyn just shared, all will discover their abilities, the potential existing within. Introspect, look within yourselves, discover them, then press them, nurture, and enhance them; remember, don't misuse them."

Hub Cap blurted out, "Remember that, Dirt."

I said, "here you go Hub Cap, always dissing me, or throwing shade?'

Dean and Sue silently listened, the **REBEL** loves it when I get the raw end of the stick, she is a hater, but I know she loves me, and just doesn't know how to show it; one day maybe she will. Sue, the **GENIUS**, simply loves being in little big brothers company, and always has my back.

As Ms. Simms spoke John Nick and Bud held an off to the side conversation.

"Bud, you're always asking dumb questions."

Bud replied, "Momma said, 'The only dumb question, is an unasked one.'"

John Nick and Bud's dialogue had Pooh, the **NEGOTIATOR** set to intervene, and settle the disagreement. A mediator is a word person, she's already thinking how to use **FRUGUL** in her next mediation. Lu, the **SMELLER**, is captivated by the tale from Chew-Bus, and like Bud, thinks the word needs explanation; Duh. The mental chaos is intentional, caused by an intruder, and silently the **BOX** beckons. I can hear it calling, vaguely, faintly, it summons me, I must go to it, and claim what is rightfully mine. Momma said Carolyn is **THROUGH BOX**, that's not possible, and if she is, then the box is technically hers. That's not fair, what happened to finders, keepers.

It's mine, we have a connection, I can now hear it clearer, it's whimpering, it doesn't want to be Carolyn's again. It says a strange thing, it doesn't want to merge with her again; it wants me, totally confusing. I do want to hold my precious **BOX** again, open it to see what's inside; and I'm dying of curiosity. The dream with the tall man has me worried, is the **BOX** safe; it's mine, I should know where it is at all times.

Ms. Simms paused a moment then continued, "Lynn, Gus is now aware of the power you possess, you injured him, and hurt his pride. He is aware of your gift, and not only does the **SUG** know, so does it's master; assassins will come for you."

Carolyn became alarmed by Ms. Simms' words, we all did. Her safety is now at stake, and her life is in jeopardy. Ms. Simms then shared information she discovered while in north Louisiana.

"My trip to north Louisiana was a fact finding mission, my sister Betty shared some of the things going on in her neck of the woods. The same strange things are happening there as is here. People are changing, lifelong affiliations are ending, and **EVIL** is giving birth to never before seen creatures lurk. An **EVIL** presence is ominous; something is building."

We all listened, but are also into our own little side dialogues, our attention is divided, and our interest isn't focused. The surface and face of Broussardville is in transition. Scrunges are now seen by day, Night Stalkers have emerged from the shadows, and Ratwolves prowl once hallowed grounds; all signs our mother's warned about are happening. Shook by what Chew-Bus shared, talking back to Hub Cap, and desiring to hold my **BOX**. My thoughts are everywhere, on numerous things.

Once Ms. Shirley finished speaking, she looked over to L.B.M.N., who looked at us all individually. Lu smelled something, detecting a strange presence now permeating the backyard, sitting amongst us. **EVIL** arrived from the depths of hell, disguised as the wind, reclined at the table. Momma felt the existence of something airborne, as did Ms. Simms. Momma intensified her gaze, released Carolyn from her arms, realizing the intent of the intruder. She allowed Ms. Simms words to sink in, but noticing the mental division amongst us scolded.

Momma shouted, "Children, listen; you bicker amongst yourselves, and don't see the writing on the wall? The time of preparation is over, **WAR** is at hand, and the way we will prevail is **UNITY,** not disarray. **EVIL** wants to create division, once divided, it will conquer. It grows, has an agenda, and is near, very near. It can see it's goal in sight, and has but one objective; the **BOX**."

She then yelled, **"Behind me, you Satan."**

We all froze, snapped out of our selfish indulgences, amazed. Momma talks directly to **EVIL**, and has first-hand knowledge of it's power. She then looked directly at me, knowing my thoughts, and rebuked me.

"My poor son; all you think about is that **BOX**, the **BOX;** the **BOX**. Don't allow it to obsess, control, and merge with you; once it does, there's no turning back."

"And so it begins!"

THE END!

Tribute to:

Kernel Menard & Erline Menard

also

Irma Lee Gonsoulin aka Miss Zoo-Bee

331

Self-published by:

Keith J. Nickerson in association with

Kindle Direct Publishing

Lafayette, la.

cldlucille@aol.com

Keith J. Nickerson
421 St. Charles St.
Lafayette, La. 70501
cldlucille@aol.com

Made in the USA
Middletown, DE
08 September 2018